WHEN DEVILS SING

FIRST INK

WHEN DEVILS SING

XAN KAUR

First published in the US 2025 by Macmillan Publishing Group USA

First published in the UK 2025 by First Ink,
an imprint of Pan Macmillan
The Smithson, 6 Briset Street, London EC1M 5NR
EU representative: Macmillan Publishers Ireland Ltd, 1st Floor,
The Liffey Trust Centre, 117–126 Sheriff Street Upper
Dublin 1, D01 YC43
Associated companies throughout the world
www.panmacmillan.com

ISBN 978-1-0350-4517-4

1 3 5 7 9 8 6 4 2

A CIP catalogue record for this book is available from the British Library.

Typeset by Intype Libra Limited
Printed and bound by CPI Group (UK) Ltd, Croydon CR0 4YY

For my mother and my aunt.
I made sure it wasn't all for nothing.
&
For B and M.
Wish You Were Here.

In the Southern night everything seems possible, the most private, unspeakable longings; but then arrives the Southern day, as hard and brazen as the night was soft and dark. It brings what was done in the dark to light.

—James Baldwin, *Nobody Knows My Name: More Notes of a Native Son*

PROLOGUE

SECRETS OF THE SOUTH

SEASON 4: TEASER

(INTRO THEME SONG)

HOST: Down in rural Southwest Georgia, there's a sleepy town called Carrion. It's in this town, every thirteen years, that a swarm of millions of cicadas crawl out of the earth, rising from their extended slumber.

Then, as one, they begin to scream.

FORMER CARRION RESIDENT, LEE WATKINS (phone): Now, I ain't lived in Carrion in some years, but I still remember the sound of those damned things. Make you go deaf, if you not careful. But let me tell you this: Those cicadas bring nothin' good. And that's all I'm gonna say on that.

(phone call ends abruptly)

HOST: What makes a town? Is it the people who live there, or the secrets they keep?

In this season, we will explore the history of a dying small town in Southwest Georgia, the wealthy lakeside community that keeps the region afloat, and the mysterious deaths and disappearances that occur on the water every thirteen years.

Because for the townspeople of Carrion, the arriving cicadas are more than just a scientific marvel. They're an omen.

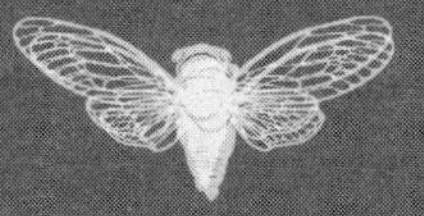

PART ONE

There's the devil you know
The devil you don't
The devil you wish you'd never met

CHAPTER 1

SAM

Perched unsteadily next to her brother's limp body in the back of an ambulance, Sam Calhoun prayed. To who, she didn't quite know.

She gripped the railing of the gurney as the ambulance picked up speed, rounding the corners of Carrion's dusty backroads. Outside the windows, there was only all-consuming dark. The population in the sticks was too sparse, too spread out for the county to justify the cost of lighting nothing.

The moon was covered by smoke that night, which only made the darkness worse. It was the last day of burning season in Langley County, the final chance for residents to burn the piles of leaves and brush on their property before it became illegal for the summer.

Sam's throat ached.

Maybe the fires were to blame for the accident. Maybe it had been too smoky to see clearly.

Sam knew it was a ridiculous thought as soon as it crossed her mind. The blame for the accident fell squarely on the person who hit her car and drove off, leaving her and her brother for dead.

Sam leaned forward to brush Ben's red hair from his face. His left eye was closed, his right swollen shut. He was a mess of blood and wounds. His small frame looked even smaller against the size of the gurney, made worse by the tubes and equipment attached to him.

Her brother had already been unconscious when Sam had crawled her way out of the wreckage, and he hadn't stirred when the paramedics showed up and set to work. Sam didn't know what kind of pain her brother was in. She hoped he couldn't feel it, wherever he was inside his own head.

The paramedic across from her studied Ben's vitals on the monitor. He frowned and shouted something in medical code to the driver, but Sam couldn't follow.

"What's wrong with him?" she asked, growing more frantic by the second. "What're you sayin'?"

The paramedic ignored her, his focus wholly on her brother.

Sam stared at the monitor—it was only a flurry of lines and numbers, none of which she understood. Save for one.

Ben's heart rate was slowing to a crawl.

Sam's own heartbeat thumped harder within her chest in response.

Ben's pulse stopped.

The machines began to scream.

The paramedic grabbed a pair of scissors and sliced Ben's T-shirt open from collar to hem. Sam winced as the defibrillator pads were placed on her brother's bloodied skin.

One shock.

His body jolted.

Two shocks.

His body jolted again.

But his heartbeat didn't return.

The paramedic shouted to the driver once more. The ambulance made another sharp turn. Sam gripped the gurney harder to avoid flying off the bench.

Moments later, the vehicle lurched to an abrupt stop. The

back doors of the ambulance swung open, and bodies in blue scrubs shouted to one another in more medical code as they rushed Ben's gurney onto the ground and through the doors of the hospital.

Sam trailed after them, watching as Ben and the gurney disappeared behind a set of doors, putting further space between her and her dying brother.

A nurse in scrubs appeared and motioned Sam into a nearby room. Her lips moved, but Sam wasn't listening. She started toward the doors at the end of the hall, but the woman moved in front of her.

"No, ma'am," the nurse warned, "you can't go where he's goin'."

Sam kept moving. Distantly, she was aware of the dull, throbbing pain in her right ankle. A stinging welt across her ribs from the seat belt. The nauseating tightness of whiplash along the length of her neck. She was aware of it all, but she didn't feel it. Not really. She needed to get to Ben.

The nurse was still talking. She reached out and grabbed Sam's arm.

Sam jerked back. "Don't you touch me," she snapped.

The nurse sighed. "Your brother is in good hands. You won't be helpin' a thing if you try and follow him. Understand?"

Sam crossed her arms. Something in her shoulder popped a little. "Fine."

"All right," the nurse said. "Now, let's get you looked at."

Sam followed the woman into an examination room. She motioned for Sam to sit on the table, but she hovered along the wall instead. The tiny space felt like a cage.

"Someone will be in shortly," the nurse said. She hesitated at the door, then asked, "Is there anyone you need me to call? Your parents?"

Sam blinked, then swallowed. "Yeah. My daddy. Wiley Calhoun."

The nurse's eyes widened. "Is that right?"

"Yes, ma'am." Sam recognized familiar fear bleed into the woman's face. It was theå same fear her daddy inspired in everyone around Carrion, including herself. Being the one to call about Ben was out of the question.

She scrawled down the number Sam recited. "Anything you want me to tell him specifically?"

Sam's chin quivered. "Tell him his son is dying."

The nurse gave her an awful, pitiful look. "We don't know that."

Sam turned her eyes to the hard tile floor. "I can feel it."

The nurse left Sam without another word. A few minutes passed. Sam's body shook from adrenaline. Her head pounded. The room began to spin and shrink around her. She peeled away from the wall and opened the door, finding the hallway empty. The fluorescent lights lining the ceiling buzzed overhead. It was too loud, too much.

Sam stumbled down the hall, through the hospital doors, and out into the smoky summer night, her vision swimming.

Angry, fearful tears streaked her freckled cheeks as she stood outside Clearwater Regional Hospital. The tears of a girl who believed her brother was dying somewhere in the building behind her.

And it was all her fault.

Sam never cried. Not at the hands of her daddy, nor the sharp tongue of her mama.

But this was *Ben*. Her baby brother who crawled into her bed during thunderstorms, or when their daddy was three bottles in, searching for something to hurt.

It felt as if the things she'd tried to protect Ben from had added up to nothing. Misfortune had a way of befalling her like a tornado leveling a town, taking everything with it.

Sam swiped at her face, trying to wipe away the tears, but it only left her skin feeling grimy and half-wet. She glanced around the dark, quiet parking lot. There was nowhere to go, nothing to do. She couldn't go back inside to the tiny, claustrophobic exam room. Couldn't just stand there, waiting for an ambulance to run her over.

She walked. Whatever direction her feet would take her.

As she stalked along the rows of parked cars, Sam fumbled in her pocket for her phone—although who she planned to call, she had no idea. Her former best friend, Dawson Sumter, was the one person she used to go to when things got bad. But they hadn't spoken for weeks.

Not since their fight a month ago that had severed the connection between them.

Sam wanted to scream. She resisted the urge to throw her phone onto the paved ground of the parking lot, but she wanted to break something. *Needed* to break something.

She was like her daddy in that way.

Sam lashed out with her fist and hit the nearest parked car. Less of a punch and more a slap across steel. It stung her hand, but what was one more injury, one more little ache? She hit the car again, and then again. Over and over until her good hand was numb and red, her knuckles swelling with fresh blood.

Sam stood there, breathing hard, her hand throbbing in time with her pulse. The vehicle didn't have a scratch on it. No trace of her hand, of her fury.

No matter how hard she tried, she just couldn't leave a mark.

"You look like you could use a light," a voice said.

Sam whirled. A man leaned against an old Jeep a few spaces down, the car caked in Georgia red clay and dirt. He took a drag on a cigarette, his silhouette barely visible beneath the dim parking lot light.

"Sorry." Sam stood there, too numb from the accident to feel frightened. Or to feel much of anything at all. "I thought I was alone."

The man shrugged. "I've seen worse in this parking lot. Rough night?"

"Yeah." Only one word, but even that came out strained.

The man extended an unlit cigarette out to her.

Sam inched closer, studying him with a wary eye. He had a young face with a shadow of facial hair. Dressed like any Carrion man—tattered button-down, sleeves rolled up to his forearms. Faded jeans with fraying bottoms. His work boots were dull and weathered.

But it was his eyes that stood out to her. Irises so dark they looked black. Even in the glare of the parking lot light, his gaze was razor-sharp.

"Care to talk about it?" The man exhaled smoke from his nose. "I'm a fine listener."

Sam hesitated, then reached out to take the cigarette from his hand. He leaned closer and flicked his lighter. Sam watched the tip of her cigarette glow bright orange in the dark. She put the filter between her lips but didn't inhale. The man stared at her as she held the cigarette like it was a prop.

"You don't smoke," said the man. Less a question and more an observation.

Sam shook her head. "My little brother asked me to quit for his tenth birthday." Hot tears welled up in her eyes.

"Smart kid."

"He . . . is." Sam's green eyes turned toward the hospital. "He's in there right now."

The man's dark eyes followed hers. "What happened?"

"Car accident." Sam turned the cigarette over in her hand, careful not to burn herself. "We were run off the road into a ditch. The person that hit us just . . . drove away."

The man said nothing. Sam kept her eyes on the cigarette as she turned it around and around, but she felt his gaze fixed on her.

Her throat went tight. "I don't think he'll make it through the night."

The man whistled a sad tune under his breath. "That is a terrible thing." He may have been a stranger, but his tone sounded sincere. Or maybe he just had a talent for pretending.

Sam dropped her cigarette and snuffed it out with her high-tops, noticing fresh blood smeared into the canvas. Was it her own, or her brother's? "It's my fault. If he'd never gotten in the car with me tonight, none of this would've happened."

"You know what I think?" The man eyed the crushed tobacco smeared across the asphalt. "Blame is a poor use of your time."

Sam looked up. "How the hell else am I supposed to feel?"

The man held her gaze for a very long time. "What if I told you," he said slowly, leaning forward a little, "that I could save your brother's life?"

Sam froze. Quietly, she said, "I would say you're full of shit."

The corners of the man's mouth turned upward slightly. "That's fair. But it don't make what I'm sayin' untrue."

Sam studied his face, looking for any sign of malice. There was none to be found. "How could you possibly save him?"

He put out his cigarette, too. Crushing the embers beneath his heavy boot. "You have faith?"

"Faith in what?"

"Anythin' at all."

Sam snorted. "If I did, there's not a lot of it left."

"It don't require much." The man gave her a wry grin. "I can save your brother's life. All I ask is the favor be repaid in turn."

"What kind of favor?" Desperation pooled in Sam's stomach. "I don't have a whole lot to offer."

"Ah," the man said, his tone sly. "Now, if that were true, I wouldn't be standing here before you."

"I'm serious," Sam huffed. "I don't have money. Nothin'."

The man laughed dryly. "Money is no good to me. You see, my currency is only in bargains and souls."

Sam recoiled. She braced her weight against the nearest car, the world tilting around her as she realized who—no—*what* stood before her.

"You're . . . the devil, aren't you?" Sam murmured.

"One of three," the devil said plainly.

It wasn't such a strange thing, for a girl grown up in Carrion. Everyone in town knew of somebody who knew somebody who sold their soul. They were tragic tales, whispered over beers and bonfires. Most stories ended poorly—while others ended, at best, with one's face on a missing persons poster, and at worst with an early grave.

Only fools sell their soul, her mama used to say. *Hell ain't a forgiving place, and it's at our doorstep. Don't you ever welcome it, Samantha.*

Sam glanced uneasily around the empty parking lot as the humid night air grew thick, nearly suffocating in its intensity. She struggled to steady her breath.

"I can't," Sam whispered.

The devil frowned. "And here I thought you'd do anythin' for your brother."

"I would," Sam snapped.

"But not this?"

Sam looked back at the hospital. How long had it been since

her brother's heart had stopped? Had it been minutes since they arrived? An hour? How much time was she willing to gamble away for Ben?

"What do you need me to do?"

The devil offered her a gallows smile. "Lie."

"A *lie* for my brother's life?" Sam shook her head in disbelief.

"What's a life worth, anyway?" the devil asked, still smiling in a way that made Sam's skin itch.

"I suppose it's nothin' to you."

"I suppose not," the devil said with a shrug. "In the comin' days, I'll find you and tell you everything you need to know. For now, we can either shake on it, or you can walk away. Let your brother die. It's up to you."

Maybe it was the crash, or the guilt, or the presence of this strange man—the *devil*—but Sam's head still wasn't all the way there. She was tuning in and out of reality, like a car radio on Carrion's backroads. But if she did nothing, Ben was not long for this world.

Hell didn't seem so bad in comparison to a life without her baby brother.

Besides, according to her daddy's backwoods beliefs, she would be sent there just by existing.

What's one more damnation?

Sam held out her unsteady, bloodied hand to the devil. He took it in his own, and they shook.

She asked, "That's it?"

"That's it."

She pulled her hand back. Her skin was hot, tingling as if held to a flame. Silence fell between them. Sam was anxious to get inside—to get away from whatever it was that stood before her. Whether the devil spoke true or not, she was desperate to see Ben. But the devil didn't move to go, and she wasn't sure if she should, either. "You got a name?"

The devil looked contemplative. "You can call me Jack."

Sam didn't know why she did it, but she said, "My name's Sam."

"Well then." Jack smiled, baring again those sharp, white teeth. "I guess I'll be seein' you soon, Sam."

Her skin crawled at her name in his mouth. It sounded *wrong*, like the moment glass breaks. "See you, Jack."

AS SAM WALKED away, leaving the devil behind in the parking lot, the night seemed darker, as if it crowded around her. The humid air heavy and hot on her skin. Beads of sweat pooled at her T-shirt collar, clinging to her damp neck. At the hospital entrance, she glanced back, but Jack and his Jeep were nowhere to be found.

Once inside, the nurse from before led Sam to her brother's hospital room. She felt like she was being walked to the gallows.

As soon as the elevator doors opened, a woman's high-pitched wailing reached Sam's ears. Her mama. Sam's feet were heavy as she was led down the nearest hallway, the wails growing louder with each step.

Sam stopped as they turned the nearest corner. There was her mama kneeling right there on the hall floor, keening at the feet of a grim-faced doctor. Sam's daddy was crouched beside her, his arms wrapped around her shaking body, his face buried in her neck.

"*My baby boy,*" her mama screamed. "*My baby boy!*"

Sam looked to the nurse, desperately searching her face.

The woman's expression was grim as she guided Sam down

the hall. "You need to be with them."

No.

A choked sound escaped Sam's throat. It was a primal thing, somewhere between a sob and a scream. "Is he—?" She couldn't give voice to the word.

Dead?

Her daddy glanced up then. "Samantha." His voice was a low rumble, the kind of distant thunder you hear before a summer storm.

Without meaning to, Sam's good hand went to the splint around her left wrist. He'd done that to her, the last time she saw him.

"I'm sorry," she whimpered those familiar words. She'd spent eighteen years apologizing, but it was never enough. "I—I tried to—"

What could Sam even say? That she thought she'd made a deal with the devil to save her brother's life? Standing in the sterile hospital hallway, her bargain with Jack suddenly felt foolish. *Of course* Ben was dead. She saw his heart stop. How could she believe otherwise?

"Do you realize what you've done? *Huh?*" Wiley demanded, rising from the floor. He was all tension, the bottled-up inertia before a punch collides with its target. His grief was indistinguishable from his rage. The feelings needed a way out, and he was itching to lay it all on her.

Sam flinched as her daddy drew near. She wondered if he'd hit her right then and there. Who would stop him? Behind Wiley, the doctor hovered anxiously, clearly unsure of what to do. A few nurses lingered in the doorways of other rooms, watching.

They all were surely thinking the same thing: Wiley Calhoun was untouchable.

Sam's voice cracked as she said, "Just let me see him. *Please.*"

It was a phone call that saved her in the end. An obnoxious trill rang from the back pocket of Wiley's jeans, rendering him frozen. Even if Sam no longer lived under her daddy's roof, she knew who called. A master and his hound. Not even Ben's death would stand in the way of him answering.

Wiley sucked his yellow teeth but stalked down the hall to take the call from his boss.

The doctor, taking advantage of her daddy's absence, showed her into Ben's room. He eased the door shut behind them with a soft thud, silencing her mama's lingering whimpers at once.

Sam looked onto her brother's lifeless body, lying limp in a hospital bed. The oxygen had been removed from his nose. IVs stripped from his bruised skin. The heart rate monitor was dark and still. There was no sound in the room, except Sam's own labored breathing.

She knelt beside him, reaching for his hand. His freckled skin was still warm. Fresh tears ran down Sam's cheeks.

"We couldn't revive him," the doctor said, and Sam startled. She'd already forgotten he was there. He kept talking, but his voice sounded distant to her ears, like he was speaking to her from underwater. "Injury to the brain . . . excessive blood loss . . . body went into shock . . ."

Sam brushed away the hair that stuck to her brother's forehead. They shared the same red hair, always falling in front of their eyes. She swept it back again and again—repeating the motion, realizing she'd never have another chance to do so.

"I'm sorry, Ben," Sam choked out. Tears streamed onto the bed in a steady rhythm. "I'm so sorry."

Sam wanted to crawl into the bed beside him, to hold him like she always did when he was scared. To fall asleep and wake up to his smiling face. For the sun to rise and to discover it was all a terrible dream. She didn't know how long she knelt there, weeping over her brother.

The doctor cleared his throat. "We need to move his body soon."

"He's not a *body*," Sam snapped. "He's my baby brother." She needed more time with him, but she knew there would never be enough. Not when a wolf was at the door, hungry for blood.

Sam squeezed her brother's hand one last time, holding back a choked sob.

Ben's fingers twitched.

She froze, loosening her grip on his hand. Her pulse thudded in her ears as she stared at his fingers, loosely curled inside her larger palm.

They twitched again.

His fingers gave another tremulous movement, like the muscles were waking up, and then Ben's hand gripped her own.

Sam's gaze went to her brother's face as his left eye fluttered open.

The doctor whirled into action. He pulled a small flashlight from his front pocket. He checked Ben's pupil, then his pulse with his fingers.

"My God," the doctor whispered. "He's alive."

But Sam *knew*—God had nothing to do with it.

CHAPTER 2

NEERA

It was only in the late hours of night when Neera Singh found time to play her guitar. The best time to practice was *always,* but the second-best time was when she was meant to be scrubbing blood off the walls in her grandparents' motel.

Neera sat on the cool tile floor in Room 11's bathroom. The small space reeked of bleach and lemon, but she didn't have the luxury of being picky. The acoustics of the room were just too damn good. She hit record on her phone and set a timer, giving herself thirty minutes before she had to continue cleaning. That's all she had most days—those precious thirty minutes.

The last of the Colonial Inn's housekeepers were gone. All that remained was Neera and her mom, Kiran, to keep the place clean while her grandparents ran the front desk in shifts.

Before long, the timer on Neera's phone rang, signaling an end to her session. She played back the recording as she donned rubber gloves and dipped a sponge into a bucket of cleaning solution.

Neera kept her mind on the music, listening intently, as she got to work on the blood-spattered bathtub. Red streaks covered the yellow-white tile, seeping into the cracks. It wasn't often that there were bloodstains left over when guests checked out, but it was common enough that Neera knew better than to ask questions. She learned young that the motel, while a home for her, was merely a pit stop for others. Gone were the days when the Colonial housed bright-eyed snowbirds on the way to Florida. If the rooms were booked at all, occupants were often running *from* something, even if it was just themselves.

Nothing surprised her anymore, but Room 11's last occupant had given her pause.

The man—well, *boy*, really—had checked into the Colonial in a frenzy, stumbling through the lobby's door. He had looked about Neera's age, with a shock of white-blond, tousled hair and blue eyes that had seen better days. As he lingered at the front desk, she noticed the whites of his eyes were bloodshot and the skin around them swollen pink and puffy.

It had taken Neera a moment to recognize him. She knew Dawson Sumter from her second job, bussing tables up in Lake Clearwater on the weekends. Except the boy that had stood before her was a ghost of himself. While he usually ran with the Clearwater crowd, rich kids dripping of privilege and bravado, Neera could *tell* he was from Carrion. It was how he always took extra care with his posture, the tidiness of his clothes, the clean parting of his hair. He had the peculiar look of a marionette doll moving through the world as someone else pulled the strings.

Neera had asked, as she passed him Room 11's key, "You okay?"

"Yeah." Dawson kept his eyes trained downward as he grabbed the key, and Neera swore there was dried blood on his pale hands. But he had merely said, "Relationship problems."

It was a lie, and they both knew it.

It'd been a week now since Neera had last seen him, but his room was paid for through the day. She continued to scrub the walls, wondering just what Dawson had been running from.

Neera didn't know when exactly her grandparents' motel became the last place people wanted to find themselves. Somewhere between the last recession and the impending one. But all that mattered to Neera was getting the hell out of Carrion, for good. If she and her family could do that, they'd be all right.

Without stopping her scrubbing, Neera glanced at her Yamaha guitar. Her ticket out—for all of them.

Neera's phone buzzed twice, yanking her from her thoughts. A text from her mom.

Jason said yes. Tomorrow at 3

Jason managed the Tavern Bar & Restaurant in Lake Clearwater, where her mom tended bar and she bussed tables. He was also in charge of selecting musicians for the upcoming Cicada's Song, an open-mic competition that happened during the Cicada Festival—though it wasn't *really* an open mic. The contest was a special event, only held every thirteen years during the festival, and the Clearwater folks were highly selective of who they allowed onstage.

There was a *chance* the winner of the Cicada's Song could walk away with a record deal at Blue Mountain Records, run by Grant Langley himself—Lake Clearwater summer resident and kingmaker of the Nashville music scene.

Neera frowned at Kiran's text. She hadn't really expected her mom to pull through. Getting an audition was as likely as winning the lottery, especially for someone like her. But it didn't help that Neera's usual confidence vanished when performing in front of an audience. Her throat would get tight, her voice would warble and falter. She'd shrink away from the lights and the crowd until people started pulling out their phones, leaning across tables to chat with their friends.

Neera wrote back: *Any chance I could audition Tuesday instead?*

The reply came a moment later: *No. This is it. Do you want it or not?*

Neera's fingers hesitated over the keyboard for a second. *Yes. Thank you.*

Neera leaned back on her heels and sighed. She sat there for a second, staring into space, then hit play on the song recording for the third time.

It still wasn't good enough.

She gave the bathtub one last swipe with her sponge and tossed her supplies back in the bucket, grimacing at the dirtied water. On her way out of Room 11, she returned the rags and bucket to the cleaning cart, then scanned the room a final time to make sure she hadn't missed anything.

Something glinted beneath the chair in the far corner, catching her eye. Neera crossed the room, digging beneath the dusty upholstery. Her fingers found something cool to the touch—a key ring with one key and a worn leather key chain embossed with a deer antler logo.

Neera wouldn't have given the design a second thought if it weren't so strange looking. Around Georgia, deer antler iconography was as common as the cross, but this was different.

This buck's eyes were covered with a blindfold, while the antlers spread across the leather like sprawling, twisted tree branches. A unique design choice if she'd ever seen one. She slipped the key chain into her pocket, intending to return it to Dawson next time she saw him at the lake.

With a final look, Neera stepped out into the night and shut Room 11's door behind her.

The distant smell of burning leaves hung in the warm night air, turning her throat scratchy. She checked her phone. It was after midnight, and there was still another room to clean. Yawning, she descended the short flight of stairs to the ground floor and made her way toward the laundry room.

Passing by the glass windows of the motel lobby, Neera paused. Inside, Nanaji sat at the front desk, his enormous glasses sliding down his nose as he read the *Punjab Times* newspaper. An American news channel droned from the old television in the corner. Harsh, fluorescent light shone down on him, casting his brown skin in a dull shade of gray.

Looking in on her grandfather, Neera had one of those rare moments of sadness for him. There he was, a man far from his homeland, reading about Punjab in the run-down motel he had sold everything to own. As though he could feel her pity through the smudged glass, Nanaji looked up. His face immediately pinched into a frown at the sight of her, his heavy eyes sliding to the Yamaha resting across her back. Her tenderness for him evaporated at once.

Neera couldn't be heard practicing without upsetting her grandparents, but being *seen* with the guitar was somehow worse. The instrument was a physical reminder of her uncle, Ajay—a memory best kept buried for them all.

Nanaji waved her into the lobby like he would call for a dog. Reluctantly, Neera rested her guitar at the lobby's door then walked inside.

"All right, Neera?" Nanaji said by way of greeting, his voice low and accented.

"Yeah." Neera hung in the doorway, letting moths fly in. "I just have Room 6 to clean, then I'll be done."

Nanaji nodded absently. "How are your studies?"

It was a question he asked so often that it was almost funny. Neera's lips thinned as she said, "I don't start college until the fall, Nanaji. I don't have anything to study right now."

He looked up from his newspaper. "Oh? There is always something to learn."

Neera wanted to say that she was learning a new fingerpicking technique on guitar. That her recent cover of a Reverend Gary Davis song was pretty damn good. Her songs on SoundCloud were picking up in streams. But those were all useless things to him. Nanaji measured success by dollar signs and commas, despite his own struggling business.

Fine. He was a simple man of a different time, a different place. She just wished he wasn't such a dick about it.

And then there was the other issue—Neera didn't intend to go to college at all. She hadn't told anyone that yet, though, not even her mom.

Neera opened her mouth to remind him that for all his talk of education and success, his granddaughter spent her summer nights cleaning blood off the motel's walls. But her grandfather's cell phone rang. He glanced at the screen, his graying eyebrows furrowing, and rose from the desk to take the call in the back office. The door shut behind him with a dull thud.

Neera stood awkwardly in the motel lobby. This time of night, it had to be a relative from India or England calling. Nanaji could be on the phone for an hour or more. The right thing to do would be to watch the desk until he got back.

Neera didn't often do the right thing.

She turned on her heel and walked out into the balmy Georgia night. Lightning bugs blinked in and out of sight along the tree line surrounding the motel. A symphony of katydids and tree frogs reverberated around her. The parking lot light flickered occasionally, casting the concrete in stilted shades of dark. A television blared from one of the rooms.

Guitar slung over her back once more, Neera made her way to Room 6. It faced the back of the motel, overlooking a weathered swimming pool and the broken fence that surrounded it. Beyond the pool were longleaf pines, towering and swaying with the night breeze. When the wind hit the trees in *just* the right way, Neera swore she could hear a song. Summers in Carrion were wondrous like that if nothing else.

By the time Neera finished cleaning Room 6, it was two in the morning. As she trudged toward her room, the sound of shouting made her slow, then pause. There was her grandfather's voice, taut and angry—and he was shouting in English. It wasn't uncommon for Nanaji to get into vicious phone arguments with his brother, but it was *always* in Punjabi, his preferred language for anger.

Neera took a few cautious steps forward and peered through the smudged glass of the lobby window.

A burly man stood across from her grandfather at the front desk, hands resting casually in his worn, stained blue jeans. His face was turned away from Neera, but she recognized him by his shaved head, the dozens of raised scars that ran down his forearms, and the dented toolbox that sat on the counter. Wiley was the motel's handyman, but he was rarely helpful. Each time he showed, her grandparents were visibly on edge.

"I will pay it back soon," Nanaji insisted. His voice carried through the lobby's propped-open door.

"I need you to be more specific." Wiley stepped forward, resting his hands on the counter. His skin was pale and muted, but his scar tissue shimmered beneath the harsh fluorescent lobby lights. "As I'm sure you know, my boss ain't a forgiving man."

"*Soon,*" Nanaji huffed, his expression indignant. "A few months. I will have it all by then."

"Months?" Wiley snorted. "Way I see it, you got a week. Until the Fourth of July." He stepped away from the desk, taking in the dingy lobby. His beady eyes darted quickly, then met Neera's through the window. "Otherwise, you *and* your family may end up just like that son of yours."

The threat was a simple thing. Quiet, and unassuming. It hung in the air for only a breath, swallowed up by the buzzing of the tiny front desk fan and the drone of the newscaster on the old TV.

Nanaji blinked, then slammed his hands down on the desk, rattling the tools in the toolbox. "Get out!"

"July Fourth, Mr. Singh," Wiley said casually. He grabbed his toolbox with ease, giving Neera a quick, impersonal nod as he stepped out the lobby door and disappeared into the night. His Chevy pickup peeled out of the parking lot and onto the dark, two-lane highway the Colonial sat on.

Neera lingered in the doorway once again, fear twisting in her gut, while Nanaji slumped in his chair, rubbing his eyes. Shame crept across his face.

Neera didn't know what to do. Ever since Ajay died, her grandfather had a weak heart, at a high risk for heart attacks. Fighting with the handyman in the middle of the night was the last thing he needed. But her grandfather was stubborn to a fault—the type of man who would refuse water in a drought if it was given and not earned.

"Are you . . . okay?" Neera asked finally. She resented the question, wanting, instead, for Nanaji to ask that of her. To comfort *her*—to offer her the illusion of safety, if only for a moment.

Nanaji wouldn't look at her. He kept his gaze trained on the front desk, absently shuffling pages of the open newspaper. "I am fine," he said flatly. But even from the doorway, Neera could see his trembling hands.

Seconds gave way to minutes, but Nanaji refused to say anything more. He was content to leave Neera with unanswered questions and Wiley's threat echoing in her head. With one last look at her grandfather's slumped form, Neera slipped away from the lobby and continued to her room.

Neera shared Room 4 with her mom. She unlocked the

door to the sight of two twin-size beds, a tattered dresser missing one of the drawers, and a TV that was older than she was. All the belongings to their name sat in trash bags along the wall. A handful of boxes stacked in the corner.

It was the most stable home Neera had ever had in her life. The Singh women had a knack for leaving, which meant they also had a knack for returning. Whenever Kiran broke up with a new boyfriend or was in between jobs, they'd always return to Room 4 at the Colonial until her mom was on her feet again.

They'd been back at the motel for about a month now. With Neera recently graduated from high school, and her mom's newest ex out of the picture, they no longer had any ties elsewhere. The pair could stay for as long as it took to move forward again.

Or so they thought.

The night's events proved that the motel's stability was clearly barreling toward an end. It was no secret the Colonial was in the red, but Nanaji owing money to a mysterious person was a surprise. He was meant to owe money to the *bank*, just a few small business loans to keep them afloat until business picked up for the Cicada Festival. But to be threatened in the dead of night—owing money to someone's *boss*—none of it seemed normal, much less legal.

What exactly had Nanaji done to keep the motel afloat? Was it worth their safety—their *lives*?

But where else is there for us to go? The thought sent an uneasy tremor through Neera's gut. She collapsed onto her bed fully clothed and shut her stinging eyes. She had no answers. No solutions for her family's mounting problems as they grew suffocating like the humid, summer air.

"NEERA," A VOICE said. "*Wake up.*"

Neera's eyes opened. Her mom was standing over her, still in her bartending uniform from her shift at the Tavern. Kiran's face was exhausted and stricken.

"What's going on?" Neera struggled to sit up. She'd fallen asleep in her grimy housekeeping clothes again, shoes and all.

"We gotta go." Kiran pulled Neera from the bed. "There's a fire."

Her mom's words cleared away the last haze of sleep, then Neera smelled smoke. She stumbled out of bed and followed Kiran out the door. The sharp tang of smoke and gasoline hung heavy in the air. Somewhere in the distance, the roaring siren of a fire truck.

A bolt of fear hit her, and Neera stopped walking at once. "My guitar!" She spun on her heel.

Kiran grabbed her arm, pulling her back. "The motel's fine. Come on." She dragged Neera to the front of the Colonial.

In the motel's parking lot, a car was on fire. The flames rose high in the sky, billowing black clouds of smoke into the air. The few guests staying at the Colonial stood outside their rooms, bleary-eyed and curious. A couple of them recorded the inferno with their phones. Neera's eyes darted around the scene, searching, until she spotted her grandparents standing in the lobby. They stared at the flames with open mouths.

Kiran dragged Neera across the lot and into the lobby, where she finally let go of her arm. "The fire department is on the way."

Nanaji responded in Punjabi, and the adults continued the conversation that way. Neera was never taught Punjabi, save for a few words like *hello, yes,* and *no*. Useless in a moment like this. But Nanaji wouldn't look Neera in the eyes. He kept his gaze trained away from her, as if she wasn't there at all.

Neera moved to stand next to her grandmother, wrapping

her arms around her small frame. Nani patted Neera's face, smiling sadly. Tears fell from her eyes. Neera didn't understand why her grandmother was crying. In the Singh household, the only emotion that ever got out was anger and the repression of it. Sadness was reserved for the places behind closed doors.

But then she looked again at the flaming car.

It wasn't just *any* car on fire, it was her grandfather's car. His '87 Cadillac Fleetwood. Camel colored, with tanned leather interior. The car itself wasn't worth much, but it was one of the few things her grandfather treasured. His gift to himself when he immigrated to America. Neera's vision blurred as she stared into the flames.

The car's engine exploded, lashing orange flames into the air. Glass shattered across the lot as the windshield gave out. Onlookers screamed and moved away, back to the safety of their rooms.

Neera could only stare as the Cadillac burned into a blackened heap of metal.

CHAPTER 3

REID

The hunting rifle in Reid Langley's hands shook. He sat in a ground blind beside his father, observing their prey from an elaborate hidden fort in the woods. About a hundred feet away, an animal grazed in the dark, oblivious to their presence and the rifle scope Reid had trained on it.

"*Careful,*" Russ, his father, chided in a low voice. "Steady."

There was no way his father could see his shaking hands in the dark predawn hours, but somehow, he still sensed Reid's weakness. Reid squinted down the scope of the rifle, staring at the exotic creature cast in green night-vision hue. A scimitar oryx, something akin to an antelope with horns like long, curved blades. The rest of its herd was nowhere in sight.

It was possible the others had been hunted already. Scimitar oryx were extinct in the wild—they only existed in zoos and places like *this,* their elaborate horns a sought-after wall decoration in every exotic hunter's home.

Reid tightened his grip. If the oryx truly was all alone, perhaps it would be a mercy to shoot the animal.

An animal with no herd is as good as dead, he thought.

But his hands continued to shake. His palms were slick against the stock. Reid moved to wipe the sweat from his forehead, but his father placed his gloved hand over his, steadying his rifle.

"Focus," his father said.

Reid leaned into the weight of the rifle, bracing the stock

against his shoulder. He'd shot a rifle more times than he could count in his nearly eighteen years, practicing at the shooting range for hours with his siblings and his father. But he always avoided hunting trips.

When it came down to shooting a living thing, he just couldn't follow through. That was precisely why his father had dragged Reid to the Oakbill Hunting Range that night.

"Go ahead," his father whispered. "*Now.*"

Reid inhaled, aiming for the high shoulder of the oryx. The most ethical way to kill—break the spine, paralyze the central nervous system. The animal drops dead within seconds. It was also one of the more difficult shots to make, especially from their distance and the angle of the blind.

Crosshairs aligned, Reid braced himself for the shot. There was no way around it. His father was quite literally breathing down his neck. If Reid didn't make the shot now, he'd simply spend another night in the blind until he did.

This is merely a means to an end, Reid reminded himself. He had little more than a week left in Carrion. His eighteenth birthday was fast approaching on the Fourth and with it, he'd finally have access to his trust fund. While most Clearwater kids blew their inherited wealth on things like yachting on foreign waters, Reid saw the trust fund as his one-way ticket out of Lake Clearwater for good.

But he had to play the game of the dutiful Langley son just a little longer. Then, he would be free.

At least, that had been his singular plan until a week ago. How could Reid leave it all behind when his closest friend had just vanished without a trace? He wanted to be rational about Dawson's radio silence, but his gut said otherwise. In fact, it *screamed* there was cause for concern. Desperately, Reid hoped he was wrong because what would he do if he wasn't?

Reid pulled the trigger. The stock kicked back violently against his shoulder, and he jerked backward with a pained grunt. With the silencer on, the sound was nothing more than a fast, sure *pop*.

The oryx went down.

The woods went quiet, absorbing the reverb of the shot, stilling. Through the scope, Reid stared at the animal's body. A wave of nausea rolled over him. At least he hadn't eaten earlier—too nervous for their excursion—or he would've vomited at his father's feet.

Reid turned toward his father, attempting to search his face in the spare light of the moon. But his expression was impassive. His father lifted the night-vision goggles to his eyes, fixed on the downed oryx. Without lowering the goggles, he reached behind him for the hunting knife he'd set on the little camp table. "Field dressing. You remember how, don't you?"

Reid could only manage a nod. He hadn't expected to field dress the oryx, too. He'd made the shot. He'd thought he was done. His empty stomach clenched.

His father grabbed the electric lantern and another knife, motioning for Reid to follow as he made his way to the carcass. But Reid watched him for a moment, frozen.

There was no refusing his father, not now. He'd already come this far.

Before his father could bark at him to hurry up, Reid followed him out of the blind. In the darkened woods, a chorus of crickets and katydids hummed around them. Animals skittered above in the treetops.

They were miles outside of Langley County. The Oakbill Hunting Range sat on private land, over a sprawling five thousand acres. Gated, well-guarded, and exclusive, it was one of many playgrounds for the residents of Lake Clearwater.

Reid fell into step beside his father as they approached the fallen oryx, their path lit by the dim glow of the lantern light. Their shadows cast elongated shapes on the forest floor. Pine needles crunched beneath their boots. A barred owl hooted overhead. Far in the distance, there was the subtle tang of smoke.

As they neared the oryx, the lantern light began to flicker.

Once.

Twice.

Then it went out, shrouding them in the heavy cloak of night.

"Goddamnit," his father hissed. He reached into his duffel, searching for a flashlight.

Reid fumbled for his phone in his camo-printed pants. But before he could turn on the flashlight, he paused. He had twenty-three missed calls and a dozen texts, all from his older brother, Jonah. His phone had been on silent. The most recent text, from ten minutes earlier: *answer the fucking phone!!*

His father cleared his throat. Reid wasn't supposed to have his phone on him. It made for a more "authentic" hunting experience.

"Uh, my bad," Reid said, scrolling through the log of missed calls. "Jonah called me, like a lot."

"It can wait. Come on."

Even as the words came out of his father's mouth, the screen lit up with another call.

"Jonah," Reid answered. "We're busy. What's—?"

His brother cut him off. "Give the phone to Dad. Right fucking now. *Please.*" His voice was frantic, his tone taut like a bowstring about to snap. Reid had never heard him sound so undone.

"I—I did something," Jonah choked out. "I just need Dad . . . I need his help."

The Langley siblings had been born with silver spoons in their mouths. They rarely asked for help because they never needed it. The whole world had been laid at their feet. All they had to do was take it.

"What did you *do*?" Reid asked, more bewildered than anything.

His father had been observing this whole time. He extended his hand. "Let me talk to him."

Reid did as he was told. His father took the phone and motioned for Reid to tend to the oryx. He hesitated—ears still pricked with curiosity over what Jonah had gotten himself into.

But with his father, it wouldn't do to be told twice.

As he made the short trek across the clearing, he slapped the electric lantern a few times, knocking it back on. Reid's heart began to pound once more in his chest as he neared the oryx. He sidestepped the pool of blood seeping into the damp grass, staining it black.

Even in the dim light, the beauty of the creature humbled Reid. He crouched at its side, marveling at its massive size, the curved horns that could easily impale a man. This was no Georgia buck. How would Russ and his hunting buddies fare against the creature without their rifles and blinds to hide behind?

Reid glanced over his shoulder. He could just make out the silhouette of his father in the dark, but he was too far for Reid to overhear the call. And too far for his father to see Reid's reluctance.

Reid let out a shaky breath. He placed the knife on the oryx's stomach, piercing the topmost layer of flesh. But just before he could sink the blade in, he paused. Up close, in the stark, eerie glow of the night, there was the subtle rise and fall of the animal's rib cage.

The oryx was still alive.

Reid stumbled back on his heels, thumping softly onto the ground.

He'd failed his shot. The oryx was dying slowly in front of him. Suffering.

What were his options? If he shot the animal again, putting it out of its misery, his father would know he'd done the first shot wrong. His father's way didn't allow for mistakes. But Reid couldn't stomach more senseless death.

He glanced at the knife, still embedded in the animal's heaving side. Dark blood welled up around the edges of the blade. He couldn't continue field dressing while it was alive, either. That would be cruel beyond comprehension.

And it would *bleat,* signaling to his father that Reid had messed up.

Footsteps sounded behind him. "Forget the animal," his father said. "We need to go."

Reid looked up, willing his face to appear calm. "What happened?"

His father glanced past Reid, observing the oryx. The animal's breathing was nearly imperceptible. Reid hoped whatever Jonah had done was distraction enough.

"Your brother . . . ," his father began, shaking his head. "I need to fix it."

Reid hesitated, then asked, "Are we leaving the oryx behind?"

His father scoffed. "We don't waste good meat, son. I'll have someone pick it up. Let's go."

His father reached out his hand to help him up from the ground, but Reid hesitated to take it. An innocent animal was dying slowly beside him—*because* of him—and this was his final chance to make things right. To help the oryx die in dignity, with little pain. All it required was a quick action.

A slash of the carotid artery.

A bullet through the skull.

A snap of the neck.

But no matter how much Reid wished otherwise, he was still a Langley. Cowardice and cruelty were in his blood. He made no move to ease the oryx's suffering. Instead, he took his father's hand, allowing Russ to pull him up.

In the dark of night, the pair walked out of the clearing together, while the lone oryx was left to bleed out in the dirt.

REID'S DRIVEWAY HAD never felt so long.

Actually, that was a lie. There had been another time, six years ago, when the half-mile drive wound and twisted for what felt like hours as he sat in dread of what lay at the end.

The night they found Mom.

But that was a memory he'd spent years tamping down. Now was not the time to falter. Reid squinted, refocusing himself on the dark road beyond the windshield.

And if he was honest, what he felt right now was not dread at all—it was anticipation. Almost . . . *excitement*. His older brother, adored by his father and peers, had done it. Jonah had made another mistake. One that prevented Reid from the humiliation of owning up to his own. But he pushed the nauseating thought of the oryx away, burying it in the same way he did the memories of his mother.

For the first time in a long while, Reid wasn't the fuckup.

Reid glanced at his father. Outwardly, he seemed calm. Unfazed. The only indication of his rage was his white-knuckle grip on the Ford's leather steering wheel.

They rounded a bend, and the sprawling Langley estate

came into view, lit by the bright outdoor lamps that dotted the lakeside landscape. Reid scanned the property, searching for some clue as to Jonah's mishap. Everything was in its place, just as they left it. Except for the eighth door of their ten-car garage. It sat ajar, warm light spilling out onto the smooth pavement of the driveway.

Of the ten cars in their garage, six were antiques, all of which belonged to his father. He tended to the cars nearly every day, caring for them with a tenderness he had never shown Reid.

There were only two rules in the Langley household.

Rule one: Never tarnish the family name.

Rule two: Don't touch the cars.

Reid couldn't help the smug smile that crossed his face. *Jonah wrecked one of Dad's cars?* It was a fate worse than death.

His father parked the Ford in its usual spot. Reid watched him take three long, deep breaths before turning off the truck's engine and climbing out.

"Bring the gear inside," his father said over his shoulder before he walked away, disappearing inside the front doors of their home.

Reid set about hauling the heavy gear to the house, but he slowed his steps as he passed the open garage door. Inside, his father's '73 Aston Martin was in shambles. The front hood was smashed and twisted, exposing the car's engine. The windshield was cracked, though still intact, and the left side of the car's body was badly scratched, dirt and mud covering most of the burgundy paint job. Reid whistled low under his breath. Jonah must have hit a deer.

It still didn't explain the peculiar panic he'd heard in his brother's voice over the phone.

Something isn't right. Reid hefted the gear bags higher on his shoulder and continued to the front doors. He stepped inside the house, quickly disposing of the hunting gear in the nearest closet. He hesitated at the sight of the taxidermic buck's head that hung over the entryway of their home, its antlers nearly spreading the width of the wall.

A moment later, he found his family's private doctor, Dr. Simmons, pacing in the living room, but there was no one else there. The doctor held a cell phone against his ear, speaking in a hushed tone to someone on the other end.

"Evening," Reid said awkwardly.

Dr. Simmons paused, giving Reid a strained, polite smile, then returned to the call.

Distantly, the kitchen faucet ran. He followed the sound, finding his older sister, Farris, rinsing a bloodied towel in the sink.

"Where's Jonah?" Reid asked.

Farris didn't glance up as she said, "In Dad's study, but I'd wait a few minutes if I were you. He's angry." The sink water ran red as Farris continued to rinse the towel.

Reid studied his sister's dirtied hands. "Is Jonah badly hurt?"

Farris scowled, meeting Reid's gaze. "He will be once Dad's through with him." She paused, eyeing Dr. Simmons in the other room. His sister's gray eyes flashed with delight as she said, "Jonah fucked up. *Big time.*"

Reid made his way out of the kitchen, down the long hallway of their home. He passed several rooms before reaching the door of his father's study. He didn't know if curiosity or sympathy propelled him forward. Perhaps it was both.

Hovering near the study door, he rested his ear against the polished wood. Jonah could be heard crying on the other side. His sniffling was unmistakable to Reid, as his older brother had always been a dramatic crier.

Knocking once, Reid opened the door.

Jonah sat in one of the worn leather armchairs in the corner, his face buried in his hands, shoulders shaking. His father leaned against his ornate desk, eyebrows raised as Reid peered in. "Dr. Simmons is here."

His father nodded once, wiping freshly bloodied knuckles on a towel. He gave Jonah a parting, disapproving look, then peeled away from the desk and stepped out of the room.

Reid eyed his brother, debating whether he should comfort or taunt him. But as Jonah continued to cry into his hands, Reid's earlier elation began to disappear. Violence was a tool their father wielded carefully. Their father was the hand that broke them, and the hand that made them whole again.

Reid cleared his throat, causing his brother to look up.

Jonah had a fresh black eye, the bruise already turning purple. His bottom lip was swollen with blood crusting around his mouth. He wore a white-collared shirt that wasn't very white anymore; bloodstains turned the fabric a crude shade of brown.

"Get out of here," his brother croaked.

Reid frowned. "You look like shit."

Jonah's gray eyes were glassy. "I know."

"I saw the Aston Martin." Reid took a seat in the armchair beside his brother. "Looked like the deer did a number on it."

Jonah shook his head. His voice came out rough, strained. "There was no deer."

Reid's eyebrows furrowed. "Then what the hell did you hit?"

"Another car." Jonah buried his face in his hands again. "They went off the road into a ditch." His voice hitched. "I didn't know what to do. *I didn't know.*"

Reid hesitated. "So . . . what *did* you do?"

Jonah didn't answer for a long moment. "I tried to see if they were okay." A sob escaped from his brother's throat. "The kid . . . he wasn't moving. There was so much blood. It was everywhere."

Reid stayed quiet, waiting for his brother to continue. To say what he'd done next, but Jonah only continued to whimper into his hands.

"Did you call 911?" Reid pressed.

Jonah shook his head. "I'd been drinking. I couldn't get another DUI. Dad would fucking *kill* me."

Reid leaned away from his brother, his thoughts racing. Disgust and revulsion pulsed beneath his skin. All his previous excitement was snuffed out. "Do we . . . do we know what happened to the kid?"

Jonah's shoulders gave another tremulous shake. He wound his dirtied hands into his brown hair, staring at the polished wood floor. His words a hoarse whisper, Jonah finally said, "I don't know."

The realization of what Jonah had done fully dawned on Reid. He struggled to look at his brother at all. "And the driver?"

"It was Samantha Calhoun," Jonah whispered, meeting Reid's gaze. "She's alive . . . I think."

Reid blinked. "You mean . . . ?"

Jonah nodded, fear etching across his beaten face. "I hit Wiley's kids. Wiley's. Goddamn. Kids."

Wiley Calhoun was a weapon of a man, wielded exclusively by the Langley family. A discharged war vet whose affection toward violence made him a useful asset to their father. You didn't want to be on the receiving end of the kind of work he did for the Langleys. Reid feared how their father would handle this, and if Jonah would even survive it.

Before Jonah could say anything else, their father appeared in the doorway with Dr. Simmons. He looked between his two sons, giving little away. "Our good doctor has news."

Dr. Simmons knelt before Jonah with a leather bag of medical supplies. He turned Jonah's face upward with gloved hands so he could inspect his cuts and scrapes.

"What happened?" Jonah asked, sounding almost pitifully eager.

"My colleague called me several minutes ago," Dr. Simmons said, his hands hovering over Jonah's bruised eye. "The driver sustained minimal injuries, while the boy . . ."

Jonah swallowed hard, eyes widening as Dr. Simmons applied an ointment to his face. "What—what happened to him?"

Dr. Simmons cleared his throat. "The boy was confirmed dead at 2:04 a.m."

Jonah struggled to speak. His eyes darted between their father and Dr. Simmons, as if this was an elaborate joke. "No, no." He shook his head, gray eyes wide and pitiful. "Dad, *please.*"

Reid couldn't discern if his brother felt guilty, or if he was simply ashamed of being caught. Their father studied Jonah for a long time, no doubt trying to discern the very same thing.

"However." Dr. Simmons cut his eyes to Russ, who gave him a small nod, before saying, "He has since been revived. Aside from a few broken bones and fractures, the boy is in a remarkably stable condition."

Jonah's bruised face paled. "He's *alive*?"

"Lucky for you, son," their father said. "It seems a medical miracle occurred at Clearwater Regional tonight."

CHAPTER 4

ISAIAH

To: secretsofthesouth@kmail.com
From: dawson.sumter@kmail.com
Subject: Missing Teenager In Carrion, Georgia

>If you're receiving this email, it means something bad happened to me. Whatever the local news says in the coming days, I'm not dead.
>It's all connected to the Lake Clearwater community. Find out their secrets before more people go missing.

Not even the roosters could wake Isaiah Johnson that early morning. Only the rough shake of his grandmother's hands as she pulled him from deep, dreamless sleep. He jolted upright, finding himself seated at his desk with his laptop as a pillow.

Grandma Bee frowned down at him. "Baby, you were sleeping like the dead. Nearly gave me a heart attack."

Isaiah winced and rubbed his stiff neck, struggling to clear away the haze of exhaustion that hung over him. "What time is it?"

"Almost sunrise. You would've slept through the harvest if I didn't wake you." Grandma Bee cast an evaluating look at him. Her eyes narrowed, and Isaiah's cheeks warmed. "What were you doing up all night?"

Isaiah's dark brown eyes slid to his laptop. "I was transcribing a hearing," he lied. "Took longer than I thought. I must've passed out."

"Those boys at the law firm are already working you silly, aren't they?" Grandma Bee didn't look satisfied but, thankfully, didn't push further. "Well, almost everybody is here. Hurry and get ready so you can eat before harvest."

"Yes, ma'am," Isaiah said as his grandmother left his room, leaving the door ajar. Bright light spilled in from the hallway, illuminating his untouched, perfectly made bed.

Isaiah bemoaned another night spent at his desk. He hadn't slept properly in days. Not since he'd received *that* email. Once he was certain his grandmother was downstairs, he opened his laptop, navigating to the encrypted messaging service he used. For what felt like the hundredth time, he reread the ominous tip that had appeared in his inbox a week ago. The email that could change the entire trajectory of his summer, if not his life, if he let it.

"*Shit.*" Isaiah buried his face in his hands, massaging his temples.

It wasn't that Isaiah had never received tips for his podcast before. *Secrets of the South* was in the "Top 10" list of all true crime podcasts across all streaming platforms. He had hundreds of thousands of listeners, which meant a large audience of amateur sleuths, often pitching him the next big thing through email.

But this one was different. The email was about a kid from Carrion, *his Carrion,* and that didn't sit right with Isaiah. He hosted the podcast anonymously. Admittedly, a large part of its success was due to the mystery of the person *behind* the mic. No one knew a Black teenager from Georgia ran it, and he intended to keep it that way. But what were the odds someone would pitch him a story about his hometown?

Carrion was a small, insignificant town in rural Southwest Georgia. A place no one had heard of unless they were from the area. What made Carrion remotely significant wasn't even the town at all, but the neighboring, unincorporated community of Lake Clearwater. It was *too* coincidental, and Isaiah wasn't one for coincidences. The same question repeated again and again and again in his head.

Why now?

"Boy, you best get up quick!" Papa Charles called playfully from down the hall. "Or else I'll eat all the eggs!"

"Be down in a minute!" Isaiah called back, returning to the world in front of him. He logged out of the email and shut down the laptop, placing it in the drawer of his desk. His eyes lingered on the open curtains of his bedroom window. The sky was slowly changing from blackened night to the purple-and-orange gradient of early morning.

Isaiah stumbled through his morning routine—including eye drops and the eight-step skin care regimen his mom had taught him—anything to make himself look less tired, even if he was just going to be kneeling in the dirt for the next few hours.

Once downstairs, he walked into the kitchen just as Grandma Bee pulled a fresh tray of golden biscuits from the oven. Bacon sizzled on the stove, and Papa Charles handed him a cup of freshly brewed coffee.

"You look like you need it," he said with a laugh and a wink before heading out the front door.

But Grandma Bee wasn't smiling as Isaiah sipped the coffee. He sidled up beside his grandmother, offering her a one-armed hug to placate her.

"Most everybody's already outside and fed," Grandma Bee said with a nod toward the door. She handed him a warm plate topped with all the makings of Southern comfort food. "They were tired of waiting on *Mister Harvard*," she said in a teasing, singsong voice. "Hurry up and eat, then head outside."

"Yes, ma'am." Isaiah smirked at the light jab, carefully cradling the plate to his seat at the kitchen counter. That morning was the first day of the summer harvest for his family's farm, but it was also the first time everyone was together since he received his Harvard acceptance a few months prior. It was meant to be a celebration of not just the farm, but of him.

Isaiah was the second on his father's side of the family to attend an Ivy League school, the first being his father, Laurence. Isaiah had worked tirelessly to get accepted. But with high school graduation newly behind him, doubt brewed in his stomach. He still wasn't sure whether Harvard was what he wanted, or if he was simply fulfilling the path his father forged for him.

As Isaiah finished stuffing his face with grits and eggs, a car's engine sounded from a distance. His ears perked at the rumble before he craned his neck to peer out the kitchen window, eyes searching.

Grandma Bee followed his gaze, frowning ever so slightly. "Your father's not coming, baby."

Isaiah repressed a sigh. "He never said no, Bee."

"Maybe so. But he never said yes, either." Grandma Bee fixed him with a level gaze. "You and I both know, good and well, that this farm means little to nothin' to Laurence these days. He's too proud to be digging in Carrion dirt."

"I know." Even so, Isaiah had hoped differently. But hope was a fickle thing when it came to the actions of his father.

"Don't worry yourself over nothin'." Grandma Bee's gaze turned sympathetic as she wiped her hands on her kitchen apron. The fabric was adorned with handsewn bees of different sizes and stitching. Each one affectionately sewn on by a member of Isaiah's family—a gift for her seventieth birthday.

"There's plenty of folks who *are* happy to be here."

Isaiah nodded, walking his plate to the sink. He scrubbed the dish absently, wondering what was more important to his father than this. He supposed that list was long, growing longer with each day as his father grew increasingly involved with his work as a judge for the state. But Isaiah had suspicions there was more on his father's mind than just the docket.

"Papa Charles and I were going to wait to give your graduation gift to you," Bee said, interrupting Isaiah's thoughts. She held something behind her back, a wide smile spreading across her face. "But you know me—I've never much been a patient woman."

Isaiah dried his hands with a kitchen towel. "Oh, Bee. I told you that you didn't have to get . . ." His voice faded away as his grandmother revealed a bow-wrapped film camera. Vintage, boxy, with an attached leather strap to rest around his neck. He'd been eyeing one just like it on eBay for months. "I—I don't know what to say." He stepped forward, his fingers delicately assessing the body of the camera.

"It's what you deserve, baby." Grandma Bee beamed.

Isaiah gently set the camera down on the counter, then wrapped his grandmother in a tight hug. He struggled against the joyous tears welling up in his eyes. "I can't thank you both enough. For everything."

Grandma Bee stood on her tiptoes, clutching the sides of his face. "Just be sure you'll put the camera to good use this summer, all right? I don't want you getting in your father's habit of workin' more than living." She clapped her hands together. "Now, let's get going. We've kept everybody waiting too long."

Once Isaiah finally stepped outside on the screened-in porch, he was greeted by bright cheers and animated claps. Aunts, uncles, cousins, family friends—all gathered around him with hugs, kisses, and shoulder squeezes, drowning him in the kind of love that made summers in Carrion special.

"How does it feel to be a Harvard hotshot now?" Aunt Tamera teased as Isaiah hoisted his eleven-year-old cousin, Keisha, onto his back for a piggyback ride.

Flashing his signature smile, Isaiah said, "Pretty good." He continued to field questions left and right about his acceptance for the fall, all the while trotting in circles with Keisha on his back.

Dawn just barely broke along the horizon, casting the farm in the soft, warm hues of morning. Cardinals sang all around them, calling to one another from the pine trees. The chicken coop hens clucked around their enclosure, the roosters still crowing over them. Somewhere on a neighboring farm, cows mooed, the sound carrying through the dewy air. Isaiah took advantage of every spare moment, photographing the beauty of the world around him.

A few more cars bounced down the gravel driveway of the Johnson farm—last-minute stragglers, cousins and neighbors and people from the Carrion community. Isaiah's grandparents were loved by many, and their farm was treated just the same. Grandma Bee greeted them with paper plates of breakfast, parceling out food like it was a party. Before long, Isaiah was dizzy from hugs and laughter and the warmth of being completely at ease.

Eventually, Isaiah joined everyone by the shed, donning gardening gloves and sorting crates for the vegetables. He changed into dirt-caked work boots, gazing out across the tidy rows of crops that stretched across the flat landscape. A smaller harvest than usual, but it was no surprise. Over the years, the once-sprawling acreage his family owned had been sold off, piece by piece.

According to Papa Charles, farming wasn't what it once was, especially for Black farmers. Every year the profits grew slimmer as massive agricultural companies bought up the land of Southwest Georgia, turning the art of cultivating food into a sterile practice, one driven by profit over a reverence for the earth.

A whistle cut through the air, silencing the farm. Papa Charles, adorned in his signature overalls, waved everyone over to him. The Johnson family and friends finally gathered in front of the shed for the usual Papa-Charles-Harvest-Day speech.

"It's nothin' short of a miracle that we're here today," Papa Charles began, his dark eyes glistening. "We are truly blessed to have this land and these people to tend to it. Thank you for coming out to help. Now, let us harvest the crops and feed those we love."

Isaiah looked onto the community of people that showed up for his family. The smiles and the care that was as clear as the morning sun. For a breath, Isaiah wanted there to be nothing more to Carrion than what was in front of him. No unnerving email. No secrets. Nothing buried in the soil other than the seeds his family planted.

But reality was never that simple, and he knew it as best as anyone.

Everyone broke off in pairs, with Keisha and Isaiah assigned to pick the green peas. His cousin worked the lower part of the trellises, while Isaiah reached for the higher ones. Before long, they'd filled two crates' worth. As a team, they hauled the full crates onto the pickup truck, chasing each other around the wire trellises, laughing and carrying on as they worked.

Once they were done, Keisha ran off to help Aunt Tamera with the tomato vines, while Isaiah joined his uncle Cedric and grandparents as they harvested the eggplants.

Grandma Bee smiled as Isaiah approached, making a dramatic show to hug Cedric's arm. "Look here, Isaiah. Ced just told us he was up fightin' fires *all* night, yet he still made it to the harvest. That's my boy."

Uncle Cedric was the youngest of his father's siblings, Laurence being the oldest, Tamera in the middle, and then Ced, Grandma Bee's favorite. A fact she was incredibly vocal about. Papa Charles chuckled at Bee's dramatics, while Ced playfully rolled his eyes, then planted a kiss on the top of Grandma Bee's head. "It's nothing, Ma. I was only doing my job."

Papa Charles snorted as he wiped sweat from his forehead. "Your night didn't sound like nothin' to me."

"What happened?" Isaiah asked as he helped pluck plump eggplant from leafy, overgrown bushes. "Did the burnings get out of control?"

"It was a wild night," Ced said casually. He took a long swig from his water bottle before continuing. "Everythin' from unruly fires to a couple bad car accidents. One thing after another. Never seen a night quite like it."

Papa Charles and Grandma Bee exchanged a curious look, something unspoken passing between them.

Ced continued, oblivious to the looks of his parents, "There was even a fire at that motel off the highway. Y'all know the one?"

Papa Charles grunted. "That's the Singhs' motel still, ain't it? They all right?"

Isaiah froze, nearly dropping his basket of eggplants on the ground. "What?"

Ced nodded. "They're fine. Their car caught on fire. Nasty business, but no one was hurt."

"Thank the Lord." Grandma Bee frowned. "That poor family. They keep goin' through it." Her dark eyes flitted to Isaiah. "You should go pay 'em a visit after harvest. Take a crate of produce over."

Papa Charles nodded in agreement. "That'd be real nice. Let 'em know we're here if they need anything."

"I'll do that," Isaiah said slowly. He wasn't excited about the idea, but it was the right thing to do. He and Neera Singh had once been best friends, but that was firmly in the past. After what happened three years ago, the possibility of seeing her again felt heavy inside his chest.

Once the eggplant bushes were picked clean, Isaiah wandered to the tree line and squatted in the dirt, yawning into his elbow.

Isaiah couldn't help but smile at the land, at how different life was below the fault line. He'd spent most of his life in gated Atlanta suburbs, the environment sterile and cookie-cutter, with the people to match, but summers spent down at the farm were where he truly felt like himself. Even if he was still figuring out exactly *who* that was.

Ginger, the farm's cat, strolled over, weaving between Isaiah's legs. He scratched her ear, dusting fresh dirt off her pink nose. Ginger was the only stray allowed inside Grandma Bee's house and she knew it. The farm was her dominion. She nuzzled Isaiah's hand and flopped onto her back, purring loudly.

A gust of wind picked up around them, rustling the trees.

Ginger was on her feet in an instant, eyes locked on the tree line with pupils blown wide. She hissed, every bit of fur along her back standing straight up. Isaiah grabbed for her, but she swatted at his hand.

"Ow!" Isaiah recoiled, pulling his hand back to his chest. Ginger took off at a sprint, back toward the house. Isaiah inspected the cut. She had left three bright red slashes across the back of his wrist.

"What'd you do to my cat?" Papa Charles called, his tone playful.

Isaiah shook his head. "Nothing. She was just acting strange."

Papa Charles opened his mouth to respond, but something

made him pause. He turned slowly toward the wood, his head canted to one side. Listening. His usual smile faded from his sun-worn face. "You hear that?"

Isaiah strained to listen, too. "I don't hear anything."

"Exactly," Papa Charles said, his voice coming out low.

He was right. There was no sound at all. No birds chirping or frogs croaking. Even the roosters and hens were silent. The wind moved through the trees, but it seemed to have taken sound away with it—not even a rustle of branches.

"Pop," Isaiah whispered. "What's going on?"

Papa Charles shook his head. "We need to get inside. Come on."

They walked quickly back toward the house, their footsteps strangely muted. Isaiah had never heard such silence before. A total absence of sound. The farm's attendees all shuffled inside, their movements quiet and hurried.

Grandma Bee was already on the porch when they reached it.

"Where's Keisha?" Papa Charles asked, a little breathless.

"Inside with everybody else." Grandma Bee looked past them, out to the forest.

"What's going on?" Isaiah repeated, struggling to keep the frustration out of his voice. "*Please.*"

"It's the cicadas, baby," Grandma Bee said, but she didn't take her eyes off the tree line.

Isaiah looked between his grandparents. Their faces were grave. He hadn't ever seen them look so . . . *afraid*. He followed their line of sight, looking into the trees, expecting something to happen.

For a moment, nothing.

Then the cicadas began to scream.

CHAPTER 5

NEERA

By the time the police arrived at the Colonial, an ungodly sound had descended upon Carrion.

Neera had heard cicadas all her life, but the awful shrill coming from the surrounding pine forest was the sort of sound she hadn't heard in years. Not since she was small—the first time her mom brought her to Carrion. To the Colonial. Even as a child, she had known the shriek of the cicadas was *wrong*.

One moment, she was standing outside the motel with her mom, watching firefighters tend to the burnt remains of the Cadillac. The next, a neon-red sun peeked over the horizon, and with it came the screaming from the woods.

At first, Neera thought it was a jet engine flying overhead. But it didn't pass.

Every thirteen years, the town held a festival to herald the arrival of the periodical cicada brood. In South Georgia, regular cicadas, or *annual* cicadas, could be found quite commonly every summer, but the thirteen-year creatures were something else entirely. The massive, winged insects swarmed up out of the ground in late June by the millions, each one as big as a grown man's thumb. Masses of chittering legs and writhing, grubby bodies scrambling over one another in their bid for freedom and fresh air.

Neera had only been five the last time a brood had emerged, but she'd heard the stories long after. The insects blanketed the town all summer long. Nanaji took to fishing them out of the Colonial's swimming pool every morning, and ladies leaving church each Sunday could be seen shielding their heads as they walked to their cars—lest a pair of cicadas fall out of a tree, mid-copulation, and get stuck in their hair.

Neera didn't fully understand why the town pretended to love them, why they celebrated them—the nuances of Carrion traditions were as foreign to her as the Singh family's culture was to the town.

As the only South Asian family in a hundred-mile radius, they never quite belonged. Her family had immigrated to Carrion from England in the midnineties. Back then, as British-Punjabi immigrants, they were regarded with disdain by much of Carrion's population. And now, over twenty years later, Neera didn't think it had much changed. She found that rural Southern towns were often smaller in mindset than size.

But she supposed Carrion's celebration of the cicadas was better than the other option. They were creatures better worshipped than damned, or else they'd probably bring the plague with them.

Kiran, wincing from the noise, jerked her head toward the hotel lobby. Neera nodded and followed her mom across the parking lot.

The glass door of the lobby thudded shut behind them, and it was like putting in earplugs. The buzzing of the cicadas could still be heard—no longer a piercing siren shriek but a dull, ominous drone that made the thick hairs on Neera's arms prickle with unease.

Nanaji was already in the lobby, talking with the two cops who'd been sent to the scene. The sight of the police made Neera's skin crawl. She kept her eyes trained on the ground as she ducked behind the front desk, keeping her distance.

The last time there had been cops in the motel lobby was a night she'd spent the past three years trying to forget.

"So you're sayin' the car just caught fire randomly?" one of the officers asked her grandfather, chewing tobacco like it was bubble gum. Neera recognized him from that night years ago—Sheriff Buckley. His partner, Officer Taylor, listened along with his arms crossed over a protruding potbelly.

"Yes," Nanaji said. "It is an old car. Bad engine."

Kiran tensed, shooting her father a look. "That's not true. We think it was arson."

Officer Taylor raised his eyebrows. "That's a bold claim, ma'am. You got any evidence?"

"Parked cars don't catch fire," Kiran said evenly.

Nanaji clicked his tongue, holding his hand up at her. "No, it was not arson. My daughter knows *nothing*."

Kiran opened her mouth like she meant to fire something back but stopped herself. With a sigh and a shake of her head, she stalked off, disappearing through the door that led to the kitchen. Neera watched her go, wondering exactly what she knew about the motel's debts.

"So which one is it?" Sheriff Buckley kept probing Nanaji. "Accident or arson? We don't got all day."

"Accident," Nanaji said firmly, his British-Punjabi accent in sharp contrast to the deep-fried Southern men before him. "Nothing more."

The smell of warm cloves and cardamom carried through the room. A moment later, Nani stepped out of the kitchen carrying a small silver platter with two cups of chai resting on it. She gently placed the cups before the officers, nodding once, then stepped back. It was a kind gesture, one that the officers were not deserving of, but that was Nani's nature. Kindness in the face of unkind things.

Officer Taylor sniffed the glass. "You got any sweet tea instead?"

Neera spoke up before Nani could respond. "That's all we have." Her words were final, definitive.

Sheriff Buckley picked up his cup, seemingly to take a sip, but instead he spit his dip into the chai. The force of the blackened wad sent the drink spilling onto the table. "Oh, would you look at that," he said benignly, making no move to clean it up. "Forgive my clumsiness."

Neera bit down hard on her tongue. She grabbed napkins from behind the front desk and cleaned up the spilled chai without looking either officer in the eye. Her grandfather watched in silence, while Nani just stood there, wringing her wrinkled hands, looking lost, before she turned and went back to the kitchen. There was something so *shameful* about the whole thing.

But Neera would rather feel that shame a thousand times over if it meant her grandmother didn't have to. She finished wiping up the last of the tea and straightened, forcing herself to meet Sheriff Buckley's eyes. Willing her own gaze to burn into him, as if to say: *I was once afraid of you, but not anymore.*

The sheriff stared right back. His gaze felt wrong. "What about you, huh? You see anythin' suspicious last night?"

The memory of Nanaji's yelling match with the handyman flashed through her mind. Wiley's threat was fresh, lingering on the tip of her tongue. If Langley County police were a just or honest group, Neera would've told the officers everything. But the Singh family intimately knew that they were neither. "No, sir. Nothing."

Sheriff Buckley squinted at her. "All right, then. I suppose we're done." He reached into his pocket for a business card and tossed it onto the damp, sticky table. "If you feel so inclined to report anything else that may happen around here, you can just call us directly." Both cops rose and made for the exit.

Officer Taylor tipped his thick head by way of goodbye.

"Y'all take care," Sheriff Buckley said from the doorway, with a deliberate look first at Nanaji, then Neera. He wrapped his knuckles twice against the doorframe on his way out.

Nanaji picked up the business card, folding it twice, and placed it in his pocket. He didn't look at Neera as he said, "You'll work the front desk today." Without giving her a chance to protest, he left the lobby.

WITH THE COPS gone, Neera stood in the small kitchen connected to the lobby, nursing her third cup of coffee, and went through the day's roster book. There were no check-outs or check-ins scheduled. They were at half occupancy, which was strange for the beginning of summer, especially with the Cicada Festival coming up.

Every summer, thousands of tourists came to Lake Clearwater to enjoy idyllic paddleboarding and lakeside golf. But the Cicada Festival was special—those years, the tourists swarmed the manicured lawns in numbers rivaled only by the insects themselves. Cicada summers on Lake Clearwater came to a dramatic end with the last day of the festival, held on the Fourth of July. There was no better place in all the Deep South to celebrate being American.

If only the motel's occupancy could reflect the upcoming influx of tourists. Maybe then her grandfather's debt could be paid.

Neera took another sip of her coffee, gazing out the small kitchen windows with dry, heavy eyes. It was barely past eleven, but the cracked parking lot already shimmered with midday heat, as the land hadn't been blessed that day with a breeze. Beyond the lot, the longleaf pines stood still, their sparse canopies towering high above. From the branch of the nearest pine, a lone crow took flight into the cloudless blue sky.

As the bird flew, it seemed to mutate and multiply, transforming from one bird into dozens—then hundreds. Thousands. The crows moved through the sky like starlings, twisting and dipping in the air, drawing circles around themselves until Neera could no longer see the individual birds. There were only black wings dancing, morphing, rapidly shifting into shapes she couldn't make sense of, but she was unable to look away.

The bell above the lobby door dinged sharply. It was like breaking a soundproof seal—the shrieking of the cicadas startling Neera back to reality. She rubbed her eyes, then looked again to the sky, finding a singular crow flying off into the late June day.

Neera shook off the moment before setting her coffee down and hurrying to the front desk.

A tall teenage boy stood in the lobby, his arms full with a heavy crate of leafy greens and vegetables. He wore shining sunglasses that covered his eyes, while a bushel of mustard greens covered half his face. His outfit, a pair of fitted dress pants and a striped polo, had the neat, crisp look of someone who had spent a fair amount of time choosing exactly what to wear.

"Where can I set this?" he asked as he kicked the door closed with his polished leather shoe.

"Oh, there's fine." Neera motioned to the sticky table where the cops had sat earlier.

"Thank you," the boy said as he laid the crate on the table. He dusted invisible dirt off his clothes, then turned to Neera and smiled, removing his sunglasses. It was a smile she once knew well—an infectious sort of joy she envied since she was little. "Hey, Neera."

"Isaiah?" Neera was frozen in shock for all of a second, then she stepped forward and offered him an awkward one-armed hug. They pulled apart, eyeing each other, unsure of what to say. "Why're you here?"

Isaiah smiled sheepishly. "Just dropping this off. My family wanted to send it over after what happened last night." His sharp eyes took in the small lobby, as observant as he had been when they were kids. His gaze lingered on the burnt remains of the Cadillac in the parking lot. "My uncle Ced was one of the firefighters on the scene. Grandma Bee wanted to help in some way. You know how she is."

"Yeah, I remember," Neera said, hesitating for a moment. Taking him in. "Well, thank you."

Isaiah Johnson had been Neera's first real friend. She and her mom had moved so much while she was growing up—her childhood a whirl of ever-changing zip codes and schools—she'd never lived anywhere long enough to make a lasting friend. Until Isaiah, friendships had been strictly made from survival.

But that had changed the summer Neera was eight. Her mom had dropped her off at a daycare on the outskirts of Carrion. Inside, her eyes had been drawn straight to a boy playing a Nintendo DS by himself. He was playing *The Legend of Zelda*, and Neera badly wanted to join. But she knew from experience that expecting someone to share was a losing battle. She hesitated, looking around the room at the other kids, their friendships and hierarchies already formed. At least the Nintendo boy was alone.

Neera sat beside him, content to just watch him play.

He offered his DS to her almost immediately. "You wanna try?"

Isaiah and Neera became fast friends.

And for a long time, they stayed that way; no matter where Neera moved to, they picked up each summer like no time had passed. But their friendship faded after Ajay. Neera stopped responding to Isaiah's texts, ignored his calls, no longer feigned connection through social media.

Everything good in Neera's life had withered away after what happened three years ago.

"What're you doing in Carrion?" Neera asked as they each took a seat at the lobby table. "I thought you'd be moved up to Massachusetts by now." She'd seen his college announcement during her brief return to Instagram a while back. She quickly added, "Congratulations on Harvard, by the way. I always knew you'd get in."

"Thank you." Isaiah's tone was distant but appreciative. "My father actually got me a law internship up at Lake Clearwater. But I also wanted one last summer in Carrion, you know? It's supposed to be a special one this year." He angled his chin toward the window. "The cicadas are . . . interesting, aren't they? I barely remember them as a kid."

"They're certainly *something*."

Isaiah cleared his throat. "What about you—how've you been? Business still good?"

"Everything's . . . fine," Neera lied. She looked down at her hands in her lap. Her knuckles were chafed and dry from all the scrubbing she'd done the night before. There she was, still at the same motel in the same shit rural town, with not a thing to show for herself.

Then there was the death of Ajay. The black hole that lived in the corner of her vision, widening just a little with each day.

Sometimes, it felt like her grief was a force on the scale of a hurricane. How was she? How could she answer that truthfully?

Three years ago, the sun went out in my life, and it never returned.

Neera turned her palms over, brown eyes lingering on the guitar calluses on the tips of her fingers. Despite everything, there was one thing greater than her grief. She finally offered Isaiah a genuine smile. "I'm trying out for the Cicada's Song. My mom scored me an audition."

Isaiah's eyes lit up a little. "*Whoa.* That's big, Neera. When is it?"

"Today, actually." Neera's stomach twisted. "Can't say I'm not scared out of my mind."

"You'll do great. You've always been incredible at guitar." Isaiah leaned back in his chair, eyes turning toward the ground. He was still for a beat. "Ajay would be proud."

Neera's breathing hitched. No one spoke Ajay's name aloud since he died. Names were tricky like that. In the Singh family, his memory was buried so deeply Neera was shocked he was remembered at all. Not even a photo of him remained in their rooms, on their walls. They had all but erased him from their lives.

Even for her, the only way Neera could bear to remember Ajay was through guitar strings and sheet music. Anything more and she'd come undone.

Isaiah got a faraway look in his eyes. "You know, I'll never forget that time you got picked up from daycare early—it was your birthday, right? We looked outside and your uncle was sitting in his truck bed with his guitar, singing that song he wrote for you. Everyone was cheering. It was like a little concert." He looked at Neera again, his brow furrowing. "Did I say something wrong?"

Neera shook her head. Despite how precious the memory was to her, she worked to get the words around the tightness in her throat. "We don't really talk about Ajay anymore."

His name *burned* in her mouth.

Isaiah's expression turned solemn. "I'm sorry . . . I was just—I was just trying to . . ." Discomfort flashed across his face. It was a look that Neera knew well. The face of someone who hadn't yet experienced grief in the way she had.

"It's all right." But it wasn't, really. It was never going to be all right.

The loss—it was something that *happened* to Neera. An unspeakable thing that gnawed away at her with every passing day. There was only the time before Ajay passed and there was the time after. Living in the after didn't feel much like living at all.

Neera inhaled through her nose, willing herself back under control, returning to the present moment. She found Isaiah studying her with his watchful eyes. "What is it?"

"I'm curious," Isaiah began slowly. "Do you still get many locals renting a room these days?"

Neera was grateful for the change in subject. "Sometimes, yeah. Though not as many as we used to. The Colonial's not exactly in its prime. Why?"

"It's nothing." He looked at his phone in his hand. "Well . . . *something*. Do you know this guy?"

Isaiah set his phone on the table, the screen displaying the Instagram of an eerily familiar face. The Carrion boy from Room 11. Neera took the phone, pretending to consider, despite recognizing him immediately.

The key chain Dawson had left behind was still in her pocket. An unspoken confession.

She shrugged. "I've seen him at the Tavern sometimes when

I'm working, but we've never really spoken. He hangs around with the Clearwater kids."

Isaiah's dark eyes seemed to light up a little. "Which ones?"

Neera considered for a moment. "The Langleys." As the founding family of the county, the Langleys were hard to miss. It wasn't so much how they acted but how others behaved around them—Dawson included. "Why're you asking?"

"It's just internship stuff," Isaiah said as he rubbed his jaw.

He's lying, too, Neera thought. Isaiah had always been an excellent liar, but even after three years, she remembered his tells.

It seemed truth was something that needed to be earned between them again.

Isaiah looked at his wristwatch. "Look, I gotta get going, but would you want to grab food later? Catch up?"

Neera's instinct was to decline, but nothing would get better in her life if she didn't, at least, try. "When?"

"A morning later this week? I'll text you," Isaiah said. "But you have to respond this time, all right?" His words were playful, but Neera detected an edge to them. Heat warmed her cheeks.

"Yeah, I will."

"Before I go . . . ," Isaiah started, eyes still glued to the burnt car. "Can I take a look at it?"

"The Cadillac?" With a shrug, Neera said, "Go ahead."

As they rose from the table, Isaiah asked, "Any idea what caused the fire?"

Neera hesitated. Though she didn't fully understand the fight she'd witnessed the previous night, she knew Wiley's threat was more than just words. The burnt skeleton of the Cadillac was proof enough.

After a long pause, she said, "No idea."

As they exited the lobby, Neera covered her ears with her hands. The cicadas had only grown louder as the sun rose in the sky. Her teeth vibrated in her skull as the sound reverberated around them. A cluster of cicadas barreled past, diving toward the simmering cement. Neera dodged around them as they collided with the ground.

The pair approached the car, sidestepping burnt debris. Isaiah circled the Cadillac, gaze serious. He pulled out his phone and made another circle of the car, taking photos from each angle. Leaning in close to inspect the gaping holes where the windows once were. Crouching down to examine the gas valve.

Finally, he stood and turned back to Neera. He said something—she could see his lips move—but his words were snatched away by the roaring cicadas.

What? Neera mouthed, gesturing to her ears.

He frowned and typed something on his phone, then passed it to Neera.

In his Notes app, he'd written: *I think an accelerant was used to start the fire.*

Neera feigned shock. She typed her response: *Why do you think that?*

Isaiah pointed to the car's lack of windows and typed: *Windows don't melt like this in a normal car fire.* He watched her with those serious, earnest eyes for a long moment before typing another line: *Why would someone do something like this?*

How could Neera respond? The truth was too absurd. A threat of death hung over the Singh family like a curse, and she had to pretend otherwise.

Carrion was dying. All of Southwest Georgia was in the throes of ending. Why did they have to stay? Why did *she*?

Neera only hoped she and her family could make it out of Carrion before it ate them all alive.

CHAPTER 6

SAM

Sam shuffled through the labyrinthian halls of Clearwater Regional, her muscles and bones screaming in protest. Last night, she'd run out of the exam room before anyone had looked at her, and now she regretted it. It didn't matter, though. She had no health insurance and no money to pay for medical bills. She winced, thinking of what the ambulance ride alone was going to cost her.

Despite not being able to sit at her brother's bedside, Sam had waited to leave until he was safely out of surgery that morning. She'd waited until she knew he was alive and well. She'd waited until she knew, without a doubt in her bones, her bargain with the devil rang true.

Because against all medical and mortal odds, Ben lived.

Sam stopped in the middle of the hallway after having passed the same door twice. This was pointless, and if she walked in another circle she might vomit.

"Samantha Calhoun—you not gonna speak?"

Sam tensed at the sound of her full name, but eased a little at the sight of a familiar face approaching from down the hallway. "Mrs. Sumter?" She hadn't noticed her at all, overwhelmed with worries about her brother. "It's been . . . a minute."

Sam hadn't seen Andrea Sumter in months, and she wanted to keep it that way. Despite that, she barely recognized the woman she once knew. Andrea's face was gaunt, cheeks hollow. Her blue eyes were dull. The contrast was stark, compared to the once-smiling woman she knew as a kid.

"Yes, ma'am, it has." Andrea pulled Sam into an unwilling hug, then looked her over, blond eyebrows furrowing. "What happened to you? You're covered in blood."

"I, well . . ." Sam took a gracious step back. She shifted her weight from one foot to the other. "Ben and I got into a car accident last night."

Andrea's eyes widened, which only made the dark bags beneath them look worse. "My Lord. I didn't know that was you."

"You heard about it?"

She nodded. "There's talk all over the hospital. They're callin' your brother a miracle."

Sam snorted. "Yeah . . . something like that."

Andrea's dried lips thinned. "Well, I'm glad to hear it. God bless his soul. Not all of us can be so lucky."

Sam's eyebrows furrowed. "What do you mean?" That's when she noticed a thick stack of paper in Andrea's hands. Peeking over the top of her fingers were familiar blue eyes. "What're you holdin'?"

"You don't know?" Andrea's eyes turned watery, her chin trembling. She struggled to speak, offering Sam one of the papers. It took a breath for Sam to realize what she was looking at. In her hands was a missing person flyer for Dawson Sumter. According to the *last seen* date, he'd been missing for a week. "Have you heard from him?"

Sam's throat went tight. Before high school, Dawson Sumter's backyard had been Sam's favorite place. Back then, she ate dinner at the Sumter household more often than her own. But Andrea always knew Sam's bruises and cuts weren't just from falling on the playground. She never did anything about it, other than offering her the food at her table.

No one ever did anything. Not her teachers. Not the school nurse. Not her soccer coach. Sam learned early on that people were rarely good, but they were also rarely bad. Instead, they were neither wholly committed to either side, which, in her eyes, was much worse.

Shaking her head, Sam said, "We haven't talked in a while."

Andrea nodded and handed Sam a thin stack from the pile. "Could you put these up around town for me?"

"Yes, ma'am." Sam tucked them under her arm. "What'd the police say? Are they looking for him?"

"They told me this was normal for an eighteen-year-old boy. That I'm overreacting. Saying he'll come home any day now." Andrea stepped closer, lowering her voice. "But I *know* somethin' ain't right. I can feel it."

Sam wanted to pull away from her. Andrea's eyes were wild and desperate. She wondered if the woman was using again. If so, it made sense why Dawson was avoiding her. "Like what?"

Andrea frowned, hesitating for a moment. "I think Dawson got mixed up in something he shouldn't have up at the lake."

Sam blinked. "What makes you say that?"

Despite Sam and Dawson being best friends since elementary school, they had grown apart the past year. They both got part-time jobs working at the lake last summer. But while Sam grew to hate the Clearwater community more with each shift, Dawson grew to love it. Last she saw, he was buddying up with the Langley kids and was well on his way to becoming an honorary Clearwater member.

Andrea looked around, her voice low and quiet. "He was spendin' too much time out there. He started not coming home after his shifts, being gone for days at a time. You know Dawson—that ain't like him." Her watery eyes went to the tile floor. "He moved out about a month ago. Got his own place somewhere."

His own place?

Sam bristled, reconciling the idea of the Dawson she grew up with versus the person he had become. "I'm sure he's fine. I bet he got flown out on a trip with some Clearwater kids. You know how they party. He'll be back any day now."

For a long moment, Andrea stared at Sam with a look she couldn't discern. Was it anger? Frustration? *Guilt*? Sam didn't know.

She supposed Andrea expected Sam to be more upset about Dawson's disappearance, but Sam wasn't worried. The white trash of Carrion all had dreams of being accepted into Clearwater's exclusive community, but it often came at a cost. And for Dawson, that cost was clearly his former life, including his friendship with Sam, and now his association with his mama.

"I hope you're right." Andrea sighed, trying to compose herself. She hovered a little too closely to Sam, wringing her hands. "You'll let me know if you hear anything from Dawson, won't you?"

Sam took another step back while resentment swelled in her stomach. She wished her own mama cared for her half as much as Andrea did for Dawson. "Of course." She cleared her throat, then asked, "Can you point me to the elevators? I got all turned around in this place."

Andrea nodded, then gestured down the hall. "Take the first left, then go through the double doors on the right."

"I guess I'll get goin' then." Forcing a thin-lipped smile, Sam said, "Take care of yourself, Andrea. I mean it."

"You too, Samantha," Andrea said. "Please . . . watch yourself up at that lake."

"I always do."

Once Sam reached the elevators, she was grateful to disappear within and gather her thoughts. It was only then that she realized she had never pressed a floor number. The elevator was still—stuck, waiting for Sam to choose whether it was time to go down and home, as she was in desperate need of sleep.

Before she could decide, the elevator began to move. Gravity shifted and it went down, bringing her to the ground floor. When the doors opened, her daddy's boss stood before her.

"Oh." Russ Langley gave Sam a once-over, evaluating her, then donned a strained smile, barely more than a stretching of his lips. "Hello, Samantha."

Sam didn't return his smile or the greeting. There was no point in pretending with Russ. As he stepped into the elevator, she merely asked, "What floor?"

"Five."

Sam paused, eyeing him. That was the same floor where Ben was. "All right," she said, curiosity keeping her firmly in place. She pressed the button, leaning against the wall for support. Her heartbeat thudded loudly in her chest. She gripped the elevator railing tighter. Now was not the time to look out of sorts. Trying to steady herself, Sam took in his appearance.

Russ carried himself well. His outfit, a polo with slacks, was crisp and clean—a uniform of wealth every Clearwater resident wore with pride. His posture easy, limbs loose as his hands rested in the pockets of his khakis. Russ Langley moved through Carrion as if he were its king. But it was Sam's daddy who was the attack dog that slept at the king's feet.

"I'm sorry to hear about what happened with you and your brother," Russ said, his tone even and professional. Like he was sorry for rain interrupting a sunny day. "But I'm glad you're both okay."

"I wouldn't say that Ben is okay," Sam said. "He . . . he nearly *died* last night. He's far from okay."

"I heard." Russ nodded sympathetically. "Well, he is in wonderful hands here. In fact, a family friend of mine will be treating Ben personally."

"Is that right?" Sam huffed. She struggled to smooth her wrinkled T-shirt, despite it being ruined with her brother's blood.

"That's why I'm here, as a matter of fact," Russ continued. "I'll be paying for your brother's medical expenses after what happened."

"You're shittin' me," Sam blurted, her eyebrows furrowing. "Daddy's been struggling to pay for my mama's dialysis for years now, but all of a sudden you wanna cover our medical bills?" Sam knew she was being too blunt, that she should mind her words with a man like Russ Langley. But she was tired, and hurt, and didn't have it in her to play nice right then.

"It's called goodwill, Samantha," Russ condescended. "It's not unheard of around here. Besides, your father is a fine employee. It's the least I can do after such an accident."

A hysterical laugh bubbled up in her chest. *A fine employee.* The work her daddy did for the Langley family wasn't exactly the kind of thing for which they put up a plaque in your honor. Wiley Calhoun must've had more blood on his hands than half the surgeons of Clearwater Regional. Russ had honed her daddy's penchant for violence, wielding it for whatever nefarious activity he saw fit.

Though Sam wasn't privy to the details, she knew enough. Power came at a price, and Russ Langley was the most influential, and *feared,* man in town. Even in all Southwest Georgia. His influence hadn't merely been bought or handed down to him because of his last name.

No—the fear Russ Langley inspired around Carrion had been well and truly earned.

The elevator dinged; they'd reached the fifth floor.

Russ made to step out first but paused. "You know," he began, "despite what you may believe, my family and I prayed all night for your brother's well-being."

"Yeah?" Sam met his cold, gray eyes. "I prayed, too."

"Well . . ." Russ Langley looked contemplative, as if considering his next words carefully. "It's truly incredible what prayer can do, isn't it? Even the impossible can be made possible." Without another word, he stepped out of the elevator and out of sight, disappearing down the hall.

Sam hung back, her mind racing. The elevator doors shut, leaving her alone again. She didn't know if the sleep-deprivation was getting to her, but Russ's parting words carried a noticeable edge to them.

Shaking the thought away, she dug for her phone in her pocket. There were two text notifications on the home screen. One was from her roommate, Bailey:

Rent's due by Friday, FYI. Also, where the hell have you been all night?

The other was from her boss, Jason, at the Tavern restaurant on Lake Clearwater:

Can you come in early today? There's been some call outs.

All of Sam's fighting energy drained from her body. According to her phone, it was nearly noon, and she'd barely even sat down since she'd left the ambulance last night, whatever time that was. She ignored Jason's message, responding to Bailey instead:

I'm at Clearwater Regional. Can you pick me up?

SAM COLLAPSED ONTO her bed. Well, it was less a "bed" and more a dingy mattress on the floor of a tiny room in a single-wide trailer, but after the night she'd had, it felt like the best place in the world. She closed her eyes, but she could still feel Bailey standing in her doorway, staring at her.

Maybe Sam was just exhausted, but that look only pissed her off. It was hard to swallow pity from her ex-girlfriend, especially when crashing at the place Bailey shared with her new boyfriend.

"You're really gonna lay in your bed all filthy?" Bailey asked.

Sam buried her face into her sheets. "I'm too beat to care."

The mattress dipped. Bailey had perched herself at the edge. Sam tensed at the other girl's soft touch on her ankle. Gently, Bailey pulled her bloodied Converse off, tossing them in the corner with her flip-flops.

"Watch it," Sam yawned, glancing up. "Those are my favorite shoes."

Bailey rolled her eyes. "You've had them since we were in the ninth grade."

"And? You gonna buy me new ones?"

"Maybe I will." Sam could hear the teasing smile in her voice.

"Uh-huh." Sam burrowed deeper into her bed, yawning dramatically.

Bailey grabbed a plastic bowl of water and a washcloth from the kitchen.

"Let me sleep," Sam groaned. "I need to nap before work."

"It'll only take a minute." Bailey knelt beside the bed. "Sit up a little, come on."

Sam pushed herself up, so she was sitting with her back against the paper-thin wall for support. Bailey dipped the cloth in the water, then brought it to her face. The water was warm. Sam closed her eyes.

Bailey gently wiped away the blood and the dirt from the previous night. Still, Sam winced when the cloth touched the cut on her forehead—the one from when her head had smashed into the steering wheel.

"Jesus," Bailey whispered. "You're really cut up."

"I know," Sam breathed.

Bailey moved the cloth down Sam's neck, her fingers brushing the fresh bruise from the seat belt. Sam tensed again. Her cheeks went warm; she averted her eyes to the floor. That happened, sometimes. When Bailey—or anyone, really—touched her. Every muscle in her body went rigid and tight. It didn't matter that Bailey was being kind or gentle. Because in Sam's life, a touch was rarely just a touch. It was a command, a reprimand. A crossing of boundaries. *A punishment.*

Sam could tell Bailey had felt her go stiff. She knew as well as anyone how Sam got, sometimes. But her careful strokes with the washcloth did not falter. And piece by piece, Sam began to relax.

"It's all right," Bailey murmured.

Bailey's fingers were featherlight against her skin as they lingered over her collarbone, then found their way to the nape of Sam's neck. Without even meaning to, Sam leaned into the touch. Sam wished she could live in that one moment. Where there was no boyfriend of Bailey's, no Carrion, no Clearwater. Just Sam and Ben and Bailey—like a little family. Perhaps they'd even get a house by the ocean, like she always wanted.

Sam's green eyes snapped open. She swatted Bailey's hand away. "Stop."

Bailey's sun-bleached eyebrows furrowed. "What's wrong?"

Sam couldn't look her in the eyes. "You're playin' games again."

Bailey leaned forward and gently grasped Sam's chin, turning her face to look at her. "I'm not playing at anything, Sam."

"But you are." Sam's words came out strained. "You have a

boyfriend who lives in the same fucking house as us. What do you think Clayton would do if he found you in here like this?"

Bailey's eyes turned molten. "What if I want to be with you both? Is that so wrong?"

Sam yanked her chin from Bailey's grasp. She scooted backward on the mattress, putting necessary distance between them. "It's absolutely wrong and you know it."

"We had a good thing. You can't tell me we didn't," Bailey said.

Sam shook her head but didn't say a word.

"You broke up with me, you know." Grabbing the washcloth, Bailey tossed it in the bowl filled with now-murky water. Droplets splashed onto the grimy carpet, staining it further. "Remind me again why you did it? Oh yeah. To please your daddy—the man who wishes you'd rot in hell. Was it worth it?"

And there it was. The *real* reason why she and Bailey could never really work. Bailey's bite was stronger than her love. Her affections ran deep, but her cruelty ran deeper.

Any other day, Sam would've fought back, but there was nothing left. "Get out."

Bailey rose from the floor, leaving the bowl and washcloth behind. The bedroom door slammed as she went, shaking the thin walls with its force. Sam rolled over in the tiny bed, wincing as she did. On the floor, Dawson's face stared up at her from the stack of flyers Mrs. Sumter had given her.

Life after high school wasn't meant to be like this. Sam and Dawson had always dreamed of bigger things, of better places. Leaving Carrion far behind. Before Dawson had given his loyalty to Clearwater, the duo would sit together at lunch every single day, reading about all the faraway places they wanted to visit and eventually settle down in. The people they could be if the world would only let them.

"What'd you do, Dawson?" Sam whispered to no one. "Where'd you go?"

With a sigh, she pulled up Dawson's number in her phone and called him. The line didn't ring but went straight to voicemail.

Reluctantly, Sam began, "Hey, Dawson. I, uh, ran into your mama today." She paused and rolled onto her back, staring up at the popcorn ceiling of the trailer, eyes tracing shapes in the patterns. "She's really worried about you. I know you're probably busy or whatever, but could you let her know you're okay? You know how she gets. I mean—she thinks you're *missing*, for God's sake, so please . . . just give her a call or somethin'."

As Sam burrowed into the thin sheets of her lumpy bed, welcoming the relief of sleep, the night's events returned to her. A memory of the precarious deal she'd made with Jack. *A lie in exchange for Ben's life?* She trusted the relief of her brother's survival about as much as she'd trusted one of her daddy's good moods—fortune never hung around her long.

What exactly would the devil ask of her when it came time to collect? A lie could be a volatile thing, far-reaching in its consequences. Sam wondered if the anxiety, the uncertain *fear* of it, was all part of Jack's game—a predator playing with its prey.

The earsplitting scream of cicadas swelled around her, pulsing to the rapid beat of her heart as she recalled the accident. The trailer's AC unit sputtered to a stop outside her window. A gnat that wandered in from outside hovered beside her ear, just out of reach, and the cloying stink of cigarette smoke still lingered on her fingers like a mark of sin.

All at once, Sam made a promise to herself: *No matter what it takes, this will be my last summer in this godforsaken town.*

CHAPTER 7

ISAIAH

Isaiah idled at the gates of Lake Clearwater, waiting to be let in.

"What'd you say your name was again?" the security guard asked Isaiah, eyeing his car. "I don't see your license plate in the database."

It was the third time the guard had asked. He was clearly new to the job. The last one normally let him in without a second glance, but this one was being deliberately *obtuse*.

Isaiah wanted to blame his obstinance on the cicadas, but he knew the guard could hear him clearly. Unlike in Carrion, the cicadas were merely an unobtrusive hum on this side of the water.

"Isaiah Johnson." He sighed, watching as the guard held on tightly to his license. He hated what he was about to do, but time was not on his side that morning. "I'm the son of Judge Laurence Johnson and I'm running late."

The guard's eyes went wide, quickly handing Isaiah back his ID. "Oh—oh, I'm sorry, sir. Of course." The guard fumbled for the button to open the gate. "Just be sure to get a new visitor pass decal before you leave today. Security's tightening this summer for the festival."

"Will do." Isaiah reluctantly gave the man his signature country-club smile. He checked his watch for the third time. Ten minutes late to an internship he'd only just started was a bad look.

The gate opened before him, and Isaiah made sure to tip his head at the guard one last time as he passed through to the bridge that crossed the water. A physical border, one that marked the divide from the southern, public side of the lake to the northern, private side.

Dirty public beaches and faded boat docks gave way to a sprawling peninsula filled with elaborate, genteel mansions and services only the incredibly wealthy required. Golf courses, plastic surgery offices, a boutique gym and yoga studio, an organic food market, a landing strip for personal helicopters and jets. Sights that couldn't be found anywhere else in Southwest Georgia, the most impoverished region in the state.

As Isaiah continued down the tree-shaded, winding road, he passed an expansive antebellum-era property, complete with ornately trimmed columns and an unnaturally green lawn. One of the many "community centers" on this side of the lake—a place for the Clearwater folks to gather for political fundraisers and the occasional wedding. This one occupied the remains of a former plantation. Because nothing conveyed love better than reciting your vows at the site of former slave quarters.

Isaiah pulled into the small parking lot of Clearwater & Co. Law Firm, one of two firms that sat upon Lake Clearwater. He parked between two gleaming cars that cost more than a year's worth of Harvard tuition.

That's how he measured things these days—the price of an elite education he wasn't sure he even wanted.

Isaiah opened his car door with care. As he crossed the lot, he spotted a familiar Tesla a few spaces down.

"Seriously?" he groaned.

Inside, Isaiah was greeted by the distant laughter of wealthy white men, as well as the controlled chuckle of his father. He paused at the entryway mirror, smoothing the lines of his collared shirt. Now that he was inside—the cool of the AC in stark contrast to the dense, soupy heat of Georgia in summer—his clothes clung to him like a second skin.

He found his father and the two Clearwater & Co. attorneys seated around a glossy teak wood table in the reception area. Each held a glass of scotch, sipping and smiling. The attorneys, Rutledge and Leblanc, greeted Isaiah, raising their glasses in his direction as one. He had checked his watch enough times to know it was barely past noon.

"Ah, there's my son," his father said.

It was a strange, slightly unsettling surprise to see his father here in Lake Clearwater, unannounced and schmoozing. Laurence Johnson wasn't a man who *schmoozed*. Usually, it went the other way around.

Isaiah greeted his father and the attorneys like it was just another day. Except, it wasn't. Since the cicadas swept over Carrion that morning, the email from Dawson Sumter clung to Isaiah like a millstone. He had never wished more for a tip to be untrue. In fact, it was normally the opposite. For the podcast, he relished every possibility of a story. The potential of scandal and secrets to uncover was a special kind of thrill—one he'd indulged in while his parents' marriage slowly fell apart over the past three years.

>It's all connected to the Lake Clearwater community. Find out their secrets before more people go missing. Everyone knew Judge Johnson was among the most powerful men in Clearwater—a rising political figure in the whole state of Georgia. If there was even an *ounce* of truth to Dawson's email, it meant Isaiah's father could be involved.

The thought was enough to make his palms sweat. But did it mean Isaiah had to go digging? He didn't owe his investigations to anyone or anything. *Secrets of the South* had started as a distraction. A mere hobby. Why couldn't he let it end as one, too?

Isaiah pushed his anxious thoughts away and pasted on an easy smile.

"Afternoon, everyone," he said. "What's the occasion?"

The men laughed as if they were all in on a private joke, not bothering to answer.

Isaiah just kept smiling. The bland, polite smile he'd mastered for situations like this. He took his seat at his small desk in the corner. His father and the attorneys resumed their discussion of some new legislation that had just passed, and Isaiah riffled through case files, started a pot of coffee, and began the arduous process of photocopying a pile of documents left on his desk.

It was meaningless work, very little of which would prepare Isaiah for a career in law. But it wasn't what he did during the internship that mattered—it was about whose hands he shook. And if he made a good impression here, the next internship would be an even better one. Maybe something in a high, gleaming office overlooking Washington, DC. After all, he'd learned from the best.

Isaiah glanced up from the folder he was filing, watching covertly as his father took another sip of his scotch, his posture relaxed and easy in his chair. He wore a dark gray suit that complemented his deep brown skin, his short hair freshly cut, and sat completely at ease. Isaiah didn't know how his father did it—but he commanded every room he stepped into.

"We best get out of here for the luncheon." Rutledge, the older of the two attorneys, stood and polished off his scotch. "I don't need Russ chewing our heads off for being late."

"*Luncheon.*" Leblanc grimaced. He had neatly kept, dark brown hair with a bit of silver shining through, and wore designer tortoise-print glasses. A man from old Southern money who liked to pretend otherwise. The kind that voted libertarian and recycled. "My goodness, I'll never get used to it."

"Man up." Rutledge gave Leblanc a hard slap on the back. "It's only once every thirteen years. You can handle it."

Leblanc rolled his eyes, turning to Isaiah's father. "Laurence, you still joining us?"

It was a simple enough sounding question, but Rutledge and Leblanc looked expectantly at Isaiah's father. He eyed the scotch in his glass, then knocked the rest of it back. "Of course," Isaiah's father said as he rested the empty glass on the table. "But I need to speak to my son for a moment. I'll be right behind you."

As the two attorneys gathered their keys, Rutledge paused at Isaiah's desk. "If you could continue going through the folders dated from the past two weeks, that'd be great. Once that's done, you can head out early."

"Water the plants today, too," Leblanc said, following behind Rutledge. In a lowered voice, he added, "And don't worry about any calls of mine while we're out. There's been so many spam calls recently. The damn thing just keeps ringing and ringing."

Once the front door of the firm shut behind them, Isaiah relaxed just a bit. Turning to his father, he said, "I didn't know you were in town yet, considering you never showed for the harvest this morning."

"I'm afraid this luncheon took precedence." Laurence stared out the bay windows, gazing at the glistening lake water. "Being invited is a significant honor."

Isaiah fished, "What's the big deal with it anyway?"

"It's a Clearwater tradition of welcoming the cicadas." Laurence motioned outside. "Don't you hear them?" His dark eyes cut to Isaiah, his gaze heavy. Isaiah instinctively straightened his posture, tilting his head a little higher. His father's stare had a way of making him aware of every part of himself that needed improvement. "You were fifteen minutes late today." His tone was measured, calm. A voice honed through years of playing God in a courtroom.

Isaiah hesitated, considering whether to tell his father about the security guard at the gate—or just drop it. He sighed, relenting. "I need a new visitor's decal for my car. The guard almost didn't let me in this morning because of it."

Laurence bristled, ever so slightly. "I'll take care of it."

It most likely meant *him,* and Isaiah had a feeling he wouldn't see that specific guard working again. That was how his father handled things. Laurence believed there was nothing in this world he couldn't achieve without enough wit, money, and a calculated handshake. Isaiah understood where his father came from, but it didn't mean he had to agree. He knew well enough that wealth and power weighed differently in their hands.

"We also were carried away with the harvest," Isaiah said. "Would've been faster if we had some extra help. Grandma Bee really wanted you there." *I really wanted you there.*

Laurence's gaze returned to the window. "Your grandmother knows, good and well, I don't play farm boy anymore."

Isaiah balled his fists at his sides, a reflexive habit he had when he wanted to challenge his father. But there was a time and a place, and this wasn't it. "It's not *playing,* Dad. You know that farm means the world to them."

Laurence stepped toward the desk, looking over Isaiah with inscrutable brown eyes. "If it weren't for me, that land would've been clear-cut and turned into a poultry factory by now, and they'd be without a home."

Isaiah tried not to roll his eyes. "They know that."

"It's best you prioritize this internship over running around on that farm." His father brushed a bit of lint off Isaiah's shirt. "Big things are on the horizon for us both."

"Yes, sir," Isaiah said, his cheeks turning warm. "I understand."

Laurence gazed at Isaiah for a long moment, then pulled him into a hug. Isaiah relaxed as he embraced his father. "I've missed you, Dad," he said into his shoulder.

Laurence pulled away, his lips set in a tight line. "I've missed you, too."

Isaiah hadn't seen him in several weeks. With his parents officially separated, Laurence spent more and more time *working*. Isaiah thought being in Carrion for the summer would mean more quality time with his father, as he recently purchased a summer home on the lake, but so far, that hadn't been the case.

"This internship could open a lot of doors for you, son," Laurence said as he gathered his briefcase. "Don't squander it."

His father didn't give him a chance to respond before he was gone. Once Laurence's Tesla pulled out of the parking lot, Isaiah locked the front door, hovering for a breath. His head spun as he thought again of the email.

Isaiah turned on the flat-screen that sat in the common room of the firm, switching to the local Carrion news station for background noise. He *almost* expected there to be a report on Dawson, but there wasn't anything of note.

As Isaiah went through the usual tasks as an intern—water the plants, scan case law—a phone began to trill in the room across the hall. Isaiah jumped at the sudden noise, waiting for it to end. It was coming from Leblanc's office. The phone rang and rang, then stopped. A moment later, it rang again. Three calls passed and he had enough.

Annoyed, Isaiah stood, abandoning the watering can on the floor. He crossed the hall to Leblanc's office, walking on soft, creeping feet, even though no one was around. As he opened the office door, it finally cut to voicemail.

A pause.

Then the answering machine beeped. Of course, this old Southern law firm hadn't updated its phones in about twenty years.

"Casey . . . Casey Leblanc," a woman's slurred voice hissed over the line, echoing through the empty building. "You can't hide behind those gates forever. You gotta face me sometime." There was shuffling, followed by a long pause. "I know about you and my son. No one else has to know if you just bring my baby back to me. *Please* . . . where is he?"

The woman's desperate, hissing voice made the hairs on his arms prickle.

"What the hell?" Isaiah whispered to himself, as he played the message again, then again. When it ended, he took out his own phone and recorded the voicemail as an audio file: a reflexive gesture when it came to his podcast.

He had no idea who the woman was. Who her son was. But the pain in the woman's voice was unmistakable. He saved the recording and scrolled through the caller ID history. The number had a local area code, and she'd called Leblanc dozens of times in the past few days.

So much for spam calls, Isaiah thought. Leblanc clearly didn't want him to know about the calls, but he hadn't accounted for the possibility of voicemail.

He pulled out his own phone again and typed the unknown number into Google. The first page of results pulled up nothing. He kept scrolling. Nothing but useless links claiming they could do reverse number lookups—those never worked. And then something different: a result for a public Facebook Marketplace post containing the woman's number.

The number belonged to a woman named Andrea Sumter.

A familiar pinprick of recognition crawled down Isaiah's neck.

The email from Dawson Sumter.

>*If you're receiving this email, it means something bad happened to me.*

Was Dawson Andrea's son? What did Leblanc have to do with any of it? Isaiah struggled to make sense of the pieces. Composing himself, he looked around Leblanc's office, taking in the space with fresh eyes.

Everything was painfully normal. A desk, filing cabinets, a bookshelf lined with leatherback texts, a Harvard Law degree hanging on the wall. A framed photo of his family on a boat—Leblanc and his wife, two small daughters, each with a designer dog in their laps.

As he shuffled through a stack of papers on Leblanc's desk, a gold-embossed envelope peeked out from underneath. It had already been opened, the contents half spilling out. An invitation, also embossed in gold and written in delicate, hand-lettered cursive. It read:

Please join the Langley family for a luncheon
honoring the arrival of the cicadas of Carrion
and the town's creation.
June 28
1 p.m. at the Langley Plantation
Note: A twenty-four-hour fast is required to attend.
One's body must be cleansed before partaking
in the celebration.

Isaiah snapped a photo of the invitation, then put it back in its place, feeling more confused than ever before.

CHAPTER 8

REID

Reid was almost five years old when the cicadas last arrived in Carrion, but he had been too young to attend the celebratory luncheon. He'd stayed home with his mother, watching as his father and siblings disappeared out the front door in their finest Sunday best. That's how it often had been, when Caroline Langley was still with them: Caroline and Reid were one unit; Russ, Jonah, and Farris, another. But the thing Reid remembered most about that day was how badly his stomach had hurt from hunger.

As soon as his family had disappeared down the driveway, his mother pulled out a small bag of frozen grapes. They'd been tucked away in one of their many freezers, hidden beneath a layer of ice cubes. At the time, Reid was too young to understand why his father had locked away all the food, not yet privy to Lake Clearwater's traditions.

He'd eagerly eaten the grapes with his mother, sitting outside on their dock on the water. Geese from the lake swam over. Reid and his mother shared their paltry meal, laughing as they watched the geese bicker and compete for the same scraps of food.

"My stomach still hurts," Reid had whined to his mother after devouring the grapes. "Why can't we eat?"

"We're honoring the cicadas." Caroline patted his head, tousling his brown hair. "It's *tradition*, Reid."

"Well, I don't like the cicadas," Reid said with childish defiance. He tossed loose pebbles into the lake water, watching them sink. "They're creepy and loud."

"They are, aren't they?" Caroline gave Reid a sly grin. "Can you keep a secret?"

Reid nodded eagerly, gray eyes lighting up at sharing something special with his mother. "What is it?"

She leaned forward, their foreheads nearly touching. In a soft voice, she whispered, "You won't ever have to be hungry again."

"How?" Reid whispered back.

He remembered how his mother's face had turned serious. "Because the next time the cicadas come, you and I will be far, far away from Lake Clearwater."

Thirteen years had passed, and Caroline Langley had been unable to fulfill her promise to Reid. This time, he had to attend the luncheon with the rest of the family, his mother a noticeable, painful absence. Sitting at the long outdoor table on the lawn of the Langley Plantation, Reid could almost taste the icy-cold burst of grapes on his tongue as his stomach growled. He frowned down at his own abdomen.

"You're such a child," Farris said from beside him. "How can you not handle fasting for one day?"

"Sorry." Reid scowled, fanning himself with his hand against the midday summer heat. He craved a cold sip of water, but even that was forbidden until the feast began. "I don't have as much practice starving myself as you."

Farris rolled her eyes. "It's called *intermittent fasting,* Reid. It enhances your body."

Jonah snickered. Farris hit him in response.

"*Jesus,*" he yelped, clutching his arm. "I'm injured. Have some respect."

"You're an embarrassment," Farris snapped. "I can't believe

Dad let you show your face today."

"It would've looked worse if I *hadn't* shown up. I'm the eldest son," Jonah fired back. Farris had applied a hefty layer of makeup on his face that morning, but it wasn't enough to fully cover the black eye and swollen lip. Reid still wasn't sure if his brother's injuries were from the car accident or their father.

Farris adjusted the large sun hat on her head. "People are staring."

Reid followed her line of sight. It was true; the well-dressed guests in attendance were staring and whispering among one another. Gossiping, no doubt. "People are *always* staring."

Even though the Langley siblings were virtually untouchable, the gilded children of the founding family of Clearwater, they weren't immune to the community's judgment. It was no secret how others felt. Reid had heard the snide comments all his life.

The Langley bloodline was tainted when Russ Langley had children with that woman.

How do we know the children won't grow up to be just like their filthy mother?

There's something not quite right with the youngest Langley boy.

Before Reid's mother had become a Langley, she was Caroline Cochran. Born *elsewhere* but reared on the outskirts of Carrion in a run-down trailer park. Her parents barely raised her past the crib, with her father in and out of prison and her mother drug-addicted and absent, and she eventually settled down with an aunt in Carrion when she was nine.

Then at the age of thirteen, through what his mother had said was *wit and sheer, dumb luck*, Caroline was accepted into the private Clearwater Academy with a rare full-ride scholarship, awarded to two "disadvantaged" students each year. Caroline enrolled in the eighth grade, met Russ Langley sometime in high school, and the rest was history. What made Caroline so resented was that she not only *survived* Clearwater Academy, but graduated at the top of her class, with the affections of his father in tow.

"Your father would've followed me to the ends of the earth if I had chosen to leave Clearwater. He would've left it all behind for me," Caroline had confessed to Reid in a rare moment of reflection when he was ten. He'd been bullied again that day. A classmate pushed him to the ground and taunted him about his mother. "That fact scares a lot of people around here."

Reid's mother had upended Clearwater's strict social conventions when she married into the Langley family. She was labeled a *tick*—a cruel word reserved for the impoverished outsiders of Lake Clearwater who found their way in.

Some people even believed Caroline's outsider ways *infected* Russ Langley, made him soft. But Reid knew better. There had never been anything soft about his father. And if there had been, in some small way, it was extinguished six years ago: the day they found his mother's body washed up on the shore of Lake Clearwater.

Reid looked to the water lapping on the shore a few yards away. His mother was gone, and now Dawson was, too. He couldn't stomach any more loss; it would be his undoing. He had to believe Dawson was okay. He kept replaying their last conversation in his head, kicking himself for what he'd said.

The pair had been lounging on one of his family's deck boats in the early evening.

Reid had asked, "When I leave after my birthday, why don't you come with me?"

"Not this again." Dawson shook his head. "You don't gotta feel responsible for me."

"I don't—you're not—" Reid stuttered, struggling to find

the right words, as he often did. "I just . . . what's keeping you here?"

Dawson had merely said, "I have *obligations*."

"You mean, to your addict mom or to your secret boyfriend?"

"Low blow, Reid." Dawson sighed, gaze lingering on the dusky orange sky above. "I'm not your charity case, all right? I wanna earn my way on my own."

Reid had dropped it, but he hadn't heard from Dawson since they'd parted ways that night.

Jonah cleared his throat, bringing Reid back to the present moment. "You think they know about the accident?"

"Of course not," Farris scoffed, waving politely at a group of elderly women hovering near their table. They wore massive pastel sun hats and obnoxious pearly jewelry, fanning themselves with white gloves and floral paper fans as they no doubt tried to listen in on their conversation. "Dad made sure of it."

A heavy hand squeezed Reid's shoulder. *Speak of the devil.* His father's face was fixed in a friendly smile, but Reid fought not to wince at the iron grip on his shoulder.

"Are you three incapable of doing what's expected of you?" his father asked in a low voice.

Jonah's cocky expression vanished. He looked down at his lap, like a dog that had been kicked. "Sorry, sir."

Farris beamed. "I'm keeping them in line."

His father kissed her cheek. "I can do that just fine, angel. Now get off your asses and socialize with our guests."

Reid stood at once—an almost Pavlovian response to his father's command, instinctive and unconscious. Jonah and Farris were already walking off into the crowd. Reid watched as Jonah joined a group of his friends, slapping one of his buddies on the back. They disappeared off behind a blooming dogwood tree to do Lord knows what. Farris had made her way to the wraparound porch that overlooked the grounds, where she stood beside their grandparents beneath a massive, slow-moving fan.

"Kiss-ass," Reid muttered.

He shoved his hands in the pockets of his pressed khakis and started walking, wandering through the crowd of guests. His stomach growled again. The gnawing feeling only worsened the dizziness from the heat of the midday June sun. That was the point of the luncheon, though—to mimic the conditions in which his great-grandfather, William Langley, had founded Carrion.

It's important to remember where we came from, his father had explained to him when he was little. But now, Reid only saw it all as archaic traditions calling back to a time best kept in the past.

Taking up a spot in the shade beneath a peach tree, he observed the attendees. There were about one hundred or so, each person a significant figure in Lake Clearwater *and* beyond the gates. Everyone from politicians to musicians, medical doctors, hedge fund managers, CEOs. The wealthiest people of the lake—even of the whole of the Southeast.

With a sly move of his hand, Reid pulled out his phone from his pants pocket and began recording a video of the lawn. He wanted to share the moment with Dawson, to laugh with him over the absurdity of it all. His friend was meant to be with him that afternoon, his designated plus one, but Dawson never showed.

Reid texted him the video anyway. Once again, the message didn't deliver.

And once again, a tremor of fear rattled through him.

What if this is just like Mom?

"Always the loner," a voice joked from behind Reid. His uncle, Grant Langley, threw an arm around Reid's shoulder as he took a squat beside him.

Reid hid away his worry, then leaned into his uncle's hug. "You're one to talk. When'd you get in? Dad didn't think you were coming."

Grant plopped onto the grass, not minding the dirt that would surely stain his khakis. He scanned the lawn, his gaze lingering pointedly on Reid's father, who was gathered with some of his attorneys. "That's because my brother still expects the worst of me. Can't say I blame him." He gestured dramatically around them. "*Fuck* this dog and pony show."

Reid let out a genuine laugh.

For Reid, Grant was the only redeeming member of his family. Younger than his father, he was honest to a fault, moving through Lake Clearwater with a devil-may-care attitude, in sharp contrast to the carefully cultivated Langley image. As it stood, Grant was the most nontraditional member of the family, as the head of one of the biggest music labels in the South. He carried himself like a rock star, even though his own music career had been lukewarm at best.

Grant *made* stars, but he'd never be one himself, no matter how much he pretended otherwise.

"How long you home for?" Reid asked.

Grant tugged at the roots of his dirty-blond hair, mussed and wavy, falling to his ears. "Through the Fourth, actually. I'm overseeing the Cicada's Song in person this time around."

Reid's eyebrows raised. "You expecting anyone big this year?"

Grant smirked. "Anything is possible." He then nodded across the lawn, to the sight of Jonah as he came from around the dogwood tree, rubbing his nose. His makeup had begun to melt off from the unbearable heat. "*Goddamn*—what happened to your brother?"

Reid plucked a handful of grass from the ground. "Russ happened to him."

There was a beat of silence between them.

"Fair enough," Grant finally said. "And you? Your birthday's coming up in a week. Any big plans?"

Yeah, to get the hell out of Lake Clearwater and never look back, Reid thought. Except, his best friend was missing, and he had to pretend it was just another summer. Instead, he answered with a shrug, "Same old, same old."

Harp music sounded from the porch, thankfully interrupting any further interrogation.

"It's starting," Grant sighed, rising from the ground. He helped Reid up, then dusted dirt off his slacks.

"Any tips?" Reid asked in a low voice as they approached the long, white-cloth table at the center of the lawn.

Grant chuckled. "It's not so bad. Just, uh, hold your breath."

All around them, attendees gathered at their respective seats. Elegant, shining dishes and glassware had been placed before each person. Reid took his seat near the head of the table, where his father would sit. The harp's melody gathered speed, reaching its crescendo.

Then the grounds went still.

Heads turned toward the house. The quiet was pierced by the sudden scream of cicadas. His father then descended the white steps of the Langley home, flanked by Reid's siblings. Pointed gazes flicked to Reid, undoubtedly taking note of his absence beside his family.

Each of the Langley siblings had been offered a role in the ceremonial luncheon that morning, but Reid politely declined. "The cicadas make me squeamish," he'd said. "Besides, you only need two sets of hands and there's three of us."

"It's for the best," Farris had agreed. "You'd probably trip anyway."

His father hadn't challenged him but merely replied, "Son, there will soon come a day when you can no longer go against what's expected of you."

Thankfully, today is not that day.

His father held a large wire cage in his hands, the sides supported by Jonah and Farris. Inside were hundreds of swarming cicadas, fresh and bright from their thirteen-year slumber in the earth. They vibrated within the confines of the cage.

Murmurs and veiled grimaces rippled among the guests, but they fell silent as the buzzing cicadas drew closer. His father took his place at the head of the table. Farris and Jonah scrambled to help him set the cage on the tabletop.

"From the earth they rise, and to the earth they return," his father began, his voice somehow louder than the cicadas themselves. "We gather here on this momentous day to celebrate this bountiful land and the cicadas that bless our community every thirteen years. To our founder, William Langley."

To William Langley. As one, the guests murmured in agreement. Reid found himself murmuring, too.

His father smiled, meeting the eyes of every person, lingering on Reid. "Let us feast."

He opened the cage. Reid expected the cicadas to swarm out, but they only continued to seethe and scream inside the wire bars. His father reached his hand inside. When he pulled it out, his arm was covered in dozens of pulsing brown insects that clung to his skin.

His father picked a live cicada off his arm and held it up, whether to inspect it or to show it to the crowd, Reid wasn't sure. With his eyes looking out across the assembled guests, expression placid, serene—he placed the insect in his mouth and swallowed it whole.

SECRETS OF THE SOUTH

SEASON 4: EPISODE 1

HOST: The acclaimed Southern writer Janisse Ray once said that in South Georgia "everything that comes you see coming." There's no better way to describe the land, flat and yawning toward oblivion. Unlike the foothills of Appalachia or the swampy marshlands of the southern coast, there is nowhere to hide in these flatlands. Even thunderstorms can be spotted, miles and miles away, long before they flood the muddy earth.

In Carrion, they have a saying: The devil can be seen coming from a mile away. That is where our story begins.

(Intro theme song)

All towns have legends that shape them.

Before there was ever a Lake Clearwater, there was Carrion. And before there was Carrion, there was nothing. Nothing but a plot of nameless land owned by the likes of a man called William Langley.

The records say that he was a farmer at a time when the land was barren, the soil was dry, and dust blew across the United States in apocalyptic black clouds. With that dust went any hope for survival in Southwest Georgia.

But William Langley was a devout man. He prayed every morning and every night for rain to bless the scorched earth and give life to long-dead crops. He prayed for a savior. He prayed for relief.

That relief never came. His wife grew gravely ill while the last of their food supply ran dangerously low, and then empty. They had nothing left to their names but their withering bodies, a shotgun, and two shells.

The legend goes that William ended his wife's misery before turning the gun on himself, but he was unable to fire, as the shell was a dud. Bereft, he stumbled through the barren farmlands until he collapsed at a crossroads, where trade was once lively but had since died out. William cursed his Lord, angry that he couldn't have the dignity of a quick death.

William prayed for his suffering to end.

But it wasn't *his* God that answered.

It wasn't long before he heard the grating caw of a corvid, its wings casting long shadows across the dry earth. A crow as dark as starless night landed before him, carrying something dull and rounded in its black talons. An offer in the form of a single shotgun shell.

William Langley's fingers twitched toward the shell, longing to join his wife in the next life.

But he did not succumb to the creature's offer. Instead, he shouted the bird away, cursing as it disappeared into the swollen blue sky above with the shell in tow.

The sun bore down on William as he lay in the dirt. If starvation didn't kill him, sunstroke surely would've. But another creature appeared, a sharp hiss moving through the cropped, dead wire grass that bordered the crossroads.

A cottonmouth viper with mud-brown scales slithered toward William. Round and round the snake went, circling his body, drawing nearer with each lap. The snake stopped inches from William's outstretched hand, going still as a statue and ready to strike. It waited for an answer, as if to say, *One bite and your suffering will end*. That's all it would take. His fingers once again twitched, inching toward his death.

But William did not succumb to the creature's offer. He swatted the snake away, watching it disappear into the dead wire grass from which it came.

It is said then, that when the sun had nearly set and was at the lowest point in the sky, a silhouette of a man appeared, far off in the distance, walking straight toward William Langley. His shadow was as long as the day, spreading behind him like the wings of a cicada.

The shadowed man knelt before William and said, "You have shown a great deal of strength, William Langley. You were not tempted by the proclivities of my brothers. For that, I shall help you."

"Who are you?" asked William.

"Merely a man with a proposition," the man replied. "If you feed me, then I shall feed you."

But William insisted, "I have no food, sir. I haven't eaten in weeks. My wife is dead. There is nothing left."

"Ah," the man said. "I don't require crops, you see. Only flesh. If you bring me a warm body, I will bless your lands and your soil. As long as I am fed, you will live like a king for the rest of your days."

And so, the story goes that William used the last of his strength to crawl back to his home. He carried his wife's body to the crossroads. By the time he returned, he was so weak he could do nothing but collapse in a heap beside his wife's corpse.

When he awoke, he found his wife's bones laid neatly beside him, picked clean, as if by vultures. And standing at the crossroads now was not a man but a tree. A fully grown tree, overflowing with ripened peaches, ready to be picked.

And on that tree sat a cicada, screaming to the heavens.

In his journal, years later, William Langley would write, *The cicada sang the most glorious song, more beautiful than anything my ears had ever encountered or have encountered since.*

William devoured the peaches from the crossroads tree, regaining his strength. He carried his wife's bones back to their farm and buried them in the earth. A storm appeared along the horizon. Rain returned and blessed the arid grounds. The next day, long-dead crops began to spring from the topsoil.

It wasn't long before word spread that William Langley had been blessed by God. That he had healed the earth. Destitute farmers from far and wide flocked to the Langley land, begging for food, for water, for shelter. Langley fed them as best he could, but the food turned to ash in their mouths. Water ran dry in their throats. Roofs collapsed above their heads.

Langley returned to the crossroads, demanding answers from the shadowed man. He wanted to feed his people. To shelter them. To protect them. To give them a bountiful life, as he was promised.

The crossroads man appeared once more and simply said, "You know what I desire. If you feed me, then I shall feed you."

And so, it began. With each family that sought refuge on the Langley land, William was forced to demand a sacrifice in flesh and blood.

Legend goes that after the thirteenth body was left at the crossroads, the man appeared once more and said, "No more, I am fed. But I will return in thirteen years' time. Listen for the call of the cicada and know that I am coming."

CHAPTER 9

NEERA

"Mom, where are the car keys?"

Neera shook her mom's shoulder. Kiran was sprawled on one of the twin beds in Room 4. She groaned something indiscernible in her sleep. After long shifts, her mom slept like the dead. Waking her was an impossible task. As a kid, it used to scare Neera, the way her mom would disappear into her body, dead to the world for what felt like days at a time.

And then, of course, there was the time Neera had needed her. *Really* needed her. The minutes Neera spent begging her to wake up had felt like hours—hours where she was completely alone.

The phone had been ringing. That was the memory that cut through it all, three years later. A high, persistent trill. On and on and on. Neera hadn't bothered to move from her bedroom floor. She'd known her mom wouldn't answer it, but a perverse kind of stubbornness kept her playing chicken with her drunk mom. Just how long could it go on before Kiran noticed?

On and on and on. Ringing and ringing and ringing.

Neera had been studying for finals into the late hours—quadratic equations, she remembered even now. The dull, inconsequential detail forever stuck in her mind.

Eventually, Neera lost the game of chicken. The ringing was just too annoying. She trudged into the living room, sighing to herself the entire way. Kiran was passed out on the sofa, five beers into the night. Her phone was on the coffee table, vibrating incessantly.

Neera remembered rolling her eyes. She'd delicately picked her way through the maze of beer cans to approach the couch.

"Mom, someone keeps calling." She shook Kiran's shoulder. "Wake up."

Kiran grunted but didn't move.

"*Mom.*" She shook her again, perhaps a bit rougher than she needed to. "It could be work."

Without opening her eyes, Kiran swatted feebly at her. "Leave me alone." Her words were slurred, her breath stale.

Frustrated, Neera unlocked her mom's phone, scrolling through the log of missed calls. There was Ajay's name, having called a handful of times earlier in the night. Then another number she didn't recognize. They kept calling.

After what felt like minutes of jostling and shaking her mom's limp body, Kiran finally groaned and sat up. She grabbed the phone from the coffee table, shooting her daughter a disgruntled look.

Kiran rubbed her eyes as she answered the call. A pause. "Yes . . . this is she."

Before a tornado touches the ground, the air becomes entirely still. Forever after, Neera would remember that moment of stillness. The sudden absence of sound, the phone no longer ringing. Still on the phone, Kiran's face contorted. Her bloodshot eyes went wide. Her mouth twisted in agony.

"No," she whispered, shaking her head violently. "*No no no.*" Her trembling hand scrambled to her mouth, tears spilling down her cheeks. The phone slipped from her grasp and fell onto the carpet with a muted thud.

Now, in Room 4 of the Colonial, years away from that tiny apartment and that horrible night, Neera squeezed her eyes shut. A swell of rage surged inside her, furious with her mom for sleeping. For scaring her.

For making her remember.

For everything.

She swallowed. Neera didn't have time for anger today. No time for memories, either. Her audition at Lake Clearwater was in less than an hour and the car keys were missing. Any other day, she would've just taken the Cadillac, but now it was a burnt corpse in the parking lot.

Neera spun on her heel and speed-walked out of the room. There was a spare key for the Nissan somewhere in the lobby's back office; she just had to find it.

Careening through the lobby's entrance, Neera yelled, "Nani! Do you know where the . . ." She went quiet at the sight of her grandmother seated at the front desk, head wrapped in her signature silk chunni, reciting her daily Gurbani.

The sun's early-afternoon rays filtered in through the window, reaching Nani's brown skin, casting her in a warm glow. Her silk scarf glimmered around her head, tufts of dyed-black hair with bits of silver peeking out from beneath the fabric. Her lips moved quickly, voice barely even a whisper as she performed her paath, bent over a tiny Sikh scripture book with a worn leather-bound cover.

"Sorry," Neera whispered, letting her grandmother be.

Disappearing into the back office, she scanned every surface of the claustrophobic room for the keys. At last, Neera yanked open the drawer of a steel filing cabinet and found a pile of mismatched keys—the spare Nissan key thankfully among them.

Neera shoved it into her pocket and started stuffing the drawer's contents back inside. The edge of a photograph peeked out from underneath the crumpled mess of papers. It was folded and worn, browning at the edges. Neera paused.

With hesitant hands, she slid the photo out from the stack, smoothing the folds to get a better look.

An old photo taken on a cheap, disposable camera. Her grandfather and Ajay standing in front of an unimpressive brick building. What made the photo notable were Nanaji's and Ajay's grinning faces, their joy clear as day. A look she hadn't witnessed in her family in years.

Neera traced a finger over Ajay's face. It was strange to see him so *happy*. The date on the back of the photo placed it four years ago, but Ajay still looked so much younger, not yet let down by the world in the way she remembered him.

Although admittedly, she didn't remember his face well at all anymore.

Her uncle's memory had become blurred and messy. The image of him that lived in her head wasn't a smiling photograph or a sun-soaked day spent together. It was a clinical Polaroid dated from that night. The night of the ringing phone. The night he died.

It was his body lying on a steel table in a morgue, a sheet covering his bruised and bloodied skin.

It was his head blown partially off by the gunshot that killed him.

"Neera?"

She jumped at the sound of Nani's voice. Her grandmother stood in the doorway of the office, chunni still wrapped around her head, eyes lingering on the photograph in Neera's hand.

"I was looking for the spare car keys," Neera said quickly, shoving the photo of Ajay into her back pocket, praying Nani didn't see. But her grandmother's glistening dark eyes said otherwise. Neera cleared her throat. "I found them."

An uncomfortable silence lingered between them. Neera shifted on her feet, unsure if she should say something or just go. There were many things not discussed in their lives, and Ajay *always* sat at the top of that list.

Neera had wondered more than once what his legacy would've been like, had his death not been ruled a suicide. He'd had no proper funeral, not in the way of Sikh death, at least. Family members from all over the globe didn't flock to Carrion to help them mourn. There was no handwashing of his body, or surrounding him with flowers in an open casket. The nearest gurdwara—three hundred miles away—didn't host his service. There was no formal reading of the Guru Granth Sahib. No langar. No community. No shared grief.

Ajay's body was merely turned to ashes and given to Kiran in an unmarked box. Neera and her mom took a weekend trip to the Blue Ridge Mountains and found a river on the highest peak. They poured his remains into the rushing water, watched as they disappeared, then drove home.

Neera was no expert on her family's culture, but she knew death was *never* meant to be solitary. Whole villages would grieve over the loss of someone in Punjab. Even in the small town her family was from in the UK, Punjabi immigrants from neighboring areas would grieve as a community over those who died.

But Ajay wasn't given that respect. His death was a scandal, rippling across their extended family scattered around the globe, rivaling that of Neera's own birth. He was meant to be forgotten because remembering was too painful.

Neera gave herself a mental shake. The most important audition of her life was happening today, and the Singh family tragedies were like quicksand—threatening to pull her under.

"Where are you going?" Nani broke the silence.

Neera hesitated. She'd wasted enough time already, she couldn't afford to be honest. "I got called into work."

"Oh?" Nani studied her face. "It is not the weekend."

"I could really use the extra money," Neera partially lied. "It's not like we have much going on here anyway." She checked the time on her phone. "I'm running late. I'll see you later." Before Nani could say anything more, Neera gave her a brief hug and darted out the lobby door.

Only once she was in the Nissan, doors locked, did she dare to look at Ajay's photo again. She traced his face once more, then froze, her finger lingering on the T-shirt Ajay wore. With spindly, branchlike antlers splayed across his chest, the shirt bore an identical logo to the key chain she'd found in Room 11 the night before.

CHAPTER 10

SAM

Sam yawned into her elbow as she worked on the giant box of unrolled silverware that sat before her, prepping for the evening's service at the Tavern Bar & Restaurant. Not even a night spent in the hospital could get her out of work. Not that it mattered; she needed the money more than she needed to rest.

One day, things will be different. It was the promise Sam repeated to herself in moments like this. More and more lately, it seemed.

Someone kicked the legs of her chair. "Sam, you listenin' to me?"

Sam startled. Her boss, Jason, was staring down at her. "Huh?"

"Did you get a concussion in that car accident or what?" He snapped his fingers near her face. "Pick up the pace."

"I'm fine, just tired," Sam said, yawning again. "Thanks for your concern, though."

Jason checked his watch. "It's gon' be a busy week around here. Can't afford to dick around." His pocket began to vibrate. Jason answered his phone, disappearing into the private lounge on the other end of the restaurant.

Sam scowled at his retreating back. She then fell into the quiet, methodical task of rolling silverware, mind drifting. Rent was due in less than a week and the only thing standing between her and homelessness was the upcoming day's tips. A totaled car and shitty insurance coverage didn't help anything, either.

Time dripped by as Sam struggled to finish another box of silverware. Her wrist was still messed up and splinted from before the accident. The stressors just kept adding up. Eventually her body was going to give out beneath the pressure.

Sam pulled out her phone, checking to see if she had any missed calls or texts. She didn't want to admit to herself she was hoping to hear from Dawson, but there was only radio silence.

Her thoughts were interrupted when the Tavern's front door swung open, revealing a flustered Neera Singh rushing inside.

Neera greeted her with a smile, a little breathless. "Please tell me Jason's still around."

"Yeah, he just took a call in the back." Sam noticed the guitar case slung over her shoulder. "Wait, does this mean you scored the audition?"

Nodding sheepishly, Neera said, "My mom pulled through."

"No fucking way," Sam yelled, nearly leaping up from the chair in excitement. If she was the hugging type, she would've embraced Neera, but she held back. Touch had always been a complicated longing for Sam, despite how much she wished otherwise. It didn't help that being in Neera's presence turned that reluctant wanting into a desperate ache. "Jason's not gonna know what to do with himself. I'd bet he's never heard real good music a day in his life."

Neera laughed. "We'll see, won't we?" She glanced around the empty restaurant, brown eyes lingering on the table full of unrolled silverware. "Let me help you." Without waiting for Sam's response, she sat down and got to work.

Sitting across from her, Sam protested, "Come on, don't do free labor for these assholes."

"I'm not doing this for them." Neera gestured to Sam's

splinted wrist. "I'm doing this for you."

Heat warmed Sam's freckled cheeks. She didn't like to admit to *herself* the splint was a hindrance, much less to anyone else. She didn't like to acknowledge it at all—the physical reminder of all her failings. "Well, uh, thanks."

Nervousness had been a foreign concept to Sam until she'd met Neera Singh a month ago. There wasn't a person on the planet Sam couldn't talk to with ease, but it was different with Neera. She grew abashed and a little awkward and she *hated* it.

"So"—Sam cleared her throat, motioning to Neera's guitar case—"did you decide what you're gonna play?"

"Not yet." Neera considered for a moment. "I'm really into blues right now. Bluegrass. Stuff like that. I suppose any of it will work."

"Ooh, bluegrass." Sam hummed. "Folks here would like that."

Neera looked thoughtful. "I hope so. Never played for a place like this before."

"Just give them what they want, and you'll be fine."

"Oh yeah?" Neera asked, "what would that be?"

Sam shrugged, smirking. "I know these people. They like *easy*. They like comfortable. You could play some sweet, sweet country. The type of song they hum to themselves on their wraparound back porches, drinking sweet tea and expensive whiskey."

"So . . . what you're saying is, I should be what they want. Not who I am."

Sam nodded. "Yeah, exactly. You're gettin' it."

"Noted." Neera gave her a wry grin, and Sam's heart stuttered.

Jason appeared from the back. He took in the sight of the pair of them, his thin lips forming a tight line. "What's all this?"

He then checked his watch. "Oh, right." He waved for Neera to get onstage without giving her a second glance.

Neera let a brief expression of annoyance flash across her face before smiling pleasantly. Guitar in hand, she marched over to Jason and extended her hand proudly.

"Thank you for taking the time to let me audition," she said smoothly.

Jason looked at her hand, then her face, before finally extending his own. "Uh-huh." He then turned around, facing Sam. "You just gonna sit there or what?"

Sam rolled her eyes, grabbing the remainder of the silverware and carrying them to the bar. She began slowly polishing the wineglasses that hung overhead, while Neera stepped onto the stage, pulling a stool to the center. With efficient, methodical movements, she opened her guitar case and pulled out a shining acoustic. She slung the guitar's worn leather strap over her shoulder before taking a seat on the stool. Her brown eyes scanned the restaurant, meeting Sam's.

You got this, Sam mouthed, giving her a thumbs-up.

Jason grabbed his clipboard from the nearby table and clapped his hands for Neera to begin.

"Any song requests?" Neera asked as she tuned the strings.

Jason didn't bite. "Honestly, I really don't care."

Neera nodded, chewing her lip. "Okay then." She glanced at Sam again, then down at her feet. "This is 'Old Man' by Neil Young." She strummed the guitar for several notes, then began to sing.

Sam thought the song was an odd choice at first. The flow wasn't easy, and the lyrics told a story more than it moved an audience. It took several lines before Neera really leaned into it. But as the chorus picked up, the song flowed like water. Neera's whole demeanor changed, growing loose and languid. There was a subdued yet beautiful way about how she played, picking at the strings with ease.

Sam stood with a wineglass in hand, frozen with the rag mid-swipe. Watching Neera perform was like seeing a sunrise early in the morning, soft and wondrous. Nearly impossible to look away.

But Sam noticed movement at the back of the room, by the side entrance. Grant Langley, the Tavern's owner, leaned against the wall, arms folded across his chest, watching Neera just as intently as Sam had been. She didn't know when he'd arrived but hoped for Neera's sake he liked what he heard.

The song came to an end. Neera strummed the last part slowly, the notes echoing in the near-empty restaurant. She had closed her eyes as she played, but she opened them now, looking squarely at Jason.

Jason cleared his throat and leaned forward in his chair. "You're not bad."

Neera exhaled, her shoulders visibly relaxing. She didn't say anything, and the silence stretched on between them. She chewed her lip, shifting underneath Jason's appraising stare. Whatever she put into her music, it seemed to equally take out of her.

Finally, she asked, "Can I enter the Cicada's Song or not?"

Sam tensed, waiting for the answer. She'd seen Jason turn down dozens of other perfectly talented people hoping for a slot. It was damn near impossible to get onstage if you weren't already part of the Clearwater community in some way. Someone like Neera couldn't make it just by being good—she had to be perfect.

Luckily for her, Sam thought she was pretty damn close.

Jason was quiet for too long, Neera's question hanging in the air between them. Finally, he let out a short, breathy chuckle.

"You and your mom are somethin' else. You know that?" The way he said it, it seemed like neither a compliment nor an insult. "Yeah, you can enter."

Sam did her best to hide the smile that spread across her face.

"Not so fast, Jason," Grant interrupted as he peeled away from his hiding spot in the back and approached the stage.

Neera's eyes widened at the sight of Grant. Sam wondered if Neera knew who he was. Judging by the size of her eyes, it was safe to assume she did. Jason stood abruptly from his chair, his demeanor quickly changing from a man with power to a man without.

"Oh! I didn't know you'd be back so soon," Jason said quickly, fumbling over his own words. "Of course, it's up to Grant here if you can enter. It's his competition after all."

Grant Langley looked at Neera as if she were a zoo animal. Sam couldn't tell if he was impressed by her performance or repulsed. His expression was unreadable.

"How many years you been playin'?" Grant asked.

"Since I was five years old," Neera said defiantly. "I was taught by the best. By . . . by my late uncle." She cleared her throat. "Ajay Singh."

Grant rubbed his chin, studying her for a beat. "You ever performed in front of a big audience? What about a crowd like Lake Clearwater? You know what stage presence is? Because to be in this competition, much less *win* it, you gotta be more than just a pretty young thing with a guitar and a Neil Young cover."

Neera's face blanched at Grant's rapid-fire words, while heat boiled under Sam's skin. She bit her tongue, struggling to temper her anger.

"Yes, sir," Neera said weakly. "I understand."

Grant continued to stare at Neera with that same strange

expression. Finally, he said, "The crowd here is a tough one. If you're not prepared, they'll chew you up and spit you out. They'll boo you off the stage without so much as a second thought. All I'm saying is: You gotta be someone *worth* seein'. You think you can do that?"

"I'll do whatever I have to." Neera rose from the stool and began packing up her guitar. Once it was safely in the case, she faced Grant, looking down on him from the stage. "What time should I get here on Thursday?"

Jason chuckled to himself, struggling to conceal it with a cough, while Grant stayed quiet. Several tense seconds later, a smirk crept across his face. He extended his hand to Neera. "We'll see you at six sharp."

"See you then," Neera said, shaking his hand without skipping a beat. Without exchanging another word with either of them, she walked out of the Tavern, guitar in hand, and into the warm afternoon light.

Jason blew out a heavy breath, turning toward Grant. "You sure she's worth the risk?"

Grant shrugged. "Either way, it'll be good entertainment."

Sam threw down the rag she'd been holding, trotting out from behind the bar. With a huff, she called over her shoulder, "I'm takin' my fifteen."

CHAPTER 11

NEERA

If Neera had any skill other than guitar, it was her ability to hold back tears. She only had to *decide* not to cry, and she could fix her face so that she'd go numb all over.

It was a learned talent, honed since childhood.

Sitting in her parked car outside the Tavern, Neera channeled that sense of hardness. Getting onstage had been terrible, but she'd done it. Forced herself to push every doubt, every squirming emotion all the way down to the place where she could pretend it away. Her first time playing on a *real* stage, for someone other than Ajay or a coffee shop with disinterested patrons, and it had, for the briefest moment, felt like magic.

But then Grant Langley, an asshole in khakis, had popped her shimmering, golden bubble. Made her feel like she was standing on the stage naked, having been weighed and found wanting. Laughable to think she could play for the residents of Lake Clearwater and, even more ridiculous, win the contest.

Neera needed to be better. She *had* to be. There was no other option.

Movement in the rearview mirror caught her eye. Sam was walking toward her car. Neera rolled down the driver's side window as she approached.

"How bad was I?" Neera asked self-consciously. "Be honest."

Sam shook her head, dismissing the question. "Look, Neera . . . you gotta play on Thursday."

"I don't know if I can," Neera admitted.

"I'm serious." Sam leaned in close, shielding her green eyes from the sun with a splinted wrist. "Yeah, Grant's a dick, but you're *good*. He knows it, too. I haven't seen him show up for any audition other than yours."

"Jesus, really? That has to count for something, I guess." Neera stared ahead at the empty parking lot. She didn't know how to react to Sam's kindness, unsure if she was even deserving of it. "You're too nice to me."

"You don't give yourself enough credit." Sam beamed a little. "I mean, you were like Hope goddamn Sandoval in there."

The soft hum of the cicadas pulsed through the air, filling the space between them. Then, distantly, Neera heard cheering echoing across the lake. Or was it yelling? *Screaming?* Sound always seemed to travel strangely on this side of the water.

"You hear that?" Neera asked, angling her head around, scanning the lot, then the lake's shore.

Sam followed her gaze. "It's probably from the Langley luncheon."

"What's that?"

Sam rolled her eyes, seemingly at the thought of it. "It's basically a super exclusive, fancy pregame party for Clearwater's *finest*." She didn't bother hiding the bitter edge in her tone. "But I really have no idea what those rich folks get up to. All I know is that it's held to celebrate the arrival of the cicadas. Personally, I can't stand the little buzzin' fuckers."

Neera couldn't help but laugh at Sam's blunt phrasing. "I didn't think it was possible a bug could be so *loud*."

Sam laughed with her, tilting her head back into the rays of the sun. Her skin shone with hundreds of freckles, while her red hair shimmered with streaks of gold and copper. Frizzy, tangled, in a loose braid down her back. She somehow looked how summer felt: warm and wild. But then Neera looked closer, noticing fresh cuts peeking out from beneath her shirt collar, scabs and bruises dotting her arms. Nicks and scrapes along her fingers and hands.

Neera pulled her eyes away.

Sam leaned in close again, wiggling her eyebrows. "Town legend says that the Clearwater folks owe their riches to the cicadas. That without them, all their good fortune would vanish. That's why they damn near worship 'em."

Neera wrinkled her nose at the thought. "You think there's any truth to that?"

"I think small-town superstitions rot the brain," Sam said, her gaze going distant. "Though I suppose anything's possible around here."

Sam didn't need to elaborate for Neera to understand what she meant. There was a palpable *strangeness* to Carrion, felt especially during the summer months, even more so with the arrival of the thirteen-year cicadas. Everything, both wonderful and horrible, felt equally likely then. As if the sticky, muggy air buzzed with a sense of tremendous possibility.

"I know what you mean," Neera murmured.

Sam looked up then. "Yeah?" They held each other's gaze for a breath. The moment felt significant in a way Neera didn't quite understand, but she didn't let herself consider it further.

"I gotta get going," Neera blurted, turning her attention to the car's steering wheel.

"Wait one sec," Sam said, still leaning through the Nissan's window. She pulled a pen and napkin from her server's apron, quickly scrawling something onto it. "Here, in case you think of backin' out between now and the Cicada's Song."

Neera took the napkin, finding a phone number on it. "And I'm supposed to do what with this?"

"Call or text me whenever." Sam smirked. "I'm volunteering my time as your number one hype person. I'll be around if you need me."

"Thanks," Neera said as heat warmed her cheeks.

Sam gave her a dramatic salute and then she was off.

Once Sam was out of sight, Neera groaned, running her fingers through her thick hair, and pressed her forehead against the warm steering wheel. There was no way in hell she could perform in a matter of days, not in a room full of people like Jason and Grant goddamn Langley. It was obvious Grant had given her a chance just to see how she'd fare onstage, though it felt like more of a test than an opportunity. But he was right. She had to do more than sing a pretty song. Neera needed to win over a crowd of people who'd rather see someone else behind the mic.

But it was too hot to sit in her car doubting herself. Neera pulled out of the Tavern's parking lot and onto the two-lane road that wound through Lake Clearwater. It was barely the start of summer and already the heat felt oppressive—too thick and wet for even the AC to contend with.

Neera put on her favorite Pearl Jam album, cranking up the volume as she drove along the smooth, manicured roads. Not a pothole in sight. The world was so different on this side of the gate. If Carrion was a dingy, sepia-toned old photograph, sun faded and creased, Lake Clearwater was like the set of a sitcom, all crisp lines and oversaturated color. Even the cicadas were somehow quieter.

While she sat idling at a stop sign, the sun flared off the lake and into Neera's eyes. She lowered the sun visor, the picture of Ajay fluttering down from where she'd tucked it away, landing in her lap. Long-buried thoughts about her uncle resurfaced. And with them, her overwhelming grief.

Ajay had taught Neera everything: how to swim, how to drive, how to dream. But he hadn't taught her the most crucial of life's lessons—how to live without him. It never made sense to her that he'd done it, that he'd truly taken his own life. It was a truth she couldn't seem to reconcile, even after three years.

A car's horn blared behind her, shocking Neera to the present moment. She hit the gas, desperate to shake her thoughts away.

Ajay was gone, and he was never coming back. No amount of overthinking was going to change it.

CHAPTER 12

SAM

Late that humid June night, the devil waited for Sam in the Tavern parking lot. She spotted him through the windows as she flipped the last table of chairs. She lingered as Jason counted out her meager tips for the evening, even asking him to count again, if only to avoid walking out the front door. She volunteered to mop and toss the trash in the dumpster, much to the busboys' endorsement but not to Jason's.

"Go on home," he barked. "I'm not gonna pay you extra to hang around."

Once outside the Tavern, Sam met eyes with Jack. Across the lot, he leaned against his clay-covered Jeep, cigarette in hand. He watched her with an unblinking gaze.

Sam was meant to ride home with Bailey, her de facto solution until insurance provided a rental. But it seemed Jack had other plans. She texted her roommate not to worry about the ride, then made her slow trek toward the devil.

"Hey, Red," Jack greeted as she approached, his mouth upturned in a sly smile. "Up for a drive?"

Sam hesitated a good yard away. "I got a choice?"

Jack shrugged, tossing his lit cigarette onto the ground, and climbed into the Jeep. He turned the car's engine and flicked on the headlights, nearly blinding her.

Sam shielded her eyes, blinking rapidly. She gave the Tavern one last look before crossing the lot, then climbed into the Jeep's passenger seat. Buckling her seat belt, she asked, "Where to?"

Jack backed up the car, pulling out of the parking lot with ease. "There's somethin' I want you to see."

They drove in silence, while a bluegrass tune played quietly on the car's radio. It was hazy and muddled, like it was broadcast from a faraway radio station. It took a moment before Sam recognized the song: an old Carrion folktale known as the "Three Brothers."

Except, she hadn't learned it from the radio but on the playground during school. Carrion kids knew the legend of the three brothers as a local folktale, passed down from older generations. They were the region's very own boogeymen—the three devils who longed to either help you, trick you, or eat you alive.

Which one is Jack?

Jack whistled along to the tune, completely at ease. Sam looked around the Jeep, finding it surprisingly threadbare. It only reeked of cigarettes and the way her daddy used to smell when he worked at an automotive shop when she was little. Everything about it was so painfully normal that Sam almost doubted that the devil sat beside her.

Almost.

In the spare light of the Jeep, Jack gave her a once-over, his unnatural black eyes lingering on her face. "How's your brother?"

Sam eyed Jack right back, despite her skin prickling with unease. Being in the presence of the devil was a lot like seeing a predator in the wild. The number one rule: Never let it know you're scared. "Alive."

Jack snorted. "Ain't you the least bit curious how I did it?"

"No," Sam said. "I know who you are. Sorry—*what* you are. That's all I need."

Jack looked intrigued. "Oh, really? Tell me, Red, what am I?"

Sam squirmed in the passenger seat. "You're the devil."

Jack only laughed. "One of three."

Sam expected Jack to drive them straight out of Lake Clearwater, but to her surprise, he stayed inside the gated community. Within ten minutes, they arrived at a boating launch tucked behind a thick row of pine and oak trees. It was a secluded little fishing spot, unremarkable and hidden from the road.

"What're we doin' here?" Sam asked as Jack parked the Jeep.

Jack reached into the back seat and materialized a worn bookbag. "You ever heard of the saying 'patience is a virtue'?"

Sam rolled her eyes by way of response, then climbed out of the Jeep, following behind Jack to the lakeshore. Gravel crunched beneath her shoes, giving way to grass and then sand.

She took in their surroundings, quickly realizing they were entirely alone.

If things went south between her and Jack, she made a mental note of a trail marker close by. She could disappear into the cover of the woods and make a run for it.

Jack knelt on the tiny strip of beach that lined this part of the lake. "Tomorrow, local news is gonna report on a missing boy's disappearance. They're gonna say they found evidence of the kid at this fishing spot. They'll say he was seen out here drinkin' some days before." His heavy boots sank beneath him as he dipped his hand in the small, lapping waves hitting the shore. "And you're gonna corroborate it."

Sam's heart sank. "Who's the boy?"

"Judgin' from that look on your face," Jack said, "you already know."

In the dim light from the Jeep's headlights, Sam recognized the backpack over Jack's shoulder. The worn army-green bag belonged to the boy she'd eaten lunch with nearly every day since she was five years old. The boy who not only *dreamed* with her, but encouraged Sam to be better than the decaying town in which they lived. "Where's Dawson? What'd you *do*?"

"I never laid a hand on him." Jack pulled a handle of vodka

from the bag, as well as a six-pack of beer. He popped open the bottles, one by one, and lazily poured their contents into the shallow lake water. "But let's get one thing straight, Red. I don't go around *fucking* with the lives of innocent people, despite what you may believe."

Sam shook her head. "Is he . . . dead?" The word came out quiet, barely a whisper.

Jack's gaze lingered on the black water of the lake. "Not yet."

Blood rushed to Sam's head, pounding in her ears. "Why're you doin' this?"

"We all answer to someone," Jack said, his usual bravado absent from his voice. He rose, bridging the distance between them. He gently placed the handle of vodka in Sam's hands. "Pour."

Sam wanted to smash the horrible thing across Jack's face, but the urge quickly passed as reality set in. *This* was the cost for saving her brother's life—covering up the death of another. Of the person she once called her best friend.

"This isn't right," Sam murmured as she slowly unscrewed the cap, watching as the clear liquid disappeared into the sloshing lake water.

Jack was quiet as he pulled a pair of Dawson's scuffed-up Nikes from the bag. Sam remembered when he'd bought them, right after his first paycheck came from caddying last summer. Jack buried them in the sand, then splashed them with water. He tossed the bag, empty beer bottles, and Dawson's shoes onto the grass in a pile.

"What's the story then?" Sam asked, guilt lacing her words. "How am I supposed to help you cover this up?"

Jack held out his hand, gesturing for the bottle. "You'll say that last Wednesday, after your shift at the Tavern, you and Dawson met up out here around ten. He was upset. Drinkin' heavily. Kept asking you to swim with him, but you declined. You drove home while he, supposedly, waited on a friend to take him home. After you left, one thing led to another, and Dawson went for a solo swim and never came back. And well . . . you know the rest."

Sam squeezed her eyes shut for a long moment before opening them again. "What if I refuse?"

"Then your brother dies like the good Lord intended," Jack said evenly. "*Bottle*, Red."

Sam tossed the empty vodka handle toward Jack, not minding the intensity of the throw. He caught it with ease, then added it to the pile that now painted a pathetic, fabricated picture of the end of Dawson Sumter's life.

"What's gonna happen to him?" Sam's gaze was fixed on Dawson's bag.

"Somethin' that won't happen to you as long as you keep your head down and mind your goddamn business," Jack cautioned, then his expression softened as he met Sam's eyes. "I'm not intendin' to be cruel here. Just trying to help you out."

"You can help me by being honest," Sam snapped in return. "I deserve that, at the very least."

Jack heaved a heavy sigh, rubbing the shadow of facial hair along his jaw. "What's happening to Dawson is punishment. For somethin' he did. It pissed some Clearwater folks right off. There're some forces at work here that you don't wanna be involved in for your own good. Got it?"

Sam nodded, not wanting to hear any more. It seemed Andrea had been right all along—Dawson *had* gotten mixed up in something bad at Lake Clearwater. Something that was going to kill him. And there wasn't a thing Sam could do about it without risking Ben's life.

"Can you take me home?" Sam asked in a small voice.

"Not just yet." Jack hesitated before he said, "There's another stop we need to make first. WCLB News. For your eyewitness statement."

CHAPTER 13

NEERA

The next day, Neera was out running errands for the motel's cleaning supplies when her grandfather surprised her with a phone call. She'd just left Walmart in the next town over when her phone began to vibrate on the passenger seat. She debated simply not answering it, as she was unwilling to do whatever asinine task Nanaji was surely to ask of her. Her stubbornness was, perhaps, one of the worst Singh traits she carried.

With a dramatic sigh, she fumbled for her phone, putting the call on speaker in her lap as she drove.

"Neera?" Nanaji's aggressive voice rang out. "I need four lottery tickets. Four, okay? Two Powerball and two Mega Millions. All right?"

"Got it," Neera told him, swallowing back a groan. Her grandfather only spoke to her about two things these days: college or the lottery. Finding success with either was equally unlikely.

"You have cash, yes?"

"Yep."

He hung up the phone without warning. If Nanaji truly thought the lottery would be the solution to his debt, they were all surely dead.

Neera sighed, fumbling to enter the address for the nearest gas station into her phone. She and her mom had lived at the motel on and off for years, but she still didn't fully know her way around Carrion. Everything looked like the same backroad, a dizzying maze of pine and oak trees and overgrown kudzu. It was a wonder anyone got around at all.

Twenty minutes later, Neera arrived at a tiny Chevron. It was the early evening now, the sun sitting low in the sky, casting the world in warm shades of orange and long shadows. The cicadas had quieted, their raucous screams an annoying hum rather than a deafening cry.

Several good ol' boys hung out in the parking lot, sitting in the beds of their trucks, shooting the shit, and drinking cheap canned beer. One truck had a Confederate flag pitched proudly on the back. The air was flat and breezeless, the faded cloth falling limp against the dusty truck. Country music blared from one of the radios—not the kind Neera loved, with soaring harmonies and sad, twanging guitar, but the kind they played on the radio that was machine-made pop music, only about trucks and freedom and beer.

As she walked across the sizzling asphalt, Neera was careful not to make eye contact with any of the drinking country boys. They leered but otherwise paid her no mind.

Outside the gas station, two other men stood in front of the missing persons' wall that this Chevron was known for. Most of the dates went back years, some even before Neera was born.

A brightly colored flyer caught Neera's eye as she neared the Chevron's entrance. Her stomach sank as she recognized the blond teenage boy who had checked into the Colonial with tearstained eyes and blood on his hands.

According to the flyer, Dawson Sumter had gone missing during his stay at the motel.

A scarred hand snatched the paper away before she could examine it further.

"What the *hell,*" Neera snapped. "I was reading that." Her anger sputtered out as she realized who towered over her.

Wiley, the handyman from the motel, crumpled up the flyer and tossed it into the garbage bag. With an exaggerated frown, he said, "No point now. Didn't you hear?"

Neera slowly shook her head. "Hear what?"

Wiley nodded to the trash pile. "They just found that Sumter boy's car abandoned near a fishing spot on Lake Clearwater. Were a couple empty liquor bottles on the shore, too. Like mama, like son, I suppose."

A cocktail of guilt and dread mixed in Neera's stomach. Was she the last person to have seen him? Could she have stopped him? "I—I gotta go," Neera stuttered, turning away from Wiley. What was there to do? She couldn't go to the police, especially not after Sheriff Buckley's thinly veiled threat the day before.

Wiley called after her, "My sympathies 'bout that fire."

Neera froze, her hand hovering above the handle of the Chevron's entrance. Wiley's comment was meant to taunt her. To make her feel small and scared and helpless. While she was afraid, she was also angry.

In the dreadful lingering heat of the late summer day, Neera turned on her heel and approached the man who had threatened her family. "How much?" she asked.

Wiley blinked, his smug grin quickly fading. "Beg ya pardon?"

Neera fixed her face into something hard. "How much does my grandfather owe your boss?"

"You *really* wanna have this discussion here?" Wiley sucked his yellow teeth, his beady eyes darting around. Neera looked around them, too. The good ol' boys had turned their music down, now staring their way. Pam, the cashier who always sold Neera lottery tickets, looked on from inside the gas station.

Everyone watched with cautious, distant interest.

"Yes, I do," Neera said with as much confidence as she could muster.

"All right, then." In a quick motion, Wiley grabbed Neera's arm in an iron grip, pulling her away from the front of the Chevron. He dragged her around the corner, not letting go until they were out of sight, hidden away at the back of the building near the employees' entrance.

Neera fought against the urge to scream. To kick Wiley in the balls and run away. But this was what she wanted, wasn't it? Answers? "How *much*?"

Wiley looked at her like a gnat that wouldn't disappear. "Half a million, give or take."

"Wh-what?" That wasn't the number she was expecting at all. "I don't understand how that's possible."

"Your grandpa bit off more than he could chew. Big loans mean bigger interest." Wiley shrugged. "I thought you people were supposed to be smart with money?"

You people? Neera's anger was quickly fading to the hollow feeling of defeat. She swallowed hard, forcing down the lump in her throat. "Who's your boss?"

"Why? So you can talk to him yourself?" Wiley snorted. "It won't change a thing. You can't get your grandpa out of this, kid. He dug his grave with his own two hands."

And our graves, too, Neera thought with a shudder.

"Your grandpa has until the Fourth of July," Wiley continued. "Or, well, there may just be another fire at the Colonial." He studied Neera's face, his eyebrows furrowing in false, exaggerated sympathy. He dug in his pocket, pulling out his wallet. He licked his fingers, counting out ten dollars. "You're here to buy lotto tickets for your grandpa, right? Take this. My treat."

"I don't want—"

Wiley didn't give Neera a chance to decline before he

grabbed her hand and wrapped her fingers around the small wad of bills. He treated her like a rag doll, merely a thing to manipulate for his own amusement. "Today may very well be your lucky day," he said with a wink, then a glance at his phone. "I'm sure I'll be seein' you again soon."

Wiley walked away, disappearing around the Chevron's corner. He left her alone with ten dollars in hand, a freshly bruising arm, and a clear understanding of her family's precarious situation.

If Nanaji didn't pay his debt in less than a week's time, he'd pay in not only his life, but in *all* their lives. In horror, Neera imagined the Colonial going up in flames with them in it, trapped inside as the building burned to ash and rubble. The cause would be a gas leak, or a haywire fuse gone wrong. Something easily glossed over by police. A cruel, fitting ending for the Singh legacy, and Neera felt powerless to stop it.

The harsh caw of a bird sounded nearby. Neera startled, looking up to find a single crow staring down at her from the power line above. The crow held her gaze, refusing to look away, even when she did. It cawed again, louder this time, then cocked its head.

The crow taunted Neera, as if to remind her that, despite everything stacked against her, she still had one option left.

NEERA WAS FIVE years old when she met her grandparents for the first time.

The day had started normal enough. Her mom had taken her to mini golf and then they'd gotten ice cream. But afterward, they took a different route home. Way past home. Hours went by. Neera needed to go to the bathroom, and her stomach felt funny, having had nothing but ice cream all day. But Kiran was immune to her whining, only telling her to wait a little longer. They'd be there soon.

She wouldn't tell Neera where "there" was.

When Kiran finally put on her turn signal and pulled off the road, they'd arrived at a motel, situated just off the highway and surrounded by forest on all sides.

Her mom parked the car in the lot and turned in her seat to face her. "Neera, would you like to meet your grandparents?"

Neera didn't even remember answering. The next thing she knew, she was staring up at the people her own mom called parents.

They were both foreign and familiar. She could see herself in their features, in the shape of their frowning mouths, the depth of their brown eyes. Their cheeks flushed the same way Kiran's did when she was upset.

At first, the adults all just stared at one another. They barely said a word, but Neera thought they must be communicating silently, because the air between them was heavy with hurt and bitterness so strong it made the hairs on her arms go rigid.

Then the strangers shifted their attention to Neera, looking down at her like a tattered, broken toy on the doorstep of their motel. In turn, they each pulled her into an embrace, then pushed her back to get a good look at her. Her grandmother's eyes had the glossy sheen of unshed tears. Her Nanaji's mouth kept twitching as he stared at her, like he was holding himself back from saying something sharp.

Neera had the sudden feeling of having come up short in their appraisal.

They went into the motel for chai. Despite the awkwardness, things were going well enough until the word *father* came up. Neera didn't know anything about her father, and she had never really cared to—her mom and uncle gave her all the love she ever needed. A third parent seemed excessive.

But everyone else seemed to care about this whole father business quite a bit.

Neera was sent to wait in the motel's lobby, where there was a tiny television in the corner. A game show was on. But the contestants' delighted shouting could not compete with the voices yelling in Punjabi from behind the closed door.

Neera did not understand. It was a secret language. The room seemed to shrink around her.

It felt quieter outside. Neera shut the glass lobby door behind her, and the sounds of yelling were silenced, swallowed up by the shriek of the cicadas in the trees. She wandered around the edge of the motel.

A door slammed, and Neera tensed like a gun had gone off. She turned and saw her mom comforting her grandmother through the smudged glass windows of the lobby. Her Nani wept while her grandfather was nowhere to be found.

A sense of *wrongness* swelled up around her. Neera knew it was her fault, that she had somehow caused this badness that hurt everyone else so much. She hadn't meant to. She had no idea what she'd even done. But they were all yelling and crying because of her.

So, she ran.

Tears blurred her vision as she ran past the fence, past the tree line. Into the depth of the nearby forest. There was safety among the trees.

It was late afternoon. In the motel's parking lot, everything had still seemed sunny and bright. But the woods were already dark. Shadows tilted around her as she ran, deeper and deeper into the trees, and over a babbling, slippery stream.

Neera tripped over a tree root and fell, slicing her knee.

Rocks dug into her soft palms. Pine needles scraped against her bare skin. She didn't bother moving, just sat there with her legs folded against her chest and cried, her small frame hidden among the soaring pines.

A figure moved in the shadows.

Neera froze, her hiccuping tears stopped at once.

No longer crying, she noticed the woods had gone silent—the usual chatter of birds, cicadas, and chorus frogs eerily absent. She peered into the shadows, searching for the source of movement. Her eyes fell upon a creature she had no name for. His large body was partially concealed in the shadows, the rest exposed to the dusky light.

Neera was too stunned to scream. The thing towered over her in the form of a mighty bird, looking like he had emerged from the dirt itself. His wings were spindly like twigs, but his body was covered in iridescent feathers that shimmered like an oil slick—some black as night, others green as grass after a summer rain. His beak was nearly the length of her arm, and sharp talons rested on the forest floor. They flexed, like the claws of a cat.

A voice like that of the earth and the trees whispered, "Why do you weep, child?"

In the face of this monstrous creature, Neera could do nothing but tell the truth.

"I want them . . . to love me," Neera whispered back. "Why don't they love me?"

The creature shifted slightly, creaking like branches in the wind. "In time, they will."

Neera sniffled weakly. "How do you know that?"

The creature swayed, his wings fluttering against his body. "I know many things."

Neera appraised the creature, desperate to understand the

thing that loomed over her. Even though he was monstrous, she was unafraid. She had a vivid imagination, preferring stuffed animals over dolls, the nature channel over cartoons. The birdlike monster wasn't much different from the creatures she dreamed up herself.

"Can you help me?" Motivated by her wet tears and aching heart, Neera asked, "Can you make them love me? I don't want to make my family sad anymore."

The creature was quiet for several heartbeats. "I cannot."

Heaviness returned to Neera's chest as tears threatened to pour down her face once more. She whimpered, "Why not?"

"One day," the creature began as he moved forward, inching slowly like freshly spilled ink. The tip of his long beak, covered in moss and dried leaves, nearly touched her nose. "You will desire something greater than love. It will be more powerful than anything you can imagine. I will be here to will it, but *only* that."

Despite the sudden closeness of the creature, Neera was still unafraid. Curiosity threatened to eclipse her sadness. "You promise you'll be here to help me?"

"Yes."

Neera looked around, eyes struggling to discern the woods in the dark. "Do you live here? In the trees?"

"Yes." Branches cracked and snapped all around her. "And no."

Neera felt saddened by that. "How will I see you again?"

"You may call on me when the time comes," the creature said. "But *only* if you are willing to pay the cost of your desire."

Neera nodded slowly, too young to fully understand the weight of the creature's words. "I don't know your name?"

The creature was silent for a long time, as if he weren't used to being asked about himself. "I am nameless," he said finally.

Neera scrunched her nose. The creature looked like the black birds perched outside her window every morning. The ones that sometimes left buttons on her doorstep. "I can call you Crow?"

His black, bottomless eyes blinked slowly. "As you wish."

Compelled by a force beyond her, she said, "My name's Neera."

"*Neera.*" Crow repeated her name as if the wind itself spoke it. "May we meet again."

Without another word, the creature stepped backward, into the bramble and the pines. His eyes stayed on Neera as he backed away, but then she blinked and Crow was gone, absorbed by the leaves and the earth and the night.

Sound returned. Frogs croaked and crickets hummed all around her. Lightning bugs dotted the night in sudden yellow bursts. The cicadas pulsed and whined to the rapid beat of her heart.

Later, Neera emerged from the woods to find all the adults frantic and scared. Even her uncle Ajay had been called to join the search party. She'd been missing for three hours. It had felt like minutes. It had felt like days.

As Kiran fussed over her—alternating between hugging her too tight and scolding Neera for scaring her—Neera could only ask one question. "Mommy, do they love me?"

Her mom hesitated, then pulled her in for another hug. With Kiran's cheek pressed against her own, Neera could feel her begin to cry. She did not answer the question. Ajay looked on from beside them, resting a weary hand on her mom's shoulder and another on Neera's back.

A bird cawed overhead. Neera tilted her head up and up and up, watching a crow disappear into the summer night.

CHAPTER 14

ISAIAH

Isaiah sat on the living room floor of his grandparents' house, surrounded by puzzle pieces. The puzzle, an oversaturated ocean scene, was his little cousin's idea. But Keisha sat beside him, more interested in the contents of her summer homework than helping him create a sunset.

It was early evening, the house abuzz with laughter, clattering pans, and the sweet smell of cornbread. Papa Charles and Uncle Marcus fumbled around in the kitchen, while Grandma Bee and Aunt Tamera were happy to sit at the dining room table, sipping sweet tea and watching their husbands whip up dinner. The local news station played on the living room flatscreen, a dull background noise for the night.

It was all, apparently, too much for Keisha, who gathered her study materials in her arms and excused herself to go upstairs.

Frustrated with the puzzle's slow progress, and Keisha's indifference to it, Isaiah pulled out his phone.

Without really thinking, he then found himself in a new message thread with Neera. He'd typed up a text to her earlier in the day, yet he hadn't the courage to send it. To ask her to breakfast felt like another complication to his already weighted summer. Was he ready to entertain a friendship with her again?

"Oh, that poor boy," Grandma Bee said from the dining room.

Isaiah looked up at the TV. Drone footage played of Lake

Clearwater, with a BREAKING banner flashing across the bottom of the screen. He stood up, crossing the room to better hear the news report.

"Carrion teenager Dawson Sumter has been presumed dead this afternoon. Police found the deceased's car on the north side of Lake Clearwater, parked on the banks of a secluded fishing location." An aerial camera panned over the gated side of the lake, hovering over a heavily wooded inlet. "The teen's shoes were left at the scene, along with several empty bottles of alcohol. A witness has since stepped forward, claiming to have seen Dawson Sumter swimming in the water the night he was reported missing. Recovery of the body will not be possible, due to the treacherous layout of the lake, posing a safety risk to the county's Search and Rescue team.

"We have Samantha Calhoun with us to discuss her eyewitness account of the events leading up to Dawson's death," the news anchor announced. "Samantha, you were with Dawson Sumter the night he drowned, is that correct?"

"Yes, ma'am, I was," Samantha Calhoun said in a thick Georgia drawl. She shifted uncomfortably in front of the camera. "He was really tore up about not getting accepted to the colleges he'd wanted. I often found that drinking was his only way of coping with things. That night was no different."

"Would you say he drank more than average? More than your peers?" the news anchor asked pointedly.

"Yes, I would." Samantha cleared her throat. "It was all he knew how to do. Grew up around it, you see."

"What a shame," Papa Charles said from the kitchen, and Isaiah turned the TV down. "Such a young life lost. Nothin' but tragedy in those waters."

Grandma Bee joined Isaiah, shaking her head at the screen. "I remember reading about him in the paper a while back. He raised money for the Langley County animal shelter, kept it from closing up."

Isaiah struggled to keep his composure at the news. It was reported like the email had said. A chill went down Isaiah's spine as he considered the gravity of it. What had Dawson gotten himself involved with for this to happen? All at once, Isaiah began to feel this was bigger than him—bigger than his podcast.

He leaned against the couch for support. "Is it normal for them not to search for a body?"

Grandma Bee nodded. "They haven't in decades. Last time they did, the divers never resurfaced. It's Old Carrion that lies beneath the water, baby. An entire town's ruins on that lake floor. It's too dangerous. That's why we always drove down to Florida if we wanted to swim in the summer. I'd rather face a shark than whatever hides in Lake Clearwater."

Isaiah's eyebrows furrowed. "What do you mean by that?"

"The lake's haunted," Bee said simply. "Anyone with sense knows it. Only townsfolk looking for trouble and clueless tourists would set foot in that water. Each year those cicadas return, the bodies seem to pile up. It's as if those cicadas wake the spirits and disturb their peace."

Isaiah nodded, though he'd never been one for superstitions, preferring fact over feelings. But through his podcast, he'd learned that folklore and legend were often rooted in a kernel of truth, one just had to dig deep enough to find it. "I'm gonna go check on Keisha."

Isaiah disappeared upstairs before anyone could object. He found his cousin splayed across his bedroom floor, surrounded by notecards and neon highlighters, still engrossed in her textbook. "How's the reading going?"

"Just fifty pages to go," she mumbled absently.

Here she was, barely eleven and already studiously trying to assemble a future for herself from flashcards and outdated textbooks. Keisha had a chance of being accepted into the coveted Clearwater Academy in the coming years, and she was already fighting hard for her future, just like his father had done when he'd been accepted at fourteen.

"Take your time," Isaiah whispered, carefully stepping over her on the way to his desk.

Isaiah pulled out his laptop, mentally preparing himself for an evening of relentless research. He began with Dawson's email, wondering if the IP address could provide anything of note.

He inspected the email's metadata, copying the address into the tracking software he often used for his podcast. It took him several minutes to filter through the numeric noise before he learned the email was sent from a public Wi-Fi network.

Specifically, from a business in Carrion.

The Colonial Inn.

Dawson had been connected to the Colonial's internet when he emailed Isaiah a week ago. His heart stuttered a little as he considered what this meant: Neera had lied about seeing Dawson, and he was determined to find out why.

Isaiah looked again at the text he'd begun to type earlier in the day. Pushing back his complicated feelings, he sent it.

Waffle House off Antioch Rd in the morning?

To Isaiah's surprise, Neera replied a moment later: *Sure, does 7 work for you?*

See you then, he responded, and his chest felt heavy again.

Isaiah looked out the bedroom window, dark eyes lingering on the farm's oldest oak tree, the branches thick and sprawling, heavy with Spanish moss. For a moment, he allowed himself to remember the contours of their friendship: the worlds they'd created when they were younger, when they'd climb into that very tree and weave elaborate stories between each other—little gods above the flatland. The way that, when things were good, Isaiah had felt as if no one would ever truly see him as Neera did.

But they weren't children anymore.

"Isaiah?" Keisha asked. "You okay?"

Isaiah blinked the memory away, finding his cousin staring up at him with a furrowed brow. "I'm all good." He fixed his face with that easy smile.

Once Keisha was absorbed again in her schoolwork, Isaiah pulled up Dawson's Instagram, looking once more for anything that stood out. Despite his profile being public, he was a private person. The only thing Isaiah could gather from the paltry photos was that he had an affection for rescued animals and a passion for golf. It didn't tell him anything about *who* Dawson really was or who his friends were.

Isaiah went to Andrea Sumter's Facebook next. She was less social media savvy, with her account entirely public, including an archive of hundreds of photos spanning years. Over the next hour, Isaiah went through every single photo album. Every cheesy caption. Studying all the comments.

A number of the photos featured Samantha Calhoun, the girl from the news, alongside Dawson, dating all the way back to their childhood. But the photos stopped abruptly about a year ago. The pair seemed close, but they didn't follow each other on Instagram.

Then he noticed someone else had replaced Samantha in Andrea's recent photos—Reid Langley. There wasn't much to go off of, as the number of photos tapered off over time. But there was Dawson's eighteenth birthday back in March, with Reid sitting proudly beside Dawson at a steakhouse in Lake Clearwater.

Isaiah leaned back in his desk chair, trying to make sense of his thoughts. Then he took to his keyboard, typing into a new Word document. He wrote down the fragments of everything he knew so far.

Missing teenager, Dawson Sumter (possibly dead?)—reason unknown

Cover-up by Lake Clearwater—motive unknown

Colonial motel—connected to Dawson's disappearance?

Strange voicemail from Dawson's mom, Andrea Sumter, to Clearwater attorney, Casey Leblanc—connection unknown

Samantha Calhoun—lied to police??

Reid Langley—Dawson's best friend?

As Isaiah stared at the meager bit of information he had, his anxiety about his father returned. If he were to investigate Lake Clearwater in the same way he'd done for the past three seasons of *Secrets of the South,* he was terrified of what he might find. Afraid there was, in fact, something insidious going on in Carrion.

What would that mean for his father?

For his family?

For himself?

CHAPTER 15

REID

Someone called Reid's name.

He lay on his fiberglass paddleboard in the middle of Lake Clearwater, having come here to escape his family, and stared up at the night sky. His arms dangled off the side of the board, skin growing pruned from hours spent floating.

Someone called his name again. In the stifling humid air, Reid swore it was his mother's voice. But that was impossible. His mother had been dead for six years.

"You're just cross-faded, Reid," he mumbled aloud to himself, while rubbing his face.

After he'd seen the news of Dawson's drowning earlier that day, Reid grabbed his vape pen, one of his father's flasks, and vanished to the water. It was full dark now, but he didn't want to return to land because it meant he would have to confront the fact that everyone he loved had left him.

Reid reached for his vape, inhaling for as long as he could bear it. Only nothing happened. His pen had finally died, and the flask was now empty. He cursed, struggling to right himself on the board. His head felt heavy. His vision swam. And that voice—it kept calling for him.

From his anchor point far from the dock, Reid could just barely make out the blur of guests gathered outside the Langley estate, lingering like flies, their laughter echoing across the dark water. Reid was so sick of the endless parties and posturing and pretending. Sitting fully up, he squinted against the cloudy haze in his head, only to see his sister's faint figure waving him in from the shore.

Coming, Reid reluctantly signaled.

As he paddled back to land, the memory of the day he'd met Dawson was still clear in his head, nearly a year ago to the day. Jonah had dragged Reid onto the lake's most difficult golf course, Kingdom Waters. His brother was on a mission to impress their father, and Jonah was in desperate need of an ego boost after nearly being kicked out of UGA for selling prescription stimulants on campus.

That blistering June day, Dawson Sumter had the misfortune of being Jonah Langley's golf caddy.

Jonah took one look at Dawson with his oversize, ill-fitting polo and khakis, eyes lingering on a scuff mark on his white golf shoes. He was clearly a kid from Carrion, yet he wore his uniform with pride. "Do they let just anyone work here these days?"

Despite Jonah's unbearable rudeness, Dawson smiled through it with ease. All eighteen holes of it. He always handed Jonah the best clubs, advising him appropriately on his swings, his posture, the tips he learned from caddying other golfers.

But for all of Dawson's patience and help, Jonah had a terrible round. There would be nothing for Jonah to boast about around the Langley dinner table that night. Jonah felt small, but he needed someone else to feel smaller.

"Next time, you'd do well to *not* be my caddy," Jonah warned as they parked the golf cart outside one of the many golfing clubhouses that dotted the shores of Lake Clearwater. "Otherwise, you'll be lucky to get a job picking up dog shit on the green, much less caddying."

Jonah stalked off like a petulant child before Dawson could get a word in, leaving him and Reid alone with the myriad of golf equipment as the sun set along the lake. Wordlessly, Dawson climbed out of the golf cart, making to grab the golf bags and walk away. He didn't bother concealing his disappointment. Four hours of being bossed around by a Langley and all he got out of it was a threat to his job security.

"Wait," Reid said, finally speaking up. He pulled out his own wallet, counting out several hundred dollars. Extending it to Dawson, he said, "For putting up with my awful brother."

Dawson didn't move to take the bills. Dryly, he asked, "Pity money from a Langley?"

Reid flinched but kept his hand extended. "For a job well-done."

With a firm shake of his head, Dawson said, "I'll pass. Thanks, anyway."

Reid sighed. He hadn't stood up for Dawson while Jonah was around, but that didn't mean he couldn't do better now. "When's your shift end?"

Dawson blinked, then looked at the cheap watch on his wrist. The band was made of worn, sun-bleached leather, and the face was cracked down the center. "Another two hours. Why?"

"You're seriously skilled on the green." Reid gestured to the sprawling golf course at their backs. "If you have time, why don't you teach me some pointers? Imagine my brother's face if I get good enough to best him on Kingdom Waters."

A smirk crept across Dawson's face. "I would pay to see that."

"Well, I can't make it happen on my own." Reid waved the money in his hand. "Think of this as payment for teaching me not to suck. I mean, you saw me. I can barely hit the ball."

"That's true. You're terrible." Dawson snorted, his shoulders relaxing a little. "Fine, I'll do it. But I don't want your money unless you beat Jonah's score. Fair?"

Dawson eyed Reid's outstretched hand, then took it in his own, signaling the start of their unlikely friendship.

The summer came and went, and with it, Dawson Sumter and Reid Langley became close friends. After a childhood bullied by both his peers and siblings, Reid had never known friendship in the way he and Dawson shared it. It had been difficult to make friends in Clearwater *before* his mother died, but it was nearly impossible after.

Reid went from being the runt of the Langley siblings, meek and unassuming, to the social pariah of Clearwater after Caroline's death. It didn't help he went mute for two years, unable to speak to anyone at all after she passed. Not even his family—*especially* not his family.

In the year they knew each other, Dawson had allowed Reid to be more than the title that preceded him. In many ways, Dawson reminded Reid of his own mother, with their shared kindness and fresh perspectives on the world around them. For the first time in a long time, Reid was able to envision himself as more than just the weird Langley son who still grieved the loss of his long-dead mother. Around Dawson, he could simply *be*.

But that was in the past now.

Because, according to the news, Dawson had drowned.

If Reid allowed himself to see beyond his grief, for even just a moment, there was a part of him that knew something wasn't quite right. He had the nauseating sense that history was somehow repeating itself.

This is just like Mom.

Having floated back toward the shore, he lingered beneath a cypress tree growing out of the dark water. Spanish moss hung from the branches, brushing Reid's shoulders. A cicada fell from the overhanging tree, landing on the edge of the paddleboard. The heavy, winged insect squirmed on its back, struggling to right itself. He studied the cicada, suddenly feeling sick at the memory of eating one the day before.

He had been taught from an early age to respect the skittering creatures, to treat them with reverence. To do anything less was practically sacrilegious. But those teachings never settled right with him.

Reid gripped the end of his paddle. In a fast, sure motion, he squashed the whining cicada, silencing it with a steady, killing blow.

CHAPTER 16

SAM

The sound of screaming jolted Sam awake. In the haze of sleep, she forgot where she was. Her heart pounded in her chest as the distant yelling conjured images of her daddy on the other side of her bedroom door, threatening to destroy everything in his path to get in. She fumbled for the meager switchblade she kept beneath her pillow, then flicked it open.

Reality set in as Bailey's and Clayton's voices pierced the thin walls from across the trailer. They were fighting again, as they often did. The pair had a penchant for alcohol-fueled arguments in the same way her parents always had, and it set her nerves ablaze.

When Sam was kicked out of her house a few weeks back, she'd never intended to move in with her ex and her ex's boyfriend. It had been a decision made from desperation—after her fight with her daddy. The broken bedroom door. The bruises. The fractured wrist.

Her new place was so small, you couldn't so much as sneeze without it being heard across the single-wide trailer. Sam didn't much care, as she was grateful to have a place to stay at all. But when Bailey and Clayton fought, Sam felt like she was back home. Her muscles tensed. Her heartbeat soared. Her body braced for something bad. She didn't know how to force her mind to tell her body that she was going to be okay.

That Wiley wasn't going to charge through the door at any moment.

That she was safe.

But was she *really* safe? What would stop Clayton from doing the same thing to Bailey and Sam that her daddy had done to her, all her life?

The fighting continued.

I can't do this, Sam thought. *Not tonight.*

Not after what she'd done to Dawson—what she'd done to save her brother.

A life for a life.

Sam untangled herself from her sheets, and something rough and unfamiliar grazed against her bare legs and feet.

She jumped out of bed and turned on the light.

Peeling back the sheets, she found several feet of dried snakeskin tangled in her bed. It took everything in her not to scream. Her skin prickled with goose bumps as she realized the snakeskin's origins.

A taunting message from Jack.

Sam understood then which devil he was, recalling the town's legend. There was the cicada, the crow, and the snake. It finally clicked. Whatever shred of disbelief she still had for Jack had all but vanished. He truly was what he claimed to be: a serpentine devil walking among them.

Frantically, she stripped the sheets, wadding the fabric into a tight ball, hiding the molted skin within. Without another thought, she opened her bedroom window and tossed the bedding outside, watching it fall to the ground.

Sam climbed out the window, landing barefoot on the warm grass. She carried the sheets to the trash cans at the road, then kept on walking, desperate to rid herself of the sensation of the snakeskin against her legs.

Clayton didn't come from much, but his family owned the ten acres his trailer sat upon. It was forgotten farmland, with old buildings scattered across the property.

Taking refuge in a run-down barn, Sam relaxed into a chair she'd squirreled away for moments like these. It was made of cheap plastic that she'd been burning holes into every time she came out here. If she was gonna light a cigarette and not smoke it, she might as well entertain herself in other ways.

Except, that night, Sam craved a cigarette something awful. She'd promised Ben she would quit. But she *needed* one after what she'd just seen. What she'd just done. As she looked onto the shadowy flatland that spread for miles outside the barn, she placed the cigarette between her lips, hesitating for a breath. She studied the old lighter in her hand, with its worn American flag design.

It was a joke gift, one given to her by Dawson last summer. Before their fight that had ruined nearly a lifetime of friendship. Sam turned the lighter over, fingertips brushing over faded letters scrawled on one side with permanent marker.

Two words.

Call me.

Just like her brother, Dawson had once been invested in helping Sam quit smoking. The difference was that Dawson had known *why* she did it to begin with. To quell her ever-present anxiety. To allow herself a moment of peace when every nerve in her body was on fire. Dawson had understood that if Sam couldn't find release in one way, she'd find it through another.

For many years, Dawson had always been there for Sam in those desperate moments. He picked up the phone every single time she called. Until he didn't.

It was last fall when Sam began to notice the fissures growing between her and Dawson. They were walking the halls of Langley County High during lunch, as they often did. Their high school was run much like a prison, and it looked like one, too, but Dawson had a way with teachers. They'd let him roam the halls if he kept out of trouble, and she tagged along.

Just outside the cafeteria doors, a military recruiter had been setting up a table as they walked past. The uniformed man had put up signs about traveling the world on the government's dime, as well as attending college for free in exchange for service. It was a predatory practice, not uncommon in town.

"Sumter!" the recruiter called out. "You finished up your paperwork yet?"

Dawson's face blanched. "No, Sergeant Davis. Not yet."

Sergeant Davis nodded. "Well, get it to me soon. The army could really use a bright fella like yourself."

Sam waited until they were out of earshot. "Are you fucking serious?"

Dawson shook his head. "I was *considering* it. That's all."

"What about college?" Sam stepped in front of him. "I thought you'd heard back early from your picks?"

Dawson shrugged, leaning against the nearest locker. "I'm not going."

"Like, which one? UGA? Tech?" Sam asked. "There's still the smaller schools, right? They're fine. You can always transfer out."

"None of 'em, Sam," Dawson sighed. "I didn't get accepted into any."

Sam blinked. "I don't . . . *how*?"

"It doesn't matter. I just—I didn't get in." Dawson scowled. "Why're you houndin' me? It's not like you bothered applying."

"School's not for me. You know that." Sam crossed her arms, eyeing her best friend. He looked ready to crawl out of his skin. "What're you gonna do then? Be shipped off somewhere halfway around the world? That's how you wanna see it, in uniform with an assault rifle in your hands?"

"*Jesus,* you can be so self-righteous sometimes," Dawson fired back. "Military's not an option anyway. My heart thing disqualifies me from even applying."

"Oh, right." Sam was quiet for a beat. "You deserve better than this place is all I'm sayin'."

"I get it." Dawson fumbled with a broken belt loop on his jeans. "I actually got a job lined up after graduation. It's good money. Could pay for my mama's treatment, you know. Finally get her some help."

"Where at?" Sam asked. "Up at the lake?"

"Somethin' like that," Dawson said, but he wouldn't look at her.

Sam never got the chance to ask anything else before the bell rang. They went their separate ways to class, but at the time, Sam couldn't shake the feeling Dawson was keeping something from her.

And she'd been right, despite how much she wished otherwise.

Months later, Sam's lighter was no longer a comfort, but an aching reminder of not only the dear friend that she'd lost, but what she'd *done* to him. It was bad enough to know that their stupid fight a month ago had been her fault.

It was worse realizing that, because of her, he may truly end up dead.

CHAPTER 17

NEERA

Waffle House was a strange place at sunrise.

Customers were slumped over in slippery booths, faces nearly buried in plates of syrupy waffles and greasy bacon. Waitresses in black aprons, covered in kitschy pins, ran plates to tables filled with obnoxious drunks. The cooks shouted orders from the exposed kitchen, wiping sweat from their foreheads while they flipped piles of steaming hash browns on the stove.

Waffle House was the best place to be without really having to be anybody at all. Was that why Isaiah had suggested it?

A hazy country tune played on the jukebox beside the door as Neera hovered by the entrance. No one paid her any mind as she walked to the corner booth in the back by the tall windows and waited for Isaiah to arrive.

"Two waters and coffees, please," Neera said to a waitress as she slid into the cold seat.

A moment later, the sticky tabletop was filled with drinks and several laminated menus. Neera blew on the scalding-hot coffee as she pretended to consider what to eat.

Neera's fingers drummed against the table, at first absent and anxious, keeping rhythm with the thoughts racing through her head. She kept thinking about seeing Dawson at the motel, the blood on his hands, in his room. And now, he was dead. But then she found the tune of the song playing over the speakers—Johnny Cash singing about shooting a man in Reno—and she eased ever so slightly.

The parking lot was unchanged. No sign of Isaiah's white BMW. Insecurity bloomed inside of Neera, like a kudzu vine snaking around her throat. Would he stand her up? Not bother to show because he knew there was nothing between them worth salvaging?

In the ways of real friendship, Neera had always been lacking. But she supposed Isaiah had once truly known her. He knew the girl who hadn't yet lost the sun. There was something special about that—something worth protecting. Because whoever she met from then on, they only met a girl that had been broken and hardened by grief.

But it was music that kept her safe all those years, and it was music that was going to change her life for the better. It couldn't judge or hurt her. Music would never leave her.

Neera's phone buzzed on the table.

Isaiah: *Ten minutes away. Really sorry!*

Frowning at the screen, she responded: *No worries. See you soon*

Neera's hands were sticky from drumming her fingers on the dirty table. She rose in search of the bathroom, so she could wash up before Isaiah arrived. Down a narrow hallway, she pushed open the squeaky door, only to find a woman in wrinkled scrubs slumped on the floor, hovering over the toilet. The bathroom reeked of piss and bile.

"Ma'am, you all right?" Neera asked, covering her nose with the neckline of her oversized T-shirt.

The woman blinked slowly, wiping her mouth with the back of her hand. She waved Neera away with a grunt. "I'm . . . fine."

"You don't look fine." Hesitating for a moment, Neera knelt to the woman's level. "Is there anyone I can call to come get you?"

The woman shook her head as silent tears slid down her worn, sun-spotted face, falling quietly into the toilet. "There ain't nobody left," the woman whispered, her words a barely audible slur. "Ain't nobody left," she repeated, her eyes bloodshot as she stared at nothing.

The woman was clearly intoxicated, beyond point of reason. Neera didn't know what to do. She couldn't help but think of her mom as she stared at the woman. She'd found Kiran in the same position more times than she cared to remember after Ajay's death. Curled up on the bathroom floor, begging for him to come back. But no amount of drinking would change anything. It only made the grief worse.

If Neera knew nothing else, it was that solace wasn't at the bottom of a bottle. She'd like to think it could be found in better things, like her Yamaha resting across her lap. But who was she without it? The thought shook her to the bone.

"I'm sorry," Neera said, and she meant it. She was sorry for the woman, as she recognized the loss written across her face. Neera didn't know her, but she felt her pain, even on the grimy bathroom floor of a Waffle House on the edge of town. "I'm sorry for whatever happened to you."

The woman blinked a few times, then her cloudy blue eyes locked with Neera's. "They'll . . . get you."

Neera's thick eyebrows furrowed. "What?"

In a hoarse whisper, she said, "If you ain't careful . . . they'll get you, too." The woman's eyes went glassy again as she began to heave, then vomited in the toilet.

Neera grimaced, quickly rising from the floor, and stumbled out of the bathroom and into the other one across the hall. Her heartbeat thudded loud in her ears. She tried not to take the woman's words to heart, but it was impossible not to in a place like Carrion.

As she dried her hands, Neera noticed the wall riddled with writing. There were phone numbers of people looking to hook up, initials of couples enclosed within poorly drawn hearts, but then there was handwriting in small, crooked lettering that was barely noticeable at all. But Neera saw it, clear as day, as she tossed her wet paper towel in the trash can.

The devil went down to Georgia and never left

Neera recognized it as the lyrics from a folk song Ajay had taught her years ago—a folkie blues ballad, slow and methodical. Relentless and haunting.

The devil went
Down
Down
Down
Down to Georgia
The devil went
Down
Down
Down
And never left
They say
You meet the devil
At the crossroads
Down in Georgia
When there ain't no options left

The tale was an old Carrion legend. It warned that, in Southwest Georgia, there was not one devil but three. They were known as brothers, each one more wicked than the one that came before.

There's the devil you know
The devil you don't

The devil you wish you'd never met

Years ago, Ajay taught Neera the song as a music lesson but also as a cautionary tale.

"The three devils are as cunning as they are cruel," Ajay had told her one hazy summer afternoon, leaned over the body of his Yamaha guitar. "They each prey on desperate people, offering them the one thing they want most."

With a child-sized guitar in her lap, Neera, five and wide-eyed, gulped. Intrigued, she had asked, "*Really*? Could they give me a pet tiger? One that can talk?"

Ajay smirked, ruffling her long black hair. "The brothers can only give what's already in your heart." Then, Neera remembered clearly—how her uncle's face had turned serious. His playful brown eyes went dark. "Nothing in this world is given freely, Neera. There is always a cost. Never forget that."

"Okay," she said in a small voice. "I won't."

Light returned to Ajay's eyes, warm and comforting. "But you know what to say if any devils ever come around with an offer, don't you?"

Neera smiled, nodding quickly. "I say *no, thank you,*" she recited proudly, puffing her chest.

"That's right," Ajay said, strumming the song's melancholy tune with a grin. "That's all the devil needs to hear. *No, thank you.*"

Be careful of the devils
Down in Georgia
There ain't no coming back
From the pact

In the Waffle House bathroom, Neera nudged the trash can with her shoe, finding the rest of the lyrics scribbled onto the wall. All the way down the words went, written to the place where the wall molding met the dirty tiled floor.

But then, she noticed something else. Scrawled beside the familiar song were three crude drawings, childlike in their depictions.

A cicada.

A snake.

A crow.

Neera ran her hand over the drawings, her calloused fingertips lingering on the crow. She'd seen the corvid three times since her confrontation with Wiley at the Chevron. Sitting on the fence around the Colonial's pool. Perched on the hood of the Nissan in the late afternoon. Hovering above her on the low-hanging power line. She had no proof it was the same bird each time, only a feeling. A sense of familiarity as the black eyes of the crow tracked her every step.

A life-changing decision loomed over Neera as the Cicada's Song approached.

ISAIAH

A HALF-EATEN WAFFLE and rubbery blanched eggs sat between Neera and Isaiah.

After initial pleasantries and half-assed catching up, there was little among them in the way of conversation. Neera kept fidgeting, glancing behind Isaiah at something he couldn't see. But Isaiah was no better.

He heaved a heavy sigh, deciding to focus on the only thing he had an ounce of control over—repairing his friendship with Neera. "So . . . how'd the audition go?"

Neera swirled a spoon in a cup of black coffee. "To be honest, kind of terrible."

"How do you mean?"

Neera shrugged. "Grant Langley was there. The Blue Mountain Records guy. Made me think I wasn't worth getting onstage. Like *I* wasn't enough. But he's letting me perform on Thursday, so . . . we'll see."

Isaiah frowned. "Don't let him get to you. I know you'll do—"

"Stop." Neera cut him off, no longer swirling the coffee, then set the spoon on the table with a *clang*. Meeting Isaiah's gaze, she said, "Don't do that."

Isaiah blinked. "Do what?"

"*Pretend,*" Neera said bluntly. "You're pretending right now, I can tell."

Isaiah was taken aback. He was so accustomed to bland politeness and people always talking around their words, that Neera's bluntness threw him off. "How exactly am I pretending?"

"Honestly, I don't think you would've reached out if it weren't for the fire," Neera said. "We've barely spoken in three years. I just feel like you're bullshitting to smooth things over between us."

Isaiah opened his mouth to argue but stopped himself. Neera wasn't exactly wrong. He truly had missed their friendship, but was there anything left to return to? The Neera Singh he once knew no longer existed. "I just wanted to try."

"I'm not sure there's a point."

Isaiah glanced around the brightly lit Waffle House, his eyes eventually lingering on the window nearest them. The early-morning sun painted this side of Carrion in a bright shade of pink. A crow circled overhead, like a vulture. He then saw past the parking lot, to the peanut field across the road, how it stretched for miles until it hit the pine forest. That's all Isaiah saw, flatness in every direction.

Quietly, he said, "You know, you were the one who stopped responding. After . . . what happened, I reached out. I texted. I called. But it was radio silence from you. What was I supposed to do? We were *fifteen*—we were just kids. I didn't know any better."

Heavy silence hung between them, filled only by the clanging of dishes, the murmur of customers, and the sizzle of waffles cooking.

"You stopped trying, Isaiah," Neera said. "You stopped . . . *caring*." She choked on the last word, her chin beginning to tremble.

Isaiah studied Neera then, really taking in the girl he once knew. She had the unsteady energy of a tiger caught in a cage. The kind you'd see pacing in a run-down enclosure at some roadside zoo in the Florida swamps.

Despite what had changed between them, Isaiah was reminded of when they were little kids. Neera had that same energy when they were on the fenced-in playground in the dead of summer. That desperation to be anywhere but where they were. The only time he'd seen Neera truly at ease was with her uncle.

He had been so jealous of their bond. Ajay had treated Neera like she was his entire world. It was the kind of love that Isaiah had longed for from his own father: the kind which asked for nothing in return.

"But I don't blame you," Neera continued, her golden-brown eyes welling up with tears. "I blame *me*. For being so fucked up after it happened. I pushed you away because I wasn't worth being around anymore. And I'm not sure that's changed."

"Neera," Isaiah began, but nothing followed.

In that moment, his heart truly ached. For the years lost between them, for the guilt he felt, and for the pain Neera still clearly carried within her.

Despite the time that had passed, their friendship was worth fighting for.

"I'm sorry. I am truly sorry I wasn't there for you when you needed it the most. You're right. I *did* stop trying. We can't change the past, but . . ." Isaiah inhaled a steadying breath. "I'm here now."

A heartbeat passed, then Neera met Isaiah's gaze. "I'm here now, too." Her chin still trembled, but she managed to keep her tears at bay. "I'm sorry. I want to be better—I really do."

Isaiah gave her a smile. It wasn't the fake, country-club one he often wore, but a genuine, heartfelt expression. Neera returned it, and for the briefest moment, there was a glimpse of the girl he once knew.

Neera's phone vibrated on the table, taking her smile with it. With a groan, she said, "I'm being summoned back to the motel. I should probably get going."

"Wait." Isaiah hesitated for a breath. "If we're gonna really do this again"—he motioned between them—"we need to be honest with each other."

"I agree."

Isaiah asked, in a low voice, "Why'd you lie about seeing Dawson Sumter at the Colonial when I asked you the other day?"

Neera went still. "You asked if I knew him, not if I'd seen him. I didn't technically lie."

Isaiah's eyes narrowed. "So, you *did* see him?"

"Yeah, he got a room and now he's dead. What do you want me to say?" She let out a heavy sigh. "Sorry, I don't mean to sound rude. But why're you asking about him at all?"

"It's just . . . I have a gut feeling something isn't right," Isaiah said, the hypocrisy of his words not lost on him. He wasn't *technically* lying, either. But this wasn't the time or place to tell Neera about his podcast or Dawson's email. *This is merely delayed truth,* he thought. He glanced around them to make sure no one was listening. "Was there anything *off* about him?"

"I mean, yeah. When I first saw him, it looked like he'd been crying. And . . ."

"And what?"

"I think Dawson had blood on his hands," Neera whispered. "There was blood in his bathtub. Not a lot, but not a little, either."

"*Blood?*" Isaiah repeated. "Jesus Christ, Neera."

"It's not that uncommon at the Colonial," she insisted. "I didn't really think anything of it until I saw that he'd, you know, drowned."

"Anything else?" Isaiah asked, his mind now racing.

Neera's eyes went to the tote bag sitting beside her. She dug around in it for a moment, then placed an object on the table between them. An old leather key chain with a peculiar buck antler logo carved into it, as well as long-faded letters he couldn't decipher. "I found this when I was cleaning his room. And then . . . I saw this in the motel's office."

She reached into her bag and pulled something else out. A photo of her uncle, Ajay, wearing a shirt with the same blindfolded deer logo. She set it on the table between them. "What if the fire, Dawson's key chain, and this photo are all connected? I just don't know how or why yet."

Isaiah sat in silence for a beat, processing what he'd just heard. He picked up the key chain to look at it more closely, comparing it to the photo of Ajay. "This building in the background . . . what if Ajay worked there? Dawson, too? Just a coincidence?"

"Maybe," Neera said skeptically. "But I don't know. It's *too* coincidental." She went quiet again, her gaze focusing beyond the window. "There's something else," she said. Her voice was, suddenly, so *small*. She was no longer a tiger but the memory of one. "The guy who threatened us—Wiley. He said something weird. He mentioned Ajay. Said we'd end up just like him if my grandfather's debt isn't paid."

"*What?*" Isaiah leaned across the table, drawing close. "Neera, I thought—I thought he . . ." He wasn't willing to say it aloud.

Neera met his gaze. "You know, what if he *didn't*? What if it wasn't suicide after all? I've always thought it, but didn't have any proof. Just another goddamn feeling. And I'm having that same feeling right now, after finding the key chain and this photo. What if Wiley didn't just mean dead, but *murdered*?"

"Maybe the same thing happened to Dawson," Isaiah said, reconsidering everything he'd learned so far. "I can do some digging—property records, public debt, that kind of thing. See if I can find out who your grandfather owes the money to, who this boss of Wiley's is. Maybe then it'll make all this a little clearer."

"Thank you, Isaiah," Neera said solemnly. "But whatever happens, I'll figure something out, okay? This isn't your responsibility."

"All right," Isaiah agreed, except he didn't mean it one bit. Because this was one side of Neera he recognized: stubbornly independent. Terrified of asking for help. He owed it to them both to try.

When the two said their goodbyes, they hugged, but it wasn't the awkward, tense embrace from a few days before.

It felt genuine and certain.

ONCE NEERA'S CAR had pulled out of the Waffle House parking lot, Isaiah went to the counter to pay for their meal. As he hovered at the register, a woman's yell sounded behind him. A middle-aged white woman was being escorted from the bathroom, cussing and yelling all the while. Her voice was familiar, but he couldn't quite place it.

The cook, a gruff man covered in tattoos, guided her to the exit as she made a scene, dragging her feet along the tiled floor. He led her out the front door and onto the sidewalk, plopping her firmly on the ground before returning inside.

Their waitress, Jo, rang up Isaiah, shaking her head at the scene.

"What's that all about?" he asked.

"Just a woman taking no responsibility for herself," Jo said as she scribbled onto a yellow receipt pad. "Ain't nothin' new around here."

"Did something happen to her?" Isaiah prodded as he folded the change into his wallet.

"Her son died and she's going around blaming the whole town for it, instead of making right with God." Jo rolled her eyes. "Everybody in Carrion wanna blame somebody else for their problems instead of lookin' at themselves."

Isaiah realized then where he'd previously heard the woman's voice. The voicemail in Leblanc's office.

I know about you and my son.

The belligerent woman was Andrea Sumter. Isaiah swallowed hard, trying to keep his cool.

"Thank you for the meal," Isaiah said by way of goodbye.

All around Isaiah, people glared and turned their noses up at the sight of Andrea outside, bent over on the ground, her face buried between her knees. He fought the urge not to grimace at their harsh lack of sympathy.

The early-morning humidity was stifling as Isaiah considered his options outside the front door of Waffle House. This was his chance to speak to Andrea, to hear her side of the story about Dawson. But she wasn't what he expected. He wasn't sure she was in a state to have a conversation about the weather, much less the death of her son.

Isaiah rubbed his temple. He had been trying to track down Andrea for nearly two days without any luck, and here she was, emerging from the woodwork of Waffle House. He supposed it was now or never.

"Ma'am," Isaiah began, kneeling on the ground. "Are you, by chance, Andrea Sumter?"

"Who's askin'?" The woman met Isaiah's gaze, her blue eyes watery and bloodshot. She had the same eyes as Dawson's from the photographs he'd seen. The same thin nose.

In a quiet voice, Isaiah said, "I'd like to talk to you about your son."

"There's nothin' to talk about." Andrea's chin trembled. "My son's gone."

"I know, and I'm really sorry about that," Isaiah said. "But I'd like to talk to you about what happened. What *really* happened, if you'd be open to it?"

Andrea's eyes narrowed, studying Isaiah. "You a reporter?"

"No, ma'am," Isaiah said with his most mollifying smile. "Not yet, at least. I'm studying journalism at SCAD. I read about your son's drowning and felt his story deserved to be told." He felt bad, telling another lie to a woman who was drowning in them, but through his various investigations for *Secrets of the South,* Isaiah had honed his ability to obfuscate. To wrap up the truth in a blanket of dishonesty. It was his protection.

"Oh," Andrea said, placated. She sniffled, rubbing snot from her nose and onto the back of her pale hand. "I'm really in no shape to talk to anyone," she relented, grimacing at her vomit-stained scrubs. "But I'm open to talkin' another time. Later today? After I clean myself up."

Isaiah nodded. "Yes, ma'am, of course. Here's my number." He rattled off one of the many Google Voice numbers he used for interviews. "And my name's Jordan Harris." For most things relating to his podcast, he erred on the side of caution, but this felt different. Riskier, somehow. Was it because this was so close to home?

Andrea finished typing the number into her phone, then eyed Isaiah once more. Her gaze alternated from present to gone, like she struggled to remain here or was somewhere lost in her thoughts. "You have the same sort of eyes as my boy. Kind. Trustin'."

"Thank you."

"It ain't a compliment." Andrea shook her head. "Not anymore."

Isaiah's chest felt heavy as he climbed into his car and made the drive back home to the farm. He rolled the BMW's windows down, willing himself to breathe the fresh morning air, to think clearly about the story unraveling before him.

Of the town he loved taking shape into something he no longer recognized.

As he drove down the flat stretch of the two-lane road, the cicadas sounded with their morning rallying call. All at once, their cacophonous screams echoed around Isaiah, doing little to drown out his racing thoughts and the uneasy feeling burrowing beneath his skin.

CHAPTER 18

SAM

That afternoon, Sam recognized Sheriff Buckley guarding the closed door of Ben's hospital room like a pig-faced sentry.

What the hell is this?

It'd been three days since the accident, since Sam had last seen her brother. She hesitated around the hallway corner, frowning at the paltry gift in her hand. A hazelnut chocolate bar that had already turned soft from the heat of the late June morning. Ben wouldn't care if it was melted—he'd never been picky like that. The gesture alone would bring a smile to his face, showing his freckled cheeks. But as she eyed the sheriff down the hall, Sam feared she wouldn't even get the chance.

Approaching the door with confident steps, Sam pretended she didn't notice Sheriff Buckley. Once he spotted her, he began to slowly shake his head.

"You can stop right there, Samantha," Sheriff Buckley said. "Go on ahead and turn around before this gets ugly."

Sam slowed. "What're you talking about, *Buck*?"

The sheriff snorted at the nickname reserved for use by friends and family. He'd been a longtime family friend of her parents, as was most trailer trash of Carrion, where everybody knew everybody. And *everybody* did well to stay on the good side of her daddy.

Wiley Calhoun and Sheriff Buckley were as thick as thieves. If her daddy was Russ Langley's attack dog, Sheriff Buckley was the authority that looked the other way when someone got bit.

"You ain't allowed in there," Sheriff Buckley said, chewing on a black wad of tobacco like a grazing cow. "More specifically, you ain't allowed within fifteen hundred feet of here." He materialized a manila folder from the nearby chair, pulling out several sheets of legal papers and extending them to Sam.

"A *restraining* order?" Sam took all of a moment to look it over before shoving the papers back into the sheriff's hands. "My parents can't keep me from Ben. They have no right."

"Sure they do," Sheriff Buckley said. "You threatened your brother's life with that accident. You're an endangerment to a minor. It matters not that he's your blood."

"I never endangered him," Sam snapped. Her fingers twitched into a fist as she stared at the sheriff's satisfied face. He was the kind of person who derived joy out of cruelty, and she wanted to punch him for it. "Why don't you do your damn job and find the person who's actually responsible?"

"What was that?" Sheriff Buckley's expression turned hard, his cheeks going ruddy. "You wanna spend a night in county?"

Sam's jaw went tight at the threat. "I just wanna see my brother. That's not a crime."

The sheriff waved the restraining order in her face. "It is now."

Sam took a step back, ready to bolt before he could make a grab for her, but she froze before she could. She found her mama standing a few feet away, her arms filled with a bouquet of vending machine food. The two stood in a gridlock, assessing each other with the green eyes they both shared. Maggie Calhoun may have been Sam's mama, but it was in title only. She was as motherly as a lion that eats her cubs.

"Buck," her mama began. "Can you give us a minute?"

Sheriff Buckley nodded, then peeled away from the door.

He shot Sam a pointed look before walking down the hallway, disappearing around the corner.

"Was the restraining order your idea?" Sam finally broke the silence. "Or Daddy's?"

Maggie held Sam's gaze. "I couldn't let you hurt my baby again."

"Have you lost your damn mind?" There was no sense of self-preservation for Sam in that moment. She bridged the distance between them, causing Maggie to drop the plastic-wrapped food in her hands. "Since when have you *ever* cared about Ben's safety?"

Despite the shock of Sam's closeness, her mama remained resolute. "What you did to Ben is far worse than anything Wiley has done."

Sam blinked. "I saved him."

"Bones and bruises heal," Maggie said slowly. "But people . . . they don't just come back from the dead. What you did was not savin'."

Sam's anger began to sputter out, giving way to fear. The sort of fear that had been taught to her since she was a kid, when her mama would whisper warnings of devils and desire and all-consuming hellfire—teachings she'd spent years trying to unlearn. But Jack appearing two days ago, and performing the inexplicable, upended it all. Now, she wasn't sure what to believe.

"Ben didn't die," she said weakly. "He survived—I made sure of it."

"I know." Maggie sniffed, then grimaced, as if she caught whiff of something rotten. "I can smell the sin on you like a stench."

"You're delusional," Sam spat.

"Call me whatever names you like," her mama said. "But I

know what you did, Samantha."

Sam struggled not to shrink herself in the face of the woman who was meant to protect her but had only ever turned the other cheek. "Tell me, Mama. What'd I do?"

"The devil came knockin' and you answered." Maggie didn't look at Sam like she was her daughter but a sickly mutt that she couldn't wait to put down. "Come hell or high water, I won't let you ruin Ben like you've *ruined* yourself."

Sam stood there, frozen in place by her mama's words as Maggie picked up the food from the hospital floor. Finally, she whispered, "You and Daddy ruined us a long time ago."

Maggie said nothing else before she called the sheriff back. "Buck! We're done here."

A moment later, Sheriff Buckley stood sentry at the door, and her mama disappeared within, the door slamming firmly in Sam's face.

CHAPTER 19

ISAIAH

In the silence of Isaiah's bedroom, the singing cicadas pulsed like a frantic heartbeat outside. An anthem that could only be escaped in the night or behind the gates of Lake Clearwater. Several cicadas crawled along the window, skittering across the glass. They droned and hummed with a fervor that mirrored his own anxiety.

Isaiah was so close to *something*. He could feel it in his bones, and it terrified him.

"Isaiah, baby." Grandma Bee knocked on the door, then pushed it open with her foot, poking her head in. "I forgot to give this to you the other day. Got caught up in all the excitement of the harvest. It's the rest of the equipment that came with your camera." She stepped into his room, a worn cardboard box in her hands.

Isaiah eyed the box's contents. There were a few more lenses, rolls of old film, a dusty carrying case, and faded negatives nearly buried beneath it all. "Where'd you find this anyhow?"

Bee chuckled. "At the Carrion flea market, of all places."

"That's a lucky find," he said, admiring the vintage equipment. Isaiah was fascinated by analog. He preferred his devices uncomplicated by modernity, appreciating the artistry of how things were made with care in the past.

Bee looked Isaiah over with her inscrutable brown eyes. "What're you all dressed up for?"

Isaiah's expression turned sheepish. "I'm spending the night with Dad. Finally gonna see his new house." It was the half-truth, as he had another stop along the way, but Grandma Bee didn't need to know that. "Sorry, I meant to tell you sooner."

Disappointment crept across his grandmother's face. "Oh, all right then. That's fine. Is Laurence too busy to come here for a bit first? Or too proud?"

Isaiah shrugged as he wrapped Bee in a bear hug. "I'll be back in time for breakfast, bright and early."

Grandma Bee squeezed him tightly, then pulled back, cupping his face in her warm hands. "I really, *really* don't like you going up to that lake every day."

"I'll be fine, Bee," Isaiah said, but the words didn't sound as convincing as they left his lips. "You act like I didn't grow up in Alpharetta of all places."

Grandma Bee frowned. "You and I both know that being Black up there and being Black down here are two very different things." Bee sighed. "I only say this because I know your father won't."

"I hear you." Isaiah stepped back, tugging at the collar of his shirt. The air in the room suddenly grew warmer. "But you don't need to worry. Everyone knows Dad. They know me. And I know this town. Nothing's gonna happen to me."

Grandma Bee crossed the room, gazing out the window. "Lake Clearwater has always been a dangerous place, baby. It doesn't matter who your father is, or how many connections he has in high places. Neither of you will ever really belong there." She then slapped the window with her palm, shooing the cicadas from their perch on the windowpanes. "Don't you ever forget that."

ANDREA SUMTER LIVED at the end of a long dirt road, the nearest neighbors hidden behind overgrown kudzu and dense rows of slash pines. Isaiah's BMW stuck out like a sore thumb, parked in front of the narrow trailer. But he was grateful to be shielded by the overgrowth that defined most of rural Southwest Georgia land.

Isaiah reminded himself why he was there: to learn the truth, even if it was only Andrea's version of it. In all his investigations for the past seasons of *Secrets of the South,* he had learned every story had at least two sides. And sometimes, two opposing stories could be true at once. What really mattered was *how* those stories were told—how they were presented to an audience that wasn't there to witness them unfold.

The doorbell was broken, the button nowhere to be found. Isaiah knocked instead, softly at first, but there was no sound on the other side of the door. No movement behind the sheer curtains that hung in the window. Then he knocked harder, praying Andrea remembered their meeting.

"Andrea?" Isaiah called through the door. "It's . . . Jordan."

Isaiah was ready to give up when a light switched on inside the house. The curtains parted, revealing one of Andrea's bright blue eyes, followed by the *click* of a lock. The front door opened, with Andrea hovering in the doorway, clad in stained, oversize pajamas.

"Afternoon," Andrea said, her gaze going past Isaiah to the empty front yard beyond, then back to him. "Thank you for comin.'"

"Yes, ma'am." Isaiah flashed his winning smile, hoping it would put Andrea at ease, if only a little bit. "Thank you for having me."

"Come on in." Andrea shuffled backward in torn slippers, leaving the doorway open.

Isaiah gave one last glance behind him, then stepped into Andrea Sumter's home. It looked on the inside much like it did on the outside. A small, cramped place, with mismatched furniture and dim lighting. The smell of cigarettes and stale air clung to his skin.

Andrea led him to the cluttered dining table, clearing away stacks of magazines and mail. "Can I get ya anything?"

"Water would be great," Isaiah said, taking a seat in a rickety wicker chair. While glass clanked in the adjoining kitchen, he took note of the chaos that surrounded him. Isaiah wasn't one to judge, but he wondered if Andrea's home had always looked this way, or if it was due to her fresh grief.

A moment later, Andrea sat a glass of water before Isaiah, joining him at the table. She shifted uncomfortably in the chair, wringing her hands in her lap. "How does this sorta thing go?"

"Well," Isaiah began, as he pulled his notepad and tape recorder from his bag, setting them neatly on the table. He recited the lie he'd practiced. "As I mentioned before, I'm writing this article on Dawson and how a town treats a tragedy. It's a wide-scope look at small-town life. Your perspective is, of course, the most important part of the story."

Andrea's gaze lingered on the tape recorder. "And that?"

Isaiah held it up for her to better see. "With your permission, I'd like to record our conversation. That way, nothing gets lost in translation in the article."

Andrea gave him a dismissive wave of her hand. "All right, then."

With a polite smile, Isaiah clicked a button on the recorder, placing it between them. "Where would you like to start?"

Andrea was quiet for a long time, then she looked around her home, grimacing. "Dawson was the one who cleaned around here," she said. "I've never been one for it, especially with workin' nights and all. But he always took care of it."

"He sounds like a wonderful son," Isaiah said softly.

Andrea nodded. "He was the man of the house, ever since he was little, after his daddy and I split. Never acted up or anythin'—never did nothin' wrong. He was the perfect child, and I mean that. It's why this whole . . ." Her hand went to her face, hovering over her trembling chin. "It's why none of this makes sense. I *know* my baby boy didn't drown. Not like that—not like how they said."

Isaiah took notice of the empty liquor bottles lining the kitchen counter. "So Dawson didn't drink?"

"Never," Andrea insisted. "He knew better because of me. Or, at least, that's how it *used* to be. We've always been close. But he started pushin' me away. Ever since he got that caddy job at Lake Clearwater."

"What changed exactly?" Isaiah asked.

Fixing him with a sorrowful gaze, Andrea said, "Everythin'."

Isaiah let a beat pass between them. "What do you think happened at Lake Clearwater that changed him?"

"I think workin' up there showed Dawson the potential of something *more*." Andrea gestured around the trailer. "Of a life better than anything I could ever give him. He was hungry like that. I think he saw Lake Clearwater as a ladder he could climb. Someway, somehow he was gonna get out. In a sense, I supposed he did. He didn't need me anymore. Even moved out a month ago, all on his own."

"And how exactly did he do that?" Isaiah asked sympathetically. He was reminded, once more, of the beautiful life his father had given him, and how easily it could all be taken away.

Andrea shifted uncomfortably in the chair, the wicker stretching and cracking beneath her. "Off the record?"

Isaiah reached for the tape recorder between them, pausing it with a *click*. "Go ahead."

"Dawson made sure not to repeat my mistakes in life, but he couldn't escape one of them," Andrea said slowly. "Just like I once did, he fell for the wrong man. He was seeing him in secret because he's a powerful man in Lake Clearwater. A man with a wife and children, and a reputation that I'm sure he'd do *anything* to protect."

The still, recycled air of the law firm. The ceiling fan whirring overhead. A phone trilling.

Andrea Sumter's voice. *I know about you and my son.*

Every muscle in Isaiah's body tensed. He knew the answer before he asked the question. "Who's the man?"

"Casey Leblanc."

SECRETS OF THE SOUTH

SEASON 4: EPISODE 2

(INTRO THEME SONG)

ANDREA SUMTER, CARRION RESIDENT: My granmama used to have a sayin' about this town. When I would act up as a little girl, she'd tell me, "You best be careful now. You were born in Carrion, which means you're one toe closer to hell than everyone else. The devil ain't ever far."

She and my mama raised me on these sorts of stories, like most everybody around here. They used fear to keep me in line, to make sure I never did anything that'd attract the devil. If a crow was sittin' outside our window or a cottonmouth was spotted down our little dirt road, they said it meant the devil was watching, just waitin' to come into our lives.

And God forbid a cicada ever made its way inside, screamin'

and hollerin'. It meant there was a sinner in the home, calling the devil himself to the doorstep. Granmama would beat us all silly until we confessed to somethin'—anythin'. Most times, nobody had done nothin'. But she'd say those awful, thirteen-year cicadas were a mark of death. The only way to save yourself was through confession and the good Lord's forgiveness.

(long pause)

Sometimes I wish I'd taught Dawson the same stories I was raised on, even if they scared me.

HOST: Why is that?

ANDREA SUMTER: Maybe . . . *(sniffles)* maybe . . . he'd still be here if I had. Maybe he would've been more careful. Maybe he would've never gone to that godforsaken lake in the first place. *(sobs)* I'm sorry.

HOST (to audience): Andrea Sumter's eighteen-year-old son, Dawson, was the first reported drowning on Lake Clearwater this past summer. He died shortly after his high school graduation.

As a senior in high school, he had plans to become a veterinary technician after he graduated. Faculty and staff of Langley County High School described him as having a "heart of gold." Dawson was seemingly adored by his peers, his friends, everyone that met him. He even volunteered at the Langley County animal shelter on the weekends.

And like most of Lake Clearwater's deaths, his body was unable to be recovered from the water.

ANDREA SUMTER: Dawson was a lifeguard at the YMCA before he started workin' at the lake. Tell me this: How does a lifeguard drown in calm lake water?

HOST: In the police report, they attributed his drowning to alcoholic inebriation. Empty liquor bottles were found by his abandoned car on Lake Clearwater's shore.

ANDREA SUMTER: *(sighs)* Like I told you before, Dawson never drank a drop of liquor in his life. You could say it was his own personal philosophy. Probably because . . . well, all his life, he'd seen me drink. He hated it, always had. Maybe even hated me sometimes for it, too.

I'm tellin' you, on my granmama's grave, I'm certain he wasn't drinkin' that night.

HOST: What do you believe happened?

ANDREA SUMTER: I think my boy got caught up in somethin' he shouldn't have at Lake Clearwater. Saw or heard somethin' he wasn't supposed to.

(long pause)

And I think they took him because of it.

HOST: I'm sorry, Andrea. I'm not sure I'm following. What do you mean by "they took him"?

ANDREA SUMTER: I know how crazy I sound, but I can feel Dawson. I can feel that he's still alive somewhere. It's a mama's instinct, somethin' I can't quite explain. *(sniffles)* I think the Clearwater folks took my boy and faked his drownin'. The car on the lakeshore, the alcohol, all of it. The police are in on it.

HOST: Why would they do that?

ANDREA SUMTER: To protect their own, like they've always done.

CHAPTER 20

NEERA

Early that evening, Neera sat at the edge of the motel's pool, her feet pruning in the chlorinated water as she stared into the woods behind the Colonial. It was the golden hour, the sun hanging low and heavy in the sky, but the heat hadn't let up—not just yet. Absently, she picked at a fresh scab on her thigh, coaxing it off her skin. The Cicada's Song was tomorrow night, but Neera wasn't any closer to getting on that stage with a lick of confidence.

A family of four waded at the opposite side of the pool, splashing in the shallow end with floats and toy water guns. The parents laughed and cheered with the children. The dad pretended to be a sea monster, dunking his son's head beneath the water, while the daughter climbed onto his shoulders.

A flash of a memory came to Neera. She was seven years old, swimming in the Gulf with Ajay, bobbing in the ocean at his side. Seawater sprayed into her eyes as they had waded past the sandbars, to the place where her small feet couldn't touch. The air was warm, the breeze soft against her face. Seagulls swooped and dived overhead, calling to one another.

Neera gripped her uncle's arm as she struggled to find her footing, but there was no sand beneath her. Just the open ocean and the waves that carried her up and down in the salty, crystalline water.

Ajay gently untangled Neera's fingers from his arm. "Neera," he said, a grin spreading across his sun-kissed face as he floated away from her. "Can you swim to me?"

She floundered in the water, chin dipping below the surface. "I can't swim."

Ajay smiled at her. "But you can, like this." He kept gliding backward, farther into the ocean. "Don't think about it, just do it."

She kept swimming, fearing the deep ocean and the fish that darted beneath her churning feet. When Neera finally reached him—her arms and legs heavy with exertion—she wrapped herself around his torso and scaled him like a tree, climbing away from the water.

Her uncle had only laughed and wrapped his arms around her, swinging her high above the waves. "You did it, Neera!"

Neera giggled, unafraid now. She looked over the ocean as if she were a bird herself, propped up by Ajay's hands. Over on the shore, Kiran sat beside the sandcastle they'd built together, waving at her with a plastic shovel in hand.

"I can swim!" Neera had yelled to her mom, to the sea, to the world around her.

On the other side of the pool, the little boy shrieked as his sister splashed him, and suddenly Neera was eighteen again, sitting on the hot, baking concrete of the motel sundeck. Ajay was gone for good, and those glittering sea salt days with him.

That was the thing about growing up—you never noticed your lasts. You never wondered if this time was the last time you'd smile at your mom, and she'd genuinely smile back. The last time your uncle would carry you in his arms, saving you from the things that scared you.

The last time you'd ever feel safe.

"Are you okay?" The mom of the family stood over Neera.

"Huh?" Neera asked, looking up.

The woman pointed to Neera's leg. "You're bleeding."

"What? No, I'm . . ." Neera looked down. The scab she'd been picking was now an open wound. Blood ran down her thigh and onto the pebbled concrete. "Oh."

The dad and kids were no longer playing. They stared at Neera from across the pool. She stood, wincing as her movement stretched the cut.

"Sorry," Neera mumbled as she scurried out of the gated pool enclosure, seeking the refuge of Room 4. She glanced over her shoulder as she fumbled with the door to the room. The family was still staring after her as she disappeared within.

In their room, Kiran was awake and in her bartending uniform, smudging on eyeshadow before a compact mirror. "You okay?"

"Yeah," Neera sighed, leaning against the door. "What's the occasion?" Her mom rarely put on any makeup, much less bothered with eyeshadow. She grabbed a tissue from the box on the dresser and started wiping her bloodied leg.

"Jason made a comment about how tired I've looked lately," Kiran said, dabbing a brush into the eyeshadow pan. "He basically told me I can't work the festival nights if I don't 'clean up.'" Her mom made a disgusted noise, wrinkling her face in the small mirror beside the ancient TV. "So here I am, doing clown makeup."

Neera's stomach gave a sick clench. She crossed to the little vanity and prized the eyeshadow brush from her mom's hand. She pulled another tissue from the dresser and gently took Kiran's face by the chin, turning her closer. "Here, let me."

Kiran closed her eyes as Neera wiped away her botched eyeshadow job. Her mom had never been good with makeup because she never *needed* to be. She was beautiful in an effortless way with a sharp nose, deep-set eyes, and full brows that complemented her rich brown skin. Modern beauty trends had been built around her, not for her.

"You don't need to cake on a bunch of stuff, okay?" Neera said, trying to keep her voice soft.

Kiran gave her a wry, sad smile. "Just cover up these eye bags then."

Neera did as she was told, dabbing concealer on her mom's skin. Kiran was only in her midthirties, but she had streaks of gray coming through her shoulder-length black hair. The beginnings of wrinkles creased her forehead. Her hands were calloused and scarred from years of busting her ass in restaurants to keep them fed and housed.

For people like them, life drained away at you in double time.

Suddenly, Neera was just so sick of it. The constant scraping and grinding and gritting your teeth and smiling at assholes like Jason. The pretending like all this misery and struggle was something to be endured until the better days came along, rather than the blueprint of their entire lives.

Her fury curdled inside her, so intense she had to force herself not to tighten her grip on her mom's face and shake her. "So . . . ," Neera began, an edge creeping into her voice even as she fought it back. "Are we gonna talk about the fire, or just pretend it didn't happen like we do with everything else?"

Kiran sighed. "Don't start, Neera. Not now, please."

"I'm not *starting* anything," Neera argued, dusting faint blush across her mom's cheeks. "I just—I saw something the night of the fire."

Kiran's dark brown eyes shot open, locking with Neera's. "What'd you see?"

Neera hesitated, not wanting to add any more stress to her mom's plate, but this wasn't something she could keep to herself any longer. "I saw Nanaji arguing with the handyman the other night. That guy—Wiley. He said Nanaji owed his boss money. Like, *a lot* of money. More than this place could ever be worth."

"*Goddamnit,*" Kiran mumbled to herself, shaking her head. She rose from the chair, pacing the tiny length of their room. "The stubborn bastard lied to me."

"The debt's not from the motel, is it?" Neera asked.

"No, it's not." Kiran laughed dryly. "It's from four years ago. *Ajay.* He'd convinced your grandfather to go in with him on some stupid bar on the edge of town. He called it Blind Bucks, I think. But it ended up costing more money than they'd anticipated. Never even opened. They told me the debt was paid off."

"Ajay tried to open his own bar?" A sharp pang of hurt welled inside Neera. Honesty had always been a hard line between her and her uncle. "Why didn't I know about it?"

"Because Ajay didn't want anyone to know until it was a done deal. Not even me. He didn't tell me about it until it was dead in the water." Kiran added softly, meeting her gaze, "He wanted to make you proud, Neera. But he couldn't make it work in the end."

Neera looked away. She felt her mental tabulations shifting. A narrative falling a little more into place. Ajay had gone into debt the year before he died, and then he took his own life. "It's more than just the money. Wiley threatened us. He gave Nanaji an ultimatum that night. Said he had to pay off his debt by the Fourth or . . ."

You and your family may end up just like that son of yours.

Realization crossed Kiran's face. "Wiley's the one who started the fire," she whispered. She was quiet for a long moment, until she finally commanded, "I don't want you going anywhere near that man again. Is that clear?"

Weighted silence passed between them.

"What'll happen to us?" Neera realized she hadn't tempered the fear in her question, because Kiran looked at her now, her forehead creasing in a heavy line.

Her mom moved back to the vanity, spreading cheap lipstick across her mouth in an uneven line, her hand shaking ever so slightly. "I'm gonna . . . I'll figure something out."

"Okay," Neera said, her throat going dry. Whether her mom admitted it or not, it was obvious to her *everything* was on the line.

Kiran fixed her with a level gaze. "You can't end up like me, Neera."

Neera flinched. She still hadn't told her mom she wasn't going to college in the fall. She'd gotten her financial aid estimate a few months earlier—it didn't even cover her full tuition, let alone on-campus housing. Or meal plans. Textbooks. Money to get by while she was meant to take classes five days a week. But all Neera said was, "I know. I won't end up like you."

It was an old agreement between them. One Kiran repeated like a mantra. And Neera wasn't lying, exactly. She wasn't going to end up like her mom, like her grandparents. Like Ajay. She was going to make it, and she was going to do it *her* way—with the thing she loved the most: music.

They all thought being a musician was unrealistic because of Ajay, because of their narrow ideas of success, but Neera knew the truth. Their dreams were just as fanciful as hers.

Satisfied by her answer, Kiran continued to get ready, but the room felt too small now. They kept dodging around each other as her mom searched for her phone, her hairbrush, her shoes. Neera sat on her bed, trying to stay out of the way. She picked up her guitar and lightly strummed the strings.

Kiran eyed the Yamaha as she tied her nonslip work shoes.

The edge of a tattoo peeked out from beneath her black socks—Ajay's full name written in Punjabi, wrapped around her ankle in delicate Gurmukhi script. Neera averted her eyes, staring down at the guitar strings. The tattoo had suddenly appeared a month after Ajay's death, but Neera could practically count the number of times her mom had said his name aloud, since his death, on one hand.

"Don't practice that in here, all right?" Kiran finally said, eyes still sharp on Neera's guitar. "I know you're excited about the competition, but it doesn't change anything. The walls are thin." She grabbed her keys, then whirled out the door.

Once Neera was alone, she opened her guitar case, reaching again for that smiling photo of Ajay and Nanaji that she'd tucked within. This time, Neera closely studied the building behind them. The date on the back matched the same time frame her mom had given about Ajay's bar. Could this building be the defunct Blind Bucks? If so, why did Dawson Sumter have a key chain from it?

She pulled out her phone, writing up a lengthy text to Isaiah about what her mom told her about Ajay's business venture. She ended it with: *Blind Bucks—please find whatever you can on it,* then put her phone on silent.

Neera glanced at the clock. It was only seven—Nanaji didn't wake for the front desk night shift until seven thirty. Her mom's warning still echoed in her head, but if she just played *really* softly, she could maybe get a good hour of practice in.

Neera shuffled into the tiny bathroom and shut the door. The tile made for a decent sound barrier. Like moths to a flame, her fingers found the steel strings, sliding against them, carving out a melody in the quiet of the bathroom. Her shoulders unclenched, her limbs grew warm and languid.

Once more, the "Three Brothers" folk song came to her,

seeping into her practice. Like a forgotten prayer, Neera sang the words Ajay had taught her, the chords he'd practiced with her when she was little—for hours, days, weeks until she got them right.

They say
You meet the devil
At the crossroads
Down in Georgia
When there ain't no options left

Neera always remembered Ajay on hazy summer afternoons, the Yamaha resting across his knees, crooning and smiling down at her. The details of his face lost in the blur of warm, dusty sunlight. She only remembered her uncle as a memory, a *feeling*, but not a person. A moment in time she clung to as the years passed.

In these memories, he sang the "Three Brothers," not just as an obsession but as a warning.

Be careful of the devils
Down in Georgia
There ain't no coming back
From the pact

A furious pounding sounded at the door of her room—shocking Neera back to the surface. She scrambled to her feet and out of the bathroom, peeking out from behind the curtain of Room 4's window.

It was Nanaji, banging his fist against the door, rattling the thin, cheap wood in the frame. "Neera!"

She opened the door a crack. "What's wrong?"

"Where is it?" Her grandfather pushed past her like a bull chasing a flag, his eyes darting all around the room. He spotted her guitar where she'd carefully laid it on the bed and stomped over, yanking it up by its neck. His hand slapped roughly against the strings, sending a discordant hum through the room.

"Nanaji—stop. What're you doing?" Neera reached around him, grasping for the guitar. He held it away from her.

"This thing! I never want to hear it again." Guitar in hand, he stormed out of the room. The edge of the Yamaha ricocheted against the doorframe, chipping the wood.

"Stop, you're damaging it!" Neera yelled, following her grandfather into the humid night. Moths circled overhead, bouncing around the dim lights that lined the motel walkways.

"It's bad luck," Nanaji hissed, whirling around to face Neera. He shook the guitar, the soundboard scraping against the concrete in a way that made her physically recoil. "We can't keep this. You can't keep playing it."

Neera made another grab for the instrument, but Nanaji yanked it back again. "This has ruined us," he snarled. "It's *cursed* us." And in Nanaji's terrible, fearful face—his trembling chin, his wild, yellowing eyes—Neera saw the truth.

It wasn't about the guitar. It never had been. It was about Ajay, as all things were. To her grandparents, their son was supposed to be their savior, to carry on their legacy. Their name. Their blood. But he'd traded it all in for the hope of making it with his guitar.

Instead, he got a bullet to the head.

Now, Ajay was just ashes in the earth.

And all Nanaji had left was an embarrassment of a daughter and a *mistake* for a granddaughter.

"Just give it back," Neera begged. "I won't play it here anymore, I promise."

"No, it is done. No more!" Nanaji shook his head as he

turned on his heel, dragging the guitar with him. The sound of the body scraping against the ground made Neera want to retch, her stomach turning itself inside out with agony. It whited out every rational thought, every bit of care she might have had for her grandfather.

Neera sprang forward, charging at him. It was pure, feral instinct. She crashed into Nanaji in a mess of limbs and shouted words. They grappled awkwardly over the guitar's smooth body.

Then, without warning, Nanaji shoved Neera backward so hard she fell to the ground, her palms burning as they scraped the concrete. The guitar fell, too, clattering against the hard cement. Several strings snapped at once—sending *pops* into the night air.

Neera and Nanaji paused, frozen for a moment. Together they stared at the broken guitar. The neck was snapped clean off, attached only by a single, taut string.

Neera scrambled forward on her hands and knees. In a distant sort of way, she registered the sting of fresh, bloody scratches on her palms. She didn't care. Her hands hovered over the instrument, but she didn't dare touch it. She couldn't bring herself to just yet. If she did, it might crumble altogether.

Nanaji spat on the ground, a wet bit of saliva landing inches from the guitar's neck.

Neera looked up at him. Nanaji's face held no shame or remorse, still contorted in a disgusted grimace. And he wasn't looking at the guitar but at Neera. Right at her, with that look of horror and revulsion, like she wasn't his flesh and blood. She was a pest. A thing he wished he could be rid of.

They stayed like that—Neera on her knees before the broken Yamaha, staring up at her grandfather—for several long, unbearable heartbeats.

Without another word, Nanaji turned and trudged away to the motel's lobby. From within Room 3, her grandmother watched from around the curtain. Neera's eyes found hers, before Nani quickly looked away—the sliver of lamplight inside vanishing as the curtain twitched back in place.

For a long time, Neera knelt there in the dying light, knees aching on the hard concrete, staring at the shattered remains of her guitar.

AJAY HAD ONCE told Neera an angel gifted him the Yamaha acoustic guitar with its own rare guitar pick. The angel was a smooth-talking man from San Francisco who, in the sixties, had played with the likes of Janis Joplin and Simon & Garfunkel.

The Yamaha was a vintage instrument—a Red Label made in Japan in the sixties, one of the first of its kind—and worth at least several grand. Still, Ajay never sold the guitar and its accompanying pick, even when things got bad and he was pawning nearly everything he owned to get by. Not when he slept on Kiran's couch for months on end. Not when he kept a strict diet of instant coffee and bummed cigarettes to stave off days of hunger because he couldn't afford much else.

He kept it until Neera's fifteenth birthday, when he'd gifted it to her.

"Why're you giving this to me?" Neera had asked that day. "It's your *everything*. I can't take it from you."

Ajay had merely placated her with a grin, as he often did. "I've learned all I can from it. Now it's your turn."

"And your lucky pick?"

Ajay twirled the marble-green pick between his fingers, like a magic trick, then slid it into his pocket. "This'll stay with me," he'd said with a wink. "Maybe for your next birthday, I'll let you have it."

As it was, the Yamaha was the last thing he ever gave her. A lifeline thrown out to her as Ajay's own came to a horrifying end. In a tragic way, it had been easier to accept then—that her uncle had taken his own life. The alternative had been too cruel for her to consider.

But what if he had truly been murdered, and his death was covered up by the police? What would that mean for Neera and her family and this awful place they called home?

No one is coming to save us, she thought. *It's all on me.*

Discarded cicada shells crunched beneath Neera's feet as she walked through the woods behind the Colonial. The Yamaha was a broken, useless thing cradled in her arms. Her tenuous connection to Ajay, the only good memory left of him, was sustained by the single guitar string that had not yet snapped under Nanaji's wrath.

Neera felt that fairness did not fit in the vocabulary of her life. There would be no justice. There never had been, so why would the universe start now? She had spent the past three years treading water, waiting for the hand that would pull her to shore, but of course, it never came. The guitar had been the only thing keeping her head just barely above the surface. Without it, she would drown. She felt the truth of it as cold, emotionless fact.

And so, once again, Neera Singh walked into the dense pine woods with a tearstained face and a desperate prayer on her lips. She shifted her grip on the broken guitar pieces, hefting them more securely in her arms. It was full dark now, but her bare feet were steady and sure on the forest floor. Lightning bugs danced in an unsteady rhythm around her, winking in and out of existence.

The first time Neera had met the devil, she'd been a weeping child.

What was she now?

Desperate? No.

Hungry.

She walked with no direction or destination. Only farther, deeper into the trees. But her strides were purposeful, her eyes sharp and searching. Neera splashed across a cold, babbling stream, not even bothering to step over it. The cool water clung to her feet. She barely felt it. Overhead, the canopy grew so thick it blotted out the night sky above.

Still, Neera was unafraid.

Moved by an instinct she couldn't name, she slowed her pace. Quieted her footfalls. Around her, the ever-present katydids and tree frogs had fallen silent. Neera lowered herself to the ground at the base of a sprawling live oak tree, its thick, gnarled branches spreading in every direction. She laid the mangled guitar tenderly in the soft grass.

"Crow?" Neera called out the devil's name only once.

She waited, kneeling in the dirt.

There was a prolonged, heavy silence.

As a musician, Neera usually found a lack of sound uncomfortable. Unnatural. But this was different. She could *feel* the silence in those woods. It wrapped around her and held her close, like it had chosen her. As if every animal, every living being besides her, had frozen, waiting for the devil to appear.

The first sign of Crow's arrival was a quiet wind, cutting through the stillness. It rustled through the oak and pine trees, the towering giants swaying high above her.

Then came a familiar voice, like that of the earth and the trees. "*Neera?*"

Three years ago, on a humid night much like tonight, Neera

had gone looking for Crow as soon as she and her mom arrived to the Colonial. She had run into the forest, away from the harsh glow of police car lights and the sorrowful wails of her grandmother at her back. She was unaware of the briars burrowing into her skin, the thorns in her feet. There was no physical pain greater than the sudden loss in her heart.

Ajay was dead.

"Crow!" Neera had screamed once she had gone past the stream, spinning in dizzying circles. She ran through the dense woods, clambering up the trunks of trees, searching, pleading to find the creature that had made her a promise. "*Crow!* Bring him back!"

A promise, Crow had said, that was greater than love.

Hours had passed before a fifteen-year-old Neera collapsed to the ground, sobbing with a force that terrified her. "I'll do anything," she cried into the night. "Please, bring him back. *Please.*" Her desperation was ferocious and all-consuming. A wildfire burning up everything within. With each tear that fell, her hope went with it.

Neera had wept, alone in the dark, until there was nothing left inside of her.

Now, at eighteen, Neera looked at Crow, the massive avian creature that lingered in the shadows of the wood. Lightning bugs surrounded his head like a crown, illuminating in flashes the length of his long beak, the blacks of his eyes. His folded, spindly wings dusted the ground, leaving a pool of black liquid where they grazed the earth.

"You're really here," Neera breathed. It wasn't just relief she felt, but anger.

Crow nodded once. "As promised."

Neera shook her head. "Where were you when I *needed* you three years ago?" Her voice cracked.

"It was not time."

"Why?" Neera whimpered. She was a helpless child again, weeping at the taloned feet of a feathered devil.

"I rise only with the cicadas," Crow said. "It is my curse."

Neera blinked her stinging eyes, struggling to understand. "Your . . . *curse*?"

"Only in this thirteen-year time may I walk this earth. With the cicadas I rise, and with the cicadas I fall." Crow paused. "A fate forced upon me many years ago—by my brother."

"You could've told me," Neera argued weakly. "Thirteen years ago, you could've just been honest with me." Her anger faded to hollow sadness as she realized why Crow hadn't been honest all those years ago. In a hoarse whisper, she asked, "You knew Ajay was going to . . . to die then, didn't you?"

"Yes." Crow had never shown emotion before, but somehow, his avian gaze turned sorrowful. "You were only a child." He inched forward, his long talons snapping twigs and brambles as he moved closer. "But, I am here now."

"It's too late." Neera rubbed her eyes, barely aware of the fresh tears that pooled down her cheeks. She gestured pitifully to the broken guitar at her feet. Quietly, she said, "It's ruined. Everything is. It's all over."

Crow's beak hovered above the Yamaha, grazing the shining wood and the loose, untethered strings. Lightning bugs gathered around the guitar, lingering for a moment before dissipating into the dark. "Broken things cannot be unbroken."

Neera met the devil's bottomless, black gaze. "You can't fix it?"

"I cannot," Crow admitted as Neera continued to cry, unashamed now. Her tears fell in a steady rhythm on the Yamaha, sliding off the polished wood like raindrops. "However," he said, and even for a creature so ancient it sounded like a concession, "the instrument can be made anew."

"Yes." Neera nodded, willing to plead on her hands and knees if that's what it took. "*Please.*"

Crow's wings fluttered, the sound like falling leaves. "Is that all?"

A loaded question. Neera opened her mouth to say yes but paused. Another request rose within her, unbidden. A want that would be damning if she spoke it aloud. Something not about love, or death, but about power. A seething, aching desire that had been growing within Neera for a very long time.

"I want to be heard," Neera began slowly. "I want a voice the world will love." Her breath hitched in her throat, and the rest came pouring out of her. "I want to make music . . . that will immortalize me. I don't want to be forgotten."

Like Ajay.

Crow's empty eyes gazed into Neera's. "There is a cost."

"I know," Neera whispered, recalling Ajay's long-ago warning. "Whatever it is, I'll pay it."

Crow's ink-black feathers ruffled, falling from his wings and onto the forest floor, transforming into dried leaves. "One day, with little warning, your voice will vanish, and it will never return."

Neera struggled to temper the fear in her gut. "And the guitar? Will I lose that, too?"

Crow's head shook from side to side. "Consider it a gift."

The notion of a kindness from the devil felt *wrong*—impossible even, but what choice did Neera have? A creature stood before her, willing to give her the world. All she had to do was take it. To one day lose her voice was a horrible thought, but the future wasn't guaranteed, anyway. Not when the promise of death hovered over the Singh family in a week's time.

After a long beat, Neera finally said, "I accept the cost."

The heavy silence was broken by the shrill, high-pitched call of a cicada. It reverberated through the woods like a bloodcurdling scream. Neera looked all around, searching for the insect. Its call was steady and pulsing, and Neera startled with the realization it was close.

It was coming from the Yamaha.

Neera peered into the guitar's opening, finding the squirming bug within. Small and buzzing, with red veins and shimmering iridescent wings. The cicada trembled inside the guitar, echoing all around her.

"Am I supposed to . . . ?" Neera couldn't bear to finish the question.

Crow nodded once.

Gingerly, she reached into the hollow space of the Yamaha. The cicada crawled into her hand, its spindly legs sending a shiver down her spine. She pulled her hand out, staring at the insect. It pulsed and throbbed in her bloodied palm, its scream growing louder, nearly deafening in its intensity. Saliva pooled on her tongue. Neera couldn't tell if it was revulsion, or hunger.

Neera didn't hesitate as she placed the live cicada in her mouth and swallowed it whole.

"It is done." Crow's wings expanded, as if in response, stretching out fully for the first time. From her place on the ground, his wings seemed never-ending. They covered the forest, growing so large that they touched the tree canopy high above them.

As Crow's wings flapped, kicking up dirt and pine needles, Neera's eyelids felt heavy, her body growing tired. She lay beside her guitar, nestling in the earth.

The last thing she saw was the devil taking flight.

CHAPTER 21

REID

Reid longed for the days when he didn't speak, and no one expected him to do otherwise. There was the briefest reprieve in the aftermath of his mother's passing where silence was his greatest gift. His grief had been too great of a weight on his tongue, so for years, he said nothing at all.

Barely a day had passed since the news of Dawson's drowning, and Reid couldn't bring himself to get out of bed, despite the social obligations expected of him. He was afforded many luxuries in his life, but the space to grieve was not one of them.

Reid was buried in his bed in the early evening when his bedroom door swung open, sending harsh light into his eyes. "Leave me alone," he pleaded to the silhouette in the doorway. "I already told you; I'm not going to another stupid fucking party."

"You're not doing *what*?" The question came from his father.

Reid quickly sat up. "I'm sorry, sir. I meant—I can't—"

His father stepped into his room, dressed in a crisp button-up and khakis, and met him at his bedside. The sight of him here was a surprise. Reid couldn't remember the last time his father had bothered to come to his room. Russ Langley was the kind of man who called, and you answered.

"What's this business I hear," his father began, kneeling on the hardwood floor before him, "that you've been *crying* all day?"

Reid couldn't meet his gaze. "We're no longer allowed to cry in this house? Tell that to Jonah."

His father snorted. "That's not what I meant." He glanced around Reid's room as if it was a novelty to witness. "I understand what you're feeling right now, son. But there are ways to deal with it, and this isn't it."

"Yeah, right," Reid said. "I find that hard to believe."

"Watch that mouth," his father said coolly, narrowing his gray eyes. "You think it was easy for me to get out of bed every day—after what happened to your mother?"

Reid shrugged. "It seemed like it was."

"Exactly," his father said. "It *seemed* like it, and that's all that matters. We are Langleys. We are the pillars of this community, and that means there are certain obligations expected of us."

"None of this is fair," Reid protested. He suddenly felt like a child again, a scared little boy being scolded by his father.

"Fairness doesn't exist in this world, son," his father said. "The sooner you come to terms with that, the better off you'll be." He reached for Reid's hand, holding it in his own. "It's none of my business what that Carrion boy meant to you. I, of all people, can't judge you for that. However, it's my job as your father to tell you this: Wipe your tears, buck up, and get your ass out of bed."

Reid allowed his father to pull him up and into an uneasy embrace. They patted each other on the back, then stepped apart.

"Dad," Reid began, "you think we could have birthday breakfast for me this year? Like how we used to when we were little, with the homemade French toast?"

"I'm sorry, son." For the briefest moment, a distant, pained expression flashed across his father's face. "There won't be time that day. This year, the Fourth is going to be something *special* for not only our family, but for all of Lake Clearwater."

"More important than my eighteenth birthday?" Reid asked. He realized how childish he sounded, but that's how it always was with his father. He couldn't help but regress in his presence.

"You'll understand when the time comes," his father said, his tone shifting, signaling an end to any further questions.

Reid could only nod as the weight of his father's words enveloped him. His father made his way to the door, lingering for a moment. He then asked, "How 'bout we do the next morning for your birthday breakfast?"

Reid nodded. "The next morning," he agreed sadly, realizing that breakfast would never come. "Sounds good."

His father checked the time on his watch. "I'm gonna head on over to Laurence's house with your brother and sister now. I better see you there within an hour—not a minute later. Is that clear?"

"Yes, sir," he said, and then his father was gone.

And soon, Reid would be gone, too.

ISAIAH

WHEN ISAIAH'S FATHER invited him to dinner that night, he failed to mention it would include a housewarming party for his new summer home on Lake Clearwater, with dozens of people in attendance. Isaiah navigated through the house, taking the contours of it in, all while guests made a point to stop and shake his hand, congratulating him on Harvard.

It felt like his father had made sure the whole of Lake Clearwater knew of his Ivy League horizons.

His father had a way of treating Isaiah like an extension of himself. In all the ways Isaiah shined, it only made his father shine brighter. With every passing year, it felt as if the path his father laid before him grew narrower, boxing Isaiah into a role he didn't fully agree with.

And as it was, that role didn't allow for a secret investigative podcast that sought to pierce through the gleaming veneer of Lake Clearwater.

Isaiah made his way upstairs, eager for a break from hobnobbing and rubbing elbows. It appeared he wasn't the only one who wanted to get away, as he found Reid Langley sitting at the top of the stairs, his limbs tangled between the banisters, looking down on the party.

This is my chance, Isaiah thought, recalling his research into Dawson's social life. Reid had seemed like Dawson's only friend before he went missing. *He must know something.*

Isaiah and Reid weren't strangers, but they weren't exactly friends, either. He needed to tread carefully if he wanted real answers.

Reid gave him an awkward nod.

Isaiah returned the greeting and took a seat beside him. "I didn't know you were here."

Reid snorted. "I *really* hate these parties."

"As any sane person would." Sitting close to Reid now, Isaiah noticed his eyes were red and puffy, as if he'd been crying. He took in his mournful gaze and slouched shoulders. Reid looked nothing like the other Langleys, who projected a level of confidence rivaled by that of his own father. Isaiah cleared his throat. "I'm sure it sucks to be here . . . after what happened with Dawson."

Reid blinked. "How did you know we were—"

"My dad told me." Isaiah's gaze turned sympathetic. "I've been wanting to give my condolences since I heard. I'm sorry, man."

A dry, bitter laugh rose from Reid's throat. "You know, you're the first person to actually say those words to me. Not my father, not my siblings. They're treating Dawson's drowning like my fucking hamster died."

"You deserve better than that," Isaiah said simply.

"Thanks." Reid looked to the floor. "Did you know Dawson?"

Isaiah considered how to answer. He didn't exactly know how to bring up Dawson's email, if at all.

"No. But he seemed like a good guy, like he had a smart head on his shoulders."

"He is—he *was*." Reid began to pick at his cuticle until his thumb swelled with blood. "The news is making him sound like such a dick. Did you know he never even *drank*? I don't know why they're saying he was drunk. It's messed up."

"Yeah," Isaiah said slowly. "It's weird. Almost like because he was from Carrion, no one really cares."

"Exactly." Reid wiped the blood onto his khaki shorts. "It's because all these people saw Dawson as a tick. Nothing more." He looked down at the party then, his gaze turning dark. "It's what they do. They treated my mother's death the same way, like it was nothing. Like *she* was nothing. All because she was from Carrion."

Isaiah began to see a thread of connection forming between Dawson and Caroline Langley. *Two ticks from Carrion who mysteriously drowned in Lake Clearwater.* It couldn't be a mere coincidence, could it? This was where Isaiah needed to consider his next words carefully. Delicately, he asked, "Do you think . . . Dawson really *drowned*?"

Reid went visibly still. He then fixed Isaiah with a curious gaze. "What's the alternative?"

Isaiah feigned ignorance, forcing an easy laugh. "I don't

know, man. It was a stupid question to ask. I'm sorry."

Reid shook his head. "No, it's not, actually. I thought I was crazy for thinking the same thing. But you see it, too?"

Distant echoes of laughter and clinking glasses filtered from downstairs, filling the quiet between them. "I do." Isaiah inhaled a steadying breath, preparing to show Reid the email, when footsteps sounded from the stairs.

Russ Langley appeared, taking in the sight of them. Smiling pleasantly, he said, "It's time to go home, son." He waited for Reid, as if expecting him to act on command. "Your car is blocking folks in."

Reid untangled himself from the banister and rose from the ground. Before he followed Russ, he asked, "Can we talk later?"

"Yeah," Isaiah said. "You gonna be at the Cicada's Song tomorrow?"

Reid nodded and then he was gone, leaving Isaiah alone on the stairs as the party slowly died out below. He was getting closer to *something*, and he realized Reid Langley may truly have the answers he was looking for.

CHAPTER 22

NEERA

Neera awoke to the distant stream of running water sliding along slippery rocks. To crickets chirping, tree frogs croaking, an owl hooting overhead. To the wind rustling the trees and to the squirrels that scurried along the tree branches, dropping pine cones onto the ground.

Instinctively, Neera reached for her guitar. Her eyes opened as she searched the ground with her fingers. The Yamaha was nowhere to be found.

Neera slowly rose from the ground, bracing her fretting hand against the trunk of the nearest tree for balance. Her world began to spin. An awful, visceral fear simmered within her as she swayed. The thick, black hairs on her arms rose. Neera felt eyes on her. Whether it was her primal instinct telling her that, she didn't know.

But she needed to get out of the woods.

That's when she smelled it. The humid night air was laden with the sharp scent of copper, and it wasn't her own. The blood on her hands had dried and crusted along her palms. Despite her dizzying vision, Neera stumbled quickly in the way she thought she came.

A bird cawed somewhere in the distance. Just barely, Neera could see it flying above the canopy. *Crow?* Its silhouette was so faint, save for the iridescence of its wings. Neera followed the corvid the best she could. Stumbling over rocks and tangled roots of trees that splayed across the ground.

Her heart raced.

Then she heard it. Neera froze as an animal bleated loudly. It sounded like a deer was nearby—a dying one. It cried and grunted, a call for help in the dead of night. Neera pushed forward in the direction of the sound. A moment later, she found herself crossing out of the woods and stood on the side of an empty backroad.

Lying in the middle of the road was a massive buck, with antlers nearly the width of a truck. A trail of blood and entrails was behind him. The animal was faced away from her, crawling with limp back legs along the asphalt. He inched away from the bordering woods and farther into the road, thrashing his head wildly, screaming into the night.

Neera slowly approached, rounding his body, and froze. The animal's stomach was cut clean open and exposed, his bloodied rib cage a stark white against the black of the shining asphalt. The buck was gurgling, breathing heavily. Blood pooled from the edges of his mouth.

It was as if something had attacked the deer, ripping him wide open.

But as Neera peered closer at the animal, she realized most of his organs were gone from his body. Instead, tucked within the rib cage, and resting against the spinal cord, was her guitar.

The world spun. Neera stumbled to the ground, vomiting what little she had eaten that day. Braced against the asphalt, she looked again at the animal, nausea rolling through in waves.

"I'm so sorry," she whimpered to the buck as she crawled beside him. With shaking hands, she reached inside the animal's chest cavity; gripping the neck of the guitar, she slowly pulled it out. The sound of it sliding out of the buck was enough to make her vomit again, but there was nothing left within her, only bile.

The Yamaha was slick with gore, but it was no longer broken. The neck was restored to the body, the strings taut and tightened with the bridge. There were no scratches or dents. It was perfectly intact, as if Nanaji had never broken it at all. As if it wasn't a sixty-year-old instrument but a newly crafted thing of beauty.

Beside her, the dying, mutilated buck was an awful sight.

This is what a gift from the devil looks like.

Tearing her eyes away from the deer, Neera realized she had no idea where she was.

Neera willed herself not to panic. She took a deep breath, following along with the buck as he continued to crawl. Part of his antlers had snapped off. His eyes were wide and desperate. The animal sensed a danger that Neera could not see, but she absolutely felt. If Crow had done that to the buck, would that mean he would do that to her, too?

Headlights shone brightly ahead, rounding the bend of the road. Neera covered her eyes with her arm, gasping as the car headed directly for the deer, and her. In a swift move, the car braked, screeching loudly, and veered off the road and onto the shoulder, stopping just short of the trees.

It all happened quickly, but the driver's reaction was *just* fast enough. Though the car was now stuck in the ditch. Its tires spun in the dirt several times before coming to a stop.

The driver's door opened, then slammed. A tall silhouette stepped from around the car, carrying a flashlight, looking between the deer and Neera.

A young man's voice called, "Hey, are you okay?"

Neera stayed where she was, an assumedly safe distance from the stranger and his car. "I'm fine," she said, hesitating. "But this deer isn't. Can you help him?"

"*Help?*" the man parroted. He approached the deer with

little hesitation, kneeling before it. After examining him for a beat, the man, who really sounded more like a boy said, "God-damn."

"Looks like he was attacked," Neera offered as an easy lie.

The boy peered up at her, the flashlight illuminating his features to reveal a clean-cut, all-American-boy face. Adorned in worn Top-Siders, a button-down, and khaki shorts, he was, undoubtedly, a Clearwater kid. But with his straight nose and steel-gray eyes, Neera recognized him as a Langley. Her eyes flicked to his car, an old-school Land Rover, finding a small, monogrammed *RL* sticker on the back window. *Reid Langley.* Grant's elusive nephew if she remembered correctly.

Fuck.

"Must've been something mighty big to do this kind of damage," Reid said. His eyes took in Neera's appearance. The gory guitar at her bare feet, the blood on her hands and clothes. His gaze hardened slightly. "What're you doing out here?"

Neera didn't know how the hell to answer that. She barely even understood what had happened to her. It still felt like a nightmare she was waiting to wake from. "I got turned around in the woods is all." She motioned to the deer. "I heard him bleating and I followed the sound. I thought something bad was happening."

"So you headed *toward* the unknown danger?"

"Yeah," Neera said, wrapping her arms around herself. The air was warm, but she felt a chill taking root in her bones. "Could I borrow your phone? I need to call my mom for a ride."

"You don't have a phone?" It sounded more like an accusation than a question. His eyes examined her clothes, most likely wondering if Neera was a hitchhiker.

"Look," Neera began. "My family owns the motel off of Highway 40. I was out in the woods behind there earlier tonight but got lost trying to get back. I'm not some weirdo or whatever."

Reid rose from the ground, holding his hands up in a defensive gesture. "Never said you were." He reached into his pocket, holding his phone outward. "Here you go."

It was the newest model iPhone. No case. Cracked screen. She scoffed.

Neera dialed one of two numbers she had memorized. Kiran's phone didn't ring at all before it cut to voicemail. Confused, Neera called again. And again. Each time, it cut to voicemail. Her mom's phone must've been off while she was working.

Anger and fear swelled within Neera. The only other number she knew off the top of her head was Ajay's. The thought made Neera want to cry. It made her want to scream. She inhaled a deep breath, calling her mom's phone one more time.

Reid watched her intently.

Neera's cheeks flushed as she handed the phone back to him. He gave nothing away with his face.

"I can give you a ride," he said slowly. "Back to the motel. It's the Colonial, right?"

Neera narrowed her eyes. "How'd you know that?"

"Lucky guess. It's not like there's much on that highway."

Neera's attention was brought back to the buck then. She realized he was no longer bleating. No longer crawling. He sat several feet away from them, huffing quietly. There was so much blood. Entrails laid about before him. His eyes were heavy, struggling to stay open. He mewed in pain.

"All right." Neera swallowed. Her mouth tasted like bile and acid. "I'd like a ride home if it isn't too much trouble."

The boy let out a breath, checking his wristwatch. "No trouble at all."

Neera couldn't take her eyes off the deer as she asked, "Is your car stuck in the ditch?"

"It's fine," Reid said. "But stand clear as I get it out."

Neera knelt by the deer as the boy climbed into his Land Rover and maneuvered out of the ditch. The buck was dying slowly. It was the worst kind of death. Neera wished she could give him mercy, end his suffering.

Looking at the mutilated animal reminded her of Ajay. Of her worst intrusive memory—Ajay's dead body. His brown skin turned ashen. His bruised eyelids. His skull partially missing from the gunshot wound that had killed him. She clutched her forehead, willing the image away.

Reid's voice brought her back. "Hey, hey. Are you okay? *Hey.*"

Neera blinked rapidly as warm tears fell down her cheeks. She'd done it again. Lost herself in the memory of him. It took her a moment to realize the Clearwater boy was kneeling beside her, his face concerned. "Sorry," Neera said, her voice shaky. "I just really want to help him."

"Look," Reid said, looking between her and the buck. "There's nothing we can do for him. Let me just take you home, all right?"

Neera eyed the boy for a long moment, before finally saying, "All right."

They approached his Land Rover, which sat idly on the road's shoulder. Dirt coated the tires and splayed across the side of the otherwise clean exterior.

"You can put your guitar in the back seat," Reid said, opening the rear passenger door for her.

Neera peered inside the dimly lit vehicle. There were no signs of suspicious items or anyone hiding out in the back. Though Neera knew *she* seemed like the dangerous one, she had to be cautious herself. Eyeing the front seat, she decided there was enough room for her to sit the guitar between her legs as they rode. "The front's fine."

They sat in silence for a long moment, as the boy clutched the steering wheel, his eyebrows furrowed.

"What's wrong?" Neera asked.

Reid sighed. "I need to do something. Just . . . give me a minute." He climbed out of the car, walking around to its hatchback. Neera watched him in the passenger mirror, prepared to jump out of the door at a moment's notice. But Reid didn't return to the driver's seat. Instead, he grabbed something from the trunk, then walked back over to the deer.

The boy hovered over the animal for a moment, then pulled out a handgun and shot the buck in the head, right between the eyes. It was quick and it was loud. Neera clutched her ears as they rang from the shock of the shot. The deer had gone completely limp, his body unmoving.

Returning to the car, Reid returned the gun to its place, then shut the hatchback. He slid back into the driver's seat, his gaze pained and distant. "Sorry," he said under his breath. "I didn't want him to suffer anymore."

They rode in silence as the Land Rover slowly pulled onto the road and headed away from the bend and the dead buck. As they drove off, Neera watched the deer in the side mirror.

When they were nearly out of sight of him, she saw the animal's body being dragged off the road and into the cover of the woods and the night. It happened so quickly that Neera blinked, and the buck was gone, as if the animal had never been there at all.

CHAPTER 23

SAM

That night, gunshots rang outside Sam's bedroom window, courtesy of Clayton and his buddies playing target practice behind the trailer. Instead of drowning out the noise with headphones, she decided on a walk around the property.

Ten minutes away, on a worn dirt path, Sam went to another one of her favorite spots, a massive pecan tree covered with a single tire swing dangling from the branches. It was quiet and isolated, just how she preferred things to be. Sam's anxieties about Dawson and her brother and her predicament in Carrion threatened to consume her, so she took to the sky. She relaxed into the swing, churning her feet as a warm summer breeze reached her skin.

Sam swung until her legs burned and her head was dizzy. When she planted her feet on the ground, she found she was not alone. Jack sat at the base of the pecan tree, a shit-eating grin spread across his face.

"A bit old for swings, ain't ya?"

"We all have our simple pleasures, Jack," Sam said, coming to a stop with her heels in the dirt.

"We damn sure do."

Sam flexed her bare feet in the grass. "Why're you here? I did what you asked."

"I've come to make you an offer," Jack said coyly. "A mutually beneficial bargain, if you will."

"Nope." Sam shook her head. "I don't want nothin' else from you."

Jack laughed, rising from the ground. He dusted dirt off the back of his worn blue jeans. "It's not polite to lie to the devil, Red."

"I'm not a liar."

Jack drew closer. "How's that wrist of yours? Must be mighty hard to wait tables with one good hand."

"It's fine," Sam lied. "I'm *fine*."

"Tell me this," Jack said, placing one hand on the rope swing and his other around her splinted wrist. "When your daddy did this to you—were you scared? Or were you *angry*?"

When her daddy had fractured her wrist a few weeks prior, it wasn't due to something she'd done. Ben had spilled his spaghetti on the floor by accident. Their daddy had been fine that whole evening, nice even, but the moment the plate hit the floor, it flipped a switch inside of him.

He'd always been that way. Sam knew it was coming, like lightning before earth-shattering thunder.

She hid Ben away in her room, desperate to placate their daddy, but she was no match for his wrath. Not even her locked and barricaded bedroom door could keep him out.

Sam had done everything she could. But by the end of the night, both she and her brother were bloodied and beaten. And Sam had already turned eighteen. Wiley was no longer legally obligated to offer her a roof over her head. Her standing up for Ben was the final straw. She was tossed outside without a second thought.

"Neither. I wanted to make him feel the way he made Ben and me feel," Sam said, her voice low. "I wanted him to suffer."

Jack nodded eagerly. "What if you could? What if I told you that you could scare your daddy? That you could *kill* him if you wanted to?"

Sam yanked her wrist away from Jack's grip. "That's too far."

Jack looked contemplative. “Is it? What happens when Ben goes home from the hospital? When he angers your daddy again and you’re not there to protect him?” Jack paused, letting the question linger between them. “I can only save a life once.”

Sam looked away into the still summer night. The cicadas had quieted down, finally resting until they returned at sunrise. “What’re you offerin’?”

“Whatever you want, Red.” Jack smiled. “You do something for me, and I’ll do something for you. No strings attached.”

“No souls involved?”

“No souls,” Jack assured her. “Like I said, this would be a mutually beneficial relationship.”

Sam stared down at her wrist. It ached in a way the rest of her body didn’t. She climbed out of the tire swing. “I need to think about it.”

“All right,” Jack said, taking a step back. “While you think on my offer, I’d like to give you somethin’.”

“What’s that?”

Jack gestured to her wrist. “Before you go to sleep tonight, place a lock of hair on your windowsill. Remove the splint. Fall asleep with your window open. Your wrist will be healed by morning, if you want it.”

Sam narrowed her green eyes. “What’s the cost?”

Jack pretended to look hurt. “You never had a gift before?”

“The devil isn’t known for being generous,” Sam said, starting down the dirt path toward home. “Even I know that.”

ONCE SAM RETURNED to the trailer, a dog howled in the distance, low and mournful. Tiptoeing inside, she disappeared into her room. Sam locked her bedroom door and pushed the small nightstand that had come with the room in front of it. The nightstand was old, and creaked as she moved it, but was heavy enough to serve as a decent barricade for the door. She wondered if she'd barricade her bedroom door for the rest of her life.

Old habits, as they say.

Her head spun and her body hurt all over. Her fractured wrist throbbed. She considered Jack's gift, supposing it wouldn't hurt to at least try. Reaching into her backpack, she dug around for an old pair of scissors. They were dull and rusted, but they did the trick, as she cut a lock of hair from around her face. She placed the hair on the windowsill, then pushed open the window by a few inches.

Sounds of wildlife trickled in. The neighbor's dog continued to howl at nothing. Katydids chirped. The wind blew softly through the pines. They were the familiar sounds of a Georgia summer night that hummed with life.

Sam unbuckled the splint around her wrist, wincing at the pain and the smell. She was grateful for not having to wear plaster, but the pain of removal still ached. Once the splint was off, she closed her eyes, but sleep didn't immediately come. Instead, recurring, dreadful images flashed behind her eyelids.

Dawson's hurt, angry face the last time they spoke. Ben crumpled and bloodied in the back seat of her car. Her daddy's fist barreling toward her.

Squeezing her eyes tighter, Sam forced herself to imagine she was on a beach, sitting cozy in a cushioned chair, overlooking the ocean with her brother. They would play cards together or a board game. Ben would paint with the watercolors he liked so much, not afraid of making a mess in fear of their daddy. They could laugh loudly and freely. Stay up as late as they wanted and sleep in as long as they wished.

It was Sam's ritual every night to envision that dream. The fantasy kept her grounded—focused on what she needed to do. Her only goal was to support herself and Ben. To make enough money and adopt him—to spirit him away from their parents and from Carrion altogether. Sam had to get them out, and she was willing to do anything to make that a reality.

Jack's offer of a mutually beneficial relationship rang clear in her head as she eventually drifted off to sleep.

THE NEXT MORNING, Sam woke slowly. Her eyelids heavy. She crawled out of bed, shifted the nightstand from in front of her door, and stepped into the hallway, stumbling into the bathroom. Once she was done, she returned to her room. Yawning and stretching like a cat.

It was then, as she tilted her palms upward, she realized she felt no pain in her left wrist. She turned her hand every which way, poking and prodding her skin. There were no bruises, nothing swollen or abnormal. The doctor had said it would take several months for the fracture to heal. But it had only been a few weeks, and there it was, as clear as day: her mended wrist. It was as if there had been no fracture at all.

Sam padded over to her window, hesitant. The curtains swayed slightly, blowing gently in the morning breeze. A bluebird sat on the tree branch outside her window, putting on a show for the sunrise. Her lock of red hair was gone. In its place on the windowsill sat something else.

A small, bloodied bone picked clean of flesh.

She examined the bone but knew little of anatomy to understand what she was looking at. She couldn't even confidently say it wasn't human.

"What the fuck!" Clayton's voice rang from outside, followed by Bailey's high-pitched scream.

Sam scurried out of her room and outside. She found her roommates standing in front of the hickory tree that stood before their single-wide. Warm, bright sunlight filtered through the branches of the tree, casting the land in a soft glow.

"Who's fucking with me?" Clayton questioned, his masculine bravado faltering. His thick fingers wound through his light brown hair, while Bailey covered her face with her hands. They were looking at something dangling from the hickory's branches, but Sam couldn't see from the porch.

"What's going on?" she asked as she took the steps by two.

Bailey turned toward Sam, her face fixed in a grimace. She collapsed into Sam, still in her pajamas, and threw her arms around her neck. "It's awful, Sammie. It's so awful."

Sam pushed Bailey's bleached hair out of her face, looking past Clayton's glaring expression. Dangling from their fully grown hickory tree was a gruesome sight. It took Sam a breath to understand what she was looking at—a bloodied raccoon trapped within the grip of a swollen cottonmouth viper. Both animals were dead, arranged in a deliberate display of gore from the tree branch.

Untangling herself from Bailey's grip, Sam stepped closer, trying to make sense of it all. It was as if the animals had been frozen in place, the raccoon half-eaten by the snake, and hung from the tree. Dark, nearly black blood dripped from the raccoon in a steady rhythm on the grass, pooling beneath.

Then, Sam realized the raccoon's left wrist was missing, the bone cut clean off from the rest of its arm. The same bone that now sat on her bedroom windowsill.

CHAPTER 24

NEERA

Neera woke to a phone call from Isaiah. With the dusty curtains drawn tight in Room 4, she had no sense of the time of day. Darkness hung heavy in the room like a physical thing. Fumbling for her phone on the nightstand, she realized it was barely past seven in the morning. It'd only been a matter of hours since she made the deal with Crow to better her life—to better all their lives.

And it was only a matter of hours until the Cicada's Song. Their fates would be sealed by how she fared onstage that evening.

On the twin bed across from her, Kiran ground her teeth in her sleep. The sound was anxious and grating against Neera's fried nerves. Tiptoeing into the bathroom, she shut the door and answered the call.

"Hey, Isaiah," she croaked. Despite brushing her teeth until her gums were raw the night before, her mouth still tasted of dirt and the faint memory of blood. "What's up?"

"I looked into Blind Bucks last night," Isaiah said on the other end. There was a noticeable absence of cheer in his tone. "You up for a little field trip?"

Half an hour later, Neera was safely buckled in the passenger seat of Isaiah's BMW. He pulled onto Highway 40 and passed her a manila folder. "Everything I found on your family, all at the firm."

The folder wasn't substantial by any means, yet Neera was a

little afraid of what was inside. She flipped through the first few pages, finding documents filled with dense legal jargon within. "Wanna walk me through it, future attorney?" She studied the planes of his face. "That's still the plan, right?"

"Yeah." Isaiah offered her a small smile, then a shrug. "Well, I'm not sure. There's some soul-searching I need to do this summer before I can confidently answer that."

"I get it," Neera said, suppressing a dry laugh at his choice of words.

Isaiah input an address into his car's GPS. "So, this place, Blind Bucks, was originally in Ajay's name with your grandfather as the cosigner. I found they borrowed a significant amount of money from a trust called Second Sons Inc. to fund it. Sound familiar?"

"Second Sons?" Neera repeated, flipping through the folder. "Doesn't ring a bell." She found the page with the loan amount written clear as day. There were too many zeros to wrap her mind around. "Who's behind the trust?"

Isaiah glanced her way, eyebrows furrowed. "I don't know, but Second Sons now owns the property."

Neera swallowed the thick saliva building in her throat. "Another dead end."

"It's better than nothing," Isaiah offered optimistically.

They passed the massive peanut packing plant on the edge of Carrion, a symbol of the most rural part of the greater Langley County. The land here was dry and flat as all the rest, but it felt wilder and more untouched than other parts of Carrion. There was no sign of civilization in sight. Only farmland and slash pines in every direction. Was this really where Ajay thought to open a business?

A few minutes later, Isaiah parked the BMW in front of a building that was a mix of old wood slab and brick. The parking lot was long since overgrown with weeds, a thick blanket of kudzu, and tire marks. The whole place looked eerie and postapocalyptic, a level of run-down that managed to outshine most of Carrion. The building itself was single story and wide. It boasted a massive sign, which read: BLIND BUCKS.

"Are you *seeing* this?" Neera scrambled out of the car. She pointed to the logo beneath the sign, a sprawling antler insignia. The same one from Dawson's key chain and the shirt from Ajay's photo. Looking at the building now, she realized it was the same one in the background of the old photograph, too. "I was right."

Isaiah appeared beside her, studying the building, hand shading his eyes from the morning sun. "Why was Dawson carrying a key chain from a bar that never even opened?"

"This is getting weird," Neera murmured as they approached the bar's front door, finding it chained and padlocked.

"You have that key still?" Isaiah asked.

Neera took it out of her pocket and tossed it to him. Isaiah tried it in the padlock, but it didn't open. He tried it in the door's dead bolt, too, but to no avail.

"Whatever this is for, it's not the front door," Isaiah said.

Neera tried to peek inside, but the windows were all boarded up. She could barely see through a slit in the wood, finding what looked like a stage on the other side of the wide room. A bar was in the center, tables around it, angled toward the low-set stage. The layout reminded her of the way the Tavern was designed.

"I don't get it," Neera said. "All that money for what? For this piece of shit?"

Isaiah's eyebrows knitted in sympathy. "It wasn't a bad investment for the time, you know. Apparently, there were plans in place to *revitalize* this side of Carrion. Money was being thrown around to keep the local farmers out here in business. To bring in some local commerce so they wouldn't have to drive thirty minutes into town and so on."

"Then what happened?"

"What always happens." Isaiah frowned. "Russ Langley swooped in and bought the land up for a better price, then bankrupted the farmers. Fucked over every little guy involved, while the Clearwater folks cashed their checks. Now, it's nothing."

"And people like my family are left to pay the price," Neera remarked. She kicked a nearby rock halfway across the parking lot, watching it vanish into encroaching kudzu.

"We need to figure out who's behind Second Sons," Isaiah considered aloud. "Let me look into it a bit more before we do anything rash, okay?"

"Yeah, sure."

Neera ambled out into the parking lot, glass crunching beneath her Birkenstocks. She took in the old building, the dying land, struggling to see the vision Ajay had for it. She supposed the front porch had potential if there'd been some rocking chairs and outdoor fans.

Then she walked around the side of the building and finally saw a glimpse of what Ajay had wanted. Painted along the wide brick wall was a once-colorful mural—the kind you could find in historical downtowns across rural Georgia. It was a bright design featuring an old-timey map of Carrion, cicadas, peach trees, and song notes wrapping between other iconic Southern imagery. There was even a silhouette of a young girl holding a guitar. The girl was featureless, but Neera couldn't help but wonder if Ajay had depicted her on purpose, as a message to her.

Blind Bucks could've been a lot of things, but like Ajay, it was never given an honest chance.

"Neera?" Isaiah was now standing a few feet away, looking between her and the mural, with a vintage film camera in his hand.

Neera sniffled, tempering the tears threatening to fall. "This was meant to be a place for musicians. If Ajay couldn't make it as one, he'd at least make a place for them to gather and play."

Isaiah was quiet for a beat, surely taking in the weight of her words. "Are you okay?"

Neera ignored his question. "That's new," she said, motioning to the camera in his hand.

Isaiah snapped a photo of the mural. "Just a little hobby I picked up since . . ."

Since we last saw each other, Neera thought. Another thing to add to the list of distance between them.

Sadly, she finally asked, "Why're you helping me, Isaiah? And don't say it's because of goodwill or your 'weird feeling,' because I know that's only the partial truth. I mean, really, *why*? There's something you're not telling me."

A somber smile crossed Isaiah's face. "You're the only one who can do that—tell when I'm lying."

"Yeah, well, it goes both ways," Neera acknowledged. "Why were you asking about Dawson before the news even mentioned him? It's obvious you didn't know him personally."

Isaiah heaved a heavy sigh, head tilting to the cloudless blue sky above. "Go to the podcast app on your phone and click on the true crime section," Isaiah said. "Scroll until you see a podcast called *Secrets of the South.*"

Neera didn't have to scroll far, as it currently sat at number seven in the "top shows" ranking. She clicked on it, finding a brief description about investigating small-town legends and rumors, and the real, often terrible stories behind them.

"Why're you showing me this?"

"That's me, Neera," Isaiah said plainly.

"Sorry?" Neera blinked. "That's *you*? I don't follow."

"That's my podcast. I'm behind the whole thing, from investigation to production. It's all me."

Neera didn't have to be a true-crime aficionado to see the podcast was popular. She scrolled through the backlog of episodes, finding they started the same year she and Isaiah stopped talking. The year Ajay died. Three seasons, one for each year that had passed. "I—I didn't know. This is impressive, Isaiah. Seriously."

Isaiah shrugged. "You weren't the only one going through things the past few years. My parents' divorce was . . . it was hard on me. I needed something to escape to. I'm sure you get that."

Neera nodded. "Yeah, yeah, I do. I'm sorry. Shit. And your dad—does he know?"

"No," Isaiah said. "No one does. I run the podcast anonymously. It was just for fun at first, but now it's a whole thing. There's a lot of listeners, a lot of stories coming my way all the time. *That's* how I found out about Dawson. He sent the podcast an email when he was at the Colonial."

"Can I see it?" Neera braced her cut-up hand against the mural as Isaiah showed her the email, and then he rattled off the different clues he'd picked up over the past few days. "You've been busy," she breathed, taking it all in. "What can we do now?"

"Well," Isaiah began. "I think I've found out all I can from Andrea Sumter. But there's still two people in Dawson's life that could tell us something: Reid Langley and Samantha Calhoun."

"Sam's part of this?" Neera's eyes went wide. "I can try and talk to her. We're friends. Friendly. We work together at the Tavern."

"Do that," Isaiah agreed. "I'm supposed to talk to Reid Langley tonight."

Neera's cheeks warmed as flashes of last night returned to her—of Reid finding her on the road. "Do you think Reid can be trusted?"

"Can Sam?"

Neera gave him a sad smile. "Sounds like we both have a big day ahead of us."

"Yeah," Isaiah said. "I guess we do."

SECRETS OF THE SOUTH

SEASON 4: EPISODE 3

(INTRO THEME SONG)

HOST (to audience): Picture this: a shimmering lake filled with pontoon boats, Jet Skis racing across the water, paddleboard enthusiasts coasting near sandy shores. Elaborate lakeside homes with long docks that extend out into the water. This is the image of your average American lake during the warm summer months of June and July.

But tourists from all over the country gather in droves to boat on a lake deep in rural Southwest Georgia every year. This begs the question: Why there?

ANGELA ABERNATHY, EDITOR OF *SOUTHERN MAGNOLIA LIFESTYLE MAGAZINE* (phone): You're asking me if I think Lake Clearwater is special? *(brief pause)* Well, yes. Of course. There's a unique charm to the lake and the community that surrounds it, that we don't often see in the South anymore. Clearwater has done a highly marketable thing of preserving its history, while also reinventing itself for the modern American. The Langley Plantation and Estate, for example, is a hallmark of historical preservation on its own.

HOST (phone): Could you elaborate on that reinvention?

ANGELA ABERNATHY (phone): People want to be reminded of a time when the South was genteel and aristocratic, not downtrodden and ugly, as we so often see. Tourists want to be sold a very specific fairy tale, and I think Lake Clearwater does that better than anywhere else. It's classy and it's beautiful—filled with romantic Southern grace. What more could someone want from a vacation?

HOST: It's not just the well-preserved Southern charm of the lake that attracts tourists. Every thirteen years, Lake Clearwater holds a festival that *Southern Magnolia Lifestyle Magazine* once described as both ". . . elaborate and ostentatious." They continued, "The Cicada Festival is a decadent musical celebration of what makes the South enchanting."

But the Cicada Festival isn't all dancing to country music and eating deep-fried okra served on fine china. There's a hazard to the lake that no one wants to talk about. People die on Lake Clearwater every thirteen years in ways that the local police describe as "unfortunate but not unlikely."

I consulted with a statistician who told me that the casualties were the result of basic math. The more tourists that boat on the lake's waters, the more accidents there are to occur.

But I'm not satisfied with that answer. And you shouldn't be, either. I'll leave you with this chilling audio clip until our next episode. It is a piece that was filmed for the WCLB News station in 2008. It was nearly scrubbed entirely from the internet.

ANCHORWOMAN (reporting live): Eric Wilson, husband and father of four, was last seen three days ago, while the family was boating on Lake Clearwater. Carrion police believe the man to have drowned after a long weekend spent—

(rustling audio, scratching noise)

Ma'am, stop!

MAKENNA WILSON: My husband didn't drown! I know he's alive. What they're saying isn't true. I can feel it—Eric is alive. They're lying! They're covering—

(rustling audio)

HOST: The clip ends abruptly. The only public reporting of Eric Wilson's death was this.

SHERIFF BUCKLEY OF LANGLEY COUNTY (audio clip): Unfortunately, it has come to light in our investigation of Eric Wilson's death that alcohol was involved the day of his disappearance. Accidents like this happen every summer, made worse by the festival. We try to regulate alcohol and open-container laws on the water, but it is damn near impossible. Why punish the many for the actions of the few? Most adults who come out here are responsible. This is why we advise every lake-goer of the risks before they get out on the water. But tragic accidents can and will happen at any time.

CHAPTER 25

NEERA

"Is it not good?"

Neera pulled her eyes away from the lobby's window and turned toward her grandmother's voice. Nani stood in the doorway that led into the motel's kitchen, wearing an atta-stained apron and her hair in a loose bun at her neck. She gestured to the cold cup of chai resting between Neera's cut, blistered hands.

"It's fine," Neera said. "I . . . have a lot on my mind. That's all." Like the fact that Neera had sold her soul to the devil just last night. And that, in a matter of hours, she would play onstage in front of an unforgiving crowd of people, and *pray* that Crow had given her what she begged for.

Her feelings were made worse by what she'd discovered with Isaiah that morning. Blind Bucks boarded up and decaying—another of Ajay's dreams he'd failed to realize. How could she hope for anything better than what preceded her?

Nani clicked her tongue, looking around the empty lobby. "Thinking too much is never good. Help me with dinner?"

Neera didn't feel as if she could object. Punjabi food was the only aspect of her culture that she felt any real connection to, despite the connection being weak at best. When Nani cooked, it was the only practice she could share in any meaningful way. Though it always ended with Neera burning her fingers on fresh roti or staining her clothes with turmeric.

Neera resented all the things they couldn't do together, like speaking in fluent Punjabi, watching Indian soaps, performing daily paath. Even if she didn't believe in a god, she wanted to experience the sort of blind devotion that Nani had. She wanted to understand her. She wanted to belong through believing.

The problem was this: Neera struggled to believe in anything at all.

But even still, she followed her grandmother into the kitchen behind the lobby. A Hindi soap opera played on the small TV that sat in the room's corner. A desk fan blew on the makeshift dining room table. The two small windows in the room sat open, letting out the musk of spices and smoke.

Nani handed her an apron and a roller. "Roll out the atta like this."

Neera mimicked her grandmother's movements, flattening a ball of soft brown dough into a thin pancake. They did this wordlessly until there were eight pancakes, primed to become roti. Nani dipped each one in dry flour, then placed it on the flat wrought iron pan.

Nani moved through the kitchen methodically, yet it was graceful in a way Neera couldn't help but admire. She wondered how many times her grandmother had done that exact series of motions. Nani, most likely, had cooked like that every day for the past sixty years. It was a realization that made Neera sway on her toes a little. Would her grandmother ever retire, ever vacation? Would she ever be more than a woman who worked from sunrise to sunset, for everyone other than herself?

Neera felt so foolish then. *Ungrateful.* It was moments like these where she hated herself for loving music, for choosing it above all else. All the women who came before her sacrificed so much of themselves. It felt wrong of her to want for anything else, to want for only herself.

But if her deal with Crow rang true, the Singh family would

have their well-deserved peace.

"What are you thinking?" Nani eyed her with a sharp gaze. Her deep brown eyes searched Neera's. But she didn't know how to talk to her grandmother. "I studied the psychology before marrying your Nana. I can see the worry there—in your eyes." She gestured to Neera's face with an atta-covered hand.

Neera's instinct was to lie about what was on her mind, to placate her grandmother and keep things easy between them as she was expected to do. But she was so *sick* of pretending. With a sharp inhale, she blurted, "I'm going to the Cicada Festival tonight . . . and I'm gonna play guitar in front of a huge crowd of people."

Nani's dark eyes flashed with hurt. She turned her attention back to the roti. "No."

"*Yes,* I am," Neera insisted. "I'm not asking for your permission or even your support. I'm simply telling you the truth because you asked."

Nani wouldn't look at Neera. She kept flipping the roti, turning it over again and again. She repeated, "*No.* I don't want to know anything more. This is between you, your Nana, and the God."

Neera's cheeks warmed as she glanced at the portrait of Guru Nanak hanging on the nearest wall, watching over them with empty eyes and an open palm.

"You never listen to me," Neera lamented. She yanked off her apron, folding it into a messy ball, and tossed it on the countertop. "I could *win* this competition. Don't you get that? Nani, this could change everything for us."

Nani shook her head, pulling the sizzling roti from the pan with bare fingers. One side of it was burned to a blackened, overcooked crisp, filling the kitchen with smoke. "You sound just like him—just like Ajay."

The sound of Ajay's name from Nani's mouth was enough to

make Neera pause. "Wh-what?"

Nani tossed the burnt roti into the trash, lingering beside it. "He would tell me the same things. Since he was a boy. He made so many big promises, *too many*. I could not trust a word from his mouth."

"I'm not him," Neera said weakly.

Nani looked at her then with an awful, pitiful expression. Her wrinkled forehead creasing even more, her dark eyes heavy. "I know." She crossed the small space of the kitchen. Tenderly, she patted Neera's face, leaving a bit of flour on her cheek. For a heartbeat, Neera thought her grandmother would apologize and make things right between them. Instead, she merely said, "It is not enough."

Nani walked out of the kitchen and then the lobby, leaving Neera alone, once again.

THAT EVENING, NEERA found herself climbing out of the passenger seat of Isaiah's car in the Tavern's parking lot. "I don't think I can do this," she confessed.

Isaiah adjusted the collar of his shirt in the driver's side mirror. He glanced her way in the reflection, gaze warm and sympathetic. "Neera, come on. Don't start doubting yourself now."

Panic had begun to set in. "But what if Grant Langley was right? What if I don't have what it takes to play onstage?"

What if my deal with the devil doesn't work?

Isaiah shook his head. "Trust and believe, I'll be cheering for you the entire time. If you get scared, just look for me in the crowd, all right?"

"All right," Neera repeated, struggling to temper her anxious thoughts. She adjusted the long off-white dress she wore, feeling distinctly exposed. "Thank you, Isaiah."

"Anytime." Isaiah wrapped her in a one-armed hug, guiding them across the parking lot to the Tavern's front entrance.

Everything in Lake Clearwater seemed to glitter and shine that night, even the hot, baking asphalt. They stood in the long line of people waiting to get inside. As they reached the hostess stand at the door, the two girls asked for their coats. Considering that it was the dead of summer, they had nothing to give them.

As they stepped inside, Neera opened her mouth to comment on the fanciness of it all, but her thoughts were quickly lost in the madness of Southern wealth that surrounded them. Tanned legs in khakis, cackling women in pastel summer dresses and wineglasses in hand, boisterous laughter over things like golf and climate change. TVs on every wall that displayed a different sport in bright, 4K resolution.

Neera noticed familiar red hair across the room. Sam's braids bounced through the crowd, weaving in and out of bodies with frantic energy. She disappeared through the kitchen doors before Neera had a chance to wave.

"See someone you know?" Isaiah asked.

"Yeah, Sam," Neera said, turning her attention to the bar that sat center in the room. It was there she spotted her mom shaking a mixed drink and carrying easy conversation with patrons. Kiran was in her element, it seemed.

"You can go ahead," Isaiah said. "I'm going to look for my father's table. Good luck tonight."

"Good luck to you, too." Neera gently squeezed Isaiah's arm. She didn't elaborate further on Isaiah's meeting with Reid, but he understood what was unsaid. "Text me after, so I know you're okay."

"Will do," Isaiah said, but his eyes were already looking beyond her. "You're gonna kill it, Neera."

Isaiah disappeared deliberately into the crowd, leaving Neera awash in a sea of heavily perfumed bodies. The smells made her dizzy. She pushed her way to the edge of the restaurant, moving along the wall until she found an area that was breathable. Her gaze was drawn again to her mom working the bar.

Kiran was focused and detached. Neera had spent many a night with her as she worked in restaurants over the years. There was a level of capability to her mom Neera could never quite mirror, no matter how hard she tried. Neera supposed that was the immigrant experience; it chewed you up and spat you out. Whoever you were after it all determined how far you made it in the world.

Neera realized then she wasn't the only one watching Kiran. Grant Langley stood out across the room, wearing a crisp, baby-blue button-up and shining silver wristwatch. He laughed with an entourage of men and women, the group carrying themselves with the kind of ease only obscene wealth could endow. But his eyes continued flitting toward Kiran, watching her like a hawk. Even stranger, despite the frantic bustle at the bar, her mom looked at him, too. With a subtle move of his hand, Grant raised his glass to Kiran and tilted his head down, ever so slightly.

Does Mom know Grant? Is that how she got me the audition? It wasn't an impossible thing to consider. Grant owned the Tavern after all. But why wouldn't her mom have ever mentioned they were friendly, knowing Neera lived and breathed music?

Any further thought was lost to the squeal of a microphone. Onstage, Jason the asshole tapped the mic aggressively. He bellowed, "Is this thing on?" Cheers and whistles erupted in response. "We're beginning the Cicada's Song in twenty minutes!"

CHAPTER 26

REID

The Langley siblings sat in a crescent-shaped booth near the Tavern's stage, front and center for the night's events. Flanked on either side by a cadre of their friends, the group was packed together like sardines. Under the table, Reid's leg bounced in an anxious rhythm. He scanned the crowd once more, looking for Isaiah. He had replayed the conversation between them over a dozen times in his head, dissecting every word.

What does Isaiah know about Dawson? About my mother?

"Did you forget to take your Adderall this morning, bro?" Jonah asked pointedly. "Chill out."

Reid scowled. "Fuck you."

"Ooh, scary words," Jonah taunted.

Farris laughed on the other side of him. "Seriously, Reid. What's gotten into you? You've had your whole sad puppy schtick going on the past few days. Now this?"

Reid shrugged, feigning ignorance, hoping his siblings would drop it. That night, he hoped whatever Isaiah had to say would provide him answers and, ideally, closure.

A microphone's squeal reverberated through the Tavern, interrupting the buzz of voices. Jason, the Tavern's manager, stood on the stage near where Reid and his group sat. He tapped the microphone a few times, gathering the attention of the audience. The room slowly fell quiet.

"Good evenin', everyone," Jason said, grinning. "How y'all

doing tonight?" The restaurant erupted in cheers and claps. "Beautiful," he continued. "As y'all know, this is a very special night. Not only because it's the night of the Cicada's Song hosted by yours truly . . ." A few men in the crowd playfully booed. Jason pointed to them. "I heard that, Rob. Corey. You're cut off for the night. No more free booze for you." The crowd laughed. "But also, because it's the beginning of the Cicada Festival. Our seventh one! Can y'all believe it?"

The crowd cheered once more, louder than before. People hooted and hollered. If Reid didn't know any better, he'd think he was transported to a dive bar on the other side of town. But Lake Clearwater residents were cut from a different cloth than average wealth. During the Cicada Festival, their usual Southern decorum flew out the window, replaced by a weekend of decadent, unbridled celebration.

"All right, all right." Jason waved his hand, taming the crowd. "Since it's the first night, and in the spirit of fairness, I thought we'd kick the Cicada's Song off with a newcomer." The crowd whispered among themselves. "Welcome up to the stage: Neera Singh."

At the sound of the name, Reid sat up straight. His eyes fixed on Neera walking onto the stage, a shining acoustic guitar slung over her shoulder. Though when Reid had last seen her, she'd been covered in blood and dirt, crying over a mutilated deer. The glossy version of Neera that stood onstage was nearly unrecognizable from the person he'd seen last night.

The microphone squealed again as Neera adjusted it to her height. "I'm Neera," she said softly. "Thank you for having me. Tonight, I'll be—"

Jonah cupped his hands around his mouth, then yelled, "Speak up! We can't hear you!" The demand was followed by several agreeing cheers and laughter across the audience. His brother snickered while Farris yawned.

"They always put the bad ones up first," she commented dryly. "Poor thing."

Everyone at their table turned their heads to watch Neera Singh play, their gazes hungry for entertainment. Reid held his breath.

Clearing her throat, Neera continued, this time louder, "I was told y'all like music that reminds you of sweet summer days." A few people cheered *yeahhh* in response. "So, I hope you enjoy this song. Don't be afraid to sing along if you know the words."

Reid winced a little as she adjusted herself onstage, settling onto a stool. There was a stillness to her that was at odds with the energy of the Tavern. She was a far cry from the usual musicians that gathered onstage: bearded white guys with banjos and harmonicas, or doe-eyed girls in cowgirl boots singing pop-country.

As Neera began to strum her guitar, Reid's muscles tensed.

"Almost heaven, West Virginia," she crooned. "Blue Ridge Mountains, Shenandoah River."

The room fell silent as Neera sang. Everyone's attention was fixed squarely on her, in a way Reid didn't expect. The voice that came from her was so beautiful it bordered on uncomfortable. She sang "Country Roads" with its usual rhythm, but coming from her, it was somehow even more dreamy and melancholic.

"Country roads, take me home. To the place I belong."

Reid didn't know if it was the night's energy that had gone to his head, but the room slanted a little. With every swell and dip of Neera's voice, the bodies in the Tavern shifted with her. He had the sensation of being in the back seat of a car with his parents as a child, riding through the dizzying Smoky Mountains in the early morning. Whether it was true, or simply a sensation the music made him feel, he truly didn't know.

He closed his eyes, allowing himself to be shepherded away by Neera's voice. By the soft twang of the guitar's strings. By the stillness of the Tavern, wholly enraptured in the story of the song. Reid's mind's eye conjured images of ancient trees and rivers winding through the mountains. He felt the caress of his mother's hand on his shoulder as they looked out onto the valley stretching below them, a pastel sun rising at the edge of the world.

In that moment, at his mother's side, Reid was safe.

He was protected.

He was home.

Neera strummed the final notes and Reid's eyes reluctantly opened, though his lids were heavy. The Tavern was dead quiet. He could've sworn no one was breathing. He could barely move, barely even speak. He felt a heavy weight on his chest. It was a familiar feeling—one he always had after dreaming of his mother. Dreams were cruel that way. They were brief reprieves from the pain of grief, tricking his mind into thinking she was alive.

But Reid's body knew better. Warm tears threatened to spill onto his face. It took all of his strength to prevent them from falling. *Not here, not now,* he pleaded to himself. *Grow up.*

On the other side of the restaurant, Grant peeled himself away from a crowded booth, standing slowly. He put his pinkies in his mouth, breaking the silence with a whistle that sounded more like a howl. He did that several times, before slowly, all around the Tavern, people began to clap. Whistles and cheers erupted. Reid had never seen anything like it. He clapped along with them, his sense of up and down coming back to him in ripples and waves.

"Thank you," Neera said into the microphone. Her eyes were wide and glistening as she stared down at the crowd of people who applauded for her.

Jason hopped onto the stage, his face briefly dumbfounded. "Well, *damn*. That was somethin' else. Will surely be a tough act to follow. Sorry, Jimmy." The crowd laughed, while others continued to cheer.

Neera stared at the crowd, mouth agape. Then she quickly righted herself, mouthing the words *thank you*. She took a small bow, then exited off the stage with her guitar in tow.

"Holy *shit*." The words slipped from Jonah's mouth, heavy and pronounced. His gray eyes glistened with the look of unshed tears, too. Everyone at the crescent table seemed out of sorts, all bleary-eyed and slow to speak. "That song was weird, right?"

Even Farris, normally composed to a fault, looked unsettled. "Definitely not normal," she admitted under her breath. "Unnatural, even."

"What're you suggesting?" Reid asked, sweat beading on his temple.

He still wasn't exactly sure what he'd witnessed with Neera and the buck the night before, but it wasn't his place to tell anyone. Though it was clear now *something* strange had gone down.

"I think . . ." Farris paused for dramatic effect. "That she sold her soul."

A few people at the table laughed as if she'd said Neera could walk on water. Jonah's mouth quirked into a grin, while Reid's head spun. The image of Neera beside the mutilated buck, with the bloody guitar, was seared into his brain.

It's impossible.

Reid scowled. "I thought you didn't believe in that stuff."

Jonah nodded in absent agreement. "Since when did you

start believing town legends? Come on. It's not like they're actually true—*oh, shit*." He sank into the booth, suddenly going still.

Reid followed his brother's line of sight to the next table over, where Samantha Calhoun was taking a group's orders. Once she was done, she glanced briefly in the direction of the Langley siblings before disappearing into the crowd.

"You think she saw me?" Jonah whispered, still slumped low in the seat.

In a rare moment of solidarity, Reid and Farris shared a look of embarrassment. His sister pulled him up by his shirt collar. "Stop being stupid," she barked. "You're only drawing attention to yourself."

Reid leaned close to his siblings. "You think she *knows* the truth about the accident?"

Farris pursed her lips. "It wouldn't matter if she did. I heard from Dad that Wiley's blaming it all on Sam anyway, even got a restraining order taken out on her for Ben. He doesn't care about the other driver."

The siblings looked to Jonah, whose bushy eyebrows had gone high on his forehead. "No fuckin' way. That means I'm out of the woods?"

"It means Wiley won't likely kill you, but Sam still might," Farris said wryly.

Jonah scoffed at the thought but seemed otherwise unbothered. Now that a few days had passed, his brother didn't seem particularly upset by the accident at all, which only further disturbed Reid. Sam's life had been irreparably changed by Jonah's drunken mistake, yet she was paying the price for it. The ugly truth of it made Reid feel sick.

"I need some air," he said aloud to no one in particular. With a shove, he pushed past his siblings, inching out of the packed booth. "Don't wait up," Reid said over his shoulder, before stepping into the dense crowd of Clearwater bodies, in search of Isaiah.

NEERA

NEERA COULDN'T HAVE a high without it being chased by a hellish low. She'd been camped out on the floor of the Tavern's family-designated bathroom for the past hour, listening to the other Cicada's Song musicians through the wall. After her performance, nausea had hit her like a freight train. She tried to focus on the shining mosaic squares that made up the wallpaper, desperate to calm herself.

Her performance on the stage had been more intense than she'd anticipated. The crowd seemed transfixed by her. It had been as horrifying as it was exhilarating. She'd never felt that before, as if all the energy in the room was hers to control.

But there was something *wrong* with Neera. If she concentrated hard enough, she swore there were wings fluttering inside of her. Like the cicada she'd eaten had crawled down her throat and taken root inside her stomach.

Neera rose from the ground with shaky legs, going toward the sink. She braced her hands on the black porcelain and motioned for the sensors to turn on the faucet. She dabbed a damp paper towel on her neck, then cupped the water and funneled it down her throat.

Despite her performance, she didn't feel well. She didn't *look* well. In the mirror, her normally warm brown skin was almost gray in the soft light of the bathroom.

Distantly, the boom of the microphone filtered in through

the walls, followed by Jason's voice. "It's time to announce our winner . . ."

Neera mumbled a curse, still bracing her hands against the sink. She needed to be out there—*now*. She gathered her guitar and canvas bag, then stumbled into the corridor of bathroom doors. The fluttering inside her chest was growing more noticeable, more frantic.

"And the winner of this year's Cicada's Song is . . ." Jason paused for an unbearable beat.

Neera found the nearest wall, leaning against it for much-needed support.

Come on, she thought anxiously. *Just get it over with so I can be sick in peace.*

"Neera Singh!"

Neera nearly toppled over. Without realizing what was happening, she felt hands find her at the edge of the crowd, pushing and propelling her forward onto the stage. The Tavern's lights were suddenly brighter, every sound offensive to her ears. In a blur, she shook Jason's hand, accepted a cicada-shaped trophy, mumbled a few words of appreciation into the microphone, then hurried off the stage.

Making a lap around the restaurant, Neera grew more disoriented. She couldn't remember which way she came in or which way was out. She pushed out of the nearest door and found herself standing on the outer deck that overlooked the lake. The fresh air hit her like a wave, thankfully clearing away some of the fog in her head.

Clusters of Lake Clearwater residents sat around kerosene lamps on the deck, laughing and drinking together. Couples huddled close, legs and arms entwined beneath tables. Groups of men jeered over a football game on the outdoor television screens. Neera walked past them, feeling eyes on her as she moved. There were eyes everywhere. No one was as sly as they pretended to be.

As Neera made for the steps that led off the deck, a hand stopped her. She looked down at a table of thin-lipped white men with drunken smiles.

"Congratulations, kid," Grant Langley said. "That was one hell of a performance." Of all the people in the audience that night, he'd been the first person to cheer for her. When she'd opened her eyes to Grant's whistle, for a heartbeat, she'd expected to see Ajay staring up at her from the crowd with a lopsided grin. Instead, all she had was the comfort of the Yamaha slung over her shoulder.

Neera didn't know what to say other than a polite, "Thank you."

"Apologies for my bluntness," Grant said, rising from the chair. "But I couldn't let you walk out of here without telling you how damn *remarkable* that song was." The others who sat at the table watched her with steady gazes.

Grant Langley, CEO of Blue Mountain Records, was complimenting her, but Neera could barely move her mouth to reply. She only stared at the man standing between her and everything she had ever wanted. It took a moment to gather herself. "I appreciate that, Mr. Langley."

"Call me Grant," he said. "Do you have a minute to talk?"

The cicada fluttered in her chest. "Sure."

Grant escorted her to a tall table overlooking the water, meant for sipping cocktails while standing. "I'm dying to know," he began, "did your uncle *really* teach you to play like that? That fingerpicking style . . ." He mimed his fingers plucking at an invisible guitar neck. "It's rare."

It was a loaded question. "Ajay taught me the foundations, but I learned the rest on my own."

By making a deal with the devil.

"A self-made musician then?" Grant's gray eyes seemed to light up. The way he looked at her now was different than at the audition. "Well, as I'm sure you're aware, I run this little competition here. You've now won, so you'll get to keep that trophy and receive a nice little check. But, more importantly, you'll get the opportunity to perform at the big concert during the Fourth party. Is that something you're interested in?"

"Yes, sir." Neera struggled to keep her expression neutral. To temper the desperate wanting that coursed through her veins. Her throat itched. She coughed, struggling to clear it in a way that wasn't alarming. "That's exactly why I'm here."

"Fantastic." Grant smirked. "If you keep performing like you did tonight, you may just have a real shot in this business, after all."

The cicada quivered inside of her, faster and more frantic. It was as if Neera's lungs were a trap, and the cicada was caught in the snare. She was afraid to speak, fearing she'd cough it up on the table between them. She swallowed hard. "I guess I have my work cut out for me, then."

"I suppose so," Grant said. Quietly, he added, "A voice like yours doesn't come around here too often. Could make a lot of people nervous with that kind of talent." He glanced around the patio, at the people who watched them from the corner of their eyes. "Here's my business card. Don't hesitate to give me a call if anyone gives you any trouble. I mean it."

Trouble? Neera took the card, holding it as if it could cut her. "Why would you help me?"

Grant nodded to the guitar case slung across her shoulder by way of response.

"What—because of the Yamaha?"

"Somethin' like that." Grant chuckled, easy and light. "Well, because of Ajay. We used to be old friends. In fact, we were once in a band together back in the day. Nothing serious, but it was a good ol' time. I learned a lot about music from him."

"You and Ajay? In a *band*?" Of everything Neera had learned in the past few days, this was, somehow, the most shocking. "I had no idea. My mom never told me."

Something flashed behind Grant's eyes. "You should ask her about it, as I'm not sure it's my place. Regardless, you best take good care of that guitar, kid. It's a real beauty."

With that, Grant tipped his head, then returned to his table, barely sparing Neera another glance.

Neera remained frozen, struggling to parse through what she'd just learned. Heat lightning flashed in the distance, illuminating the black sky. Unwittingly, tears welled up in her eyes. She'd always been able to keep her emotions under control, but this was different. *This* was a feeling boiling beneath her skin. The night air was balmy and electric, mirroring the energy that sizzled inside of her. Despite being in the open air, she felt as if the world was closing in on her.

Neera looked over her shoulder at Grant, but he was already laughing easy with his buddies.

Her hands trembled as she tightened her grip on the Yamaha's case. She didn't understand what her body was feeling, what *she* was feeling. All she knew was that she wanted to go home, but that didn't mean a whole lot.

The Colonial wasn't her home.

The dozens of houses she had lived in by the age of eighteen weren't home.

When Neera imagined home, it was a person. It was a feeling. It was a memory frozen in time. It was Ajay's apartment. It was his little corner of vintage guitars before he'd sold them off, one by one, over the years. It was his old piano with missing keys, his bookshelf of eighties movies and dog-eared Stephen King novels. His crate of Pink Floyd records. It was her and Kiran and Ajay celebrating holidays wherever they'd found themselves. It was a family that wasn't quite normal, but it made perfect sense to her.

Home was the past. Home was a fading memory. Home was something she would never be able to return to because, three years ago, someone took that from her.

Neera gripped her throat. The cicada was crawling inside of her. It was in her lungs, beating against her rib cage with sharp wings. Humming. Buzzing. Preparing to scream. She needed to get away.

Now.

She walked away from the patio, stumbling down the sloped, manicured grass to the water's edge. The sounds of the Tavern grew muffled behind her as she put much-needed distance between herself and the crowded restaurant.

She sought refuge on a dock, nearly hidden in a bend of the lake. Neera began to cough as she stood there, cloaked in the dark behind a weeping willow. This time, the cough was throaty and thick, as if there was something slick stuck in her throat. She coughed, and coughed, and coughed, collapsing to her knees onto the splintered wood. Her throat was closing, as if no matter how deep she inhaled, she couldn't get enough air.

The edges of her vision grew black. She coughed one last time before something twitched, moving up from her throat to her mouth. A writhing thing with spindly legs that tasted like acid and dirt.

Neera spit up onto the wood.

Covered in her own saliva was a buzzing, red-eyed cicada.

CHAPTER 27

SAM

Sam took her fifteen-minute break early into her shift that night. If she hadn't, she surely would've lost her shit on a customer and swiftly been out of a job.

After seeing Jonah Langley try to hide beneath his table, she'd figured it out, and she was *fuming*. It didn't take much to put the pieces together. Russ Langley paying for Ben's hospital bills? He'd never done an act of kindness for them before—so why now? The reason was painfully obvious. Russ was covering his son's tracks, saving him from a DUI, or worse, a vehicular homicide charge.

Not that Jonah would face any real consequences if the truth came out, other than a sullied reputation in Lake Clearwater. But he was spared from even that. Too spineless to own up to what'd he done. She considered telling her daddy, but it was only the briefest thought. He wouldn't believe a word out of her mouth, if he bothered to listen at all.

Besides, what could Wiley Calhoun do to the Langley family that they wouldn't inflict one hundred times over onto him? Or *her*? It was a losing game.

Good thing Sam was no longer playing. She had the devil on her side, with an offer in hand. The question was this: Would she be willing to do what he asked of her next?

Sam hovered outside beside the Tavern's dumpsters. She kicked the steel side one good time, letting out a cry of frustration. Her anger wasn't just from seeing Jonah—but also, Reid

Langley. The nail in the coffin of her and Dawson's friendship.

It'd been a little over a month since their fight. That night, they'd lingered in the Tavern parking lot after Dawson's last shift as a caddy. All the while Reid had idled in his Land Rover a few yards away. The sight of him had only pissed her off.

"Y'all got plans?" Sam had asked, not bothering to hide her judgment.

Dawson frowned. "You don't have to say it like that. But yeah, we do. There's a party."

"A *party*? Jesus, Dawson." Sam laughed, high and bitter. "You think these people are ever gonna accept you? Because they won't. They'll never see you as anything other than the dirt under their shoes."

"You know, hating them—hating Clearwater—ain't gonna make your life any better," Dawson had said. His voice was even and calm, as if he'd long been expecting this. "I'm just tryin' to get by, same as you, Sam."

She crossed her arms. "Oh, with your fancy new job you won't tell me about?" Her eyes went again to the sight of Reid leaning out the driver's side window. "You his personal assistant now?"

Dawson shook his head. "It's with your daddy. Workin' for the Langleys."

Sam blinked. "Huh?"

"The job," Dawson said, refusing to look at her. "I start work with Wiley next week."

Sam's mouth had twitched into a hard line. She was angry at Dawson for choosing the worst possible path, and with the worst possible man, but also at herself. For being stuck in Carrion, trapped in a place she saw no way out of. "You're no better than a tick," she'd spat, regretting it as soon as it left her lips.

Hurt flashed across Dawson's face, sharp and sudden as a wasp sting. "Maybe I am, but I'd rather be a tick than what you are."

"And what's that?" Sam had asked.

Quietly, he'd said, "You're nothin'."

Dawson started to say something more, then stopped himself. Instead, he turned his back to Sam, then disappeared within Reid Langley's car.

Those cruel words were the last things they'd ever say to each other.

It felt as if the Langleys were taking everything away from her.

Sam shook the ugly truth of that memory away, stamping down the nauseating waves of anger and regret that threatened to rise. She rounded the corner of the Tavern and headed for her secret spot down by the water. It was the only place on Lake Clearwater that Sam enjoyed.

As she neared the dock, she spotted a familiar face already there.

"Neera!" Sam called out to her with a wave. She had wanted to congratulate Neera on her win but didn't have a chance until now. But the girl didn't seem to hear her as she began coughing something awful, tripping over her own feet. Then she collapsed onto the dock, her guitar case falling to the ground with a dull thud. "*Neera?*"

Sam broke out into a sprint. By the time she reached her, Neera was kneeling on the ground, gasping for air. Fresh, red claw marks stained her throat, sending thin trickles of blood down the girl's neck, seeping into the off-white fabric of her dress. But Neera didn't seem aware of Sam's presence. Her brown eyes were locked on something Sam couldn't quite see. Moving to kneel beside her, Sam followed the girl's gaze.

A slimy cicada lay before them, covered in what Sam realized was spit. The insect's wings twitched, as if it was caught between life and death. It struggled to scream, sending a pathetic, shrill tremor into the night.

Neera looked up then, as if the cicada's call snapped her awake. She met Sam's eyes, her gaze wide and frightened.

Something swooped down from the ink-black sky above. A crow with wide wings and a sharp beak, the size of it unlike anything Sam had ever seen. In an instant, the corvid snatched the cicada from the planks of the dock. The insect's shrill hum was silenced at once as it disappeared down the throat of the crow. Then the bird took flight, vanishing into the night as quickly as it had appeared.

Sam stared after the crow's retreating silhouette as a heavy realization washed over her. It was then that she began to understand the strange connection she and Neera shared. The thin thread between them was not made of fate, but something else entirely.

They were two girls, both touched by the devils of Carrion.

"I can explain," Neera whispered.

All Sam could think to say was "I know."

Neera rubbed her eyes, smearing mascara across her cheek. "You know *what* exactly?"

Sam clarified, "I know what you did . . . because I did it, too."

Understanding washed over Neera's face. "Why?"

"My brother was going to die," Sam said. "In the ambulance, I prayed—actually *prayed*. Except, it wasn't God who answered."

Neera looked to the black sky above them. "The crow?"

Sam shook her head. "The snake."

"What'd you bargain for?"

A cynical laugh escaped her. "He said I only had to lie for him. Little did I know, that lie would cost me my best friend's life."

"You mean . . ." Neera went still. "Is that what really happened to Dawson?"

"He's not dead yet, but he will be." Sam had to look away

then. She studied the dark water, watching as ripples of light danced across the surface. "If you want nothin' to do with me now, I'd understand."

"No," Neera said defiantly. "Your bargain was to *lie,* right? That doesn't mean you can't still save him. All you need to do is play the devil's game."

Sam met Neera's gaze. "You really believe that?"

"Yeah," she said. "Maybe we can help each other."

Hesitantly, Neera's hand reached out and wrapped around Sam's, slowly tangling their fingers together in a mess of bloodied palms and calloused fingertips.

And for what felt like the very first time in Sam's life, she did not flinch.

ISAIAH

IT WASN'T DIFFICULT to find Reid. At all the Lake Clearwater social obligations Laurence had dragged him to over the years, Isaiah never ventured far from his parents' side. But he always took notice of Reid, hovering at the periphery of every event.

That evening, Isaiah found him sitting alone around a firepit, the flames casting shadows across his sharp face. He took a seat beside him without invitation, leaning back in an oversized Adirondack chair.

The pair sat in silence for a long time, as if testing the waters.

Finally, Reid spoke first. "When I was five, my mother made me a promise. She said that one day, we were gonna leave Lake Clearwater together and never look back. It was our secret." He let out a heavy, unsteady breath. "Obviously, that didn't happen, but I intend to keep my promise to her. I'm leaving Lake

Clearwater after the Fourth and I'm never coming back."

Isaiah considered the weight of Reid's words, then asked, "Why'd she want to leave?"

Reid picked again at his cuticles. "I think she looked into the heart of this place and was terrified of what she saw."

There was no one around them, yet Isaiah couldn't help but whisper, "Saw *what* exactly?"

"Hell," Reid said simply. "They like to pretend this is some sort of paradise, but she knew better. I know better now, too." He met Isaiah's gaze then. "I think Lake Clearwater killed my mother."

The statement hung in the humid air between them, heavy and haunting.

Isaiah swallowed hard. "Can I show you something?"

"Go ahead."

Isaiah pulled out his phone, opening up to Dawson's email. Gingerly, he handed it to Reid.

An unbearable minute passed.

Reid finally whispered, "Is this some kind of fucked-up joke?"

"It's legit," Isaiah insisted. "Look at the date it was sent. A whole week before Dawson was reported dead."

"Why do you have this?" Reid asked, eyes still glued to the screen.

"Ever heard of *Secrets of the South*?"

"Oh, shit." Reid looked up. "That was one of Dawson's favorite podcasts." He looked at the email again. "Wait, is this you? The host?"

Isaiah nodded. "I'm a one-man show."

Reid blinked a few times, as if filtering through what he'd just learned. "Dawson must've emailed you because he thought you were some big-shot investigative journalist. But you're just . . . a kid. Same as he was."

"Well, this *kid* is trying to find out what really happened to him," Isaiah said pointedly. "And I think I've done pretty damn well so far."

"Sorry, I just mean . . . I wanna help." Reid handed Isaiah back his phone. "Let me help you before I leave, please, Isaiah. I'm serious. You clearly know how to learn the truth of things, but I can try and fill in the gaps. Because honestly, I don't owe Lake Clearwater anything. I don't care about protecting my community. It's not like they've ever given a damn about protecting me."

Isaiah rubbed his temple. "Are you sure about this, Langley? Once we start digging, there's no going back. For both of us. Do you realize that?"

Reid answered with a firm nod. "I'm all in."

SECRETS OF THE SOUTH

SEASON 4: EPISODE 4

(INTRO THEME SONG)

ARTHUR HUGHES, DOCUMENTARIAN AND LIFE EXPECTANCY EXPERT (phone): Yes, I was originally going to feature Lake Clearwater in my documentary on life expectancy. But I didn't in the end. *(clears throat)* What I found in my research was . . . unhelpful. Inconclusive. Perhaps, even a little strange.

HOST (phone): Would you mind expanding on that?

ARTHUR HUGHES (phone): Sure. As you're aware, I look at more than the data, but lifestyles. I aim to understand what specifically makes people live longer and what, consequently, tends to cut lives short.

Initially, Langley County appeared to have a life expectancy average ten years greater than the surrounding counties in the region of . . . what do you call it?

HOST (phone): Colloquially, it's called SOWEGA. Or Southwest Georgia, if that's easier.

ARTHUR HUGHES (phone): Right, Southwest Georgia. This is a region of considerable poverty, with an average life expectancy of 69.7, compared to that of Langley County, which boasts an average of 79.5. A decade in difference from counties merely thirty or forty miles away. I couldn't believe it. I thought, this must be a longevity hotspot.

HOST (phone): And is it? A longevity hotspot?

ARTHUR HUGHES (phone): To be clear, I didn't include Langley County in my research for a reason. But technically, yes. It is. However, when I mapped the data within the county itself, I realized the longevity was concentrated in the unincorporated community of Lake Clearwater. I compared that to the town of Carrion, within the same county, and the discrepancy was shocking.

It's not the county itself that is a longevity hotspot, but Lake Clearwater.

HOST (phone): What exactly is strange about that?

ARTHUR HUGHES (phone): The data showed that every thirteen years or so, life expectancy increases in Lake Clearwater but decreases in Carrion. The numbers quite literally oppose one another on a graph. One grows while the other shrinks. I'd never seen anything like it. And I've traveled to nearly every country in the world. I study people from all walks of life, but this . . . this data doesn't align with my mission.

HOST (phone): What do you mean?

ARTHUR HUGHES (phone): *(long pause)* How would it look if I said the secret to a long and healthy life was to be extraordinarily wealthy? This is a narrative I have never wanted to promote.

CHAPTER 28

NEERA
68 HOURS

"You might wanna leave the guitar in the trunk."

The first full sentence Kiran had spoken to Neera since she'd won the Cicada's Song, and it was *that*. Sitting behind the Nissan's steering wheel in the Colonial's parking lot, she cut her eyes to her mom in the passenger seat. She'd enthralled an entire Clearwater crowd, received praise from Grant Langley, vomited a living cicada, but it was her mom's silence for half the night that unsettled Neera the most.

As far as Neera knew, Kiran hadn't even seen her performance at all.

"Seriously?" Neera studied her mom's face in the low light from the motel. "That's all you have to say after tonight?"

"Can we not do this now? I'm not in the mood to fight," Kiran murmured, rubbing her temple. "I've had a tough night."

"Yeah, I know," Neera said. "I can smell it on your breath from here."

Kiran may have been a bartender, but it didn't mean she usually drank during her shifts. Instead, she saved the booze for her off days, wasted with glazed eyes in front of their ancient TV. But something about tonight was *different*. Tonight wasn't just important to Neera—it had also been a critical shift for her mom. To prove herself to Jason. To earn her place as the preferred bartender during the lavish celebrations Lake Clearwater was known for. It didn't make sense why her mom had been drinking. Carelessness wasn't like her—not when it came to her job. To matters of survival.

"I don't need your judgment, okay?" Kiran fumbled with her seat belt, struggling to unhook it in the dark. "I get it enough as it is."

It didn't matter how old her mom got—her grandfather's unending disapproval held power over Kiran in a way that angered Neera. It was why his heavy gaze from the motel lobby had kept them firmly in the Nissan for the past fifteen minutes. Because once they stepped out of the car, his wrath would be unleashed upon them. For Neera, it would be the sight of the Yamaha, unbroken and intact. For Kiran, it would be her stale breath, the slight slur to her words. Her pitiful uniform and her black apron, stuffed with wads of dollar bills.

Kiran may have been Neera's mom, but she was also Nanaji's daughter. The weight of the roles existing simultaneously only rendered her smaller. Neera understood it so well. On good days, she rarely took her mom's misgivings personally. But it was not a good day. That night, something searing and electric burned beneath Neera's skin. It charged her every move, her every word.

"Fine," Neera huffed, calloused fingers tightening on the steering wheel. "I don't care what you do. Just don't ask me to leave the Yamaha in the car. *Please.*"

Without warning, Kiran hit the dashboard with her fist, causing Neera to flinch. "I'm not asking you; I'm *telling* you. Nanaji's heart can only take so much. Do you want to be what sends him to the hospital? What kills him?"

He's killing himself, Neera thought darkly. *He's killing us all.*

"That's not fair," Neera shot back. "I'm doing more for this family than he ever has." She didn't wait for Kiran's retort before climbing out of the car, slamming the door behind her. Storming around the Nissan, she pulled the guitar from the trunk, grateful to hold the worn leather case in her hands again.

Kiran stalked after her. "What the hell is that supposed to mean?"

"Forget it," Neera said over her shoulder.

She could feel Nanaji's eyes tracking them as they walked across the lot to Room 4, her mom at her heel.

"You can't just say something like that and walk away," Kiran barked, the pitch of her voice rising with every word. She grabbed Neera's shoulder, spinning her around. "Enlighten me. How're you *helping* us? With this old guitar?"

Neera studied her mom's face, now pinched into the familiar grimace that Nanaji wore every single day. It seemed like Kiran felt the same electric charge that pulsed through Neera, as if the night air was giving life to every dark feeling in their bodies. "Did you even see me play tonight?"

Kiran opened and closed her mouth, then crossed her arms. "I was working."

You couldn't spare three minutes?

Neera ran her fingers through her thick, wavy hair, turning her head to the expansive night sky above. Ajay would've dropped everything to see her play. Why couldn't her own mom show her the same kind of love?

It felt as if Kiran didn't believe she was ever going to make it. Maybe she even hoped Neera would fail, so that she'd finally give it all up. Her dream. *Ajay's* dream. Just thinking of that possibility made her chest ache like it might cave in.

"I was fucking incredible, Mom," Neera breathed. "So good, in fact, that Grant Langley himself congratulated me on winning. He basically said I had a career in music if I keep playing like I did tonight. *That's* how I'm taking care of us."

A wild look crossed Kiran's face, her expression turning sour.

"Grant Langley?" She repeated his name slowly, then laughed, the sound awful and unfamiliar to Neera's ears. "He's not your savior, Neera. Grant's a rich prick who only cares about himself."

"Because you know him so well, right?" Acid brewed in Neera's stomach. "I saw that weird exchange between you two at the Tavern. The way he looked at you, like he *knew* you. Come to find out, he and Ajay were in a band together years ago. They were friends, apparently. It's funny how you've never mentioned that before, not once."

"Grant told you?" Kiran blinked, her anger faltering a little. "I barely know him. He's just my boss."

You're lying. Neera felt it like a sixth sense. "What're you not telling me?"

Kiran exhaled a frustrated sigh. "I'm trying to protect you, to keep you safe."

"I get that." Neera licked her dry lips. "But I'm trying to keep *all* of us safe. I have a real chance at *making it* as a musician. Why is that so wrong?"

Kiran's eyes flicked to the guitar slung across Neera's back. "Ajay already went down this path and failed. Don't you remember? He ended up with a bullet in his fucking head," she hissed. "Is that the same fate you want for yourself?"

There it was again. That hostile fear in her mom's eyes. The same fear her grandparents shared. Neera's vision began to blur at the mention of her uncle's name. "Shut up," she shot back. "You don't get to say that. You have no right to talk about him like that. All he ever did was take care of us."

All he ever did was take care of me.

"He wasn't an angel, Neera." It was Kiran's turn to cry now. Angry tears welled up in her dark brown eyes as she said, "Ajay was fucked up and selfish and chased every impossible dream instead of helping his family. And in the end, he took the cowardly way out. He left us all behind to pick up the pieces. He left *you.*"

This was the place where Neera's greatest pain lived. Most of the time, it was buried deep inside her. A raw, bloody wound that never healed. But now, beneath the dim, flickering lights of the motel's walkway, she was forced to face it. The reality that Ajay had left her entirely alone in the world, killed by his own hand. The ugly truth of it warred within her, clawing her from the inside out.

"*No,*" Neera shouted, violently shaking her head. "Don't say that!"

"It's what you need to hear," Kiran said. The night thrummed with the possibility of hurt, and her mom wasn't relenting. "Ajay fucked everything up—and now you're acting just like him."

Neera was faintly aware of Nanaji standing outside the lobby, watching their fight unfold.

"You can't blame it all on him, as if you're any better," Neera fired back. "Look where we are, Mom."

Kiran's face hardened. "I've done the best I could for us."

"*Look,*" Neera repeated, making a wide gesture with her arm. There was the chipped, peeling beige paint on the Colonial's walls. The pillars that held the building upright, new cracks appearing in the stone with every passing day. The nearly empty parking lot, save for a few beater cars and the burnt carcass of the Cadillac in the center. Then, finally, the pine trees that surrounded them on all sides like a cage they'd never be freed from. "Will we ever get out of this place? Or have you finally given up? Because to me, it seems like you're perfectly content to waste your life away with a bottle, rather than trying to make anything better."

A look of pain crossed Kiran's face, as if she'd been hit. "You have no right—"

"Enough!" Nanaji appeared beside them, shoving a rolled-up *Punjab Times* newspaper between them. He forced the two women apart with his hands. Neera hadn't realized how close they'd been standing, as if they were seconds away from coming to blows. It wouldn't have been the first time. "Why can't you both *behave* yourselves?"

It was such a demoralizing question coming from her grandfather—as if the fight was a petty thing and they were merely bickering children.

Nanaji didn't give either of them a chance to respond before his dark eyes locked on Neera's guitar case.

She took an instinctive step away from him. "Don't—"

But Nanaji was already moving. He yanked the case from Neera's shoulder, tossing it carelessly to the ground like he'd done the night before. With frantic hands, he undid the clasps, then froze at the sight of the Yamaha. "How—how is this possible? It was *broken*."

Kiran's head whipped around to stare at her. "Broken? When?"

A fresh wave of anger rolled through Neera. "He destroyed it last night when he tried to take it from me. After he shoved me to the ground." She held up her palms as proof, the cuts from the fall still swollen and red.

Kiran rounded on Nanaji then, her rage redirecting toward him. "You pushed my goddamn kid?"

Nanaji didn't respond as he collapsed onto his knees beside the open guitar case. The sight of the unscathed instrument seemingly knocked the air from his lungs. It was as if he couldn't hear them at all. He merely stared down at the guitar, mumbling in rapid Punjabi. The way he looked at the

Yamaha was different than before. Her grandfather was no longer enraged at the sight of it, but deeply afraid. His wrinkled hands hovered over the wooden body, shaking again, but he didn't dare touch it. Could he feel the *wrongness* that surrounded it after Neera had pulled it from the buck's gut?

Because the Yamaha was no longer a precious gift from Ajay, but a bloody offering from the devil.

"Dad?" The smallness of Kiran's voice surprised Neera. Her mom's anger quickly gave way to concern. She knelt beside Nanaji on the ground, clutching his arm and shoulder. "Dad, just breathe. Breathe with me, okay? What's wrong?"

Nanaji responded in strained Punjabi. He clutched his chest, pulling at the collar of his shirt. His brown skin turned ashen in the dim light from the motel's walkway. Was he having another heart attack? A stroke? Neera didn't know what those looked like in real life. She was too scared to move, for fear she'd finally drive her grandfather to the point of no return.

"Should I call an ambulance?" Neera asked weakly.

"No, don't," Kiran said, yet she and Nanaji continued the conversation in Punjabi, a hurried back and forth, push and pull.

"What're you saying?" she asked.

"He's not making any sense," Kiran began, struggling to meet Neera's gaze from the ground. "It's gibberish . . . I don't know."

"*Mom,*" Neera pushed, growing more anxious by the second. "Tell me."

"He's saying—" Kiran's voice was tense, hesitant. With a shake of her head, she muttered, "He's saying you're cursed."

"*Cursed?*" A pained, hysterical laugh bubbled up from Neera's chest. The humid night crowded around her as the weight of the word took root in her bones. She knelt before her mom and grandfather, forcing him to look her in the eyes.

She was done living in fear of Nanaji. He'd already done the worst thing imaginable to her, and she survived it. She had nothing left to lose. "That's a fucked-up thing to say to your granddaughter."

"*Neera.*" Kiran spoke her name like a threat, her dark eyes turning hard. Slowly, she warned, "Do not speak to him like that."

"I'm not taking his shit anymore," Neera said as she jerked the case away from Nanaji, shutting the clasps with deft hands. "And you shouldn't, either."

"You are not my *dohti*," Nanaji spat, his breath short and haggard. "You have never been my dohti."

Kiran's eyes went wide. "Dad, stop."

Neera didn't need to be fluent in Punjabi to understand what he meant.

Dohti.

Daughter's daughter.

Suddenly, she was five years old again, crying at the feet of the devil, begging him to make her grandparents love her. Crow had promised they would one day, but he never said *when* that day would come. She supposed thirteen years wasn't enough time for Nanaji. But she was tired of waiting. And as it was, time was no longer on their sides.

"I'm done," Neera whispered. She rose from the ground with shaky legs, the Yamaha's case clutched tightly against her chest. "I'm done wishing you'll finally love me. I don't want it anymore. You have all this anger and pain inside you and it's *killing* you. It's killing all of us."

It killed Ajay.

Nanaji had wanted life to be better for his children. He needed all his sacrifices to be worth it: leaving his life in Punjab, then leaving their little Punjabi community in England, starting entirely over in the Land of Opportunity that shouted for the Singhs to go back to where they came from.

In the end, his sacrifices hadn't been worth it. He had more debt than he could ever possibly pay off. His only son was dead. His daughter was a failure. And Neera—what exactly was she to him? What did he see when he looked at her?

That night, Neera saw only hate in her grandfather's eyes.

Perhaps, Neera embodied all his failings, wrapped up in one person. She was the product of her mom's teenage pregnancy, diluting the Singh bloodline with some stranger's DNA. She carried Ajay's passion for playing music like a torch, unwilling to consider any path other than the one he'd died desperately pursuing. She was brash and defiant and just as stubborn as he was.

In that way alone, they were alike.

"Both of you, just stop," Kiran pleaded, looking between them. The whites of her eyes were red from crying. It was clear her mom didn't know which one of them to defend, which one to condemn. Perhaps there was a kernel of truth to every awful thing spoken that night, despite how painful it was to admit.

"You know what? Maybe . . . maybe I am cursed," Neera began slowly. "But I think we're *all* cursed, and I'm gonna be the one to break it. Listen to me, Nanaji. I'm not gonna let us die here. You've practically given up, but I refuse to let us die in Carrion."

Somewhere in the black sky above, a crow called. The steady flap of its wings echoed through the air. Goose bumps rose on Neera's arms at the closeness of it. Had Crow been watching the fight unfold? Was the devil listening to every damning word?

"Go," Nanaji said. Just one word, but there was a heavy finality to it. "Go, and do not come back."

Kiran's mouth fell agape. She blinked several times, as if she didn't quite hear him. "Dad, come on. You don't mean that."

Nanaji merely held up his hand, silencing her with a gesture. "You defend her when all she has done is *lie*," he seethed. "She lies to you. To me. She lies to us all." He unrolled something from within the newspaper—a letter with a university logo on it—and handed it to Kiran.

"You went through my mail?" Neera shouted.

With slow, deliberate movements, Nanaji rose from the ground, leaning on the nearest pillar. Without another word, he turned his back to them and disappeared into the motel.

"Neera," Kiran whispered, her eyes rapidly scanning the paper in her hand. "What is this?"

"I can explain," Neera said. She didn't need to read it to know what it was. Georgia Southwestern State University had finally responded to her letter of deferment from two months prior.

Simple, merely a few sentences, but it confirmed Kiran's worst fears.

"I was waiting to tell you," Neera said quickly. "Until after the festival ended." *Until I won the competition. Until I proved you wrong. Until I saved us all.*

Kiran wouldn't look at her. "Tell me this isn't true." Hurt coated her words. "Tell me you haven't been lying to me for *months*."

"I—I," Neera started. "I knew you'd be upset, so I wanted to wait."

"Until you won the Cicada's Song, right?" Kiran asked pointedly. "Neera, I don't care what you do, but college is not negotiable. It's never been negotiable."

Neera groaned in frustration. "I'm so sick of you saying that as if it's some magical solution. You're not the one who has to take out student loans to pay for it. *I* am. And I don't want it. The last thing any of us needs is more goddamn debt."

Kiran shook her head in disbelief. "You're really not going?"

"Not this year, no." *Maybe never.*

"All right," her mom said evenly. "If you want to make your own choices, that's fine. But it doesn't mean I have to support them. You're an adult now. If you don't want to go to college, then . . . you can go live on your own."

Neera's jaw went slack. "What're you saying?"

"I'm saying . . ." Silent tears rolled down Kiran's cheeks. Sniffling slightly, she said, "Go see how hard it is to get by when you only have a high school diploma and twenty dollars to your name. Maybe then you'll realize I'm just trying to save you from the same mistakes I made."

"Mom, please," Neera cried. "Please, don't do this."

"You know, I realized I gave Ajay too many chances," Kiran said in a low, strained voice. "We all did. My mom, my dad. They babied him and I wasn't any better. Every time he screwed up and lost his job, or blew all his money on whatever bullshit he needed for his music, I picked him back up every single time."

"Don't," Neera warned. "Please." She could already sense where this was going, and she couldn't bear it.

"He never grew up," Kiran continued. "Because he never had to. Not when we would always take care of him. And you know what happened the one time I didn't help him? Huh, Neera? He *killed* himself. The one time in our whole lives I told him to figure his shit out himself—and he didn't. He couldn't."

Neera's chin began to tremble. "What're you saying?"

Kiran swiped at her eyes, smudging her mascara. "He called me that night. An hour before he did it. He begged me to let him come stay, but I . . ." Her mom's voice cracked. "I could tell he wasn't well. I couldn't let him be around you like that. Not anymore. So I told him no."

Neera's vision swam as she leaned against the nearest pole for support. Wiley Calhoun's threat rang clear in her head. She refused to believe Ajay took his own life. *He would never leave me.* In a low whisper, she said, "You don't know that. Maybe he just needed to talk to someone. Maybe he was in trouble. Maybe he just needed his family."

"No." Kiran's face turned hard. "*Ajay's* the reason he's dead. And I refuse to support that same kind of life for you, Neera. If you want to play music more than anything else, then go do that. But I'm not gonna stand by and watch you end up just like Ajay."

Neera squeezed her eyes shut, winding her fingers through her hair, damp with sweat. "You're so fucked up. All of this is fucked."

"One day you'll understand," Kiran said quietly. She glanced over her shoulder, toward the motel's lobby. "I need to check on my dad. When you're ready to take your future seriously, I'll be here. But until then, you're on your own."

Neera sniffled. "That's it?"

"I'll stay in another room tonight," Kiran said. "You can take the Nissan, but you need to be gone by morning."

Gone. Neera lingered on the word as a wedge was driven between them. Her entire life, she and Kiran had been an inseparable pair. There had never been a time where they were physically apart. For all their faults, they were the other's emotional crutch. In all Neera's daydreams of leaving the Colonial behind, her mom was always at her side.

This is all wrong.

As Neera was left alone in the walkway, she was overcome with the uneasy feeling of something *shifting* in the air, her sense of the world irreparably changed.

CHAPTER 29

REID
67 HOURS

When Reid returned home from the festival celebration that night, he dreamed of his mother.

He was twelve years old again, having awoken atop his reading nook. The shock of thunder had jolted him upright. Lightning struck, washing the sky in a blinding white. He crawled away from the window, where rain violently splattered against the glass.

He wrapped his blanket around himself and tiptoed out of his room in search of water and a snack. It was late, so late in fact that everyone else was sound asleep in their rooms. Reid saw his opportunity: He'd play the Xbox in the living room on the big TV while his siblings slept.

Once Reid was settled on the couch with chips and a glass of water, he became aware of a door creaking in the heavy wind. He rose from the couch and approached the screened-in porch that overlooked the lake. The door that led outside was partially open, swaying violently from the storm.

Reid stepped onto the porch to close the creaking door, but something caught his eye. On the porch's wooden planks were fresh, wet footprints.

Peering past the screen, Reid looked out into the rainy cover of night. Despite it, he saw movement out on the dock behind his family's home. Looking closely, Reid could make out bright yellow rain boots. The ones that belonged to his mother.

What's Mom doing?

Without thinking, Reid bounded out the door and ran toward his mother in the pouring rain. He slipped several times as he ran, but he didn't fall. He was determined to make it to her. Whatever she was doing, it was dangerous. She needed him; he was sure of it.

His mother stood in a black raincoat and carried a duffel bag on her shoulder. She was looking away from Reid when he reached her, focused on a small speedboat sloshing frantically in the water.

"*Mom,*" he yelled. "Mom! What're you doing?"

His mother turned suddenly, her face partially obscured from the hood of the raincoat. "Reid? You can't be here."

"I don't understand," he said loudly, begging to be heard over the storm. "Why are you out here?"

His mother knelt before him, pulling him close. They were both soaked and shivering, but her closeness brought him warmth.

"Go inside, Reid. Please. *Go.*"

Reid shook his head. "Where are you going?"

As Reid observed her up close, he realized his mother looked terrified. He'd never seen her so scared before. She was never scared of anything.

"I'm leaving, Reid," she said into his ear. "But I'll come back for you. I promise."

Reid gripped his mother's hand tightly. "Take me with you."

"It's not safe, Reid," his mother cried over the rain. "It's not safe right now, but I will come back for you. Please believe me."

His mother tossed her duffel bag onto the boat, then knelt before Reid again. She held him close for a long moment, then said, "You never saw me, Reid. Okay? You can't tell anyone about this. If you do, I can't come back for you. Do you understand? I'll be gone forever."

Reid didn't know what to say.

His mother shook his shoulders. "Say it, Reid. Tell me you understand."

He swallowed the spit forming in his throat. "I understand."

"What won't you do?"

Reid looked at the boat, then back at his mother. "I won't tell anyone I saw you."

His mother kissed his forehead and hugged him for what Reid would soon realize was the very last time. "Go back inside, Reid. Pretend this was all a dream."

Reid stood immobile as his mother climbed into the boat and disappeared into the stormy night.

The next morning, he was awoken by the screams of his father. Of his siblings. A chorus of people calling his name.

Reid found himself lying atop a pile of life jackets in his family's boathouse. He didn't remember how he got there. For the briefest of moments, he thought the previous night was only a nightmare.

But then it returned to him.

His mother had vanished before his eyes as he cried for her in the dark, yelling against the booms of a storm. He had stumbled into the boathouse, sobbing and hoarse. He'd cried himself sick until he succumbed on the life jackets and welcomed sleep.

"He's in here!"

Reid opened his swollen eyes, finding Farris standing above him. Her face was tired and stricken. A moment later, Reid's father and brother appeared in the boathouse.

His father rushed forward, on his knees before him. Clutching Reid's face, he asked only one thing. "Where is your mother?"

CHAPTER 30

ISAIAH
58 HOURS

Secrets of the South was born in the belly of an alligator.

Three years ago, the hurricane of the century hit the Southeast, barreling through Florida, then made landfall as a vicious tropical storm in Southwest Georgia. The storm drowned much of the rural flatland towns, knocking out power and destroying thousands of homes and businesses in its path. Lake Clearwater had been completely spared from the carnage, as it often was when natural disasters hit Southwest Georgia. The parts of Carrion nearest Clearwater were fortunate in the same regard, with only the homes on Langley County's outskirts suffering even minor wind damage.

As the Johnson family often did, Isaiah's grandparents mobilized their little community and set out to help the neighboring towns. In the months that followed, they provided families with crates of fresh produce, pantry staples, care packages, and labor to rebuild their homes. That summer, going into his sophomore year of high school, Isaiah spent most of it in the passenger seat of Papa Charles's pickup. He and his grandparents drove all over, going from town to town, aiding people in whatever way they could.

But one sizzling July day, in a neighboring tiny town, Isaiah overheard a conversation. The Johnsons were gathered at an old Baptist church turned relief center, parceling through boxes of donations for a clothing drive later that week. As was often the case with Southern folk, idle conversations turned to gossip, and Isaiah listened to every word.

At fifteen, Isaiah's ears were already trained in the art of eavesdropping. He'd always been curious, but his inquisitive nature only grew as the years passed. It was his gift of observation that prevented him from being blindsided when his parents announced their "marital difficulties" to him at the start of that summer. He'd seen it coming from a mile away—with his father taking on more cases than ever before, and his mother seeing a marriage therapist twice a week, and disguising it as *going to Pilates.*

In that dusty church, waist-deep in donated clothing, Isaiah stumbled upon the story that would become his first investigation: a little girl missing in the aftermath of the storm, and the unfounded rumors that spread as a result. It was easier for the tiny community to believe that an old alligator living in the local swamp was responsible for the girl's disappearance rather than the possibility of any alternatives.

But he instinctively knew there was more to the story.

By the end of that summer, Isaiah had ingratiated himself in the hearts of the townsfolk, and he learned the truth. The little girl wasn't eaten alive by a gator. Instead, she was taken across state lines by her estranged father, who'd taken advantage of the chaos caused by the flood. She was recovered in perfect health and reunited with her mother not long after.

The story made its way around local news stations, and Isaiah saw an opportunity. Grandma Bee had taught him his love for storytelling, and Isaiah nurtured that passion into something entirely his own. He made the alligator story his first season of *Secrets of the South,* leaning into the Southern absurdity and folklore of it all.

And each summer that followed, he spent his time in and around rural Georgia, in search of the podcast's next story.

AT THE JOHNSON farm, there was a shed at the edge of the yard. In that shed was Isaiah's own makeshift darkroom, courtesy of Papa Charles. Except it wasn't being used as a darkroom at all. At least, not that day—the next morning after Isaiah and Reid had made their pact by the firepit outside the Tavern.

The boys gathered in the shed, the space barely big enough to park a tractor, but it would suffice. They weren't in need of space but seclusion. Privacy to speak freely and openly. Outside, the storm of the summer threatened to descend upon Langley County, with waves of thunder rolling overhead, shaking the walls around them.

Their gathering began with one word scrawled on a whiteboard: *Dawson?*

From Dawson's name sprawled various lines, arrows, and question marks. They spent the better part of the day creating a complicated web of connections and speculation.

Rain began to fall steadily on the tin roof by the time the boys were ready to call it in the early afternoon.

"Leblanc, huh?" Reid asked, eyeing his name on the board. "Can I hear the voicemail again?"

Isaiah played the recording of the voicemail from Leblanc's office once more. Andrea's pleading still raised the hair on his arms, even in the stuffy air of the shed. "When I interviewed her a couple days ago, she believed Leblanc and Dawson were having an affair in secret. Do you know anything about that?"

"With Casey?" Reid blew air from his mouth, gaze going toward the ceiling. "I mean, Leblanc favored Dawson as a caddy whenever he golfed. He'd request him every time and *always* tip big." He absently tapped a marker on his knee. "I think I remember Dawson saying he'd even gotten a new job through Leblanc, but he never told me specifics."

Isaiah scribbled *mysterious job* onto the board. "Do you think it was anything more than that?"

"The only thing I know with any certainty is that Dawson kept a lot of things close to his chest," Reid said. "Even with me. I know he was seeing someone in secret. So yeah, I wouldn't doubt what Andrea said."

Silence fell between them, filled only by the patter of rain.

Isaiah asked, after a moment, "Does the name 'Blind Bucks' mean anything to you?"

Reid shook his head. "Not at all. Why?"

"When Dawson stayed at the Colonial, he left a key chain behind that came from there. It's a shuttered bar that never even opened to begin with," Isaiah said.

"Weird," Reid said. "Do you know who owns it?"

Isaiah nodded. "Neera's family owned it originally . . . but lost it. Now a trust called Second Sons owns it."

Reid blinked. "Wait, Second Sons? Seriously?"

Isaiah looked away from the board, squarely at Reid. "Have you heard of it?"

"My uncle—that's what he's always called himself," Reid said slowly. "A second son to my father."

"What's your uncle's name?" Isaiah asked, preparing to write the name on the board.

"Grant," Reid said. "CEO of Blue Mountain Records."

"Oh yeah." Isaiah scribbled down Grant's name, considering his place among the rest of the clues on the board. "He's the one who lives in Nashville, right?"

"Yeah, he made it out of this place," Reid said, almost wistfully. Then his eyebrows knitted together. "So why would he be involved with some closed-down bar in Carrion? He already owns the Tavern."

Isaiah considered for a moment. "Maybe he wanted a hand in both? Saw Blind Bucks as competition to the Tavern?"

"That doesn't seem like Grant. He's not calculating like my father. I mean . . ." Reid shook his head. "I don't know, man. It's hard to imagine him involved with any of this." He gestured to the whiteboard before them.

Isaiah was reminded of his father and the political ladder he continued to climb within Lake Clearwater, as well as beyond the gates. That familiar question returned to him: *Why now?*

He then asked, "Have you ever considered we don't know our families as well as we once thought?"

CHAPTER 31

NEERA
53 HOURS

That afternoon, Neera waited for her mom to arrive at the Tavern. She'd left the Colonial before dawn, with the Nissan packed as if she was going somewhere for only a weekend. Neera believed half a day was plenty of time for Kiran to cool down. A well-timed apology would be enough to return to her mom's good graces.

Except, when Kiran arrived for her shift, she didn't so much as look Neera in the eye. In fact, she walked right past her, pretending she wasn't there at all.

"You can't be serious," Neera called after Kiran's retreating form. "Mom, *please*."

But Kiran didn't relent as she let the Tavern's door slam in Neera's face.

The world fell quiet as a sudden downpour surrounded Neera. *It's over*, she thought as she stood alone in the rain. *It's all over*. She didn't give herself a moment to think things through before she packed up her guitar and began walking. She needed to go somewhere and gather her thoughts. Regroup.

Past the parking lot and the Tavern, down by the lakeshore, was an empty gazebo where she sometimes sat when waiting for her mom to get off work. Neera trudged toward it in the pouring rain, the soles of her Birkenstocks turning slimy from the rainwater. The storm had grown so bad so quickly she could barely see past a few feet in front of her. Thunder rumbled overhead. She slipped and struggled down the path, every inch of her soaked through by the time she reached the gazebo's shelter.

Neera collapsed onto the swinging bench, feeling weighed down by her sodden clothes and guitar. She opened the Yamaha's case, grateful to find it dry within. Resting it gently beside her, she pulled her wet phone from her pocket. She'd purposely *not* told Isaiah about what happened between her and her family after the Cicada's Song, but she no longer knew what to do or where to go.

The screen barely responded to her touch as she tried to find Isaiah's number in her contacts.

The call immediately went to voicemail. With a sigh, she waited for the *beep* at the end. "Hey, Isaiah," she began loudly, struggling to speak over the roar of the rain. "My mom and I . . . we got into a really bad fight. Could you call me back when you can, please? Thanks."

Embarrassment washed over Neera as soon as she ended the call. How exactly was Isaiah supposed to help her? Let her crash at his grandparents' farm until the festival was over? There was something so shameful about homelessness that made her feel like a helpless child again. More than once, she and her mom had been kicked out by a bad boyfriend or a scummy landlord. They'd spent more nights in the Nissan than she cared to remember. But at least they'd always been together—Kiran and Neera against the world.

This, she thought, *is different. There is no* us *anymore.* Neera was finally on her own.

There was a cruel irony to being kicked out of the Colonial when the very thing she was trying to do was save it. To save her whole family from the consequences of their failed American dream. Whether her mom could see past her hurt or not, Neera had to be the bigger person.

She only had two days to figure out how to save them all.

Pulling her legs to her chest, she laid her head on the worn leather guitar case and closed her eyes. For a long time, she lay there on the swinging bench, repeating her plan in her head.

Isaiah would call her back. He'd offer her a place to stay. She'd practice her guitar for hours for the next two days until the Fourth. She'd impress Grant Langley. He'd sign her to his label, and she'd use the money to pay off her family's debt. She'd repair the relationship with her mom. They'd all leave Carrion behind. In a couple weeks' time, everything would be okay. What was a little more struggle for a lifetime of peace?

I can do this, she thought. Over and over and over. *I can do this.*

"Hey, kid," a man's voice called from out of sight, startling Neera upright. She found Grant Langley standing at the edge of the gazebo, soaked from head to toe in athleisure. He wiped his clean-shaven face with his hand, studying the sight of her on the swing. "What're you doing out here in the storm?"

"Long story," she said, self-consciously tucking wet strands of hair behind her ear. She wasn't prepared to see him like this, looking like a mutt without a home. "You?"

Grant made a flippant gesture toward the sky. "Damn storm caught me on my run. I thought I'd wait here until it lightens up." He eyed the Yamaha's case and her own sodden clothes. "I suppose the storm caught you, too."

"I'm waiting on a friend," Neera lied, looking away. "Just waiting here until they pick me up."

Grant nodded, but he didn't look convinced. "You mind some company?"

"Fine by me."

"Fantastic." Grant stepped farther into the gazebo, wringing out water from his baseball cap. The color of his surfer-style hair reminded Neera of dirty dishwater. He moved to the railing across from her, leaning against it just enough to not be pelted by the rain. Clearing his throat, he asked, "Why don't you play me somethin'?"

Neera blinked. "Right now?"

"Now's as good a time as any," Grant said with a shrug.

Thunder boomed, briefly rattling her bones, followed by a flash of lightning across the water.

"Okay," Neera said. With hesitant hands, she pulled the Yamaha from its case. It felt awkward resting against her wet clothes, but she brushed the insecurities away. The only thing that mattered right now was how well she played. "Anything particular you wanna hear?"

Grant rubbed his chin. With easy, Southern charm he said, "I'd like to hear a song that matters to you. Something special."

Special? Neera considered for a breath, then the perfect song came to mind. "I suppose I'll play one of my favorites. 'Cross Road Blues' by Robert Johnson."

Grant folded his arms across his chest. "Let's hear it."

Once the thunder had subsided and the rain fell in a steady rhythm, Neera began to strum the Yamaha's strings. It took over a minute for her to get the tune right. The song was difficult to perform, requiring a unique sliding technique that most musicians could only dream of mastering. It was awkward and uncomfortable, but she figured she didn't sell her soul to play easy songs.

I went to the crossroad, fell down on my knees

The song was a legendary blues ballad, shown to Neera at a young age. Ajay had been enamored with not only the song, but the man behind it. Robert Johnson was a musical icon, inspiring the likes of Hendrix and Clapton, and all the burgeoning musicians that followed, including Ajay.

I believe I'm sinkin' down

When the song finally came to an end, Neera's gaze lingered on her toes. Heat warmed her neck as she noticed flecks of mud caked to her feet. She was too afraid to look at Grant, fearing disappointment in his eyes. After everything with her family, she couldn't handle more rejection. Softly, she asked, "What'd you think?"

"Neera Singh," Grant began, stepping forward. He knelt before her, his gray eyes bright and gleaming. "You're like lightnin' in a goddamn bottle."

Neera let out a heavy sigh of relief. Slowly, a genuine smile crept across her face. "You don't know how much it means to hear that."

Grant returned the smile, his straight teeth white as pearls. "Anytime, kid." He then canted his head to the side, looking up. "Hear that? Sounds like the storm is subsidin'. For now."

Past the gazebo, the world began to reveal itself. In a strange way, she wished the storm would stay, and she could remain wrapped up within it. She wasn't yet ready to face her uncertain reality just yet. "I guess you better head back before it picks up again."

"That's wise," Grant said, rising from his place on the floor. He stretched out his leg muscles, then tapped something on his fitness watch. "Is your friend coming by soon? I'd hate to leave you out here in this kind of weather. Tornado season and all that."

Neera pulled out her phone, hoping to see a text or call from Isaiah. But there weren't any notifications. It hadn't been long since she called, but she feared what she'd do once the sun began to set, and she truly had nowhere else to go. "Yeah," she lied. "Should be here any minute."

Grant looked her over again, studying her with an unreadable gaze. "I know it's not my place to say. And I say this with no judgment, but . . . I'm afraid I'm familiar with what being kicked out of the house looks like."

Neera bristled, heat warming her cheeks. "I haven't—I'm not—I'm *fine*."

"Hey, now," Grant said, holding up his hands. "It's nothing to be ashamed of. I've been there before. Many times."

"*You've* been kicked out of the house?" Neera arched an eyebrow.

Grant smirked. "Oh yeah. Plenty of times when I was about your age. I didn't come from a family of musicians if that's what you're thinkin'. No, ma'am. Born and raised to strict Southern Baptists. They wanted my life to go a certain way, and I wanted it to go another. I came out on top in the end, but the road to get here wasn't always pretty."

Neera eyed him. "Was that when you knew Ajay? In the band?"

"It was." Grant's gaze turned thoughtful. "He was a good friend to me back then. Helped me out of a couple tough spots."

"Ajay was good like that," Neera said softly. It was weird to speak of her uncle's memory with a stranger, but it felt easier somehow. Less *weighted*.

"Yeah, he was." Grant glanced around the gazebo. "What's

your plan then, kid? Camp out here? I'm afraid these Clearwater folks wouldn't take too kindly to that."

"I really am waiting on a friend," Neera said, fumbling with her phone. Still no word from Isaiah. "I just don't know how long it'll be."

"How about this?" Grant looked contemplative. "I have a fully furnished pool house that I never use just sitting in my backyard. You are more than welcome to hang out there while you're waitin'. And if you need more time, that's fine by me."

"Grant, I—" Neera began, shaking her head. "I appreciate the offer, but I don't want your charity. Or your pity. None of it."

"I understand that, I do," Grant said, his gaze turning sympathetic. "But think of it like this: From one musician to another, I'm just payin' my dues. And one day, you'll pay it forward to some struggling artist out there, too."

Struggling artist? Was that how Grant really saw her? Neera looked away, considering his offer. She checked her phone again, but still, no Isaiah. Hesitantly, she said, "Okay, I guess just for a little while. Until my friend comes and gets me."

"Just for a little while," Grant repeated as he offered his hand to help her from the swinging bench.

With the Yamaha still slung across her chest, Neera hesitated before she took Grant Langley's hand in her own.

CHAPTER 32

SAM
52 HOURS

That afternoon, Sam tagged along with Bailey and Clayton on a trip to Dollar General, though shopping was the furthest thing from her mind.

It was only minnows. Beside the discount store, and across from a cotton field, was Gator's Bait & Tackle, an old gas station that specialized in selling fishing equipment, with one barely working gas pump. Her gaze lingered on a tank of minnows visible through the gas station's window, the water a familiar shade of brownish green. It was once a place she'd loved as a kid, when she and her daddy spent most weekends fishing.

Wiley Calhoun had always been a bad man, but there was a time, years ago, when he was *better*. She wasn't sure what had caused the shift in him or if he simply grew tired of pretending.

"Hey, Gator," Sam greeted.

Gator, the store's owner, sat beside the front door on a wooden stool, shielded from the rain. He was in the middle of winding fishing line through a pole when recognition crossed his old, leathered face. "Oh, hell," he said with a toothy grin. "Trouble's found me."

Sam let out a breathy laugh. "No, sir. Not today."

Trouble was a nickname given to her by Gator back in the day.

Gator's shop was the best place in town to pick up live bait and snacks for long days spent at the pond. But every time they'd pick up fresh crickets or worms, Sam would wander to the minnow tank, content to watch them swim for hours. She used to beg, with tears in her eyes, for Gator to let all the critters go, to free them from their tiny cages and crowded tanks. The old man had always found it amusing, promising that one day he would. But her daddy found it humiliating—telling her, only once, to never ask that of Gator again.

"You headin' out to the pond today?" Gator peered up at her from beneath his sun-faded trucker hat. She'd never seen him wear another, not in all the years she'd known him. "The weather's right for it."

"Afraid not," Sam said, glancing around the building, finding everything as it had always been.

There was the rusted ice machine that sputtered and groaned depending on the heat of the day. The crate of peaches outside the doorway, through some kind of magic, were the juiciest peaches in a fifty-mile radius. In the window, the hand-painted sign with crooked letters advertising fresh bait. The price had never changed, even when the land next door was bought and clear-cut to make way for Carrion's first Dollar General.

"Best get out there before long," Gator said as he sipped from a Coke bottle. "Pond's gonna dry up and disappear by the time I'm six feet under."

There were dozens of ponds around Carrion, some worthy of names while others were not. But the pond in question was *Gator's* pond, a secret spot he shared with a handful of folks, Sam and her daddy included. No matter the weather or time of year, when you fished in Gator's pond, the catch was always plentiful.

"I hear you," Sam said with a nod. "I'd like to take Ben out there again sometime. You should've seen him last we went . . ." Her sentence trailed off as Gator's silver eyebrows furrowed at the mention of her brother. Sleep still clung to Sam and, somehow, she'd briefly forgotten where Ben was, and where she stood in relation to him. As it was, there would be no fishing trips in either of their futures.

"I heard about the accident at church." Gator stopped winding the fishing line. "How's the boy holdin' up?"

Sam shrugged, unsure of what to say because she didn't know herself. "As good as expected."

Gator grunted. "The whole town's prayin' for him. I hope he knows that."

I'm sure they are, Sam thought bitterly. She shifted from one foot to the other, gaze returning to the minnow tank. The real reason she was there. "You think I could . . . ?"

The old man turned his head, following her line of sight. He let out a smoker's laugh, then waved her inside with the fishing pole. "Go on. Take one home with you, if you want. On the house."

Sam beamed. "You're a fine man, Gator. They don't make 'em like you anymore."

"Don't I know it." Gator snorted, nodding his head toward the screen door.

Sam stepped inside, letting the door rattle shut behind her. Just like the outside, the inside hadn't changed at all. The walls were wood-paneled and faded. A distinct smell clung to the room, something like gasoline and pond water. There were only a few shelves, but they stood taller than Sam. Each one was filled to the brim in a messy array of fishing equipment and gas station junk food. Some of the candy now looked as old as she was.

Second to the minnows, Sam's favorite part was this: Somehow, there was never another person in the store. She didn't know how Gator managed to stay in business, but he did.

For a long time, she stood there, entranced by the minnows. It was quiet, uninterrupted bliss, and it was exactly what she needed. *Peace,* she thought. *All I need is peace.*

"Which one?" A man's voice pierced the silence.

Sam whirled around, fists instinctively balled, only to find Jack standing a few feet away. Her shock quickly gave way to surprise. In the daylight, he looked remarkably *human*. Like any other man around Carrion. But, she realized, his otherness was in the finer details. The way his outfit never seemed to change, which could've been a personal choice of his, but she doubted it. His dust of facial hair that never grew darker, but also, never lighter. Then there were his eyes, black as crude oil, even in the light of day.

"It's not polite to sneak up on people," Sam admonished. "Where'd you come from?"

Jack smirked as he pretended to look over a pack of fishing hooks. "That's the sort of question I can only answer with a drink in hand."

Sam tried not to roll her eyes. "I mean, I didn't hear you come in. Did you . . . materialize or somethin'?"

"Materialize?" Jack's eyebrows raised dramatically. "I may be the devil, but I'm also a man. I walk the earth same as you, Red. Besides, I have my Jeep parked out back. Don't you worry." Jack set the fishing hooks down, then took a few steps toward her. He tapped the fish tank's glass with a slender finger and said, "You didn't answer my question. Which minnow you takin' home?"

A moment before, the minnows had been swimming in synchronized chaos. Sam had spent a long time watching these kinds of fish. She recognized patterns in their frenzied behavior. But as Jack's palm lingered on the glass, the minnows moved in a way she'd never seen before. They swarmed the opposite side of the tank, clambering over one another in a desperate bid for distance and safety.

"*Stop,*" Sam snapped as she pulled Jack's hand away, his skin hot to the touch. "You're scaring them."

The minnows stopped swarming, slowly returning to their earlier directionless swimming.

Jack only shrugged. "Fish are much wiser than people give them credit for. They immediately know when they're in danger. The same can't be said for most people."

I know what you are, and I surely won't forget, she thought.

A beat of silence passed before Sam finally asked, "What do you want, Jack?"

His black eyes narrowed. "The real question here is what do *you* want, Red? I know it's more than this." He gestured lazily to the fish tank, then the bleak view of Carrion out the window.

I want to feel safe, Sam thought pitifully. But that wasn't an easy answer to give. She needed something concrete. "I want to adopt Ben, but I don't have enough saved to get us across county lines, much less take care of us."

"Then what you need is money and time," Jack mused.

Sam nodded. "That's what it all comes down to in the end, isn't it?"

"I can do that," Jack said simply. "So, I'm here with my offer."

Sam swallowed. "What is it?"

Amusement danced across Jack's face. He was neither young nor old, somehow looking simultaneously eighteen and thirty. "Tomorrow night, during your shift at the Tavern, I need you to spike Kiran Singh's drink with a little sedative. She usually has a drink she's sippin' on in a Styrofoam cup. Use that."

Sam felt sick. "Why're you askin' this of me? What's *wrong* with you?"

"Oh, don't get all bashful on me now, Red," Jack said, slowly looking more devil than man. "You sold out your best friend of nearly eighteen years. The mom of your little crush is nothin' in comparison."

"I did it to save Ben's life," Sam snapped, shame warming her face.

"And you'd be doing it again," Jack insisted. "You and I both know Ben won't last long under the care of your daddy. Think of what's at stake here."

Jack may have been the devil, but he wasn't wrong. Sam had saved her brother's life, but living under Wiley's roof was the kind of thing that ate away at you with every passing day. There were more ways than one to kill someone's spirit, and she knew it all too well.

"Why me?" Sam asked.

"Well, Red," Jack said. "Just know I wouldn't put you up to this if I didn't trust you could do it. In fact, there's not another person on God's green earth better for this job than you."

There was a sincerity to Jack's words that made Sam falter a little. It was almost like he saw something worthwhile within her, that no one else had ever seen. She shook the thought away, suddenly feeling stupid. "Are they gonna hurt her? Kiran?"

"I'd like to think not," Jack said.

"Don't lie to me."

"I wouldn't dare."

"The same thing that happened to Dawson is gonna happen to her, isn't it?"

Jack shrugged. "I am merely a messenger."

Doubt and guilt and disgust brewed in Sam's gut. She felt there was a war happening inside of her. How far would she go to get the life she deserved? How far was too far to save her brother?

The conversation with Neera from last night returned to her then. *All you need to do is play the devil's game,* she'd said. Was this not the same? Maybe Sam could spike Kiran's drink but save her like they planned to save Dawson? She only had to fulfill the *exact* terms of the bargain, then she would be free.

"Fine," Sam agreed, holding her hand out to Jack. "How should I do it?"

Jack slipped an eyedropper-sized bottle into her palm. "One drop should be enough."

Sam willed her expression not to betray her true intentions. "All right."

"All right," Jack repeated.

"You promise to keep your bargain?" Sam asked.

"It's a deal."

This time, he held out his hand for her to shake. Sam hesitantly took it, struggling not to recoil from his touch.

"I'll be seeing you soon, Red." Without another word, he disappeared around the nearest aisle, and then he was gone. It was a *feeling* more than fact.

Sam blinked a few times, righting herself. She felt like she'd been inside Gator's for hours, but when she checked the time on her phone, only ten minutes had passed since she walked through the door. With a shake of her head, she grabbed a nearby plastic container. Dipping it into the fish tank, she scooped out the shimmering minnow she'd been eyeing before Jack had disturbed her. A moment later, she was out the door, with her new pet.

"You stay out of trouble, all right?" Gator called after Sam.

"I always do," Sam said over her shoulder, eyes turning toward the sky as black storm clouds consumed the horizon.

CHAPTER 33

NEERA
50 HOURS

"Make yourself at home," Grant said casually.

Neera hung back in the entryway of Grant Langley's pool house, which sat several yards away from his much larger main house. It technically *was* next to a pool, but it was more a fully furnished home than it was a space for pool toys or cleaning supplies. It was significantly bigger than Room 4 at the Colonial, and nicer than any house she and her mom had ever lived in.

"Wow" was all Neera could say.

Grant walked around the space, his wet sneakers squeaking along the immaculate wood floor. "You got a fully equipped kitchen, one bedroom, one bathroom. I don't know if you watch TV, but there's an eighty-two-inch flat-screen over there. There's basically everything you need, except for food. I don't keep the kitchen stocked here, but if you make a list, my housekeeper can run to the store tomorrow morning."

Heat flushed Neera's cheeks. It was both too much and everything she'd ever wanted.

"Oh, no. I don't need that. I'll be gone by morning anyway." She fiddled with the strap of her guitar case. Grant had insisted on carrying her other bags, which he'd already deposited neatly by the bedroom door.

"That's what you keep sayin'." He crossed his arms, leaning against a wall filled with hanging vintage guitars. "But again, you're welcome to stay however long. I don't much use this space."

"Right, thank you," she told him, flashing a grateful smile.

"There's paper and pen on the table over there. In case the inspiration strikes." Grant nodded to a glass coffee table in the living room. "I don't know about you, but I always get the best ideas when it storms like this."

Neera nodded, still hovering in the doorway. She feared any moment Grant would change his mind and send her packing in the pouring rain. "I'll probably just go to sleep, honestly."

"*Sleep?* It's barely evening." Grant laughed easily, shaking his head. "Come on, kid. Live a little. Have some friends over or somethin'—I don't mind. I'll be out for most of the night anyway."

"Friends, yeah," Neera said. "Maybe I will."

"Just think of this as a little vacation from that dusty old motel. A musician's retreat." He gave her the grand sort of smile men like him paid good money for, before moving toward the door. "I'm heading out, but don't hesitate to call if you need anything."

Grant shut the door behind him, leaving Neera alone in the pool house. She walked around the space, taking it all in. The wall of one side of the house overlooked the pool ornamented with a stone waterfall. The water trickled down artificial rocks and slid into the illuminated water below. Another wall featured a floor-to-ceiling window that looked onto Lake Clearwater, though in the storm, she could barely see past the property's dock.

The third wall of the house was decorated with a few guitars. There were bass, acoustic, and electric. Nothing special, but the instruments were shiny and ornamental. Several glass-enclosed platinum records adorned the wall. Country music legends of Blue Mountain Records.

Neera imagined herself with her own platinum record on a wall. A folkie-blues album that would top the charts someday. The thought had always felt silly, but standing in Grant Langley's pool house, the possibility of it felt just a *little* closer.

Carrying her bags to her new bedroom, Neera heard her phone buzzing somewhere within. She dug it out, grateful to finally see Isaiah's name on the screen. Crashing on the bed, she answered the call.

"Neera, is everything okay?" Isaiah asked. "Sorry I'm getting back to you so late. It's been a long day."

"It's fine." Burrowing into the feather-soft bed, Neera let out a sigh. "Long story short, my mom kicked me out of the house because I'm not going to college in the fall."

"Holy shit," Isaiah gasped. "Where are you now? Are you safe?"

"You're not gonna believe me if I tell you. *I* still can't believe it." Neera let out an anxious laugh, looking around the strange, modernly decorated room. "I'm in Grant *Langley's* pool house. He offered to let me stay here for free."

Isaiah was silent for an uncomfortable beat. Neera could only hear rustling on the other end. She thought the signal cut out before Isaiah finally said, "Look, I'm actually driving to Lake Clearwater now. Could I swing by in thirty?"

Neera frowned at her phone, noticing a shift in Isaiah's tone. "Uh, sure. Yeah. I'll text you the address."

"Sounds good," Isaiah said. "I'll see you soon."

The call ended before Neera could say anything more.

WHEN NEERA ANSWERED the knock at the pool house door, she was surprised by two things: first, the sight of Isaiah looking noticeably *unnerved,* and second, Reid Langley standing at his heel. They both were outfitted in crisp dress shirts and slacks, as if on the way to a party.

"Can we come in?" Isaiah asked, a little breathless. His expression turned sheepish as he hovered in the doorway. "We need to talk."

"Clearly." Neera stepped aside, eyeing Isaiah and then Reid. "Do you like the place?" she asked Isaiah, settling into an armchair in the living room as the boys sat on the couch. The furniture held the distinct smell of newness, as if it'd never been used before today. "Hell of an upgrade from the Colonial."

Isaiah's gaze took in the sight of the room. His eyes lingered on the wall of guitars and platinum records, then settled onto Neera. "It's all very *shiny.*"

"You say that like it's a bad thing."

A strange, sad look crossed Isaiah's face. "Neera," he began, saying her name as if it would break with too much force. "First, Reid wants to help us with Dawson. He thinks his disappearance is connected to his own mother's death six years ago."

"*Oh,*" Neera breathed, suddenly seeing Reid Langley in a new light. He gave her a small, embarrassed wave. "Welcome to the team."

"Thanks," Reid said, his voice small. "Glad to be here."

"Second," Isaiah began, clearing his throat. "Earlier, Reid and I were going over everything we know. I mentioned Second Sons and, uh, he offered some insight."

Neera sat up fully in the armchair. "You know who owns the trust?"

"I have a very strong idea." Reid rubbed the back of his neck.

"Now, I don't know for sure, but being a second son has always been a schtick between my uncle and my father. Russ is the oldest, the golden child, while Grant's always been a bit of an outcast. He's taken to wearing the title like a badge of honor."

"Grant?" Neera went completely still. It was as if her world had been built on shaky ground, now threatening to crumble. "He's behind the threats to my family? The debt? *Everything?*"

The boys both nodded.

Neera glanced around the pool house, its veneer suddenly feeling like a cage. "What's his angle with me, then? Why is he letting me stay here?"

"I don't know," Isaiah said. "But there's no way Grant's looking out for your best interests. There has to be a motive."

Neera narrowed her eyes, insecurity bleeding around the edges of her vision. "Maybe he sees something in me, like I'm worth taking a chance on. Is that so hard to believe?"

"That's not what I'm saying," Isaiah said, rubbing his temples. "I just don't want you to be in danger by staying here."

I bargained with the devil for this opportunity, Neera thought. She wished she could confess that to Isaiah, but there was only one way that conversation would end and she wasn't in the headspace to defend her sanity. She considered her position for a long moment. "I hear you, Isaiah. But maybe we have a leg up here. Maybe, by staying here, I can find out more about Grant and his connection to Dawson's disappearance?" *To Ajay?*

Isaiah considered. "I don't know if that's wise. I mean—"

"I think she has a point," Reid interrupted. "Grant's ego is the size of the sun. He wouldn't suspect anything if she snoops around. This is probably some weird savior complex for him."

Neera nodded absently. "He thinks he's saving me from the very monster he created. I think we have the element of surprise here."

The three of them looked at one another, parceling together this new foundation of trust.

"Did you find out anything from Sam last night?" Isaiah finally asked.

Yeah, that she also made a deal with a devil. Neera carefully considered what to say instead. "It turns out that she was forced into lying about Dawson on the news. She was threatened and didn't have any other choice."

Reid's gray eyes widened. "I fucking knew it."

Isaiah leaned forward on the couch. "Does that mean Dawson is still—?"

"Alive?" Neera finished. "She said he's not dead yet, but I don't know when he will be or what that means exactly. We didn't have long to talk before she had to go back to work."

"Okay," Isaiah said. "Can you find out more from Sam and look into Grant?"

Neera nodded. "What's next for you two then?"

"Tonight is another big Clearwater party at my house," Reid offered. "Everyone will be there, even Grant and Leblanc. Could be a good time for us all to do some digging while they're distracted."

"All right," Isaiah conceded. "Does that work for you, Neera?"

"Let's do it," Neera said, her eyes going to the window, as rain ran down the glass in heavy waves. She looked past the storm, to the massive silhouette of Grant's home sitting yards away.

CHAPTER 34

NEERA
49 HOURS

Neera didn't yet know if Grant had an angle in inviting her to stay or if he'd simply taken an honest interest in her music, but she was determined to find out.

Once the boys were gone, Neera sat beside the pool house's window, anxiously drumming her fingers on her knee as she waited. For something, anything. An hour passed before the garage door of Grant's house opened, revealing him climbing onto a gleaming motorcycle.

At the sight of it, she mused aloud, "Of course he'd drive a Harley."

Grant peeled out of the garage, then out of his driveway. Once she could no longer hear the engine, she hurried to the garage. As she trekked across the expansive backyard, the open garage began to close, as if on a timer. Foolishly, she broke out in a sprint, but reached his home as soon as the garage door shuttered.

She cursed under her breath.

Neera took a step back, taking in the size of the sprawling mansion. It must've been as big as two Colonial motels, if not more. She walked the width of the house, peeking inside the windows and jiggling the doors. Nothing budged.

She shot Isaiah a quick text: *No dice on getting inside his house.*

Isaiah responded a minute later: *That's okay. You can try tomor-*

row. We're gonna check out Leblanc's boat.

Good luck. I'll talk to Sam, Neera responded before pocketing her phone.

With nothing productive to occupy her that night, Neera decided against playing the Yamaha or worrying herself sick. Instead, she dug around the front seat of the Nissan, sorting through used napkins and old receipts, until she finally found it.

A napkin with a phone number scrawled onto it.

Sam's number.

Neera cradled her phone in her hand as she paced the length of the pool house. She debated if she had the courage to call the red-haired girl who'd seen her at her most vulnerable. Sam had seen her vomit the live cicada last night, and she *knew*. She'd understood.

Was it worth exploring that connection between them?

THE SUN WAS sitting low on the flat horizon when Neera arrived at Sam's house. The rain had passed for the time being, leaving a thick wave of humidity in its wake. The cicadas had quieted, with the bellows of tree frogs replacing them in spades. Lightning bugs dotted the air.

While Neera's home at the Colonial was a cage of pines, Sam's home was an expansive vista, far-reaching and open. In the golden hour of evening, the land was warm and welcoming, coated in the shimmer of a fresh summer rain.

"This is beautiful," Neera admired as Sam came out to greet her.

Sam followed her line of sight. "It's not too bad sometimes."

"You live here alone?" Neera asked, eyeing the small trailer.

It was humble, but nothing to judge. She'd lived in many herself.

"Roommates," Sam said. Wryly, she asked, "You ever ridden a four-wheeler?"

Neera arched a thick brow. "Can't say I have."

Sam beamed. "Well, would you like to try?"

Ten minutes later, Sam navigated the four-wheeler around the property, with Neera situated behind her. She had her arms around Sam's waist, her face hesitant against her back.

"Hold on tight," Sam said before she hit the gas, sending the four-wheeler's engine roaring to life.

The four-wheeler peeled through the wet earth, kicking up mud and grass all around them. Sam went nearly forty, navigating them across flat pastures and empty fields with the ever-present pines on both sides. The wind sent Sam's braid flying, while Neera's long hair lashed wildly around her face, but otherwise it was a welcome reprieve from the muggy heat.

They rode like that for a long while before Sam finally slowed. The engine quieted as she turned her head to Neera. "I wanna show you something, but you gotta close your eyes, all right?"

"Yeah, okay," Neera conceded, smiling a little. She shut her eyes, resting her head fully against Sam's back. They rode for a bit more before Sam brought the four-wheeler to a stop, killing the engine.

"I'm climbing off, but keep 'em closed," Sam said. A moment passed before she spoke from Neera's right, "Take my hand."

Hesitantly, Neera held out her hand, and Sam took it in her own. Sam guided her from the four-wheeler to the ground, gently leading her forward. Without her sight, Neera focused on the things she could hear. As always, the katydids and tree frogs. A dog moaned balefully in the distance. In the quiet of the night, even the softer sounds came alive: the hoot of a barred owl, squirrels skittering in the trees around them.

Then she focused on the things she felt. The warm breeze that brushed against her skin, briefly keeping the thick humidity at bay. The tickle of grass and ragweed at her ankles. But it was Sam's hand that Neera felt more than anything else. The warmth of her skin, the electricity of her touch. She didn't know what to do with those thoughts. Her instinct was to pull away, but she only held Sam's hand tighter as they walked.

"All right," Sam said. "You can open them."

Neera opened her eyes, finding herself standing in a wide-open clearing with a small pond a few yards away.

Softly, Sam suggested, "Look up."

Above them was a dazzling sea of white stars, varying in intensity, coating the blackness of the night. She'd never seen so many stars at once. They blanketed the dark, shimmering and mesmerizing. There were thousands upon thousands of them, more than she could ever hope to count.

Neera swallowed, finding herself speechless. She felt entranced by the sky, her head angling up and up and up, causing her to spin in circles. It was as if her eyes couldn't possibly look at them all, but begged to.

"Cool, right?" Sam asked.

Neera pulled her gaze away, returning to Sam. "I've never seen stars like this around here."

"It's a rare thing," Sam said. "But this is my secret spot. The only place in all of Langley County the light pollution barely touches."

The two lay at the base of an oak tree and gazed up at the stars. The longer Neera looked at them, the more entranced she became. It was so expansive, so incredible, she felt foolish for thinking she'd ever seen a proper night sky before.

"How'd you find this place?" she asked after a spell of silence.

Sam shrugged. "This land's owned by a family friend. Good guy named Gator. I used to come out here a lot when I was younger to fish with my daddy."

"And now you come here to stare at the sky?"

"To clear my head. Worries seem a lot smaller when you look at all this."

Neera was quiet for a very long time before she said, "Yeah, they do."

"What're you thinkin' about?" Sam asked.

Neera exhaled a heavy sigh. "You ever feel like bad shit just follows you wherever you go? Like you'll never be free of it, no matter what you do?"

Sam hummed in agreement. "Every damn day."

"How do you cope?"

"I don't." Sam snorted. "I just break things. Don't be like me."

Neera laughed. "Well, my way of coping is running away. That's my solution for everything—getting the hell out and never looking back."

"Where will you run to next?" Sam asked.

Neera sat up on her elbows, considering her answer. "I wanna go someplace where I can see stars like this every single night. Maybe in the mountains, or by the ocean. Somewhere beautiful, far away. I'm not picky as long as it's a place I can call my own."

"Sounds like my kind of place." Sam rolled over and propped herself up, her green eyes now on Neera. "Maybe I can come visit sometime?"

Neera cracked a smile. "I'd like that."

It was then that Neera found herself leaning closer to Sam.

Their hands were touching again, brushing against each other. Sam looked into Neera's eyes, her gaze soft and searching. Neera didn't know what to do with that closeness.

In the humid night air above, a crow cawed, high and shrill, taking the moment with it. Neera pulled away, while Sam cleared her throat.

Sam looked to the sky, her eyes tracking the crow's silhouette, then went back to Neera. "You wanna talk about what happened last night? With the cicada?"

Neera's hand went to her throat, grazing her fingers over the scabbed cuts that ran down her neck. The awful memory of the buzzing cicada in her mouth. "What's there to say?"

"I saw you play up on that stage," Sam said slowly. "It was *different* from the audition. Not that you weren't good before, but that performance was something else entirely. The way your music made me feel—hell, even the whole crowd feel. It was like everyone was frozen in place while you sang. That was nothing short of *magic*."

Neera went still. When she'd made her bargain with Crow, she never expected this. A musical gift beyond simply being remembered. He'd given her something *more*—the ability to bewitch an audience. A gift of power in a world where she had very little. "I did what I had to do."

"I get it," Sam said knowingly. "I really do."

Neera studied Sam, realizing her splint was gone, but her scrapes and cuts lingered. Even in the starlight, she saw healed scar tissue all over her freckled skin. Tiny little marks from a lifetime spent bleeding. "Will your brother be okay?"

Sam's gaze turned hard. "Ben's safe for now, but I don't know how long it's gonna last." She sat up, pulling her knees to her chest. "I saved his life, but it's not enough to protect him forever."

Neera thought of Ajay—how the timing had been all wrong. How, if it had happened three years later, she could've saved him. The crow cawed again, circling overhead. "You played the hand you were dealt. There's nothing shameful in that."

"Yeah, maybe," Sam said, glancing at Neera. "When you said we could save Dawson last night, what'd you mean by that exactly?"

Neera ran her fingers through her hair, the sticky humidity tangling it into a knotted mess. "Well, where do I begin?" She filled Sam in on the trio's various theories and clues about Dawson, finishing with Isaiah and Reid's plan to investigate Casey Leblanc's boat that night.

"Wait, *Reid's* actually helpin' you and Isaiah?" Sam's tone turned acidic. "Never thought I'd see the day when he grew a pair."

"Y'all have history?" Neera asked self-consciously.

"Not in the way you're thinkin'—he's not my type," Sam said coyly. "He and Dawson became close this past year. It's hard not to blame him a little for what's happened. But I'm at fault, too." She sat in silence for a long moment. "I think I know somethin' that could help." She checked the time on her phone. "Ask them if we can all meet up tonight once they're done."

Neera nodded, typing a quick text to Isaiah.

Miles away, along the flat horizon, lightning struck.

"Looks like the storm's rolling back in," Sam said. "We should go before it gets us."

When the girls returned to the four-wheeler, Neera found the crow sitting on the handles. It watched them with its heavy black gaze before taking flight, disappearing, once more, into the cover of night.

CHAPTER 35

ISAIAH
48 HOURS

That Friday night, Isaiah roamed the edge of a labyrinth of white-cloth tables, where the flickering outdoor lamps gave way to dark. With his camera in hand, he evaded small talk with ease, choosing instead to make the person in front of him the star, if only for a moment. The guests at the Clearwater event found the camera a novelty, obliging the opportunity to be photographed by him.

He hated wasting the film, but he relished the chance to observe, rather than participate. Because on that night, participation meant shuffling at the heel of Laurence Johnson as he made his rounds around the stiff, red-tie party, and Isaiah would rather do anything else.

So instead, there he was, photographing women wearing modest black dresses holding champagne flutes, and men in Italian suits who clasped shoulders, shook hands, clinked glasses. It was a distinctly different event than the Cicada's Song from the previous night. This one felt bigger, *weightier*, as powerful political and economic denizens of the Southeast gathered like flies.

Someone cleared their throat behind him. He turned, finding Reid Langley emerging from the shadows like an impeccably tailored wraith. "Jesus, Langley. Don't scare me like that."

"My bad." Reid moved to stand beside him, grabbing a drink from the passing server's tray. He sipped delicately as his eyes roamed the party. "How was the boat ride? Anything unusual?"

Isaiah and his father had ridden with Leblanc and his wife on the ride over. He shook his head. "Nothing that I could see."

"That just means he's good at covering his tracks," Reid said pointedly. "You ready?"

It was a simple enough question on the surface, but Isaiah understood its double meaning. "Almost, just need the key."

"Right, right." Reid shifted on his feet, eyes turning toward the manicured grass. He seemed to wear his discomfort on his sleeve, doing very little to appear confident.

"Answer this for me," Isaiah said. Across the lawn, past the tables and schmoozing Southern socialites, he watched his father. He stood beside Russ Langley, in conversation with a man who looked a lot like the governor. "How *involved* do you think my father is with whatever's going on here?"

"Honestly?" Reid followed his gaze. He downed his glass of champagne, then rubbed his mouth with the back of his hand. Wincing slightly, he said, "I have no idea. But I do know he's been rising in the ranks around here for years."

Since he was a teenager, Isaiah thought. Since he'd attended the coveted Clearwater Academy. Was that where it all began for his father, leading him to this party, this very night, with this elite group of guests deciding the fate of everyday Georgians?

The handshakes on the Langley estate that night meant laws would be passed, bills would be drafted, amendments would be made in favor of those with summer homes and offshore bank accounts.

Isaiah grabbed a glass of champagne from the nearby server's tray. Like Reid, he downed the glass in a swift motion. He inhaled sharply, then said, "It's time."

Reid's head swiveled, his gaze finding Casey Leblanc across the lawn. He was sitting beside his wife, absently nursing a drink, his eyes drooping as if he were falling asleep at the table. "Let's do this."

REID

FROM A SAFE distance, Reid watched Isaiah saunter across the lawn, his steps sure and measured.

He greeted Casey Leblanc and his wife, Wendy, making a show with his camera. The couple rose, standing with their arms interlocked and party smiles on their faces. Isaiah's film camera flashed, memorializing the well-dressed pair. Small talk was exchanged before Wendy stepped away to another conversation. But Isaiah lingered with Leblanc. A moment later, the young attorney passed something to Isaiah before clasping him on the back and returning to his wife's side.

Several people stopped to shake Isaiah's hand or ask him for a photograph as he made his way back to Reid. He watched the judge's son move through the party with ease. Unlike Reid, Isaiah knew how to play the game, or at least, played it convincingly enough.

Finally, Isaiah appeared at his side, dangling something shiny in his hand.

Reid's gray eyes widened. "Just like that, huh?"

"Trust is a powerful thing," Isaiah said, smirking softly. "I told him I forgot my other camera lens on his boat. He handed me the keys without question."

"Well, damn," Reid said, impressed by Isaiah's skill. "I guess you've been doing this for a while? Investigations and stuff?"

Isaiah began walking toward the Langley dock. "I've gotten pretty good at finding out the truth of things. Sometimes, the easiest thing to do is simply ask."

"Noted," Reid said, falling in step beside him. His family's dock was no marina, which meant the handful of boats moored along it bobbed in near total dark. If they didn't attract undue attention, they could board Leblanc's boat with none the wiser.

"It's this one at the end," Isaiah said, pointing in the spare light from the party. He then noticed Reid hesitating a few feet back. "You ready, Langley?"

"I'm just . . . I'm gathering myself," Reid said, anxiously glancing around them.

"It's okay to be nervous," Isaiah said. "What we're doing is objectively stupid."

Reid relaxed a little. "I can't tell if I'm more scared of what we may find, or the prospect of finding nothing."

Isaiah nodded to the boat. "We won't know anything unless we look ourselves."

The boys waited until they were crouched aboard the cabin cruiser's cockpit before pulling out their phones, switching on the flashlights. Reid was impressed by the size of the boat. For a man who'd started a campaign for solar energy in Lake Clearwater, Leblanc seemed to spare no expense when it came to decking out the cruiser like a second home. "What're we looking for exactly?"

"I'm not sure yet," Isaiah whispered as he struggled to open the door that led to the cabin. "But we'll likely know it when we see it."

"Here, let me," Reid offered, finding the door's hidden keyhole with ease. "Not much of a lake-goer, are you?"

Isaiah snorted. "I can proudly say I am not."

Reid went down the steps first. He studied the small space, with its foldout leather couch by the bow, the kitchenette along the wall, then the tiny bathroom and stowaway closet in the corner. Isaiah shut the cabin door behind them, his eyebrows furrowing as he looked over the space beside Reid.

"Ah, there it is," Isaiah said. He stepped toward the couch, pulling his lens from between two cushions.

Reid shook his head in confusion. "Wait—I thought you lied

to Leblanc about the lens?"

"*Partial* lie." Isaiah slid the narrow lens in his khaki pocket. "Leaving this behind was my insurance."

"Jesus," Reid said. "You're good at this."

"There's no option to be anything less."

The boys fell silent as they each took to a different side of the cabin, hands combing over the cabinets, the nooks, the crannies. Minutes passed, but there was nothing out of place. Nothing that screamed to Reid that Leblanc had any connection with Dawson at all.

From beside him, Isaiah dug through the small closet. "Look at this tackle box. There's a lock on it."

Reid moved across the floor, kneeling beside him. He studied the small cabinet, seeing an array of rods and nets with the tags still on them. The equipment looked as if it had never been used. "I've never taken Leblanc to be much of a fisherman."

"Agreed." Isaiah studied the tackle box, spinning it around. "This is weird, right? Who locks up their tackle?"

Reid eyed the box. It was an expensive brand, sturdy and nearly impossible to open without a key. "Someone with something to hide."

Isaiah pulled the cruiser's keys from his pocket, and they both stared at it. Neither one moved to open the box, as if they were both afraid of what they'd find inside. Finally, he asked, "You wanna do the honors?"

Slowly, Reid took the key from Isaiah's hand. As he tried to unlock the tackle box, a howl sounded from outside the cruiser.

The boys fumbled for their phones and killed the flashlights. They remained frozen in the dark as a chorus of howls rang out, followed by laughter and heavy footsteps tapping along the dock. It must've been a group, and they were close.

"What do we do?" Reid whispered in growing panic.

"Quiet," Isaiah said. "*Listen.*"

Reid went still, straining his ears as footsteps sounded above them. Someone was on the boat. Their footfalls were uneven, as if stumbling, as they moved across the deck. The person barreled down the steps to the cabin's unlocked door, banging on it loudly. A muffled grunt sounded on the other side of it. The person then began fumbling for the door handle, jiggling it open after several attempts.

When it seemed as if they were about to push through the door, a voice called out, "That's not our boat, idiot!"

"Oh, shit," someone slurred. It sounded like Jonah's voice. "My bad, no need to name call!"

Reid crept to the cruiser's nearest porthole and peeked out the window. He watched as Jonah stumbled up the boat's steps and joined a group of his friends on the dock. They all dogpiled him as they carried bottles of alcohol and red plastic cups in their hands.

A moment later, the group boarded a different boat that was a few yards down. The engine sounded, and they were off, howling into the night.

"All clear," Reid announced, letting out a heavy breath. He leaned his head against the wall and closed his eyes, trying to calm his racing heart. "It was just my brother and his dick friends."

Isaiah was quiet for a beat, as if to give Reid a moment to collect himself. He then asked, "Do your siblings think your mom really . . . *drowned*?"

"I don't know." Reid opened his eyes, realizing Isaiah had turned the flashlight back on. The cruiser felt eerier somehow. "I'm not sure it even matters. They weren't as close with her as I was. I think they knew that there was something different about her—the way she didn't fit into Lake Clearwater. They were always more interested in pleasing our father anyway."

Isaiah nodded, his expression solemn. "That makes sense."

Reid moved across the floor, returning to the tackle box. "Okay, let's do this."

The first three keys didn't work. The lock *clicked* open courtesy of the fourth. When they flipped open the tackle box, it unfolded into tiered sections, with the biggest section filled to the brim with sharp, gleaming fishhooks. His heartbeat thudded in his chest as he carefully placed his hand in the box.

Gently, Reid dug around the tackle box's contents, fingers searching for anything that felt out of the ordinary. Then he felt it, at the very bottom. Something that wasn't a fishhook at all. But it seemed to be taped down. "There's something here."

"What is it?" Isaiah asked, his voice taut.

"I'm not sure." When Reid pulled his hand from the box, it was a butchered mess of tiny, bloody scrapes. He barely noticed the pain as he dumped the contents of the tackle box onto the floor, sending the hooks sliding in every direction. "*Holy shit.* This is Dawson's."

Duct-taped to the bottom of the box was Dawson's watch, with the familiar sun-bleached leather band and the broken watch face. Except now, the glass was shattered. Reid held the watch to the light, and he thought he saw flecks of dried blood staining the leather.

Isaiah was preoccupied with his own finding. He pulled something else from the tackle box, unwrapping it from the duct tape. "There's a key here, too."

Reid blinked, turning his attention back to Isaiah. "A key to *what*?"

"A room key," Isaiah said slowly, meeting Reid's gaze. "For the Colonial motel."

Why did Leblanc have these two things, kept so intentionally hidden from prying eyes?

A phone buzzed, startling the boys. Isaiah cursed beneath

his breath, eyeing his phone's screen. "My father's asking for me. We need to go."

Reid hesitated, looking around the tiny cabin. He'd made a mess with the hooks. If Leblanc came looking for them now, they'd be hard-pressed to lie their way out of it. "Should we take this stuff? What if he comes looking for it?"

Isaiah shook his head. "No, but we can do this instead." He snapped several photos of the key, the watch, the tackle box with his phone. Then, for good measure, he took photos of the objects with his film camera. "This is enough to go off for now. We don't want to raise Leblanc's suspicion. I mean, he clearly did *something* to Dawson."

"Yeah," Reid said, his voice coming out hard. His hands shook as he taped the watch and the key back at the bottom of the tackle box. He then scraped the hooks back in the box, while Isaiah grabbed the stray ones from across the room. A few minutes later and the cabin was in the same shape they'd found it in.

As they climbed out of the cabin and returned to the boat's helm, Reid bemoaned, "We still don't have enough to go on."

But Isaiah ignored him, looking past him to something Reid couldn't see. He whispered, "Look at that."

Reid tilted his phone's flashlight in the direction Isaiah pointed, the light lingering on a small security camera facing away from them. It was embedded in a floodlight on the stern, easy to miss for the average, untrained eye. It was angled to watch the back of the cruiser. From its position, it could reasonably record every person that walked onto the boat and walked off. Whistling low, he whispered, "We need to see what's on that camera."

Isaiah nodded. "Leblanc is smart enough to keep the recordings digitized. If I can figure out a way to get into his computer at the firm, I have a feeling we'll find out exactly what happened to Dawson."

CHAPTER 36

ISAIAH
45 HOURS

For all of Isaiah's strengths, patience was low on his list of exemplary qualities. He was entranced by the path toward knowledge, but waiting to learn something, when it was *just* out of reach, was enough to drive him mad.

Later that night, after the party had long since ended, he sat in the passenger seat of Reid's Land Rover while Reid filled in Neera and Sam on the findings of Leblanc's boat. Isaiah remained quiet, lost in his own thoughts, as he considered how he was meant to learn Leblanc's computer password.

I'm so close.

"What do you think, Isaiah?" Neera asked.

Isaiah returned to the present. "Sorry?"

"What Sam just said about Dawson—what do you think?"

Isaiah angled in the seat, turning to look back at her. The four of them were awash in artificial light from the Rover's dashboard, casting stark shadows across their faces. Storm clouds blotted dark against the night sky, blocking out any light from the moon. "Would you mind repeating it?"

"I was saying," Sam began, "that I think Dawson's disappearance is related to his new job. The one working for my daddy, and by extension, for Russ Langley."

Isaiah looked pointedly at Reid. "Did you know—?"

"No," Reid said quickly. "He never told me what the job was. Only that it paid well and could lead to something better down the line. This is news to me."

Isaiah was reminded of his interview with Andrea. The blood Neera had found in Dawson's motel room. The email. Dawson's awareness that something bad was going to happen to him. All the little puzzle pieces began to assemble before him. "If he was working with Wiley, what if that job was making him do things that he wasn't willing to do? Something related to all these people that go missing around town?" He glanced at Reid, then at Neera. "What if the job has something to do with all the people who've *died* around here in strange ways?"

Neera visibly bristled as the question settled over them, her gaze lingering on Sam. It was a strange sensation to be aware of their individual crisscrossing histories and motivations leading to this moment.

"Dawson got a new place when he started working . . . right, Reid?" Sam asked, breaking the heavy silence. "Did you ever see it? Do you know where it is?"

"No." Reid cleared his throat. "It was another secret."

"Great," Sam sighed, rolling her green eyes. "I'm willing to bet whatever's out there is something Dawson had to hide. Something that could finally give us some real answers."

"How're we supposed to find it?" Isaiah asked, frustration growing in the edges of his voice.

"One thing I know is that Russ never paid my daddy off the books," Sam said. "He washed the money through his family's various businesses, including the Tavern. Maybe Dawson was paid the same way? Maybe his new address can be found in the restaurant's office?"

Reid nodded in agreement. "My father does like a paper trail. He says it helps keep all parties involved *accountable*."

"Okay," Isaiah conceded. "The Tavern it is. Are we doing

this now?" He looked between Sam and Neera. "Please tell me one of you has a key."

"No, but I know where to find one," Sam answered.

Ten minutes later, the four of them stood outside the Tavern's back door, as Sam knelt on the ground, unlocking a tiny lockbox attached to the wall. She unlocked it with ease, then led them inside and into the pitch-black kitchen. An EXIT sign shone above them, sending shades of red glinting off the steel, sharp surfaces.

Once they were through the kitchen and the alarm was turned off, Sam and Neera led them to the back of the restaurant and to the Tavern's office door.

Neera said, "So, the plan is that Sam will stand watch, Reid will be outside the door, and you and I will look around the office. Should give us enough opportunity to split if anyone shows up unannounced."

Once Isaiah and Neera were inside, Sam shut the door gently behind them, cloaking them in near darkness.

"Should we turn on the lights?" Neera asked.

Isaiah pointed to the windows across the room. "The windows face the water. It may look suspicious if the office lights are on in the middle of the night."

"Fair enough," Neera said. "Flashlights?"

Isaiah turned his on by way of response. He moved the light around the room, taking in the space. There were the usual office features: a desk with a computer, a bookshelf, filing cabinets. On the far side of the room, beside the windows, was a chair and a guitar.

"I'll take the filing cabinet if you'll take the desk," Isaiah suggested.

Neera nodded in agreement. Isaiah began opening the filing cabinet drawers, while Neera riffled through the desk. "We're looking for what, exactly?" she asked.

"Any paperwork on Dawson," Isaiah said. "Or anything suspicious."

"*Suspicious,*" Neera repeated. "All right."

SAM

IN THE HALLWAY, Sam studied Reid Langley. She was standing at the far end, with one eye on the Tavern's front door, and the other on Reid kneeling outside Grant's office. Her gaze kept flitting back to him as if he might disappear if she wasn't looking. He'd kept his own eyes trained downward for the past few minutes, likely not brave enough to face her.

Sam thought she had her feelings under control, but the sight of Reid had sent a tremor of anger through her. He was a walking reminder of what happened to Ben, of what Jonah Langley had done to them both without any repercussions. She was reminded of the fight with Dawson a month ago, of her raw grief, of what *she'd* done—of all the awful feelings threatening to boil over if she didn't keep herself together.

Without thinking, she said, "Dawson's barely been missing more than a week and you've already made new friends. You sure move on quick."

Reid looked up. "They're not—I mean—it's not what you think."

Sam drew closer, abandoning her post at the end of the hall. "Was he just a Carrion plaything for you?" she pressed. "A trailer-trash toy you only kept around to piss off your daddy?"

"I'm hurting just as you are, Sam," Reid said, his voice low and strained. He stood up. "Or, maybe even more than you. At least Dawson and I were speaking before he disappeared. I didn't get on the news and lie about seeing him before he 'drowned.'"

Sam flinched. "Don't talk about things you don't understand."

"Then clarify for me, will you?" Reid demanded. "What was so bad that made you lie like that? It was about money, wasn't it? Tell me, Sam, what's your price? What does it cost to betray your best friend?"

"I don't owe you shit, Reid." Sam leaned against the wall. "You're no saint anyway."

Hurt flashed across Reid's face. "What does that even mean?"

"The hit-and-run accident," Sam began. The memory of the collision tasted metallic in her mouth. She could still *hear* the scraping metal, feel the way the car had contorted around her body. "How's Jonah holding up afterward? Is he okay?"

Reid's gray eyes grew wide. "How'd you . . . ?"

"I didn't know for certain, but I do now," Sam said coolly. "Tell me, Reid, what was *your* price to protect Jonah's secret?"

Reid didn't respond before the office door opened. Isaiah stepped out, holding a piece of paper in his hands. "I found something. Dawson's pay stubs from just before he went missing."

Reid struggled to wipe the shame from his face. "Yeah?" Isaiah passed the paper to him.

Sam joined them, looking it over. The pay stub detailed a drastic change in Dawson's pay in the past month, going from minimum wage to suddenly getting paid a grand per week before he'd gone missing in June. A year of that kind of salary and he would've been making twice as much as the average

Langley County resident. It was nearly the same salary her daddy made.

Reid pointed to an address line under Dawson's name. "That must be where he was staying."

"And I guess when things went bad, he must've checked in at the motel to figure out his next move," Isaiah said.

Sam murmured, "But they took him before he could talk to anyone. Or so they thought."

A shatter rang from the office, sending the three of them scrambling through the doorway.

"Neera?" Isaiah called out, shining his flashlight around the dark space. The light landed on her across the room, kneeling on the floor, surrounded by broken glass. "Are you okay?"

As Sam neared, she realized Neera's hand was bleeding. "*Shit*—she's hurt." To Reid, she said, "There's a first aid kit behind the bar. Go get it." He nodded, then sped out of the office.

"Neera?" Isaiah asked again, his voice softer. He knelt beside her. "What happened?"

Sam hovered along the wall. She wanted to be by Neera's side but recognized the closeness of the moment. It wasn't meant for her.

Neera opened and closed her mouth, seemingly unable to speak. She could only shake her head. After a long moment, she unfolded her closed palm, offering her bloodied hand to Isaiah. In the low light, Sam could just barely make out a small, triangular object. It took a second for her to realize it was a guitar pick.

"It's Ajay's," Neera said, her voice cracking a little. "His lucky guitar pick. The only one he used. He carried it on him, in his pocket. *Always* in his right pocket."

Delicately, Isaiah asked, "Are you sure?"

"It's rare. You can't even find one like it on eBay." Neera's eyebrows furrowed. "It wasn't in his things when he died. I couldn't find it anywhere." She rubbed her eyes, smearing blood and flecks of glass across her cheek. "I *looked,* Isaiah. For the past three fucking years, I've looked."

Three years ago? A terrible feeling began to build in Sam's gut.

Neera pointed to the wall. "It'd been hanging right there, in a display case. Right there. Why does he—*how* does Grant have this?"

Isaiah glanced around the room, then met Sam's strained gaze. "We need to clean this up, Neera, okay? Then we can figure this out."

Neera blinked a few times, as if waking from a dream. Her eyes came into focus as she looked around the mess at her feet. "Jesus Christ. I wasn't thinking. I just—I saw it and . . . I'm sorry." She kept staring at the pick. "It doesn't make sense that Grant has this. It's wrong."

"Should you really be going back to his house?" Isaiah asked. "I don't know if it's safe."

"He's not gonna hurt me," Neera said.

Isaiah didn't look convinced. "How do you know that?"

"Because I'm Grant Langley's newest investment." Bitterness coated her words.

"Even still, I don't know if—"

"I'll stay the night with her," Sam interrupted, peeling away from the wall. "I can keep Neera company until morning. That'll give her some time to figure out what she wants to do."

Neera nodded. "I'd like that."

"Fine," Isaiah conceded. "We can discuss any moves tomorrow."

CHAPTER 37

NEERA
44 HOURS

It was past midnight, and Neera couldn't sleep.

She was in a daze. Her strumming hand was cut to pieces from breaking the glass case that had held Ajay's guitar pick. She didn't remember breaking it—only *seeing* it through the glass, and then it was in her hands. The time between those two moments was lost.

A summer storm had since returned to Langley County, thunder rumbling overhead. She couldn't bring herself to let the pick go, cradling it in her hand.

Ajay had been a man who lived by a code of rock 'n' roll and superstition. Some were old ways learned from her grandparents, carried over from Punjab—never keep a chipped piece of dishware, as it causes ill fortune. Only wear white to funerals. Then there were others, learned from a life of music. He'd taught Neera to always keep a piece of luck on her. The object could be anything, but it must always be present.

A metal kara on her left wrist, a gift from Nani, was hers.

But the guitar pick was his.

It had a marbled, emerald-green design that matched her birthstone. She hadn't seen it in three years, yet there it was now, in her bandaged palm. She studied it in the spare light from her phone's screen, illuminating the plastic sheen of its surface. When she tilted the pick a certain way, she thought she saw some sort of engraving embedded in it. But as she looked more closely, the etchings vanished.

Must be a trick of the light, she thought.

Sighing, Neera crawled out of bed and padded into the living room.

Sam's voice came from the dark, "Can't sleep?"

Neera fumbled for the nearest lamp, then flicked it on. "Nope."

On the couch, Sam sat up, clearing away space beside her. "I can't, either."

Neera joined her. "Why not?"

Sam was quiet for an uncomfortably long time. "Can I tell you somethin'?"

"Go ahead," Neera said. She angled herself on the couch, studying Sam's face in the spare light from the lamp. Their feet were just barely touching, side by side, on the couch cushion.

"The night I made my bargain with the . . . my little brother had been with me. Ben was in my car because I was trying to protect him. He'd called me from a sleepover that night. You see, even at ten, he has a problem with wetting the bed. He was afraid to fall asleep in case he did it in front of his friends. My daddy gets so *angry* when he does it. He only makes it worse for Ben—more shameful. Life's funny that way. Ben only wets the bed because he's scared. He's scared of our daddy and that fear bleeds into his dreams."

The lamplight flickered as the power surged from the storm. "So, of course, Ben called me to pick him up. We were on the way home when the other car hit us. It was bad. I knew Ben wasn't gonna make it. When the devil appeared, when he offered me a chance to save my brother's life, I didn't hesitate. No matter the consequences. And now, my daddy made it so that I can't even legally see my brother, much less protect him.

Because that's what Ben truly needs—protection from our daddy."

"Because he's a dangerous man," Neera observed in a low voice.

Sam nodded. "My daddy is a bad man whose job is to do bad things. I've known this for a long time, like the way you know the sky is blue. But I didn't understand the truth of it until three years ago. I was fifteen when I knew it for certain. Middle of the night, and I knew he was at work. He didn't like us eating past suppertime, but I was in the kitchen anyway. He wasn't expecting anyone to be up when he walked in." Fear and memory flashed in her eyes. "But *I* was. All I saw was blood seeped into his clothes. Stained them black. He didn't yell. Nothin'. Just told me to go to bed. When I saw him the next morning, there wasn't a scar on him. Not even a bruise. The blood had been someone else's."

Neera let Sam's story settle in the air. Her gaze was drawn across the room, as the storm battered the window, sending waves of heavy rain slanting sideways against the glass. She watched the droplets fall in a steady rhythm as she began to understand the weight of Sam's words.

"Sam," she said quietly, "when exactly was this?"

"Sometime around early May," Sam said. "I remember it was around finals."

Neera's blood went cold. "May fifth?"

Sam wouldn't look her in the eye. "Yeah, that sounds about right."

There was a ringing in Neera's ears. "And you're certain of what you saw?"

Sam nodded, her freckled face grim.

Neera was on her feet and out the door before she realized what she was doing. She was running toward Grant's home in the thunderstorm. Just as she reached the back door, Sam caught up to her.

"*Neera,*" Sam yelled above the rain. "Stop!"

But Neera was barely listening, barely aware of the other girl at all as she banged on Grant's door. She struggled with the knob, desperate to push the door open. Desperate to get inside. Desperate to demand answers from Grant.

Because it was his fault Ajay was dead.

Grant had Ajay killed.

"He can't get away with this," Neera screamed, fists still hitting the door. She kept pounding the doorframe, over and over again, until Sam grabbed her wrists, then pulled her close in the rain. Neera struggled against her for only a moment before she succumbed to her fury—her grief.

In Sam's arms, Neera allowed herself to cry.

SAM

38 HOURS

BEFORE DAWN THE next morning, Sam awoke nestled in bed beside Neera. For the briefest of moments, she forgot about last night, and reached out to brush a loose strand of black hair from Neera's face. As Sam's fingers hovered near her cheek, she froze.

Neera deserves better than this, Sam thought bitterly. *She deserves better than me.*

The little vial Jack had given her still sat in her backpack, a twisted reminder of their new bargain. Even worse, Sam hadn't yet decided what she was going to do.

To spike Kiran's drink felt like more than a gamble—it

would be a death sentence. Sam looked at Neera then, still and sleeping. Wiley had taken so much from her already. Was Sam strong enough not to do the same?

The sun was beginning to rise once she slipped out of the pool house that Saturday morning. She'd left a note on the coffee table but didn't wake her to say goodbye. Guilt hung heavy over Sam as she walked down Grant's driveway in the rain, though it was only a light drizzle now.

At the end of the drive sat Clayton's old truck, idling.

"Thanks for comin' to get me," Sam said once she was buckled within the cab.

"Sure," Bailey said, navigating through Lake Clearwater's manicured winding roads. They were at the gates when she finally asked, "Do you wanna talk about it?"

Sam shook her head. She kept her gaze trained out the window as the rain persisted. Carrion was all lush green and gray skies as the flatland welcomed the storm. "Just take me home."

27 HOURS

NOT EVEN GALE-FORCE winds could close the Tavern's doors that late afternoon. Tourists and Clearwater residents alike crowded the room, watching a live baseball game on the TVs while the storm of the summer raged outside. Sam could barely hear the thunder over the obnoxious drunken yells from those watching the game.

"Jesus, I'd rather be home," Sam groaned as she clocked into work, greeting Kiran at the bar.

"You and me both," she said a little sadly as she shook a silver shaker glass.

Neera's mom wasn't exactly the friendliest coworker, though she was her favorite. She had a no-bullshit way of speaking that Sam always found refreshing. But even through the woman's tough veneer, Sam could sense something was off with her.

A man cleared his throat behind Sam, sending her head swiveling.

"My usual, if you'd be so kind," Grant Langley said as he approached the bar, leaning his elbows lazily against the counter. He held a smirk on his sun-kissed face, a wry sort of look he seemed to reserve for Kiran alone. "The weather got you down, Kiran?"

Sam tried not to acknowledge Grant's presence, pretending to be occupied with her phone.

"I'm doing just fine, Mr. Langley," Kiran responded as she poured gin into a glass. She behaved in stark contrast to most of the Tavern's employees, who all but kissed the ground Grant walked on whenever he made an appearance.

Sam didn't care about ass-kissing, either, even if he was the owner of the Tavern. But it didn't matter in that moment anyway—Grant's eyes only saw Kiran.

"I'm glad to hear it," Grant said, leaning a little farther across the bar. "I'll admit, I was concerned after I heard what happened between you and Neera. I didn't take you for the type of parent to kick the kid out. Never seemed your style."

A vein pulsed on Kiran's forehead, her whole body noticeably going rigid. "What goes on between me and *my* daughter is none of your business."

"Oh?" Grant feigned concern. "Do you even know where Neera is?" He gestured to the storm pounding against the Tavern's windows. "In weather like this, no less."

Sam couldn't be sure, but Kiran looked as if she wanted to punch him.

"Tell Jason I'm taking my fifteen," Kiran said to Sam as she moved from around the bar. "And run those drinks over to table one for me, will you?"

Grant laughed at Kiran's retreating back and then reached behind the counter, grabbing an expensive bottle of brown liquor and three glasses. He then joined his buddies across the room, sliding into a seat beside them as they cheered at the TVs.

Sam glanced at table one and froze. Jonah Langley sat among his buddies, enthralled in the baseball game playing across the Tavern. She looked between the Styrofoam cup with Kiran's name written on it and the tray of drinks. The vial from Jack felt heavy in her server's apron as her decision became clearer.

"Fuck this," Sam whispered.

With a sly move of her hand, she poured the vial's contents into one of the cups, watching as it dissolved completely. She then walked the tray to table one with a saccharine smile on her lips, careful to place the spiked one directly in front of Jonah. The group of boys barely acknowledged her as they made animal noises at the TV before mindlessly sipping the drinks.

From across the room, Sam then watched as Jonah picked up his glass and knocked it back in a greedy, indulgent gulp.

CHAPTER 38

NEERA
26 HOURS

It was the day before the Fourth, and Neera didn't want to face the world. She'd found Sam's note on the table when she awoke—*Can we talk later?*—then promptly turned her phone off.

She didn't want to talk to anyone, not even Isaiah. She needed time to think, to really consider what it meant that Grant had Ajay's guitar pick. That he was, quite possibly, the man behind Second Sons. That he was responsible for the debt terrorizing her family, all the while dangling a golden carrot of opportunity over her head. It didn't make sense.

Why is he doing this?

And then there was Sam's story from last night, when she'd found her dad covered in blood three years ago. Neera felt as if a horrible truth was forming before her.

But she was determined to get real answers that day.

Neera's gaze stayed fixed on the garage door that afternoon. She'd already heard Grant's motorcycle leave an hour ago, but then there was the housekeeper to deal with. Grant had said she was welcome to write up a grocery list. Now was her chance.

She quickly scrawled down an unnecessarily long list of groceries, then greeted the housekeeper at the back door. "Could you please get these for me today?" she asked with forced politeness.

Grant's housekeeper studied the list, then Neera. "Yes, ma'am." She checked the time on her phone. "I'll leave shortly."

Neera thanked her, then returned to her waiting perch in the pool house. She felt as if she were gearing for a fight, all the while forcing away the raw feeling of grief welling up within her. As it was, she didn't know whether to scream or weep.

Focus, Neera thought. *You don't know anything for sure, yet.*

A car door slammed. Neera turned her head toward the sound, finding the housekeeper starting her car in the driveway. A minute later she was gone, the garage door descending.

Neera ran across the lawn, skidding onto her knees and through Grant's garage just as it closed behind her.

If Grant had kept Ajay's guitar pick in the Tavern's office, what might he be hiding in his own home?

He was a collector, after all.

Neera didn't know how much time she had, so she got to work. Thankfully, aside from the music industry paraphernalia on his walls, the home was otherwise minimalist. While other McMansions in Lake Clearwater were massive just because, Grant's was modern and sparse. The spare rooms were decorated with only the essentials, making it easy for Neera to comb through empty drawers and closets.

This was his summer home, so it didn't really have much within it.

Neera had almost resigned herself to giving up, until she found Grant's study. A nearly empty room with a desk, a massive painting hanging behind it, and expansive, towering windows that looked onto Lake Clearwater. Even in the rain, with the study sitting high above the ground, it was clear the windows overlooked the world.

Neera went through the desk, which gave her flashbacks of the night before. There hadn't been anything to implicate

Grant at the Tavern, but she hoped things would be different here. It wasn't until she opened the final drawer that she found a scrapbook. An old, dusty thing that was in stark contrast to the restrained minimalism around her.

She settled onto the desk chair, flipping through relics of Grant's rebellious youth. There were photos like she'd seen in his living room, concert tickets from the nineties, lyrics scrawled on stained napkins. It was all useless to her, until she flipped a page and found Ajay's brown eyes staring back at her.

Neera rubbed her own, blinking several times.

Ajay was in a photo with Grant at a music venue, their arms slung around the other's shoulders in the way only close friends do. Then there was another one—Ajay and Grant on a stage, *performing* together. Ajay with the Yamaha, standing at a microphone, and Grant standing right beside him with his own guitar. Then, finally, Ajay and Grant sitting lazily on an old couch. Sitting between them was Kiran, laughing at the camera. They all looked so young, so *comfortable* around one another.

The world began to tilt around her. She struggled to pull her eyes away from the photos, desperate to look at anything else. Her eyes went to the painting then. It was an abstract piece, painted in muted colors but otherwise unremarkable. It wasn't the painting that caught her eye, but the way it sat slightly ajar from the wall. She eyed it more closely, noticing it wasn't affixed to the wall at all.

The painting was sitting on hinges on one side. She swung it open, revealing the sleek surface of a safe behind it. There was no handle, no keypad. Only a small glass panel, sized for a fingerprint to unlock it. She dusted her hands across the metal, looking for any point of weakness.

"This is impossible," Neera whispered aloud.

Anxiously, she toyed with Ajay's guitar pick in her pocket, hoping to pull comfort from it. She absentmindedly pressed it's pointed edge into her index finger until she pierced her skin. Pulling it from her pocket, she realized blood had welled up on her finger.

Then she eyed the biometric scanner again.

What if it isn't for biometrics at all?

Neera angled the pick in the light, finding the faintest glimpse of something etched into it, recalling a similar moment from the night before. With shaking hands, Neera pressed the pick against the scanner.

The panel turned green, followed by a *click*, and the door opened.

Inside was a handgun, several bundles of cash, and a manila folder. Her hands were drawn to the folder, and she grabbed it, laying its contents out on the desk. Among papers with *Second Sons Inc.* written across them was a copy of a birth certificate.

Neera's birth certificate.

She'd seen it before dozens of times, but why did Grant, of all people, have it in his safe?

A creeping realization was forming in Neera's mind as she looked back to the scrapbook's pages. She stared down at the final photo, the one where her mom sat between Grant and Ajay. Her eyes lingered on the date, a year before she was born. She traced her finger over the image, noticing the way Kiran's and Grant's knees touched, their shoulders leaning into each other in a way that suggested more than friendship.

"Oh my God," Neera breathed, slowly shaking her head. She shoved the scrapbook off the desk, sending it sliding across the wood floor. "*Oh my God.*"

Behind Neera's birth certificate was something else. Ajay Singh's autopsy report. Except, the copy that Grant had in his safe classified her uncle's death as a homicide, not suicide.

As she glanced up, she found Grant Langley standing in the doorway across the room, a drink in hand. "Hey, kid."

SAM

26 HOURS

AT THE TAVERN, Jonah Langley was out cold, laid face down in the booth at table one. His buddies had thought it was funny at first, as if he'd taken a little too much of whatever they dabbled in earlier in the day. But enough time had now passed to cause concern.

Once the ambulance was called, Sam began to feel sick. What if Jonah was not just knocked out, but *dead*—by her hand? He may have never cared about the lives of others, but Sam still did.

She told no one as she slipped out the back for her fifteen, yearning, once again, for a cigarette. Sam hovered beneath an awning as rain fell in waves, blanketing Lake Clearwater in a dense haze of gray. She checked her phone for the hundredth time, desperate for Neera to call or text her back, but it was only radio silence.

I owe her the truth about Jack's second bargain, Sam thought. *She needs to know.*

As she bounced anxiously, an unlit cigarette dangling from her lips, Jason popped his head out the back door.

He asked, all red and flustered, "Have you seen Kiran? We can't find her anywhere."

"What?" Sam blinked, then checked the time on her phone. "I saw her take her break a couple hours ago. She's not been back?"

"No," Jason said, blowing air from his lips. "Of all days to do this—*goddamnit.*" He gave Sam a shrewd once-over. "You know, cigarettes will kill ya."

With that, he was gone. Sam's heart pounded wildly at Kiran's sudden absence. She couldn't help but think the worst, that this was *her* fault, despite spiking Jonah's drink instead.

Sam called Neera again, but it didn't bother to ring. She began to leave her a hasty voicemail, when a figure appeared, emerging from the rain.

Jack leaned against the Tavern's dumpster a few feet away. His expression was unusually solemn. "You really shouldn't have lied to the devil, Red. We could've worked somethin' else out."

"I couldn't do it," Sam admitted. "I didn't have it in me."

"I see that now," Jack said. He gave her a sad, discerning look before vanishing around the dumpster from where he came.

Sam started to follow after him when rough, familiar hands gripped her arm, yanking her backward.

"Daddy?"

Wiley's cruel face was the last thing she saw before the world went black.

CHAPTER 39

ISAIAH
26 HOURS

That stormy evening, Isaiah and Reid were inside Clearwater & Co. Law Firm, the attorneys long gone for the day. Isaiah made a few laps to be certain they were the only ones there. He then arranged a filing setup on his desk, which looked a lot like a work in progress, in case one of the attorneys showed up unannounced.

Reid's gaze flitted anxiously around the firm. "Any word yet from Neera?"

"No," Isaiah said, checking his phone to be sure. "It's been voicemail all day."

"I'm sure she's okay," Reid murmured. "She seems like she can handle herself."

Isaiah wished he could feel as assured of Neera's safety as Reid did, but her long silence had him imagining the worst.

Once inside Leblanc's office, Isaiah sat at his desk, staring haplessly at the black computer screen.

"Go ahead," Reid said from beside him. "Don't you have the password?"

"Yeah, sort of."

He laid his phone beside him, then pulled up a video he'd recorded earlier in the day when he'd been working alongside Leblanc. It was a brief, slightly blurry video of Leblanc putting his password into his computer. Isaiah slowed the speed down, then zoomed in on Leblanc's fingers, watching the clip several times before he was sure he saw the correct input.

On the third try, Isaiah was logged in.

For an hour, Isaiah combed through Leblanc's computer, until he landed on a folder labeled *Disney World Vacation 2018*. He'd gone through nearly every innocuous file, finally ending up here. Except it wasn't vacation memories within the content's folder, but dozens of large files labeled with various dates. The thumbnail of each one showed a hazy, night-vision image that looked a lot like the back of Leblanc's cabin cruiser.

"Whoa," Reid breathed beside him. "Do you see June twenty-third?"

"Yeah, it's here," Isaiah said, suddenly feeling shaken. He couldn't bring himself to open the video file. In all his fervor to reach this moment, he hadn't prepared himself for *what* he might find in the footage.

Isaiah mentally counted down from ten, then pressed play.

An ERROR message flashed across the screen.

Isaiah cursed beneath his breath. He clicked the video file several times, but the error message continued to pop up.

"Try the others," Reid said.

And so, Isaiah did. He opened the file of every date from the past month. They all worked except for the day of Dawson's disappearance.

"They deleted it on purpose." Isaiah cursed again, low and deliberate. He buried his face in his hands, massaging his temples, struggling to think of their next move.

Reid's breath caught. "There's more. Isaiah, it's *new*."

Isaiah glanced at the desktop screen. Reid pulled up a video from that day—*that afternoon*. The time stamp read two hours ago. There wasn't anything for several minutes until there was. This new footage was rain-spattered, but Isaiah could make out enough. Leblanc and Wiley Calhoun were carrying a woman's unmoving body onto the boat.

"Is that . . . ?" A chill crawled down his spine. "I *know* her. Oh God. That's Neera's mom."

"What the fuck," Reid breathed. "Wait, there's another. Look."

As the pair had been watching the footage of Kiran, another one popped up. The time stamp was a few minutes ago. This one was similarly rain-spattered, nearly impossible to discern if they didn't already know what to look for. Another body, this one with red hair.

"Sam," they both said. But they were then interrupted by a car door slamming outside, followed by a silhouette passing the windows of Leblanc's office.

"*Hide,*" Isaiah whispered.

In a chaotic blur, Reid moved to the office closet while Isaiah dug his USB drive from his pocket and attached it to Leblanc's computer. He copied the newest videos to the flash drive, watching anxiously as the file transferred with tortoise-like speed.

The front door of the firm opened and shut as Isaiah ejected the USB, then made quick work logging out of Leblanc's computer. He scrambled into the hallway just as a familiar face in a gray suit rounded the corner.

"Dad?"

Isaiah's father greeted him with a portfolio in his hand. "I'm dropping this off for Leblanc." His father's dark eyes studied him carefully. "When you said you couldn't attend dinner earlier, you didn't mention you'd be *here*."

Isaiah did his best to look composed, despite the weight of the USB in the pocket of his slacks. "I had some work I wanted to get ahead of for this week." He quickly added, "You know, before the Fourth."

"Of course," his father said with a slight nod. "This will be a momentous Fourth of July." Yet his father's gaze was scrutinizing. He stepped forward, meeting Isaiah halfway down the hall. "What's on your mind, son? Talk to me."

"What? I—" Isaiah blinked, struggling to find the right amount of truth to share. His nerves were fraying at the seams. This wasn't the right time to face his father—to appear controlled and composed when he was the furthest from it. He settled for a half-truth. "I feel like everything's changing so quickly and I can't find my footing."

"I see." His father braced his hands on Isaiah's shoulders. "Are you nervous about Harvard? Isaiah, look at me, you were *made* for that school. You have nothing to worry—"

"It's not that," Isaiah interrupted, shaking his head. "It's *everything,* Dad. It's you and Mom separating. You buying a house on Lake Clearwater. You spending more time here than with your own family." *It's me not recognizing the man you've become.*

His father's eyebrows furrowed. "What're you so afraid of?"

Isaiah swallowed hard. He did well to tamp down his fears, but his grasp on the world grew increasingly fragile the more he discovered about Lake Clearwater. "I don't want to lose you," he confessed. *I don't want to lose you to this place.*

"You will never lose me, son." His father sighed, holding Isaiah's gaze. "Every choice I make is for the betterment of you and this family," he said. "Nothing, and I mean *nothing,* will ever change that."

He pulled Isaiah into a tight hug, and Isaiah hugged him right back. His father may not have known the real meaning behind Isaiah's words, but his embrace meant something all the same. For a breath, he allowed himself to relax into his father's arms. Isaiah wished he could be a kid again, when his father had been his hero and everything felt *right,* and he didn't have to worry whether his own father was involved in something terrible.

Isaiah pulled away first.

"Can I leave this with you?" his father asked, handing Isaiah the portfolio.

"Yes, sir," he said, composing himself. "I'll leave it on Leblanc's desk."

"Very good." His father patted his shoulder, then checked the time on his watch. "Don't work for too much longer, son. It's a difficult habit to break once you learn it."

Isaiah nodded, then walked his father to the firm's front door. He watched his Tesla disappear into the stormy night, the headlights swallowed up by the rain. Once he was gone, Isaiah locked the front door, then hurried back to Leblanc's office.

"What if Neera's next?" Isaiah asked Reid. "What if this is Grant and Wiley collecting on the debt?"

"That's possible," Reid said slowly. "But that doesn't account for Sam being taken. We're missing something important here." His face paled then. "What if Neera's already been taken? That could be why she hasn't answered her phone."

Isaiah shook his head, making a run for the front door. "We need to get to Grant's. *Now.*"

CHAPTER 40

NEERA
25 HOURS

Neera was frozen in place at the sight of Grant in the doorway. She barely flinched at his sudden appearance, still in shock from the documents strewn across his desk. "I didn't hear you come in," she said, her eyes flitting to the gun in the safe.

I don't even know how to use a gun, she thought pitifully. She needed to use her wits, because what she'd just found was definitive proof Grant was responsible for Ajay's death. If he realized she knew, she was afraid of what he might do. She needed to focus on the other damning document—the one not about death, but birth.

"You were clearly distracted," Grant said, taking a sip from his glass. "Whatcha got there?"

Neera stiffened, before gesturing to the scrapbook on the floor. "You tell me."

Grant eyed it with casual disinterest. "Ah, that."

Neera moved around the desk, putting a bit more space between her and Grant. "Is there anything you wanna tell me?"

Grant sighed, as if this was an inconvenience for him. "I need you to be more specific."

Neera felt sick, again. "Those photos—you all looked so close, like best friends. Like family."

Grant shrugged. "We were all quite close back then—me, your uncle . . ." He paused. "Even your mom."

"What changed?"

Grant took another sip from his drink, stepping closer into the room. "Me and Ajay . . . well, we didn't see eye to eye on some things. We were young and hotheaded, desperate to make a name for ourselves in music. Let's just say we had a falling-out over a business disagreement."

"Over Blind Bucks?"

"You know of it?" Grant asked, eyes narrowing.

"Yeah," Neera said. "I know all about the loans Ajay took out on it. How it never took off, yet my family was left with the debt. It's funny how Ajay wanted to partner with you on Blind Bucks four years ago. Then the Tavern opened up *one* year later. The exact same idea, only in Lake Clearwater, rather than Carrion." She shook her head. "It's like you made a career out of stealing Ajay's ideas."

Grant grimaced, swirling the brown liquor in his glass. "I can admit we were afforded very different opportunities in this industry, but I'm not a thief."

Neera mentally calculated how fast she could run into the hallway. "Why're you *really* helping me?"

Grant hesitated for a breath, then met her gaze. "Make no mistake, kid. Your talent is worth investing in, regardless of what happened between Ajay and me."

"Come on, Grant. Cut the bullshit." Neera's gaze hovered on her birth certificate. "I know it's you."

"Pardon?"

"Your falling-out wasn't really about Ajay or the music or even Blind Bucks," Neera said, more to herself than to Grant. "No, it was because of my mom, wasn't it? It was because of *me*."

Grant went entirely still, as if the wind had been knocked from his lungs. For the first time since she'd met him, he seemed at a loss for words.

"Say something," Neera snapped, slamming her hand on the

desk. "Say *anything*. Tell me I'm wrong!"

"Lower your voice, please," Grant said tensely, as if he were worried someone would hear. There was no one else there—only them.

"Oh God." Neera's whole body began to shake. "This can't be real."

Grant took a long swig from his drink, finishing it in one gulp. He stood there for an unbearable moment, staring at the empty glass. "What do you want me to say?"

"The truth!" Neera held up her birth certificate for him to see. "Why do you have this? Tell me you're not really the one who—that you're not my—oh God."

Grant grimaced. "I believe the word you're looking for is *father*."

The sound of it made Neera's skin crawl. "You're not even gonna deny it?"

"Neera, please," Grant said. "What does it matter now? It changes nothing."

"It changes *everything*." Neera crossed the room, putting more distance between herself and Grant. "So what, you knocked up my mom and bailed just like that?"

"It's complicated," Grant insisted. "I was young. I didn't know any better."

"*You* were young?" Neera questioned. "What about my mom? She was barely eighteen, raising a kid all on her own." Grant began to reply, but she cut him off. "And what about all the years since then, huh? You couldn't at least write us a fucking check?"

"No, I couldn't." Grant shook his head, his easygoing facade beginning to crack. "I had a reputation to protect, a family name, a *legacy*."

Neera went still. "A bloodline, you mean."

"If anyone had found out about you . . ." Grant's gaze fell to the floor. "Being a Langley carries weight, kid. It *means* something. There are rules in my world—consequences you can't even imagine."

Neera scoffed. "Not owning up to being a father is one thing, but did it mean you had to screw over Ajay in the process? I thought he was your *friend*."

Something dark and cruel flashed in Grant's eyes. "There was nothing friendly between us once it was all said and done. We each had our part to play—I can promise you that."

"What the hell does that even mean?" Neera wound her fingers through her hair, pulling at her roots. "Just tell me the truth, Grant. I'm owed that, at least."

"The *truth*?" Grant repeated.

Neera could only nod.

Grant sighed heavily. "When Ajay found out about me and your mom, we fought." He held up his fretting hand for Neera to see. Wiggling his fingers, he said, "In that fight, he broke my hand in three places. Severed the nerve endings in my fingers. Since that day, I've not been able to play guitar the same."

Shame warmed Neera's cheeks. "I don't believe you." She couldn't imagine a world in which Ajay would've done something so cruel to another person.

"It's true, whether you want to believe it or not," Grant said evenly.

Neera swallowed back the bile in her throat. "That's it, then? He *nearly* ruined your music career, so you destroyed him in return?"

Grant was still. "Ajay nearly took *everything* from me."

Neera glanced around the room again, laughing bitterly. "And now I'm living in your goddamn pool house."

Quietly, Grant mused, "Fate is funny that way, isn't it?"

"This is sick," Neera breathed. *I want to go home*, she thought, even though home was now a fleeting and fragile thing. "I—I need to get out of here."

Grant held out his hand, blocking Neera's path to the door. "Where're you gonna go?"

"For a walk," Neera said. "You wanna try and stop me?"

"I won't bother." Grant eyed her for a long moment, then relented, stepping aside. "I know you'll be back."

Neera sneered as she moved past him and into the hallway. She thought she heard his footsteps trailing after her, but she was gone before he could try and stop her.

With angry tears welling up in her eyes, Neera ran off the property, and absently followed the sidewalk through Lake Clearwater's winding neighborhoods in the pouring rain. After a day spent ignoring the world, she stabbed her phone's power button. To her surprise, she was bombarded with dozens of missed calls and texts from Sam and Isaiah. She held the phone to her drenched face, struggling to hear Sam's voicemail over the storm.

I think your mom's in danger.

The world faded around Neera as Sam's words settled within her.

It was happening again. First with Ajay. And now her mom. Were her grandparents next? Was this part of Grant's plan? Was he coming after Neera, too? She broke into a sprint, desperate to be far away from Grant's home, desperate to get the hell out of Lake Clearwater. But how could she leave? The community was a gilded, gated prison for someone on foot.

After a few minutes of running, a car pulled up beside her. She flipped it off, assuming it was Grant, and picked up her pace.

"Neera, it's me!"

Neera turned to find Isaiah leaning out the driver's window of his car. "Isaiah? What the hell?"

"Get in!" Isaiah yelled over the torrential rain.

CHAPTER 41

ISAIAH
24 HOURS

The car was silent as Neera held Isaiah's laptop, watching the video of her mother and Sam being taken. They were parked outside a plastic surgeon's office in Lake Clearwater, undecided on their next move.

Neera shut the screen. In a small voice, she asked, "Where are they taking them?"

Isaiah frowned deeply. "We don't know, Neera."

"Sam knew something was off," Neera whispered. "She tried to warn me. God—I fucked up. I could've called my mom. I could've *saved* her." She hit the back of Reid's seat in a fit of anger before going still.

Isaiah exchanged a pained glance with Reid, before he asked, "Should we go to the address Dawson had on his pay stub? There's still a chance that can lead us somewhere."

Neera shook her head. "What if it's not safe?"

Reid shrugged. "Safety seems a little relative right now."

Isaiah nodded in agreement as he put Dawson's address into his phone's map. "It's only thirty minutes away. Let's go."

MILES AWAY, ISAIAH and Neera stood watch as Reid Langley struggled to pick the back door lock of a peculiar, seemingly abandoned cabin.

Though standing watch wasn't much use as the thunderstorm persisted, graying out the flatland with impenetrable sheets of rain. The towering slash pines swayed violently, looking perilously close to being ripped from the ground.

Isaiah glanced over his shoulder at his parked BMW, hidden from the road behind a thick copse of trees and kudzu.

To Reid, he called out, "Come on, Boy Scout. Pick up the pace, please."

"Patience, Nancy Drew," Reid fired back. "I'm in."

Isaiah rolled his eyes as he trudged toward the cabin. He wished he'd chosen better shoes as they sank in the wet earth with every step, muddying the leather. When he and Neera reached the back door, he glanced around the property one last time before stepping inside. If the area had nosy neighbors, they were thankfully acres away, tucked behind rows and rows of dense pines.

Once inside, Isaiah shut the door behind them, locking the dead bolt in place. "Remember, no lights," he warned. He shone his phone's low flashlight around the room, illuminating a narrow laundry room that doubled as both a pantry and storage closet. Grabbing a nearby hanging towel, Isaiah wiped the mud from his shoes, then handed it to Reid to do the same.

"Got it," Reid said, passing the towel to Neera.

Isaiah wasn't big on breaking and entering, preferring his investigations to err on the side of legal. But given the dire situation, his previous methods were no longer sufficient.

"What do you think this place was for?" Isaiah asked Reid as they moved into the living room. The cabin was tiny and unremarkable, but very clearly lived in if one knew where to look.

"I have no idea," Reid said quietly.

"I'll look around out here if you two wanna take that side," Neera offered.

The boys nodded. Reid led Isaiah down a shadowed narrow hallway barely wider than their shoulders. The carpeted floor dipped beneath their shoes as they walked. Heavy sheets of rain clattered on the tin roof above their heads and slammed against the walls of the cabin.

The first door they found swung open on creaky hinges, revealing a sparse but tidy bedroom. There was a neat twin-size bed with a faded quilt, a makeshift desk made from a plastic folding table with matching chair, and stacks of perfectly folded clothes that sat in the corner.

Then Isaiah's gaze settled on a corkboard resting against the farthest wall. He crossed the room, observing the brightly colored collage up close. The board was a messy array of cutout images depicting city skylines, international locales, and college campus brochures with cheesy, inspirational quotes sprinkled throughout.

"Dawson's vision board, I guess," Reid said from behind him. "His dreams for his future."

Isaiah nodded, looking around the tiny, gray room that was in stark contrast to the vibrant, faraway life depicted on the corkboard. "Whatever he did, I guess he thought Lake Clearwater was his way out of . . . all of this."

Reid collapsed onto the edge of Dawson's twin bed, the mattress sinking beneath his weight. He rubbed his face, eyes going distant. "I told him I'd help him—pull whatever strings I could to get him out of this place, but he refused my help. Dawson said he'd figure it out on his own, in his own way." He moved from the bed to the floor, kneeling at the bedside table and leafing through the stack of books atop it.

"Why would he stay here then, rather than go home?" Isaiah asked.

"He *really* hated home," Reid replied as he closed a dog-eared book and tossed it on the floor. "Seeing his mom like that every day . . . he couldn't stand it anymore." He then positioned himself flat on the ground and began to pull plastic storage bins from beneath the bed.

Thunder crackled and boomed overhead, rattling the windows. From the rainfall growing heavier, it seemed as if the storm was becoming worse, threatening to take the little cabin with it.

"Oh, shit," Reid breathed as he emptied a plastic bin filled with folded clothes. "I think I found Dawson's journal."

Isaiah's eyes widened as Reid pulled a notebook from the bottom of the bin. He held it delicately in his hand, as if the journal could bite. "Go on then."

Reid hesitated to open it. "This feels wrong somehow. Like, really wrong."

"The answers to all of our questions could be in there, Reid," Isaiah said. "We can't draw an arbitrary line here. Not when lives are at stake."

"You're right." Reid nodded slowly. "Dawson would understand." He unfolded the journal in his lap, slowly flipping through the pages.

Isaiah's dark eyes combed the room. "I'm gonna look around the rest of the house. Let me know if you read anything useful."

"Yeah," Reid said, turning over a new page. "I will."

Isaiah stepped into the dark hallway, then joined Neera in the modest living room. He looked around the cramped space with an adjoining kitchenette, taking in the details of the cabin in the low light. There was a small table with a hunting knife sitting atop it, then above the fireplace, a gun rack with several rifles. Within the nearest closet, he found more peculiar items—rope, bleach, worn work gloves, a heavy baseball bat.

"What the hell," Isaiah murmured, snapping photos of everything.

"A lot of weapons," Neera observed.

Isaiah opened his mouth to respond when an engine

sounded in the distance.

They both froze, listening intently beyond the ebb and flow of the thunderstorm. Then came the distinctive sound of gravel kicking up along the driveway. Peering through the nearest window, he could barely make out a vehicle crawling straight toward the cabin.

Isaiah swore to himself. He instinctively crouched to the floor, motioning for Neera to do the same, careful to stay out of sight from the approaching car. Not that the person could see through the torrential downpour anyway, but he had to be safe. A moment later, a Chevy truck stopped before the home, the person not bothering to turn off the headlights as they idled outside.

"*Isaiah*," Neera breathed his name like a prayer, fear brimming in her brown eyes.

"Follow me closely," Isaiah whispered. He scrambled down the hallway, tripping over his feet as he barreled through Dawson's bedroom door. "Reid," he huffed. "We have to go *now*."

Reid looked up from the journal, rubbing his eyes as if he'd just seen a ghost. "Huh?"

The strange, pained look across Reid's face caused Isaiah to falter. "Did you hear me? There's someone coming. We need to get out of here quick."

"What? Who?" Reid shut the journal, then moved to the bedroom window. His face paled at the sight of the man outside. "This is bad."

Isaiah and Neera crawled beside him, peering over his shoulder.

"Wiley Calhoun," Neera said solemnly.

The Langley family's hired muscle was all hardness and cruelty, wearing it like a lethal suit of armor.

"Look," Reid murmured. "Are those gas canisters?"

They all glanced anxiously between one another as Isaiah said, "He must be here to burn the house to the ground and any evidence within it."

A tremor of fear nearly overcame him in that moment, but Isaiah stamped it down. He couldn't get lost in it. Not now, not when their lives were at stake. He had to keep going.

Wiley made his way to the cabin's front door, setting the red gas canisters at his feet. Then he dug in his jeans and materialized a key from his pocket. He donned a pair of gloves, then pulled a bandanna over the lower half of his face. Down the hall, Isaiah could just barely make out the sound of the front door unlocking. Reid moved across the room with deft steps, closing and locking the bedroom door before Wiley was inside.

The window, Reid mouthed. *Our only way out.*

Isaiah's hands were slick with sweat as he fumbled with the window's latch. He prayed with everything inside of him that the window would budge quickly and quietly. Now beside him, Reid helped lift the window with careful hands, but it barely slid open an inch. They continued to pull at it, but it didn't move.

What do we do? Neera mouthed.

Heavy footsteps sounded on the other side of the house while the pungent smell of gasoline wafted to Isaiah's nose. *He's dousing the entire house,* he thought grimly.

"Slide the mattress in front of the door," Isaiah commanded in a low voice as he continued to struggle with the stuck window. "We need more time." That's when he noticed the safety locks outside the windowpanes, effectively locking them in.

Reid and Neera slid Dawson's mattress across the floor, blocking the door from opening. When they returned to Isaiah's side, he pointed to the window. "We're locked in."

Reid anxiously rubbed his face, then knelt close to Isaiah. In the barest whisper, he said, "We have to break the glass."

Isaiah shook his head. "It's too risky," he insisted. "He'll *hear* us."

Reid gestured around them. "Do we have another choice?"

To Neera, he said, "Be ready to jump out first and run back to the car through the trees. We'll be right behind you." Neera nodded, while Isaiah gave him a weak thumbs-up as he glanced outside the window, grateful to find the drop to the ground was minuscule. He zipped up his rain jacket, tightening it around his chest. *Okay,* he mouthed.

Reid counted out one, two, three with his fingers, then knocked the window out with his elbow with a loud *bang*. Glass shattered across the floor, but there wasn't time to react before Isaiah ushered Neera to the window. She didn't hesitate to climb through it, glass trailing after her and into the storm.

As Isaiah braced himself to follow her, the floorboards creaked just outside the door. He and Reid went entirely still as the doorknob to Dawson's room began to jiggle.

Wiley was trying to get in.

Reid motioned for Isaiah to go, his gray eyes wide and frantic as Wiley began to pound his fist against the door, violently shaking the frame. The mattress barricade would only afford them a few extra seconds.

Go, Reid breathed. *Now!*

Isaiah flung himself out the open window, glass scraping his palms. His movements were rushed and awkward, having only ever seen people climb out of windows on TV. As he met the soaked ground with his feet, it took a heartbeat to orient himself and run for the car.

Isaiah didn't look back as he and Neera sprinted toward the tree line. He thought of nothing else but the cover of the dense pines as he ran across the muddied ground. It felt like ages before he reached the trees, but he didn't slow down until there were yards between him and the cabin. He knelt to the ground, struggling to catch his breath as he watched Reid's distant silhouette following behind.

A prolonged moment later, Reid caught up to them, and they ran the short distance back to the BMW.

"We should be in the clear," Isaiah whispered once inside the car. "I don't think he saw us."

"Yeah," Reid agreed. He collapsed in the back seat, running his fingers through his soaked brown hair, pulling at the roots. Once his breathing leveled, he said, "I know what happened to Dawson."

Both Neera and Isaiah turned to look at Reid. Adrenaline still pumped through his veins, tilting the world around him. "What?"

"He was . . . they were . . ." Reid's words trailed off as he inhaled a sharp breath. "We were almost right. Dawson was meant to be Wiley's right-hand man. Extra muscle for my community's . . . I don't even know what to call it."

"I don't understand," Isaiah said slowly. "What does that mean exactly?"

"According to Dawson's journal, he was being trained to do what we just saw. The dirty work for my family, for Lake Clearwater. Trained to kidnap—trained to *kill*." His voice came out hollow as he shut his eyes tight. "But he clearly didn't realize what he'd gotten himself into. He wrote that he was scared, that he wanted out. He was trying to figure out what to do."

Realization dawned on Isaiah. "That's why they took him. Dawson knew too much—he knew *everything*. If he couldn't be a weapon, he was a liability."

"This is huge," Neera said, brown eyes darting between them.

Isaiah's thoughts raced. "Did Dawson name names? Say specifics? *Anything?*"

"It's all in the journal," Reid said, patting his chest where the shape of the journal sat beneath his raincoat. "But we need to get out of here first."

Yards away, Wiley Calhoun stepped out the front door of

the cabin, then shut it with his foot, gas canisters still in hand. He dumped his supplies in his truck bed then climbed behind the wheel. The trio all crouched low in Isaiah's car, despite being hidden within.

Isaiah expected him to leave, but Wiley sat there instead—*watching*.

Several long minutes passed before black smoke began to billow from the opened window in Dawson's room. Through the heavy rain, he could just barely see a flicker of orange dancing along the room, igniting everything in its wake. Then from every window and door came the smoke. It wasn't long before the roof of the cabin began to cave in on itself, while the wall panels curled and slid off the sides and onto the ground. Piece by piece, the home contorted and melted beneath the heat of the fire, transforming into a monstrous pile of rain-soaked rubble.

Once there was nothing home-shaped left of the cabin, Wiley flicked on the truck's headlights, turned around, and disappeared down the gravel drive.

"Where're we going next?" Neera asked, her voice desperate. "Did he say anything about where my mom could be? Where Sam is? *Anything?*"

"Yeah, he named one place," Reid said. "Blind Bucks."

SAM

23 HOURS

SAM WAS HELD captive where the sunlight couldn't reach.

They kept her in the dark to disorient her—to weaken her. She was ashamed by how effective it was. Chained to a chilly aluminum floor, she had never felt more powerless.

In her isolation, all Sam could do was replay memories in her head. Her thoughts were stuck on an infinite loop of fear and regret as she thought of her final moments with Neera. She should've stayed that morning. She should've never left her side. Would she ever see Neera again? Or her brother? She thought of Ben and his dimpled cheeks and how she was going to leave him all alone in this world.

"I don't want to die," Sam confessed into the dark.

To which the dark answered back, "It didn't have to be this way."

Sam gasped, eyes straining. "Jack?"

"Howdy, Red." A few feet away, a single flame appeared, illuminating the devil's bottomless black gaze. "Turns out, the only thing worse than making a deal with the devil is not honoring the terms of said deal."

If Sam had the energy, she would've laughed. "Rot in hell."

The tiny flame danced across Jack's stubbled face, casting him in an inhuman shadow. He merely smiled and said, "I never wanted it to end this way for you, Red. I mean that."

In the blink of an eye, Jack was gone and Sam was left in the all-consuming dark.

Sam didn't know how much time passed before blinding light spilled into the room. The light revealed a narrow meat cooler filled with bodies. Instead of Jack beside her, she found twelve people chained up and gagged.

Including Dawson, Kiran, and townsfolk, blinking against the light.

Dawson? She tugged against the chains, overwhelmed with relief to see him alive, yet desperate to help him, to free the people in the room, but Sam was just as trapped as they were.

She opened her mouth to call out Dawson's name, only then realizing she was also gagged. The two could only stare at each other, their eyes speaking for them.

"Rise 'n' shine, folks," came the boom of her daddy's voice from the doorway. "We're relocatin'."

CHAPTER 42

NEERA
22 *HOURS*

Blind Bucks looked distinctly *monstrous* in the spare light of the moon.

It was Neera's turn to stand watch as Reid struggled to break the heavy padlock on the front door with a shovel. Isaiah hovered beside him, his phone in hand, ready to record whatever they found within. The three had been quiet since fleeing the cabin. A palpable anxiety hung between them as they feared the fate of their loved ones—if they were even still alive.

After several minutes of raucous banging, the lock and chains fell to the ground. They all stared at one another. It was one thing to *plan* to be heroes, it was another to assume the roles. Whatever they found within the abandoned dive bar, they had to be ready to meet it.

Reid didn't give Neera a chance to consider it further before he was inside the building, and she was following at his heel. They all used their phones as flashlights in the dark of the bar.

All around them was the long-forgotten branding of a place that never was. Those strange, sprawling antlers hung over the entrance, and turned-over tables and chairs were scattered about. Neera scanned the room, desperate to see some sign of life within. "Where are they?" she whispered.

"Somewhere soundproof, I imagine," Reid whispered back.

"There." Isaiah pointed to a closed door at the back of the building.

"Oh God," Neera breathed, her mind's eye conjuring something gruesome. She pushed forward, ahead of the boys. "Come on."

Glass and debris crunched beneath her feet. She shone her phone's flashlight on the remnants of this place, including the small stage—what once was and what never came to be. Ajay's legacy. Another failed dream for the Singh family. It had to end with her, this longing. She needed to see her life's dreams made reality.

It can't end like this.

The door to the back was locked. She tugged the handle, but it didn't budge.

"Here," Isaiah said from behind her. "Try this." He materialized the key she'd found in Dawson's room a week ago.

Neera put the key in the lock, expecting nothing. But it turned, then unlocked the door. There was the briefest moment of hope before it was extinguished. Inside was nothing but an empty walk-in cooler.

From behind came Reid's and Isaiah's flashlights.

"There's no one here," Neera announced flatly. "They're gone."

Isaiah crouched on the floor, rubbing his hand along smudged footprints. "These are fresh. Still wet. We must've just missed them."

Neera wanted to scream, but Reid beat her to it. He let out an angry cry, kicking the nearest wall with a force that should've broken his toes. "We're screwed."

Isaiah shook his head. "No, we're *alive*. Imagine how screwed we'd be if we were caught trying to save these people. We didn't even think this through, just acted. We're not vigilantes."

"Well, we have to be." Reid paced the length of the room.

"Their lives are in our hands. We have less than twenty-four hours to save everyone or they'll all be dead."

Neera and Isaiah whipped their heads around to look at Reid.

"What did you just say?" Neera asked, at the same time as Isaiah said, "You're not making any sense. Twenty-four hours? What is that?"

"The journal," Reid sighed. "It's all in Dawson's journal. He wrote about some *ritual* happening on the Fourth of July—tomorrow. Thirteen people are supposed to be killed to symbolize the thirteen years since the last cicada brood. They're meant to be sacrificed."

Isaiah shook his head, disbelief written across his face. He looked around the room, no doubt counting the thirteen hooks on the ceiling. "Sacrificed to *what*?"

Reid was quiet for a long moment, before he finally said, "The devil."

"No way in hell. That's just some folktale," Isaiah countered. "It's *real*?"

"Real enough," Reid shot back. "It's real to them."

"Oh, this is fucking insane," Isaiah said, tugging at the collar of his shirt. "I can't—how am I supposed to believe—"

Neera tuned out as the boys went back and forth, the tension and fear in the room creating a cocktail of anger between them. She studied the thirteen hooks hung from the ceiling, wondering where her mom had been. For a moment, she imagined how terrified Kiran must feel, but the thought was too much to bear. She shut her eyes, forcing herself to breathe. To think.

It was all painfully real to her, as she knew the devil well. One of them, at least. Like Ajay had taught her, she recalled the details of the folktale. She thought of the kind of place suitable for a ritual. Somewhere isolated, remote, but significant to the town. To Lake Clearwater. The "Three Brothers" folk song drifted into her head, as it often did.

They say
You meet the devil
At the crossroads
Down in Georgia
When there ain't no options left

It clicked for Neera then.

Thirteen bodies would be left at the crossroads for the cicada.

She had it.

"Both of you, *shut up,*" Neera shouted. The boys fell quiet, turning their attention to her. "I think I know where they're gonna be, if not already are."

The boys both looked at her expectantly.

"The crossroads," Neera said. "They're taking them to the crossroads."

"Do you know how many crossroads there are in this county?" Reid started. "At least—"

"Not just *any* crossroads, Reid," Isaiah interrupted, recognition crossing his face. "The original. From the William Langley legend—from *your* ancestor's legend."

"We'd need a map of Old Carrion to know where that is," Reid said, still defeated.

"I know where one is," Neera said.

Without waiting for them to follow, Neera was out of the cooler and crossing Blind Bucks with hurried steps. Isaiah and Reid caught up behind her as she pushed open the front door. She led them around the building, to the side, where Ajay's mural was painted across the wall.

Neera pointed up, to the map of Old Carrion drawn clear as day for them to see, even in the pouring rain. Painted beneath the cicadas and peach trees, there was the original crossroads.

"Where is that now?" Isaiah asked.

Reid replied, "In the heart of Lake Clearwater."

CHAPTER 43

ISAIAH
21 HOURS

The trio were now gathered in the tractor shed on the Johnson farm as the storm continued outside, mirroring Isaiah's own anxieties. He turned on a battery-powered lamp, sending long shadows across the old wood floor. Neera studied the whiteboard that he and Reid had been working on, while Reid paced the length of the room.

"We can't be long out here or Grandma Bee's gonna think something's wrong," Isaiah said.

"But there *is* something wrong," Reid countered.

"Yeah, but it's not like we can explain any of this to her," Isaiah said. "Jesus, Reid. I'm not trying to give my grandmother a heart attack."

Reid argued, "I never said—"

"Guys, can we focus, please," Neera snapped, tapping her finger loudly on the whiteboard. She'd just finished scrawling a simplistic map of Lake Clearwater onto it.

"What's the point? We're fucked." Reid crouched on the floor in a frustrated huff. "How're we meant to rescue anyone if they're in the dead center of the lake—for *everyone* in Lake Clearwater to see? They'll see us coming and going a mile away."

Isaiah wasn't one for dramatics, but even he didn't see an immediate solution. The original crossroads of Carrion sat on one of Lake Clearwater's many islands in the middle of the lake. There was nowhere to hide, nor blend in. They'd be spotted as soon as they hit the water. "He has a point."

"Why can't we go right now?" Neera asked, her voice taut. "It's pouring rain. It's night. How will anyone see?"

"The lake's crawling with Sheriff Buckley's police cruisers," Reid said. "Gearing up for the Fourth."

"Oh," Neera said.

"We're too late," Reid said, quickly growing deflated before Isaiah's eyes. "It's over."

Isaiah shook his head, not willing to succumb to Reid's negativity. "What if we're not too late, though? What if we're right on time?"

Reid arched an eyebrow. "What?"

"I'm saying," Isaiah began, "what if we save everyone *during* tomorrow's festivities? Is that an option?"

Reid sighed. "I'm not following."

Isaiah made an explosive gesture with his hands. "The *Fourth,* Reid. All the people, the fireworks. The lake's gonna be swarming with boats and tourists. Who will notice us then?"

"There's gonna be a concert tomorrow night, too," Neera said, writing those details onto the board. "I'm supposed to perform."

Reid went still. "That's true. We could make our move while people are distracted."

Neera's eyes lit up. "Not only distracted, but *bewitched.*"

"Huh?" Isaiah asked, eyebrows furrowing. "What're you talking about?"

"Oh, shit. I get it," Reid said slowly. "Neera's music."

Isaiah looked between them. "I'm not following."

"Come on, dude," Reid said. "You *heard* Neera play at the Cicada's Song. It was weird. Creepy, even. It was like I was feeling exactly what she was singing about."

Isaiah remembered Neera's song, albeit hazily. The whole performance had felt like a dream in a way he wasn't yet ready to contend with. "I'm not gonna ask how that's possible."

Neera looked to the floor. "I'll tell you about it if we survive tomorrow."

Isaiah smiled grimly. "I'll hold you to it."

"When I get on that stage tomorrow and perform," Neera said, "you two are gonna save the day. But this isn't gonna work unless I get back in Grant's good graces."

Isaiah said, "I like the idea, but we need to figure out specifics. Logistics. There's so much we don't know."

Reid nodded, pulling Dawson's journal from his pocket. "Maybe there's more details in here about this *ritual* that could help us."

Neera peeled away from the whiteboard, then knelt beside Reid, reading the journal with him in silence. There was only the rain falling on the tin roof and the wind howling through the pine trees. It was Isaiah's turn to pace then. He ambled around the small shed, taking inventory of everything they'd learned. Despite what he'd already seen with his own eyes, his rational mind couldn't believe the idea of coordinated kidnappings. Of a sacrificial ritual. Of devils made flesh.

The shed's door suddenly swung open from the wind, sending sheets of rain slanting across the floor. As Isaiah scrambled to shut it, he knocked over the box of old camera equipment he'd received for his birthday, badly stubbing his toe. Once the door was closed and secure, he took stock of the mess now scattered around him.

"I got it," Isaiah said, kneeling to clean it up.

He made slow work of returning the equipment to the box. He'd barely had a chance to go through it all since Grandma Bee had given it to him. He still couldn't believe what a lucky flea market find it had been for her. A half-opened envelope of film negatives caught his eye then. The antique negatives were dark, high-contrast images, barely discernible in the dim light.

He moved to the electric lamp, holding the negatives up. When the light finally caught them, Isaiah squinted against the images, struggling to make sense of what he saw. He held them closer, then froze.

They were gruesome depictions of a slaughter—of bodies strung up in trees by their feet, their stomachs cut open and bleeding.

As if the negatives were on fire, he dropped them, stumbling backward to the floor. He held his hand over his mouth, struggling not to vomit.

"Isaiah?" Neera's voice barely registered.

The negatives were clearly half a century old, at least, with time distorting and warping the identities of those in the photos. But the effect was the same—someone had photographed those poor people as they were viciously killed. And somehow, through a cruel twist of fate, the photos ended up in Isaiah's possession.

Fate wasn't a concept Isaiah indulged in, but what else could he call this? One way or another, he was meant to uncover the truth of Lake Clearwater and reveal it to the world.

"I know how we're going to save everyone tomorrow," Isaiah said, holding the negatives in his hand.

NEERA
20 HOURS

ISAIAH'S BMW IDLED outside Grant Langley's home, the massive house glowing in the late stormy night. The threat of a tornado had long since passed, leaving a steady pouring of rain in its wake.

Isaiah turned in the seat to face Neera. "You remember what to say?"

Neera nodded, recalling their hastily made plan. "I know how to make a bargain."

The three said their *goodbyes* and *be carefuls* and then she was at Grant's door. Right back where she'd started earlier that day, though it felt like a lifetime ago after everything she'd learned. But she couldn't carry that weariness or fear on her face. No, she needed to be in complete control when speaking to Grant. After all, she was about to make a business deal that would change her entire life.

When Grant answered the door, he merely raised an eyebrow by way of greeting.

"Can we talk?" Neera asked, lingering in the rain, tempering the anxiety from coloring her words.

Grant stepped aside, letting her in from the storm. He motioned her to leave her muddy shoes by the door, then materialized a towel from the nearest closet. Without another word, he disappeared down the hall.

After drying off her damp hair, Neera trailed after him into the living room. Grant sat at the bench of his vintage grand piano, his back to her as he played a familiar, melancholy tune.

"They say you meet the devil down in Georgia," Grant sang, "when there ain't no options left."

His rendition was markedly different from Ajay's. Where her uncle's singing voice had been rich and soulful, Grant's was flat and lifeless. Neera understood at once that Grant was merely the *imitation* of a musician, without any of the parts that brought a song to life. That was the difference between him and Ajay—that's why their relationship had imploded.

Grant Langley had been playing pretend while Ajay Singh had always been the real thing.

"I'm not here to apologize," Neera announced. "You don't deserve it. But I am here to make an offer."

Grant let the final key of "Three Brothers" fade out before he turned to look at Neera. "I'm listening."

"When I play at the concert tomorrow night, I'm gonna win over every single person in the crowd. I already know it," Neera began with as much confidence as she could muster. "So, let's get right to it. You should sign me because you *need* me. You need my music to take your music empire further than it's ever gone."

Grant crossed his arms. "Oh?"

"Don't bullshit me, Grant," Neera said. "You know what I did—what I *sold* to get this far. You know what I'm willing to do to see my dreams become a reality. And you know the power my music holds, maybe even more than I do."

Grant snorted. "What do you *want*, Neera? Just say it."

"I want you to protect my family," Neera said slowly. "Forgive my grandfather's debt. Call off your family's attack dog. Save my mom from Lake Clearwater's sick ritual."

"How do you know about . . . ?" Grant shook his head. "I suppose it doesn't matter now. What do *I* get out of all of this?"

"Me."

Grant rose from the bench, slowly circling the living room to stand before her. "If we make this deal, I'll own everything."

"I know."

"Your music will be mine," Grant continued. "Every song, every EP, every album. Your image—mine. Your name—also mine. When you get onstage and sing, you'll convince the audience of whatever I want you to. You'll make them *feel* whatever I tell you to. Do you understand what you'd be signing away?"

I'm signing away my soul, Neera thought grimly. *My freedom.* The irony wasn't lost on her after what she'd already promised to Crow. But what Grant envisioned was a career as a puppet. Performing not for the passion, or for an audience, but for rooms of hungry-eyed suits who thought only in profit margins, not musical notes. "Yes."

"Then I'd say we have a deal, Neera Singh." Grant held out his hand, a wicked smile creeping across his face.

"Deal," she said, shaking his outstretched hand.

Neera knew the devil well, but looking at Grant Langley now, she felt she was looking at something much worse.

CHAPTER 44

REID
12 HOURS

It was the morning of the Fourth of July, and it was Reid Langley's eighteenth birthday.

Reid thought he would pack more *things* when it came time to leave Lake Clearwater, but all he had was an overnight bag filled with the barest of essentials, and his favorite photos of his mother. In the end, he'd spent the predawn hours doing more for others than himself.

Hidden in Lake Clearwater was a parked van and a docked pontoon boat, among other things needed for that night and for their escape. It was incredible how quickly a rescue plan could come together when ample cash was involved. No language spoke louder than the almighty American dollar.

Now, Reid's only remaining task was to wait for his father's invitation that morning. There was the smallest part of him that still hoped—no, *prayed*—that his father, his only living parent, wasn't at the head of everything he'd learned the past few days. But willful ignorance was no longer a luxury Reid could afford. He had to face the truth of his family's bloody legacy head-on.

A knock sounded at his bedroom door.

He found his siblings lingering in the hallway, dressed as if they were attending Sunday church.

"Happy birthday, asshole," Jonah greeted. "Where were you last night?"

Reid tensed at his brother's question. He genuinely didn't think his siblings noticed his absence. "I was busy."

Jonah snorted. "Busy doing *what*?"

"I was with Isaiah Johnson." He added quickly, "We're . . . friends now, I guess."

"Ha!" To Jonah, Farris said, "I told you. Pay up."

Reid blinked. "Did I miss something?"

Farris smirked. "We bet on how long it'd take you to move on from Dawson."

"Yeah, and I lost," Jonah groaned, reaching for his wallet. He then passed their sister a fifty. "Nice going, Reid. I thought you'd last a little longer."

Reid didn't have it in him to fight that morning. "Can y'all just leave me alone today? As a birthday present?"

"Not yet." Farris reached out and adjusted the collar of Reid's shirt. "Dad wants to see us in his office."

It begins, Reid thought with a tremor of fear in his gut. *This is it.*

As the siblings made their way downstairs, Reid thought he'd walked onto the New York Stock Exchange. The first floor of his home was awash in over a dozen pencil-pushing suits who scrambled over themselves as they worked on laptops, spoke hurriedly on phones, and belabored over dense contracts and tax documents. The siblings all exchanged a curious look.

Once inside their father's office, Reid found his father seated at his desk, with his personal lawyers, Leblanc and Rutledge, in the armchairs across from him. Reid was nearly overcome with the urge to punch Leblanc in the mouth, but he fixed his face to remain cool. He promised himself justice would come in another form—not only for his best friend, but for many others. The three men quickly ended their discussion as the lawyers excused themselves, shutting the office door behind them.

Jonah asked first, "What's with all the suits?"

"It's an auspicious day," their father said. "A day for celebration." He gestured to the windows overlooking the ever-present lake. Dozens of boats already lingered on the shimmering water, securing their spots for the Fourth. Past the boats, in the distance, Reid could see the cluster of small islands in Lake Clearwater's center, which included the crossroads of Carrion. He tried not to look for too long.

"Yeah, God bless America," Farris quipped lazily. "We're not doing a family breakfast for Reid, right?" She glanced at him, pursing his lips. "I have plans."

Their father shook his head. "Since you three are no longer children, you are now invited to participate in Lake Clearwater's most coveted celebration this evening. It's called a Rendering." He leveled his heavy gaze at each of them. "It's an honor like no other, I assure you."

Reid looked down at his shoes, unwilling to meet his father's eyes. He couldn't be the first one to accept. It would look too suspicious.

"I thought the Rendering was, like, an old wives' tale," Farris said, suddenly sounding a little breathless. "Are you being serious?"

Their father nodded. "It's Lake Clearwater's founding come to life, and it's what keeps this community—this family—prosperous. Per Langley tradition, only *one* of you needs to attend the Rendering, but I would be remiss if I didn't ask that all three of you were there at my side."

The film negatives from last night flashed through Reid's mind, sending spots around his vision. He knew what was to come, but did his siblings?

Farris flicked her gray eyes to Jonah and then Reid, as if

waiting for them to answer first. "Hypothetically," she began slowly, "what happens if I *don't* participate?"

"Fortune favors our family regardless of your individual decision. As long as one of you participates and passes the tradition on, all is well." Their father sighed, leaning forward across his desk. "However, I don't need to remind you of how this community perceives you three because of your mother. Wouldn't it be a relief to silence everyone's suspicions, once and for all? To no longer live beneath the weight of their judgment?"

They sat in silence for several minutes, in a gridlock, unwilling to give an answer. Reid couldn't help but think that the questions their father posed were as much for himself as they were for his children.

"Okay." Reid gathered his courage, reminding himself what was at stake. He cleared his throat. "Sign me up."

His siblings looked as if they'd seen a ghost, while their father's eyebrows furrowed in surprise. "Are you sure, son?"

There wasn't any other option. "You said it yourself: I couldn't put off doing my duty to this family much longer. I'm sure," he insisted to Russ.

Reid could feel his siblings' eyes still on him.

After a long moment, Farris finally said, "I'll participate."

And then Jonah. "Me too."

"It's settled then," Russ said, clapping his hands in a gesture of finality. "Tonight, you three will perform your first Rendering."

CHAPTER 45

SAM
2 HOURS

Sam came to with blinding, early evening sunlight in her eyes. It seemed like years since she'd felt sun on her skin. It must've been a day—*hours*? She wasn't sure of anything, not even her limbs, which felt like deadweights at her side. Her vision was spotted and blurry as she struggled to make sense of the sky above. There was only a blue expanse and dense, criss-crossing tree branches that swayed from a far-off breeze. The way the branches moved almost made them seem *alive.*

Then she felt the heat. The ground burned beneath her, like bubbling asphalt on the hottest day of the year. Dirt wasn't supposed to be this hot, especially not after so many days of summer storms. It was *unnatural.*

Slowly, achingly, she struggled to sit up. The squealing clank of metal blocked her efforts. Her arms and feet were bound by rusted chains. She fought them awkwardly, floundering like a beetle on its shell. Still, she was able to raise her head enough to look around.

Sam turned, finding Dawson just a few feet away, upright but hunched over. Bound just as she was, his skin a mess of bruises and cuts. On the other side of Sam was Kiran, and she too was still.

Guilt *stabbed* through her at the sight of them both.

There were others beyond them, townsfolk Sam recognized immediately. She knew nearly all their faces, save for a few tourists. There were thirteen in total.

"Dawson?" Sam choked out, her throat dry and metallic. "Dawson, wake up. Please, wake up."

His bright blue eyes fluttered open.

"I'm sorry," Sam quickly confessed, hot tears streaming down her cheeks. She didn't know how much time they had left. There was no telling if he knew of her betrayal, of the car accident, of Ben, but it didn't matter. She needed him to hear the words. "I'm so, so sorry."

Dawson watched her for a long, long time, saying nothing. Saying *everything* with his gaze. "I'm sorry, too."

Sam finally managed to sit up properly. Scattered among the pine trees were the crumbled remains of old brick buildings, buried beneath twisting vines and kudzu. Several of the buildings were blackened and charred from a long-ago fire. In the evening light, Sam thought she saw what looked like cobblestones peeking out from the dirt. Otherwise, the earth was dry, dusty, barren. *Dead.* There was no sign of grass or wildflowers or even weeds—no sign of life, aside from the trees and long-forgotten remains of human habitation.

"Where are we?" Sam asked, still struggling against her chains.

After a long, pregnant pause, Dawson said, "Lake Clearwater."

"What's gonna happen to us?" Sam asked pitifully, despite every cell in her body sensing the inevitable.

Dawson's eyebrows knitted together, the sorrow in his gaze telling Sam all she needed to know. "They're gonna kill us."

Sam's eyes kept snagging on the cobblestones in the dirt. The longer she looked, the more she could make out the pattern. It was faint—stones missing, broken, or buried by the passage of time—but the center of the clearing looked like the barest memory of two old roads crossing.

This was the old town center, the original Carrion. Town legend said William Langley had sold his soul at this very crossroads.

And now, they were all going to die.

Despite the fate laid before them, Sam tugged on her chains. The rusty metal chafed at her wrists until they bled. "This isn't how we're gonna die, Dawson. This can't be it." Despite the bleeding, Sam kept pulling at the chains. She had to get free. For Ben. A sob escaped her throat as dread crept in. "My brother doesn't know what happened to me. He doesn't *know*."

"Sam," Dawson breathed her name like a prayer and a warning, his blue eyes pleading for her to stop.

But Sam wasn't listening. Feral fear coiled within her as she desperately pulled on the chains, ignoring the sharp pain along her bloodied wrists. Her vision swam from the white-hot tears running down her cheeks as she realized this was the end. She would never see her brother again.

"Sam, *stop*," Dawson hissed, reaching his hand toward her. "They're coming."

CHAPTER 46

NEERA
1 HOUR

"You nervous, kid?" asked Grant Langley.

Neera sat in the shade of a massive tent, on an island in the middle of Lake Clearwater, cradling her Yamaha in her lap. "Nope," she lied, tuning the steel strings with shaky hands. "You?"

Grant chuckled as his gaze swept over the audience before them—a sea of Clearwater folks, gathered along the island's shore, waiting to be entertained. "Not in my vocabulary, I'm afraid."

Neera wished she could say the same. She'd barely slept the night before, her body coursing with noxious adrenaline. Tonight was their one and only chance to save the lives of thirteen innocent people and she felt as if it all rested on her shoulders.

No pressure, Neera thought, willing her hands to stop shaking. *It's going to be okay.*

Surrounding them were Lake Clearwater's elite, wearing bright cotton and linen, lingering at cocktail tables. The sun had begun its descent that evening, but the air still sizzled with early July heat and anticipation. Neera wondered how many people in attendance were *privy* to the ritual. But you wouldn't know a ritual sacrifice was happening within walking distance, judging from the infectious energy of the party. It was all *Land of the Free* dressed up in pearl earrings and bow ties.

Squeals and murmurs rippled through the crowd as guests angled their heads to the sky above and to the ground below. Neera *heard* the periodical cicadas before she saw them. While they were normally distant and unobstructive behind Clearwater's gates, that evening, they hummed with an intensity not usually experienced on this side of the water. She pulled her feet into the chair as dozens of them skittered across the stage, while Grant ducked as more flew past his head.

The cicadas were a blanket of flying insects against the evening sky.

Across the crowd of people, Neera finally found Isaiah, her muscles relaxing at the sight of him. *Good*, she thought. *It's all going according to plan so far.* He'd just arrived with his father in their own boat, their gazes also fixed on the cicadas moving toward the island's dense forest. In an hour, at the start of her performance, everything would be set in motion.

Neera turned her attention back to Grant, who watched the crowd with a calculating gaze. "When will I know my mom is safe?"

Grant cut his eyes to her. "I'm workin' on it."

"Well, work on it harder," Neera said under her breath. "We don't have long, right?"

Grant watched the swarming cicadas, just as she did. "No, not long at all."

REID

JUDGING FROM THE gathering cicadas, it was only a matter of minutes before Reid had to be in the woods with his family, which meant there wasn't time for doubt or fear to creep in. Only action. He quickly found Isaiah in the crowd and pulled him to the water's edge.

"You remember what to do?" Reid asked.

Isaiah nodded. "Film. Fire. Flee. Got it all in here," he said, tapping his forehead. "And you?"

"Rescue. Fire. Flee," Reid recited. There was more to both their roles, of course, but now wasn't the time to mull over the details. "Remember, we'll only have a little over three minutes to do it right."

Isaiah flashed the digital watch on his wrist. "Found this old thing at the farm. Timer still works."

"Smart thinking," Reid said. He looked across the crowd of people gathered on the island, then turned his gaze to the crowded lake, where tourists and locals alike "boatgated" on the water in droves rivaling that of the incoming cicadas. He cleared his throat. "As soon as the fire kicks up, you and your father need to run. Get off the island as fast as possible, Isaiah. Don't hesitate."

"No way," Isaiah protested. "I'm seeing this through with you. You need backup."

"*No,*" Reid insisted. "If something goes wrong, it means I'm dead. You're not risking your life, too. Besides, you're the fail-safe. You need to get the truth out there, after all this. You have to. Otherwise, this will all be for nothing. Do you want that?"

"I hear you." Isaiah went quiet for a beat, before he finally said, "Film. Fire. Flee. No detours."

"No detours," Reid repeated. He looked Isaiah over, suddenly realizing the weight of the moment. No matter how the night's events went, he may never see Isaiah Johnson ever again. Their nascent friendship, if that's what this was, had been forged under less-than-ideal circumstances, but it felt significant in a way he couldn't quite articulate. "It's been real, Isaiah."

"Yeah." Isaiah snorted. "See you on the other side, Langley."

They fist-bumped and then they were off in their opposing directions.

Grant had begun speaking onstage by the time Reid reached his father's side. His voice boomed through the speakers, carrying confidently through the thick, humid air, drowning out the growing hum of the cicadas. Before long, Grant welcomed the first musician of the night on the stage to perform. Three performers in total; Neera would be last. That's when he and Isaiah would act and only then.

I have to get this right.

"It's time," Russ said as Jimmy Jones walked onto the stage with his banjo in hand.

The Langleys quietly split off from the rest of the party's attendees, slipping away into the woods on the island like wraiths at dusk, while Reid feared what he would find awaiting them.

CHAPTER 47

SAM

At the end of her life, Sam never expected to hear *music*, of all things. Not just any music, but a performance happening close by, the banjo notes ringing through the air. The final concert of summer. Was Neera there? Would she perform?

Will she save me?

Sam shook the thought away. No one was coming to save her; she felt the truth of it in her bones.

This was it.

Footsteps sounded behind Sam, heavy and slow. She craned her neck to see more people emerging from the surrounding woods carrying lanterns, torches, and buckets. They were dressed as if attending a typical Clearwater party, their clothing bright and gaudy. An anxious, terrified laugh escaped her throat as she considered how ridiculous it all looked. The clothes, the chains, the circle of people. But she went quiet as Dawson's face paled beside her.

Across the clearing, he locked eyes with Reid Langley. Sam knew guilt well and it was written clearly on Reid's face as he approached. He took his place behind Dawson, looking everywhere but at him.

An unspoken conversation passed between Sam and Dawson then. There was no way to know if Reid was there to kill them—or save them. Sam didn't have it in her to hope regardless. Even if Reid had the best of intentions, how could he possibly stand a chance against the bloodthirsty crowd gathered in the clearing? It was a losing game. But when it came to the integrity of the Langleys, it was just as likely Reid had been lying to them all along. In the end, cowardice and evil didn't look all that different.

Jonah Langley joined him, now standing behind Sam. His expression could only be described as smug. Eleven more Clearwater residents stood behind those chained to the ground, with Farris Langley standing behind Kiran. Sam couldn't bear to look at Neera's mom.

"Prepare the bodies for Him." The command came from Russ Langley in the center. "We must cleanse them of sin before He arrives."

A cashier from the town's infamous Chevron was chosen first. One person grabbed her shoulders, yanking her from the ground, and secured her upright. Her captor grabbed the bucket and held it over her head, whispering something under his breath.

Sam could only watch in frozen horror as the contents of the bucket were emptied onto her head. Scalding-hot water sent tendrils of steam up in the air as it was poured over her, causing her skin to blister. She screamed out—a bloodcurdling sound.

Sam looked to Dawson, his blue eyes shimmering and wet. It wasn't sadness in his expression, but helplessness. The kind of tears that fell when you stared death in the face.

The woman eventually stopped screaming as she collapsed to the ground. Her skin was raw and charred, swollen red.

"Who's next?" Russ asked the clearing. "Don't be shy."

Seemingly at random, different Clearwater residents offered their sacrifices to be cleansed. It was a symphony of screams against a backdrop of concert music and fireworks shooting off in the distance. It wasn't long before Sam, Dawson, and Kiran were the only ones left unharmed.

All eyes were on the Langley siblings then. Sam didn't understand it, but she could sense the watchful gazes of the Clearwater community on them. Many bore a look of judgment. She realized then that the siblings were hesitant, perhaps even *unwilling* to do what was expected of them in that moment.

How's Reid supposed to get out of this?

"I'll go," Jonah announced, stepping forward to grab her.

Sam kicked and thrashed against his iron grip, feral instinct taking over. Rough hands secured her arms and legs, holding her still. Another pair grabbed her roughly by the chin, forcing her jaw shut around her scream and tilting her face up to the late-evening sky above.

Jonah leaned forward, clutching her chin. "Your brother should've *died* in that accident," he whispered in her ear. "People like you can't cheat death."

There was the tiniest amount of give for Sam to angle her head to meet Jonah's gaze. She found only unrelenting cruelty in his gray eyes. Using the last of her strength, she bit through the skin of his hand—*hard*—until she tasted blood.

Jonah stumbled backward, screaming a string of profanities, while Sam spit up sinew onto the dead wiregrass. More hands held her now, nearly crushing her beneath their weight. She tightly shut her eyes as the bucket was brought over her head.

A voice rang out from the edge of the clearing. "Stop!"

The grip on Sam's face loosened, enough so she could jerk her head free to see Jason the asshole emerging from the trees. He escorted a bound and gagged older man who could barely stand upright.

Russ Langley crossed the clearing, then began speaking to Jason in hushed conversation. The assembled crowd all watched in silence as the men spoke, unsure of what was happening.

Several minutes passed before the group of men moved to stand in front of Kiran.

"This woman," Russ bellowed, gesturing to Neera's mom,

"belongs to Grant Langley."

Belongs? Even bound and captured, Kiran seemed to recoil.

"What does that mean?" Farris demanded. "She's *my* sacrifice."

The Clearwater folks glanced at one another, clearly caught off guard. Jonah, who still held the bucket above her face twitched, and Sam flinched away.

"Grant is providing a different sacrifice," Russ said evenly.

Farris stepped back while Jason freed Kiran, trading her for another. He guided her out of Sam's sight and into the trees with little ceremony. A heartbeat later, Sam's face was in Jonah's bloodied grip again, the bucket poised over her head.

Scalding water engulfed her, overwhelming every nerve in her body. It was the worst pain she'd ever felt; it was *all* she felt. There was nothing else besides the burning as water gathered in her eyes and her ears, silencing out the world.

ISAIAH

ISAIAH HAD SEEN enough. He was crouched down, hidden in the burnt remains of an old shack near the crossroads. He'd reluctantly recorded every unbearable scream, every desperate plea for the suffering to end. It was all on his phone, including the faces of every Clearwater resident involved. *Evidence.* Enough to indict the most powerful families of Lake Clearwater. No matter their reach in the world, no one could deny what Isaiah had recorded.

He was prepared to leak it to every independent news outlet in the country, and even beyond, once this was all over. But first, he had to make sure all of the captives made it off the island alive, though he wasn't sure how much more he could take.

The Chosen, as Dawson had called them in his journal, crowded around the first sacrifice now—a nameless woman who Isaiah didn't recognize. They unlocked her chains, working together to tie a rope around her ankles, which they secured to an overhanging branch. The whimpering woman gave a guttural cry as she was jerked off the ground and dangled from the tree like an animal before slaughter.

Suddenly, there was a glint of a blade and then a scream. Several of the captives cried out as the woman's throat was slit, her blood spraying onto the ground.

"Oh *God,*" Isaiah breathed. He bit hard on his tongue, struggling not to cry out himself. He'd thought the film negatives had been enough to prepare him for the sight of ritual murder, but *nothing* realistically could.

Come on, Neera, he thought anxiously. *Come on.*

Neither Isaiah nor Reid could act until Neera's performance. Their entire plan hinged upon her.

The Chosen watched as the woman's blood spilled to the earth below, where it flowed *against* gravity toward the center of the circle. The captives' cries were eaten by the explosion of fireworks overhead.

Once the blood touched the center, the ground beneath Isaiah began to tremble and shake. He had never experienced an earthquake before, but he imagined it was a similar sensation. Great undulating tremors rippled out from the center of the circle.

What the hell is that?

The ground rumbled again, thundering beneath the island. Everyone turned to the center of the clearing as a split appeared in the circle, spreading like cracked glass across the dirt and cobblestones.

Slowly, a tiny sliver of earth ripped apart, revealing a yawning darkness. A strange, thrumming sound emanated from the trees. *The cicadas.* Isaiah ducked lower to the ground as thousands of them swarmed down the trunks of the pine trees, sliding across the forest floor. In hundreds of lines, they marched to the center of the clearing. One by one, the cicadas crawled into the split in the earth and disappeared into the dark.

"It's time," Russ Langley announced. "We owe our good fortune and riches to our Maker—to the one who has kept us fed for the past century. May He feast, then rest once more."

With his face nearly touching the floor of the shack now, Isaiah struggled to continue recording the ritual on his phone. As he angled the camera to zoom in on Russ Langley, the screen froze, then went black. Isaiah had been *obsessive* about having enough battery that night, but his phone was suddenly dead—entirely unresponsive to the touch. He frantically pressed the side buttons, struggling to turn it back on, but nothing happened.

A growing sense of panic began to settle within him.

No no no, Isaiah frantically thought. *Please don't let the footage be lost.*

The ground continued to rumble and shake, while the sticky air grew charged with the metallic tinge of blood. More cicadas swarmed from above. Many marched toward the chasm in the center of the clearing, while others followed the trail of blood to the dead woman's hanging body, enveloping her in a pulse of winged insects. Once Isaiah could no longer discern her body beneath the cicadas, several of the Chosen gathered her corpse from the tree, then carried her to the chasm.

The woman disappeared within.

The second sacrifice was hung and killed in the same way as the first woman. The cicadas surrounded him, too. Isaiah couldn't watch any longer. Every muscle in his body was poised to act—to do *something*. But if he made a move too soon, he'd ruin everything. He had to wait for Neera.

More fireworks burst overhead, growing louder and more frequent.

The third sacrifice had been killed and their body drained

when Neera's voice finally rang through the night air.

"My name's Neera Singh," her voice echoed across the island, somehow louder than those who performed before. "And I hope you enjoy this song."

Isaiah scrambled for the earplugs in his pocket. He placed them firmly into his ears, then saw Reid crouch down and do the same thing. Before anyone could react, Neera's music rang through the trees, and everyone's attention was captivated. No one in the clearing moved except for Reid, who rose from the ground, studying the faces of those around him. They were entirely still. Reid signaled Isaiah with a whistle, and he whistled back.

Now.

NEERA

NEERA SANG THE blues in the truest way she knew how. She played "Dark Was the Night, Cold Was the Ground" by Blind Willie Johnson—a song without any formal lyrics, only a baleful surrender of the soul as she slid her fingers across the Yamaha's steel strings.

It was a risk to play a song without words that night. How could she control an audience without creating a story for them to become lost within? But part of her believed, deep down, the song was enough. Instead of words, she wove an image of the void through sound alone.

The audience became transfixed by the story Neera conjured in her head, what she believed the music represented, as well as what she felt while playing it. She imagined Blind Willie Johnson's song sent out into the ether of space, achieving immortality as the purest and most resolute form of the human spirit. Neera knew the crowd wasn't deserving of the song, but she played it nonetheless, with its slow, lilting tune that never quite reached a crescendo.

Neera closed her eyes, allowing herself to become lost in the song, in the chasm the music had conjured. For the briefest moment, there was no one and nothing else. Just her and the Yamaha and the twang of its steel strings. But then she opened her eyes and looked onto the crowd. The audience was wholly, utterly transfixed, entirely unmoving.

And she was the one who had turned them to proverbial stone.

It was the kind of melody that could be played forever with none the wiser, which was why she chose it.

Until she knew the boys had been successful in their rescue, she intended to keep playing until her fingers bled. Because Neera now knew, without a doubt in her bones, she could weave magic through her music alone.

REID

REID HAD THREE minutes and eighteen seconds. He ran to his father's side and gently pulled the key from his pocket, careful not to wake him from his dreaming state. Except it wasn't just that his father was dreaming, but something else entirely. Russ's eyes had gone entirely black, welling up with an oozing substance, as if he was weeping crude oil.

Isaiah appeared a moment later, mumbling something to Reid he couldn't understand. With their earplugs in, they relied on elaborate hand gestures and pantomime.

Reid pointed to his father's face, with Isaiah's own eyes going wide in response. They looked around the clearing, taking stock of the Chosen, as well as the captives. It wasn't just Russ with blackened eyes, but everyone. They were all frozen in place, faces pointed in the direction of the music, with dark liquid trickling from their eyes, staining their pastel clothes black.

Was this the effect of Neera's magic? What had she done to acquire such power?

Isaiah shook his head, as if he couldn't comprehend any more insanity that night.

One key, Reid finally mouthed, holding it up for Isaiah to see. *Ten people to unchain and wake.*

Isaiah nodded.

The pair made quick work of their task. Reid unlocked, while Isaiah pulled more earplugs from his pocket, shoving them in the captives' ears. A minute passed before the surviving captives were responsive, each of them struggling to wipe the black goo from their eyes. Slowly at first, then more frantic, despite their burnt and blistering skin.

Reid lingered before Dawson as the film cleared from his blue eyes and they looked at each other, actually *looked*. There was so much he wanted to say to his best friend in that moment, but there wasn't time.

The ground beneath their feet gave another tremulous rumble then, more aggressive than the ones that came before. All around the clearing, entranced bodies collapsed. Beside Reid, his brother and sister fell to the ground, too. He flinched at the sight of their blank, empty faces—black liquid seeping from not only their eyes, but their noses, their ears, their mouths. Whatever Neera sang, it was wholly unlike what she'd performed at the Tavern. This was something that affected not only the mind, but the *body*.

Is she killing them? Reid thought, guilt twisting inside his gut like a knife. He shook the question away. It didn't matter now. His family was willing to murder innocent people for their own gain. The last shred of love he had for them was gone.

Another thirty seconds passed before the captives could each see. Thirty more seconds before they were on their feet, although they were all slack-jawed and stained with blood, as well as whatever had pooled from their eyes.

The ground shook again, the sensation growing violent and angry, sending the towering pine trees swaying and thrashing above. In the middle of the clearing, the split in the earth grew wider, racing toward them. The cicadas that had disappeared into the yawning darkness began to crawl back out, spreading across the forest floor in all directions. The insects moved differently this time, pulsing and scrambling over one another as if they were being controlled by an unseen force.

Screaming, they headed for the captives.

Reid looked to Isaiah, and he understood the panicked look on his friend's face. The devil demanded its sacrifices, one way or another.

The cicadas reached Sam first. She was barely upright when the bugs swarmed her legs, crawling up her bare, burnt skin. She screamed, frantically swatting at them as they overwhelmed her entire body, sending her tumbling back to the dirt. The cicadas were dragging her into the hole in the ground. Dawson leapt forward, trying to save her, but the insects only multiplied, spreading from Sam's body to his.

Reid was frozen in place, immobilized by the horror of it all. This wasn't in the plan. This wasn't *supposed* to happen. It was one thing to stop the human captors, but how could they stop the devil?

Isaiah reacted first. He grabbed the nearest torch pitched in the ground, then buried the flame in the line of cicadas that pooled from the chasm. The fire seemed to sever the supernatural connection, sending the insects scattering away from Sam and Dawson. The pair were whole; they were alive.

Reid blinked, giving himself a mental shake. He couldn't linger in his relief for long. They had to escape. Now.

He, along with Isaiah, gestured for everyone to *run*, but most of them could still barely stand upright on their own. Isaiah struggled to pull them up, using his own body as support. Reid followed suit, helping drag people off the ground and out of the clearing. They needed to be as far from the chasm as possible.

The final minute passed, but it seemed the devil had given up on the captives. The cicadas began to swarm the dozens of Clearwater folks scattered around the clearing, their bodies still enraptured from Neera's song.

Run, Reid struggled to pantomime, praying they would understand. *Run to the shore and don't look back.*

It was only a matter of seconds before Neera's song was to end, but Isaiah, Dawson, and Sam still lingered at the edge of the clearing. They looked at Reid expectantly, but he couldn't yet follow. He shook his head, begging for them to go, as he still had one thing left to do.

A moment later and they were gone, disappearing into the dense pine trees.

The clearing was entirely free of the sacrifices once Neera's performance was over. It was only Reid, the Clearwater community, and the devil himself threatening to rise from the earth. Everyone was slow to wake as Reid raced around the clearing, knocking over the kerosene lanterns and torches that illuminated the woods that night. The dead ground was the perfect kindling as a fire quickly caught and began to spread around them, billowing up the pines and igniting in the low, dry grass.

It wasn't long before the screaming began. The hunters had become the hunted, as many people found themselves covered in cicadas that tried to pull them into the yawning darkness below.

"Reid!" His father's voice rang across the clearing, over the roar of the cries, the fire, and the rapid *pop pop pop* of fireworks. "What have you done?"

Reid Langley didn't look back as he ran into the woods, leaving behind everything he had ever known.

CHAPTER 48

NEERA

The audience was dead, until they weren't.

Neera had watched the Clearwater crowd drop like flies on the shore. She truly feared she had killed them all, but her song was now over, and they were awakening, albeit slowly. There was no time for anyone to question their collective fainting, or the peculiar black liquid that had bled from their faces, as smoke began to billow from the center of the island. That was the boys' signal.

They did it, she thought, *but where is my mom? Where's Isaiah? Sam?*

Neera untangled herself from the Yamaha, then scanned the island from the stage. The ground continued to tremble, and the Clearwater attendees grew frenzied. There was a collective panic building in the smoky night air. She spotted Laurence Johnson in the crowd, searching the tree line yards away, just as she was. Did he know what Isaiah had done?

There wasn't time for Neera to speculate further before someone grabbed her arm, yanking her backward and onto the ground. She fell into Grant Langley. He held her wrist so tightly, Neera thought he might break it. From the cruel look across his face, black tears streaming down his cheeks, it seemed like he wanted to.

"What the fuck kind of stunt was *that*?" Grant demanded, his easygoing facade entirely gone. He was clearly angry, but Neera saw something else in his gray eyes—fear. But it wasn't from the fire or the chaos that surrounded them, it was because of her. Of what she'd done to the crowd, to *him*.

Neera took advantage of Grant's uneasy stance and pushed him, sending him stumbling a few feet back. He looked wild in the uneven glow cast from the fireworks, like a monstrous thing. Neera now felt a little monstrous, too. "It was just a song."

"Just a song?" Grant repeated. He laughed darkly, winding his fingers through his sweaty hair. "Do you take me for a fool, kid?" He scrubbed away the lingering black liquid from his neck, studying his hands with a look of revulsion. "*This* wasn't part of our agreement."

"Fuck your agreement," Neera spat, pushing Grant again. Her sense of self-preservation was crumbling. "You said you'd save my mom! Where the hell is she?"

Grant opened and closed his mouth, glancing at the black stains that ran down his button-down shirt, then to the hysterical crowd beyond them. He righted himself, drawing close again. "You'd do well to remember that I *own* you and your family, kid. They are merely collateral to me. Nothin' more."

It took everything within Neera not to push him a third time, but she could only nod. The timbre of her voice turned desperate as she said, "*Please*, Grant. Just find my mom."

Grant looked to the pine trees, the fire growing larger by the second. In a low voice, he admitted, "They should've been back by now."

SAM

HELL WAS AT Sam's heels. She and the remaining captives ran through the woods, racing toward the sounds of freedom, splitting off in different directions. Somewhere along the way, she'd lost sight of Reid and Isaiah. It was only her and Dawson now. They both tossed their earplugs, running toward cheering and away from the screaming. With the fireworks going off in droves, it was almost impossible to distinguish the two, which was the point. To conceal the sacrifice within the wild celebration of the Fourth of July.

Nothing quite conveyed *God bless America* like sacrificial murder.

There was no telling how many people chased behind Sam and Dawson in the dark of the woods. She didn't look back, not once. Seconds stood between them and survival. Between her and Ben and their beach house far away from Lake Clearwater. This was it—this was all she had left to fight for.

More guttural screaming rang from behind them. Sam pushed her legs harder until her lungs threatened to give from the exertion. Her burns had already begun to blister, and now they bled from the frantic movement. She was a mess of wounds and sweat and blood.

A crowded lake peeked through the cluster of pine trees that lay ahead. Just barely, she made out the sheen of glossy boats on dark water. They were so *close*.

"Samantha!"

Sam whipped her head in the direction of the sound. She faltered, tripping over her own feet, as the boom of her daddy's voice carried through the trees nearby. Her reaction was innate, learned from her eighteen years beneath Wiley's roof. He was determined to finish what he'd started. To rid the world of his daughter. She collapsed in the dirt, hidden among the trees.

Dawson was beside in her in an instant. "Sam, get up," he begged, frantically pulling her limbs. "We're almost there, *please*."

"Samantha!" Wiley yelled again. "Come on out, girl."

Sam shook her head, frightened tears welling up in her eyes. Her daddy was drawing near; she could sense him, even if she couldn't pinpoint the location of his voice. It was over. "I can't," she choked out. "I can't—I can't face him."

Dawson's own eyes had turned teary. "It's okay," he breathed. He materialized a knife used in the ritual, the blade still stained with blood. Gently, he unfolded Sam's hands and folded her fingers around the hilt. "I'll distract him. You just need to run, all right?"

Sam blinked. "What?"

Dawson was already on his feet, letting out an obnoxious whoop in Wiley's direction. Sam could just barely see her daddy's figure stalking through the trees a few yards away. Dawson bolted straight toward him, screaming like a wild animal.

Sam counted down from five, tempering the paralyzing fear that had wound through her, then she ran. A moment later, she burst through the trees, treading down a slope, and found herself on a small shore. Hundreds of boats spread out before her on Lake Clearwater. But there was no one near enough to call for help. The island was blocked off with floating buoys that signaled boats to keep their distance.

Where was she meant to go? She spun in a circle, taking in the length of the island. She could only see so far in the dark, briefly blinded by the fireworks shooting off overhead.

Then Sam noticed a bass boat, the edge of it peeking out from a black tarp on the shore. Was this the boat they were all meant to escape to? As she sprinted toward it, her feet sank in the wet, gravelly sand, slowing her down. She was ripping away the tarp when someone grabbed her from behind, pulling her to the wet ground.

Daddy?

With the hunting knife Dawson had given her, Sam stabbed blindly behind her until she pierced flesh. She buried the knife deep.

It was Jonah Langley who screamed.

Sam crawled away along the shore as Jonah clutched his stomach, the knife embedded in his abdomen. His eyes were lit with rage. Sam crawled backward on her cut hands, reaching for something—anything to fend off Jonah with. He lunged for her. They tussled in the water as Jonah's hands went for Sam's throat.

"You don't get to escape this," Jonah panted as he squeezed her neck. He shoved her head beneath the lapping water.

Sam's vision went spotty, the edges going black. Water overwhelmed her as it pooled in her throat. Her fingers searched the ground for something to use—something to save herself with.

It can't end like this, Sam thought as she began to choke on the lake water. Blackness crept forward at the edge of her vision. *After everything I've fought for, this can't be it.*

Then she felt it. The edge of a rock in the water. Fist-sized. She grasped it with the last of her strength, then bashed it into Jonah's head. He collapsed in the shallow water.

Not giving him a moment to recover, Sam crawled on top of him and raised her arm to swing again.

"Stop!" Jonah yelled, shielding his face with his hands. "Please! I'll let you go."

In the brief lull between fireworks, screams rang from deep in the island. The screams of those who hadn't run fast enough. There wasn't any time left to waste. Sam stared down at Jonah's whimpering face. She thought of her brother, of how Jonah must've seen them in their wrecked car a week ago, and left them to die. He hadn't cared whether Ben would live.

Sam dropped the rock, then twisted the hunting knife as deep as it could go in his stomach. Jonah cried out, flailing beneath her as blood sputtered from his mouth.

Yards away, a handful of the captives swam in the water toward an unmanned pontoon boat near the shore. *The only survivors?*

She spotted Dawson among them, then Reid at his heel, followed by Wiley still chasing after them. He had an uneasy, lumbering gait, as if injured, but the survivors were faster. They didn't hesitate before climbing into the boat, then taking off, leaving Wiley in their wake. That's when Sam smelled smoke. Her gaze was drawn back to the woods, and to the inferno that began to build from the center, crawling toward her.

Sam pulled the knife from Jonah's stomach, content to let him bleed out in the water. She rolled off his squirming body, returning to the bass boat. With trembling hands, she yanked the tarp from the boat, and slid into it. As Sam cranked the engine, several Clearwater people appeared at the edge of the trees on the other side of the shore. They ran forward as the engine kicked off and propelled her away from the shoreline.

Sam didn't look back as she motored between boats filled with drunken people on Lake Clearwater. There were so many of them. Pontoons, deck boats, cruisers. It was almost impossible to steer through. Slowly, she made it work. No one paid any mind as a girl covered in blood navigated through parties of celebratory Southerners cheering at the fireworks exploding in the night sky.

Shades of blue and red cast Sam's blistering skin in an eerie glow as she rode. The wind swung her matted, bloodied hair around her face. She steered the boat toward a hidden dock on the southern part of the lake, praying there was enough gas to get her there. Sam was afraid she was minutes away from passing out. But she was so close—she had to keep going.

As Sam neared the shore, she spotted a lit cigarette glowing in the dark. It was a pitiful beacon of light. As she drew closer, she made out the faint silhouette of Jack leaning against his Jeep, cigarette dangling in his mouth. He gave her a casual, impersonal wave.

Jack met her on the dock as she approached. "Hey, Red," he said, crouching beside the boat. "You've seen better days." As he extended his hand out to her, Sam met him with the point of the bloodied knife. Jack didn't flinch but eyed it cautiously. "You're upset—I get that."

Sam stared up at him from the boat as it bobbed unevenly

in the dark water. "*Upset?*" she repeated, nearly choking on the word as angry tears threatened to fall. She could no longer parse through the myriad emotions she'd experienced that night. But looking at Jack now, one feeling grew clearer: a sense of betrayal. "You left me to *die*."

"You didn't need my help." Jack's expression softened, and she remembered how he'd looked when they met. The night she'd bargained for her brother's life. There were traces of genuine remorse in his worn face. "I knew you'd make it out."

"Just barely." Sam's hands stained the wood of the dock red as she climbed onto it, knife still in her hand. She looked over her shoulder at the inferno swallowing the island in the middle of Lake Clearwater. Dozens of people swarmed around the shore, fighting over boats and safe passage. Warily, she looked back at Jack, then asked, "You gonna try and take me back there?"

Jack slowly shook his head. "It don't matter to me what you do anymore. I'm free, Red."

"*Free?*" Sam repeated. "How's that?"

Jack nodded to the island. "Turns out, not even the devil is immune to fire. My brother's dead. It's over. I answer to no one." He tossed his lit cigarette into the water. "You're free, too."

Free? It took a moment for the finality of the word to settle over Sam.

"I'm tired, Jack." There wasn't much fighting power left in her. "What am I supposed to do now?"

Jack grinned, and it was all teeth. "As it stands, I have one good deed left in me, if you're interested."

Sam eyed him. "No more bargains, please."

Jack pulled a folded piece of paper from his jeans pocket, then handed it to her. "It's yours. No strings attached."

Sam unfolded it carefully, leaving bits of blood on the paper's edges. It took only a moment for her to understand what was in her hands. "Is this real?"

"As real as you or me," Jack said simply. He then pulled the Jeep keys from his pocket, tossing them at her feet. "I don't need it anymore."

With that, the devil walked away, leaving Sam in the dark.

In one hand, she held the finalized paperwork for her brother's adoption, and in the other hand were the keys to the devil's Jeep.

It was finally time for Sam and her brother to go home.

REID

REID MANEUVERED THE pontoon boat through Lake Clearwater, away from the screams of the Fourth celebration, away from everyone. He headed for the north shore, where he'd parked a van early that morning. Dawson was beside him, shivering, despite the warm night. He'd calmed the other captives sitting in the back, who all had grown silent.

Only seven of them had made it out and onto the boat. Seven people out of thirteen. They had truly intended to save them *all,* but the others hadn't been fast enough. But with the fire at their backs, Reid made sure there would never be another ritual again. He hoped the mysterious powers of Lake Clearwater had gone up in flames with the burning pines.

"Where're we going, Reid?" Dawson asked, his voice hoarse.

"Far away from Lake Clearwater," Reid said, drawing closer to the shore. "We'll need to go into hiding for a bit until things settle down. I've got it all covered."

"Are we gonna hide forever?"

"No," Reid said as he navigated the boat to the nearest dock. "Once I know we're safe, we're gonna expose Lake Clearwater's crimes to the world. I'm gonna make sure they never hurt another person ever again."

CHAPTER 49

ISAIAH

The island was burning, and Isaiah could only think of his father. He ran through the trees, bursting through the woods and into the open air. He couldn't look back. He couldn't hesitate. He needed to get off the island alive and expose Lake Clearwater to the world. He had to believe Reid was successful, that everything they'd done wasn't for nothing.

When Isaiah reached the edges of the party, there was only unbridled panic. Lake Clearwater residents clambered around like ants toward the boats, screaming and shouting among the rapid explosion of fireworks.

"Isaiah?"

A hand grabbed Isaiah's shoulder, pulling him close. *Dad.*

Laurence hugged him tight, and Isaiah thought everything would be okay. But then his father demanded, "Where were you?"

The question threw Isaiah off-kilter as he pulled away, bodies swarming all around them. He studied his father's face, and he only saw fire and fear reflected in Laurence's dark eyes. He knew where his son had been—he knew *everything*. Isaiah could see it now, clear as day.

"You know," Isaiah whispered.

Laurence could only shake his head before he pulled Isaiah through the crowd, his grip ironclad as they raced for the water's edge.

NEERA

"GET IN THE goddamned boat, kid," Grant hissed, tugging Neera behind him.

As the fire burned through the island, Neera refused to flee. She sank to her knees on the shore, forcing herself to become deadweight. The heat from the distant flames grew stronger, warming her wet face. "I'm not leaving without my mom!"

Grant let out a frustrated cry, his eyes searching the crowd. He was frantic, the fire a shock to not only him, but all of Lake Clearwater's elite. "There!" he shouted, pointing toward the tree line.

Neera craned her head over the frenzied bodies, finding Jason and her mom running toward them, the fire not far behind.

She made to run after them, but Grant held her back. Painful seconds passed before Kiran was before Neera. Neither one hesitated to hold each other, refusing to let go.

A few frantic minutes later and the four of them were on Grant's boat while the fire engulfed the island before their eyes. Neera looked around the polluted water, struggling to find a familiar face in the onslaught of boats. She breathed a little easier when she saw Isaiah and his father a few yards away, safely off the island.

She then thought of Sam and Reid, hoping they made it out alive. But there was no way to know, not then. Not that night. Instead, she had to sit by Grant Langley's side and watch as the heart of Lake Clearwater burned from the inside out.

EPILOGUE

NEERA

Neera Singh sat in a dressing room backstage at Ithaca House—Nashville's premier club for fresh, up-and-coming talent. Like herself.

It'd been two months since she signed with Grant Langley, yet he still had her playing small venues. Testing the waters with her *peculiar* skills.

Bigger venues were on the horizon, but Neera was fine to wait. She'd performed every night for weeks now, and the music was beginning to take its toll. Truthfully, it was already wearing her to the bone, taking more than it gave back. She couldn't imagine playing for crowds in the thousands. What would be left of her afterward?

This is what I wanted, Neera reminded herself.

After all, her family was no longer in debt from Blind Bucks. Her advance from signing the record deal had covered it all. Nanaji, finally, had sold the motel, allowing him and her grandmother to experience the joys of retirement. Though they were still figuring out exactly what that looked like. Her mom still bartended by choice, but not by necessity. She'd even enrolled in classes at a local community college in Nashville.

"This is what I wanted," Neera whispered aloud as she stared at her reflection in the mirror. She took extra care to cover the dark circles growing beneath her eyes with concealer.

A knock sounded at the door.

"It's open!"

A moment later, Isaiah Johnson appeared in the doorway of the dressing room, holding a bouquet of flowers in his hands. "This is fancy," he said by way of greeting, taking in the room. "Also, these are for you. It's customary, right?"

Neera rose from the chair, greeting him with a tight hug. "You made it," she said into his chest, grateful to see a familiar face.

"Of course." Isaiah squeezed her in response, then pulled away. "I couldn't miss you on the way up to Massachusetts."

Neera looked past Isaiah, half expecting some of his family to be trailing in behind him. "You're not making the drive alone, are you?"

Isaiah shook his head. "My mother's in the car on a work call and my father . . . he's flying in tomorrow. He and I aren't on the best of terms right now—after everything that happened. With all of us together on Move-in Day, it should be . . . *interesting*."

"I can only imagine." Neera returned to the makeup chair. "Are you excited to start school, at least?"

Isaiah waved his hand dismissively. "It's no big deal. But look at *you*—look at this. You're living the dream, Neera." A playful look danced across his face. "Have you heard from Sam?"

Neera pulled out her phone. She showed Isaiah a photo of Sam and her brother on a white-sand beach in the Gulf of Mexico. There was a modest little shack behind them. "They're all moved in."

"That's amazing," Isaiah mused. "Are there any plans for her to visit soon?"

Neera looked away, her cheeks going warm. "In a few weeks—maybe. It depends on the . . ." She gestured to the messenger bag on Isaiah's shoulder. "The podcast. Are we still doing it?"

Isaiah blinked. "Yeah." He pulled out his laptop, then set it on the counter before them, opening his podcast software. "It's all there. Every episode ready to go."

They both stared at the screen in heavy silence. It'd been easier to pretend the Fourth had only been a nightmare once Neera and her family left Carrion behind. But now, with the podcast before her, the crimes of Lake Clearwater felt all too real again. "Are *you* ready?"

Isaiah's dark brown eyes met hers. "Once we upload this, there's no going back. Everything we learned about Lake Clearwater will be out in the open. We can't know what'll happen next."

"It's worth the risk." Neera chewed her bottom lip. "What about Reid? Is he gonna cooperate with the FBI?"

Isaiah shook his head. "He's still in hiding with the survivors. Last he told me, he didn't think it was safe to come forward unless this season got a lot of attention, which I agree with. The community's power is far-reaching."

"Well, hopefully this will take them down a peg or two," Neera said. "What can they really do if the whole world is watching?"

"Right," Isaiah agreed. He leaned forward, hovering the mouse over the upload button. "Ready?"

Neera nodded. "Do it."

A minute later, her phone vibrated with a notification.

New season: Secrets of the South—The Cult and Crimes of Lake Clearwater.

"There it is," Neera said, showing it to Isaiah.

"There it is," Isaiah parroted.

Another knock sounded at the door, rattling them both.

Grant's voice rang from the other side, "You're up, kid!"

"That's my cue," Neera said, struggling to temper the exhaustion in her tone. "I'll see you after?"

"Yeah," Isaiah said before pulling her into a hug once more.

A few minutes later, Neera was onstage.

"This first song—it's a murder ballad," she said into the microphone. "This one's for the devil you know."

Underneath the warmth of stage lights, Neera held her Yamaha across her lap while a crowd of people stared up at her. Instinctively, her eyes found her family seated at a table near the front, her mom waving. They did this nearly every night—Nani watching her with pride. Nanaji watching her with a glimmer of admiration in his eyes. All it had taken was a deal with the devil to, finally, earn her grandparents' love.

Aside from her family, the rest of the crowd were a formless bunch—dark silhouettes that held clinking glasses filled with twenty-dollar cocktails. Ithaca House wasn't known for its lively patrons, but the House's stage was a stomping ground for Nashville's rising stars.

My girl, my girl, don't lie to me
Tell me where did you sleep last night

Neera supposed that's what she was now—a star burning across a night sky. She didn't exactly know what to call it, as her image was no longer her own. Blue Mountain Records dictated everything, from the way she wore her hair down to the color of her toenails.

In the pines, in the pines
Where the sun don't ever shine
I would shiver the whole night through

There was very little choice left in what Neera did as a musician. But when she overtook a stage, no one—not even Grant

Langley—could control her. The stage was her own. It was her dominion. Though she couldn't see him, Grant watched Neera from across the room. He hovered along the walls of each venue she played, no matter the size or crowd, and observed. His job was to get her on a stage, but once she was there, his power disappeared.

My girl, my girl, where will you go?
I'm going where the cold wind blows

Grant may have been a wolf, but Neera was no sheep. Her contract with him was binding, but it wasn't signed in blood. She'd continue to be Blue Mountain's next musical success story—but *Neera's* story, the one she forged on her own, was only just beginning.

SECRETS OF THE SOUTH

SEASON 4: FINALE
(INTRO THEME SONG)

ANCHORWOMAN (clip): Reports have come in of a devastating fire in the region of Southwest Georgia this past evening. In the lakeside community of Lake Clearwater, local authorities are projecting at least a dozen or more people missing in the inferno that razed one of the lake's many islands. The cause of the fire is yet unclear, though it is suspected fireworks from the Fourth of July celebration may be responsible.

HOST: As you all must know by now, this news report is only the half-truth. Like with most stories out of Lake Clearwater, the narrative is carefully controlled by those from within the community. Until the creation of this season, there were no stories of Clearwater beyond the sanitized tales they told themselves. My podcast has been an opportunity to try to change that.

Through my investigations, I learned the fire was intentionally started from the inside, by a member of the Lake Clearwater community, Reid Langley. He did this in an attempt to save the lives of thirteen innocent people who had been kidnapped by prominent residents of the lake. The townspeople of Carrion have always feared the return of the periodical cicada brood, because when they appear, locals go missing. This year was no exception. Not only did people go missing, but three innocent people died before the Fourth fire even began. They were murdered at the hands of the Clearwater residents—killed in a cultish ritual performed every thirteen years to, in their beliefs, maintain their community's wealth.

In this, I wish I could give you all a tidy resolution about Lake Clearwater and Carrion. I wish I knew the answers myself. But I don't. Instead, I will share with you the one thing that I do know. There are people in this world whose power exceeds our wildest imaginations. People with enough money and influence to make them virtually untouchable. Many of these people are prominent figures in the community of Lake Clearwater.

But before now, this community's crimes have never known the light of day. This season has sought to change that by peeling back the curtain and exposing the truth.

To my listeners, whatever happens next to Lake Clearwater lies in your hands.

AUTHOR'S NOTE

Dear Reader,

The Deep South is a place as beautiful as it is grotesque, as wonderful as it is terrifying. It's a region of incredible complexity, but it's not a place we often see in mainstream media. And if we do, it's rarely depicted with the nuance and dignity it deserves. *When Devils Sing* is my attempt to change that.

In writing this book, I was inspired by my own Punjabi family's ill-fated pursuit of the American dream in rural Georgia. I grew up among the towering pines, and for many years, I thought I'd never know the world beyond the empty acres of flatland that stretched before me. Rural places have a way of feeling expansive yet overwhelmingly isolating. Being raised in such a place was magical and painful all at once, and it's those sentiments that I aimed to imbue in this work.

When Devils Sing is equal parts a love letter to the rural South as well as a speculative depiction of the violent parts of Southern culture and history relating to the systemic inequality found here. But this is merely *one* story exploring a fictional town in Southwest Georgia. It's not meant to be an exhaustive exploration of the entirety of the Deep South.

I hope you'll walk away from this book knowing that there is a rich diversity of people, culture, and beauty in a place that is overlooked and too often demonized when it does make it into mainstream American narratives. The South deserves better.

Xan

ACKNOWLEDGMENTS

I always knew *When Devils Sing* would be the first story I ever told. It felt like an inevitable truth to write *this* book, as if I could write nothing else until this was complete. With that context in mind, writing these acknowledgments feels a whole lot like the last day of summer in Southwest Georgia, bringing with it a sense of finality and change that is more *feeling* than fact. In that, I suppose I'm finally heading out of Carrion, and there are many people to thank along the way.

To my literary agent, Pete Knapp, there is no one more extraordinary. This book would not exist without your steadfast belief in it, and I can never truly thank you enough. And to the incredible team at Park & Fine who helped, in many ways, bring this book into the world: Stuti Telidevara, Danielle Barthel, Kat Toolan. Many thanks to Claire Wilson and the team at RCW for getting *WDS* across the pond.

Brian Geffen, thank you for your brilliant editorial eye and passion for this story. You *saw* this book, and I'm so immensely grateful. Thank you to the wonderful team at Holt and First Ink for all the amazing work y'all do: Carina Licon, Sarah Gompper, Jie Yang, Tatiana Merced-Zarou, Teresa Ferraiolo, Kelley Frodel, Guy Oldfield, Emma Jones, Cate Augustin. A massive thank-you to Christina Mrozik and L. Whitt for the cover of my dreams.

Pitch Wars 2020 was where this book's journey truly began, and I'm not sure where I'd be without it, as well as the incredible people I met along the way (on hours of Zoom sprints). To my mentor, Kylie Schachte, thank you for seeing something worthwhile in the absolute mess of a draft you received. You were this book's guiding light during a particularly dark winter.

Hannah V. Sawyerr, thank you for always picking up the phone. Kat Korpi, our writing dates keep me sane. Morgan Forté, thank you for being there for me on That Very Stressful Day. Kacie Faith Kress, I'm so grateful *TRC* brought us together.

Sophia, thank you for always being the branch I can land upon. Elizabeth, I would not have survived rural Georgia without you. Maddy, to many more book conversations, beach trips, and matcha. Arianna, I couldn't ask for a better creative partner. Jamari, thank you for believing in this story before I did.

I owe everything, including the creation of this book, to my mother and my aunt. I have always wanted for the stars, and you never doubted my ability to reach for them. This book is for *us*—for all we've lost, and all we have to gain. Just a bit more time and I promise I'll dream you the world.

And to the readers from rural, misunderstood places who may see themselves within these pages: One day, things will be better, and life will be beautiful. Never stop fighting for your well-deserved peace.

ABOUT THE AUTHOR

Xan Kaur grew up in rural Georgia, where there were more gnats than people. When she's not writing, you can find her behind a camera or swimming in the nearest ocean. *When Devils Sing* is her debut novel.